The Songstress

RECORDS
OF THE
THREE REALMS

Book 1

The Songstress

RECORDS
OF THE
THREE REALMS

Book 1

Joshua Killingsworth

MYSTIC FOX PUBLISHING

ISBN 978-1-7341255-0-4 (Paperback)

ISBN 978-1-7341255-1-1 (eBook)

Edited by Cynthia Shepp

JoshuaKillingsworth.com@WriterJMK

Mystic Fox Publishing

To my lovely wife, Anna, who supported me throughout this long and crazy journey.

The Realm of Terra

Glacic Ocean

Kylyn Ocean

Trianic Ocean

Shikan Ocean

Polaric Ocean

Polar Tundra

Paitlan

Teonachi

Prudentia

Acca

Maari

Oa

Buton

Castile

The Hinterlands

Galdai

Esplaneaux

Friean

Illyria

Riata

Dardura

Eden

Edom

Magdra

Ekratta

Svokaja

Baltanna

Maos

Garlen

Mercia

Kiyira

Mirkor

Lubia

Ammon

Vidin

Kush

Ur

Nibu

Zuradon

Lesaria

Sarir

Avaar

Mylia

Akashvani

Tundier

Shika

Justia

Kunlun

Xu

Xiacau

Tochiki

Kyota

Xiang

Valezzua

Dongxiang

Bei

Namqian

Passaua

Shagu

Indalu

Ardea

Korgaera

Jauria

Mystikos

Zohan

Farkar

Tartria

Kylyn Ocean

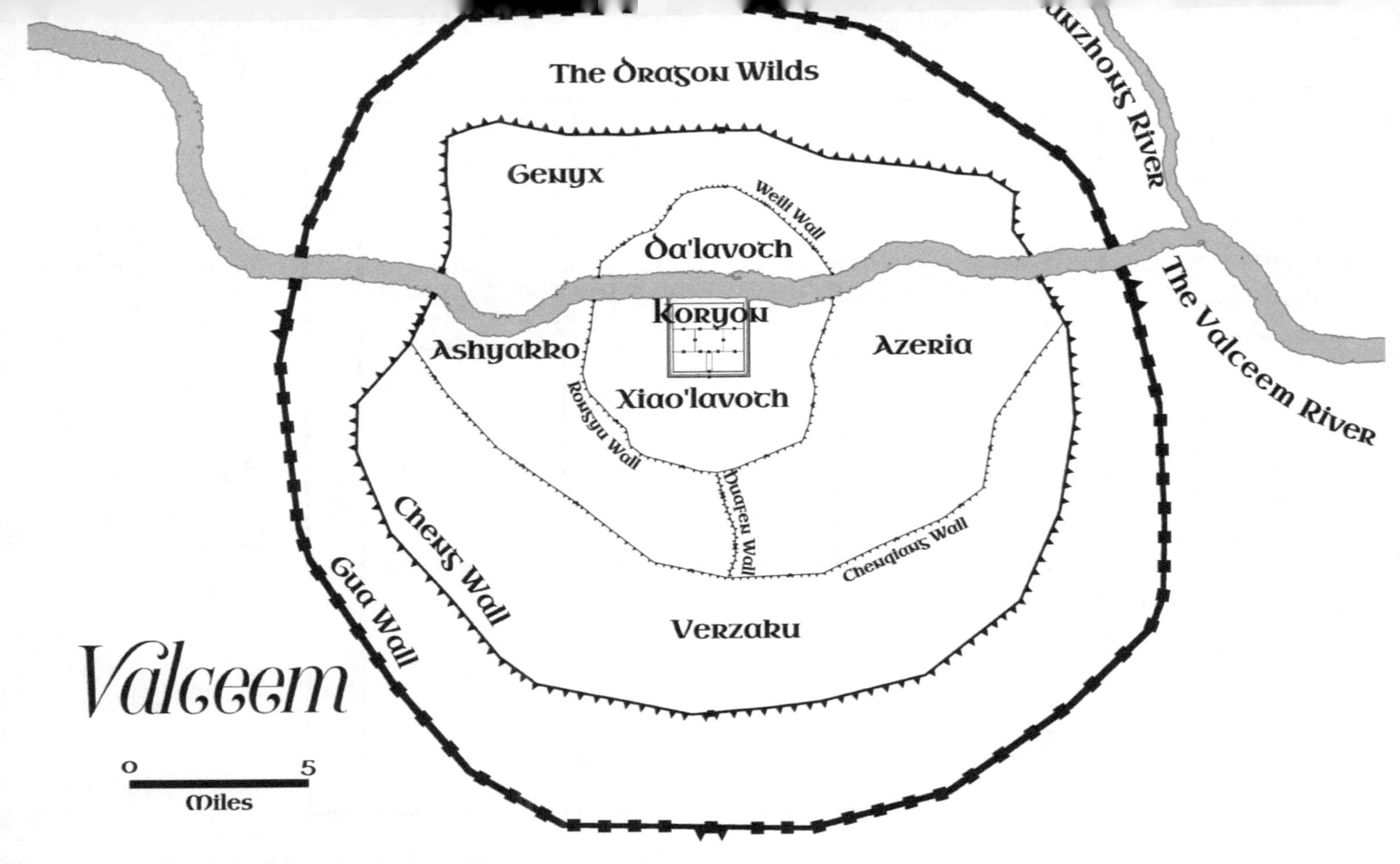

Valceem
The Dragon Wilds
Genyx
Da'lavoch
Weili Wall
Koryon
Ashyakko
Xiao'lavoch
Rousyu Wall
Azeria
Duafen Wall
Cheuzhous Wall
Verzaku
Cheug Wall
Gua Wall
Zunzhous River
The Valceem River
0   Miles   5

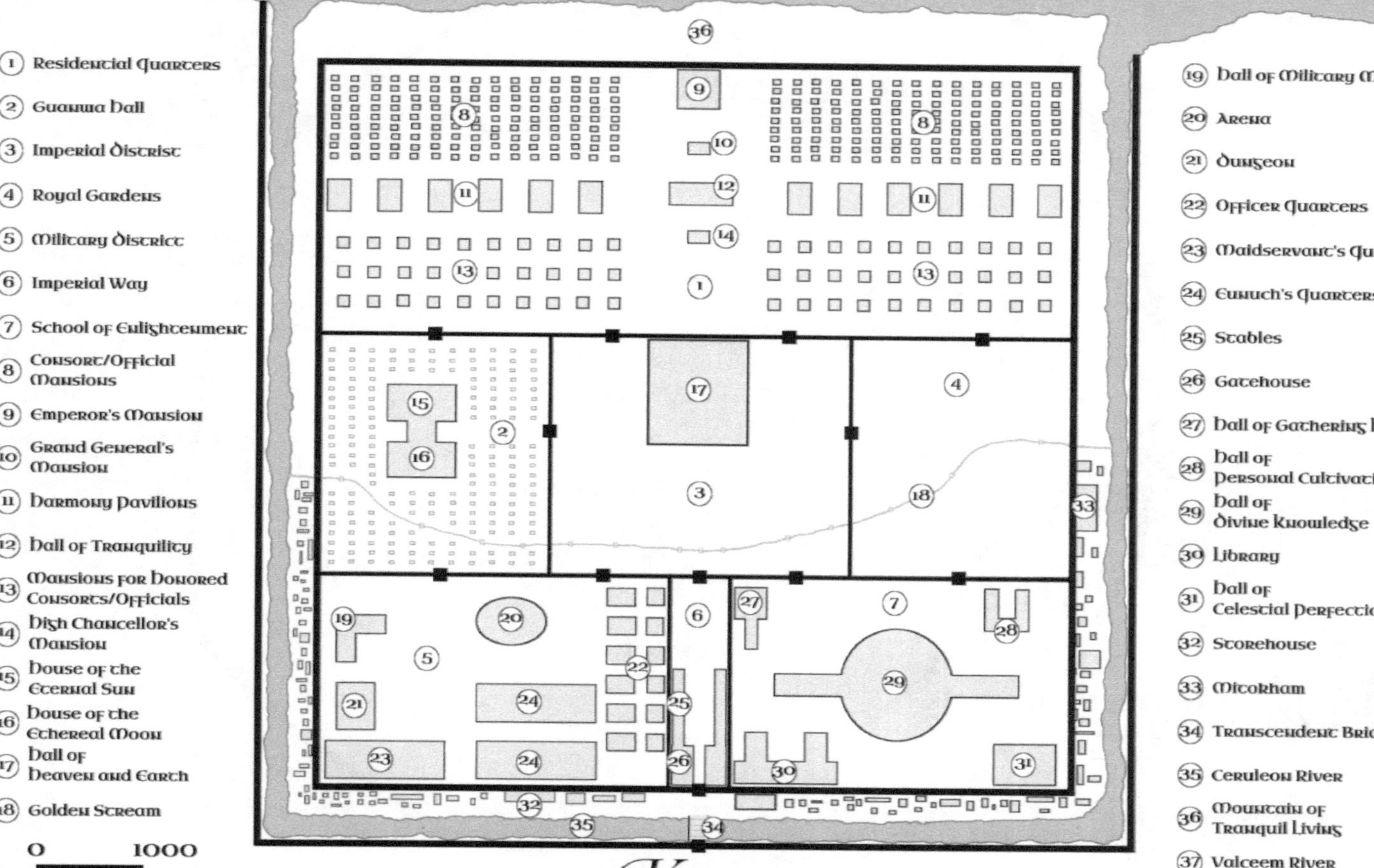

Koryon

1 Residential Quarters
2 Guanwa Hall
3 Imperial District
4 Royal Gardens
5 Military District
6 Imperial Way
7 School of Enlightenment
8 Consort/Official Mansions
9 Emperor's Mansion
10 Grand General's Mansion
11 Harmony Pavilions
12 Hall of Tranquility
13 Mansions for Honored Consorts/Officials
14 High Chancellor's Mansion
15 House of the Eternal Sun
16 House of the Ethereal Moon
17 Hall of Heaven and Earth
18 Golden Stream
19 Hall of Military Might
20 Arena
21 Dungeon
22 Officer Quarters
23 Maidservant's Quarters
24 Eunuch's Quarters
25 Stables
26 Gatehouse
27 Hall of Gathering Light
28 Hall of Personal Cultivation
29 Hall of Divine Knowledge
30 Library
31 Hall of Celestial Perfection
32 Storehouse
33 Micorham
34 Transcendent Bridge
35 Ceruleon River
36 Mountain of Tranquil Living
37 Valceem River

0   1000
Feet

CHAPTER ONE

KARI SLAMMED INTO A nearby table. It toppled over with her, its half-empty cups and saucers shattering on the hardwood floor. She clenched her aching stomach where the guard had kicked her with his armored boot. Instinct demanded she stay still and motionless beneath the heavy table, and she obliged.

"Kari!" Suying struggled against the guards as they shoved her through the teahouse doors and out into the streets of Valceem.

Kari's chest heaved with each frantic breath. She stared wide eyed as the door slammed shut and her friend vanished from her sight. She grabbed the edge of the square wooden table as if to rend it off her, but she froze instead. Her warm breath beat against the skin of her fingers.

What was she doing? Any more resistance and the guards wouldn't deal her a simple kick to the gut but rather a sword to the heart. Or worse, she would join Suying in her fate and end up being a plaything for the emperors in their harem.

"Damn it!" Kari gritted her teeth.

If it had been anyone else, she wouldn't give it a second thought. Kari would turn a blind eye, and only be glad it wasn't her that was taken. But not Suying. Kari would not let them take her without a fight. At least, that was what she told her body, but it didn't comply with her wishes. She remained still, staring at the closed door across the teahouse.

Her grip on the table's edge loosened, despite her desire to move.

Kari closed her eyes in shame as the watchful glares of the teahouse's patrons descended upon her. They were waiting to see how the songstress would respond. Would she submit and allow her friend to be taken, or would she die to protect her? No one would blame Kari for submitting. She had already done more than most. She tried to pull Suying away from the guard's grasp, only to be swatted away. No one would judge her now.

But she would.

Kari took a deep breath, trying to chip away at the boulder of fear that crushed her heart.

It was strange. She remembered stories from her childhood where gallant heroes would find the courage within them to continue to fight. The way the stories were told, courage would wash over the heroes, fueling them with the strength and will to battle against all odds, but it was fear and indecision washing over her, preventing her from moving out from under the shelter of the table.

The cool floor and wooden table served as a comforting shield against the brutality of reality, and they beckoned her to accept the safety of their embrace.

The muffled cries of Suying permeated through the teahouse walls, filling Kari's ears and haunting her thoughts. For three years, they had been inseparable. Now, in a few moments, Suying would be gone forever.

"I have to move," Kari told herself, trying to force her arms to obey her command, but her body remained still and motionless. "I have to move. I have to move *now*! Or she's gone."

"Stay down, girl," the faceless voice pleaded. Or was it her own thoughts reverberating in her mind?

"*Kari!*"

Suying's last scream pierced through the wooden walls, penetrating Kari's heart. Her whole body cried out in response as passion overcame logic, and she forced her body into action. She tossed the table to the side, leapt to her feet, and darted passed the dumbstruck patrons, out of the teahouse door, and into the city streets of the capital. The change from dim teahouse lighting to blinding sunlight strained her eyes as beams glistened off the green roofs of the cramped buildings.

"I won't let you take her!"

Kari stood defiant, facing down the guardsmen who stared in bewilderment at the young girl before them. What was she doing? The words left her lips before her mind had time to process them.

"Stand aside, girl," one guard ordered, stepping forward.

A quick scan of her surroundings revealed three carriages, each with two drivers, nine guardsmen, and a small crowd that had gathered to watch the commotion. The guards shoved Suying over to the middle carriage before tying her hands with rope. Two other girls with bound hands already sat in the carriage.

"I said you're not taking her," Kari repeated, less sure of her own resolve now than when she stood from under the table.

"Get back in the teahouse where you belong." The guard sneered. "Or perhaps you'd like it if we burned this whole district to the ground."

"You can't do that," someone from the crowd cried out.

"We're Imperial guards. We can do what we want."

"Just let them go. There's nothing you can do. You'll only make things worse for us," an old man called to Kari.

Kari clenched her fists, turning her knuckles white. The looks of panic on the faces of those in the crowd mirrored her own. They were right. There was nothing she could do, but the situation had escalated beyond repair. Her fate had been sealed the moment she stood from the floor.

The empire didn't attempt to hide its more colorful activities. Stories spread across the countryside of those who dared to question the emperors' authority. Anyone who opposed the empire was executed, whole families murdered, buildings razed, and the bodies of the dead mutilated and left as a warning to others. The emperors demanded everyone in the empire bow their heads in respect to them, and any who questioned or even showed the slightest inclination toward disobedience were brutally dealt with.

Kari's resistance would not be tolerated, regardless of what further actions she took. There was no turning back.

"You again?" The guard who had struck her in the teahouse shoved Suying toward one of his comrades, then stepped forward to confront Kari. "I've grown tired of this. Let's kill her and be done with it."

Three guards drew their swords, advancing on Kari. They wore lamellar armor of iron and leather riveted together and stained Imperial red. Even with a sword, which she didn't have, fighting three armored opponents was not wise.

Could she do this? Kari had trained from an early age to survive—a necessary skillset for her people. However, the first rule of survival was to always run when given the choice, especially in hopeless situations. Now every fiber in her body told her to turn and flee, yet her eyes were fixated on Suying. Tears streamed down the young girl's cheeks as she watched the guards advance toward Kari.

Kari had no weapon or plan, just an audience to witness her execution. She might die, but she wasn't helpless. She focused her spirit energy into her hands, her fingers tingling in response.

Kari blocked out the cries from the crowd. She couldn't afford any distractions. The slightest mistake would only expedite her death. Kari needed her full attention dedicated to the guards. She wasn't a warrior, yet she would fight, and she would die for the opportunity to protect her friend. Kari's muscles tightened, and she braced herself as the guards approached striking distance.

"Stay your blade," a man ordered, stepping out of a nearby carriage.

His black hair accented his goatee and mustache, contrasting with his crimson daopao robe. The gold edges and collar of his robe indicated him to be of nobility. By the looks of it, he was in charge of the roundup.

"It would be a shame to see such a lovely young thing carved to pieces," he said, examining her.

"You have no right to do this." Kari cursed her shortsightedness. How much more absurd could she be? Was she really challenging the man holding back her death?

"I have every right." The man glared at Kari, looking down his nose as his lips curled into a frown. "If you are ignorant as to who I am, then I suggest you occasionally emerge from your filth and familiarize yourself with your betters. I am the high chancellor to the Imperial Tian. Everything under the sun belongs to the emperors. I have every legal authority to conscript in their name."

Was this really High Chancellor Cai Ren? Why would he be leading the effort to abduct women? Not that he had a reputation of being such an outstanding individual. Quite the contrary. But it seemed like an odd task for an official of his station.

It didn't matter who he was. She had come this far and pushed her luck, so she might as well see it to the end.

"This isn't right. She's only fourteen." Kari balled her fists, planting her feet. He may be holding the guards at bay, but she wouldn't let him intimidate her.

"We are gracious enough to grant you Imperial protection. It is only fitting some of you return the generosity by serving the empire and submitting to the will of the heavens. Unless you think your lovely songs bar you from service to the throne?"

Kari's brow furred, her eyes narrowing as she glared. He knew who she was—that she was the songstress of the Bamboo Garden. Had he been spying on her and Suying? What else did he know about them?

"Don't look so surprised. We have eyes all throughout the kingdom. You have quite the reputation for your lovely singing voice, and I hear your songs have made you immensely popular among the worms in the Bamboo Garden. I wonder if your talents would be of better use in service to the Imperial throne. If that doesn't suit you, then I suggest you return to your songs."

Kari's heart skipped a beat. Her options were as she suspected, and now they were placed in front of her. However, the high chancellor was still giving her an out, or so it seemed. She could turn back now and hope Cai Ren would keep his word and her head wouldn't end up decorating the end of a pike in the Imperial palace. Otherwise, she would face certain death or subjugation.

Kari hung her head low, her eyes shutting tight. What little courage she had found earlier faded. Her legs weakened under her weight, and her muscles relaxed as her resolve dissipated.

"So that's your answer." Cai Ren chuckled, motioning to the three guards to stand down.

"Help me," Suying whimpered. She struggled against the guard as he forced her into the carriage. Her face showed her age. Her expression was that of a terrified child waking up from a nightmare—a nightmare that was just beginning.

This was no fate for a child. Kari wasn't much older, only seventeen, but she wasn't going to allow them to take Suying.

"Take me in her place!"

What had she said? The words erupted from Kari's mouth as if independent from her mind.

"What?" A wicked smile broke across Cai Ren's face.

"Take me in her place." Kari regretted the words, but swallowed her fear, burying it beneath her resolve. "I'm older and better endowed, and, as you know, I can sing and dance. I would be far better suited than Suying for the harem and to entertain the emperors."

Cai Ren stared at her, sizing her up. "Are you volunteering on your own accord?"

Kari hesitated. By the goddess, was she really going to do this? Join the harem? Volunteer for this nightmare?

Suying's eyes were wide, and she shook her head as if to say, "Not for me." Kari sighed. Unlike Suying, she would at least be better suited to escape.

"I am." Kari clenched her jaw.

"You heard that!" Cai Ren announced, addressing the crowd. "The songstress pledges herself to the service of the Imperial throne on her own accord. Let no man say otherwise."

Kari winced as a guard seized her arm, his fingers digging into her flesh.

"What about the girl? Should we release her?" a guard asked.

"No, take them both."

"What? We had a deal!" Kari lunged at Cai Ren, but the guard's grip halted her assault. She struggled to free herself from his grasp as she was pulled toward Cai Ren.

"I made no such deal." He waved her concern away with a flick of his sleeve. "I agreed to accept you as an attendant, not to release her. If you wish to dispute the arrangement of our agreement, I would be more than happy to plead your case to the court. Would that satisfy you?"

Kari slouched, staring at the ground. As high chancellor, Cai Ren was effectively the highest-ranking judge in the empire, second in power only to the emperors. It was all a farce, and the bastard knew it. There was nothing Kari could do.

"No."

"Very well. Then it will behoove you to submit to our arrangement. Bind her hands," he ordered.

A guard tied Kari's hands together, the tight ropes cutting into her wrists. She wanted to unleash her full fury on Cai Ren, but even if she could, death would quickly follow any further outbursts. She was powerless. Kari stared at Suying, who had begun to cry.

At least they would share in the nightmare together.

CHAPTER TWO

With their hands bound, the guards pushed Kari and Suying into the carriage next to the two other girls. Kari glared at Cai Ren, who climbed into the carriage and sat on the bench across from them. He met her glare with a smirk as a guard sat beside him.

Kari had never wanted to kill another human being before, but this unshakable urge to take the guard's sword and drive it into Cai Ren's smug face fell upon her like a torrential downpour of hatred. His arrogant grin cemented her rage as he wallowed in his smarmy superiority. He must have felt so proud of himself, throwing the weight of his position around to get his way.

"Cheer up, girls," Cai Ren said, still smiling, "Soon, you will be engulfed in the pleasures of royal affairs. For you to enjoy these luxuries, all you have to do is submit to royal desires with a smile on your face and a song in your heart."

A comment aimed at her, she was sure. If her hands weren't bound, she would kill him. She hated feeling this much anger toward another person. It gave him power over her. She hated him even more for that.

"I want to go home," Suying whispered.

Kari closed her eyes, nodding in agreement. She shared her sentiments, but, for now, they were trapped in Cai Ren's game, forced to play a subservient role until the opportune moment presented itself for them to escape.

Kari fought back the creeping grin that was spreading across her face. Escape would be her revenge. She would humiliate him. Make him regret deceiving her. She just hoped Suying would understand their need for patience and not despair in the meantime.

They rode in silence as the carriage made its way through the winding streets of Valceem as they headed to Koryon, the Imperial palace. Palace was such a generous term for it. Koryon was essentially a city within the city. Two grand walls surrounded the palace to separate it from the rest of the world.

The large wooden gates of the smaller outer wall opened outward as the convoy of carriages approached the Gate of Divine Majesty. The outer wall was only about fifty feet high, relatively small for a city known for its massive walls.

The outer gates slammed shut behind them as they crossed over the Transcendent Bridge and onto the other side of the Cerulean River, a manmade branch of the Valceem River that ran between the inner and outer walls separating the common world from the *Imperial dream*. A lump formed in Kari's throat. They were beyond the point of no return. This was really happening.

Straight in front of them was the inner wall and the Grand Entrance. The inner wall was a staggering hundred feet high, towering over the nearby city buildings. The wall weaved its way through Koryon, dividing the palace into its seven districts.

The carriages didn't wait for the gate to open. Instead, they turned to the west, past the military garrison, through the various houses and buildings. Lining the outer wall was a garrison of guards and the residences of various nobles and court ministers. Soldiers chattered about the new shipment of girls from outside the carriage.

The carriage stopped in front of a storehouse and the guards leapt into action, seizing the girls and pulling them out of the carriage. They untied their bindings before shoving them into the building. The storehouse was filled with merchants and smiths selling specialty armor and arms. It seemed an odd choice on where to take four potential concubines, unless of course they were planning to arm their captives, which seemed highly unlikely. Unscrupulous-looking men, all donning the crimson sash that signified them as Imperial soldiers, browsed the various wares and stalls. Anyone wearing that sash was someone to be cautious around, but better crimson than blue.

Cai Ren led the group through the store, eventually stopping at a desk in front of a large vault door. A woman with jet-black hair in a bun sat at the desk. She looked up from the book she was writing in, her dark eyes somber. Two heavily armored men with daos—single-edged swords—sat at a nearby table playing Aether.

"New additions?" the woman asked.

"Oh yes, and they are quite spirited," Cai Ren said, his obnoxious smirk returning. "Wash them up and get them ready with the rest. The emperors will be by at the start of next week for their auditions. Make sure these girls are properly trained on etiquette and obedience. And do keep an eye on the green-eyed one. She could be a handful if not broken soon, but do try to avoid damaging her voice. That's her greatest attribute."

Her greatest attribute? What a bastard. He described her like a prized horse he was getting ready for show.

"But of course," the woman agreed. She stood from the desk, then turned her attention to the group of girls. Her purple silk shenyi dress flowed with each of her movements. "My name is Zhenhua. I am the head matron of this house, and I will be your advisor. It is my job to ensure your transition from commoner to attendant is as smooth as possible. Now, what are your names?"

"My name is Tanaka Kyoko." The girl with the long braids stared at the ground. Her hairstyle was typical of young girls, and not dissimilar from the way Suying wore hers, but given Kyoko's age and the impracticality of the style for work, she had to be the daughter of a noble. Her hair looked unkempt. Clearly, she wasn't looking for a suitor. Unfortunately, that choice was being taken from her. Kyoko wore a simple ruqun with a white blouse and a red skirt tied at her waist.

"I am Hayashibara Momiji," the girl wearing the all-white ruqun said. She wore a cream-colored banbi coat over the blouse, which exposed her forearms. Her light-brown hair was held in twin twists on each side of her head, indicating working-class status.

Kari preferred to keep her own brown hair in a single loose ponytail so the front was loose and framed her face. While it was atypical of songstresses and dancers, who typically favored more ornate styles, Kari found it much easier to manage.

Kari remained silent out of defiance. She had no expectations of enjoying her stay in the storehouse, and she sure as hell wasn't going to make this a pleasant experience on her captors either.

Whether out of fear or rebellion, Suying kept quiet as well.

"And you two?" Zhenhua asked, tapping her foot on the stone floor.

"So, you're supposed to help us?" Suying asked, not bothering to look up. "What if we don't want to be here? How are you going to help me?"

Cai Ren laughed. "Good luck with this bunch." He motioned for his guards to follow as he left Zhenhua to deal with her new wards.

"You insolent little child. Unless you wish to feel the wrath of the Tian, you will soon learn some respect." Zhenhua motioned to one guard, who grumbled at having to leave his game. Kari gritted her teeth. Zhenhua was summoning a guard? What for? It seemed the slightest infraction would escalate quickly behind the palace walls.

"That won't be necessary. I'll ensure she falls in line," Kari interjected, placing her hand on Suying's shoulder. "But she does have a point. She is just a child, as you rightly pointed out, and would be of more use to the empire after maturing for a few more years."

Zhenhua motioned the guard away with a wave of her hand. "The wisdom of the emperors will determine of what use she will be. Better to mature under the watchful care of a patriarch than left to die on the street or by the sword."

Kari closed her eyes as she fought to hide her disdain. "Agreed." Her eyes met Suying's quivering stare. She would have to apologize to her later.

"So, are you her keeper?" Zhenhua sneered and turned her nose up, looking down at them.

"As a matter of fact, I am," Kari said. "Her name is Lin Suying, and I am Kari."

Zhenhua's eyes narrowed, darting back and forth between the pair. "Fine. Keep her in line. The next time she shows disrespect for me or a member of my house, she'll reap the consequences." Zhenhua recorded their names into her book, then squinted at Kari. "What sort of name is Kari? Are you a foreigner?"

"No, I am Xianese," Kari lied. She couldn't risk them knowing the truth of her heritage. She hated using it, but perhaps it was better to use her actual name for a change, at least in the presence of the empire. "My name is Hikari, but I am called Kari."

"And your family name?" Zhenhua glared at her.

"I have none," Kari replied.

"Pitiful to come from such a low class. You may follow me to your betterment." Zhenhua scribbled down the information before opening the impressive vault door. It wasn't something Kari could pick, not that she was any good at picking locks to begin with. It required both a key and a combination. Kari tried to peek at the combination, but Zhenhua shielded the dial with her hand.

The door swung open to an expansive, dimly lit room lined with small beds on raised platforms. It was nearly filled to capacity with women. There were no windows, and the only light sources were the lanterns that hung from the center of the ceiling and ran the length of the room. Smaller lanterns were affixed to the walls in between. The flickers of light cast ominous shadows on the stone walls.

The beds in the room were so close together there was barely any walking space on either side. A small wooden chest was set at the foot of each. A desk was positioned in the center of the room where two more guards in red lamellar armor kept watch. Another door, which probably led to more sleeping quarters, was opposite from the entrance.

The room was cold and barren of decoration, hardly what she expected of quarters designed to house attendants.

The walls and floor were all stone instead of wood, an odd sight in Xiang. The room resembled that of a dilapidated military barracks or a prison more so than an Imperial house.

The other women stared, loudly gossiping as Zhenhua led the four newcomers farther into the room. Kari counted fifty beds in the main chamber, with nearly as many women in here, and no telling how many more in the back quarters.

"These will be yours." Zhenhua motioned to four empty beds. "Now, listen carefully, for I will not repeat myself. Do not talk to the guards unless talked to first. Do not go into the back room unless you are being escorted by me, one of my assistants, or a guard. You will take a bath at least twice a day, and you will be suspect to regular inspections and grooming. Come, my assistant is waiting."

Zhenhua led the group into the back, which wasn't much different from the main room, just a lot smaller. Instead of single beds, it had pairs of bunk beds lining the walls. The girls glared as their party passed through, but remained silent. Was it scorn or pity in their eyes?

They made their way through the back room, then passed another guard station as they entered through a door that led into a rear hallway. The doors lining the hallway definitely weren't impenetrable on this end, but she had no way of knowing if any of the branching doors led to an exit.

Zhenhua took them into one of the many rooms. Another woman, dressed in a flowing pink silk shenyi, sat at a desk at the front of the room.

"You are to take one of the chairs from the wall and sit in front of Matron Tama." Zhenhua motioned to a cluster of odd pole-like chairs in a pile in the corner. Each chair comprised of a skinny pole with a rounded bottom and a red cushion attached to the top.

"We're supposed to sit on those? How?" Kyoko asked.

"You must balance. Sit down and fold your legs. Your feet should not touch the floor. A real lady shouldn't have any problem balancing while maintaining her posture. This will prepare you for your future duties as an attendant."

Kari sneered at Zhenhua. How was balancing on top of a pole supposed to help them? It was merely a cruel charade meant to break their wills and humiliate them.

Kari took a deep breath. She would not let Zhenhua enjoy her subjugation. She grabbed a chair and slammed it down in front of the desk, the force of the impact echoing against the stone walls. Kari sat on the cushion with her feet grounded to the floor to stabilize herself. Each movement needed to be slow and deliberate. She lifted one leg and then the other, crossing them on top of the chair. It wobbled at first, but she assumed a meditative position, controlling her breathing and the tiny movements of her muscles, which allowed her to steady the pole and keep it upright.

Zhenhua glared at Kari, who had to fight back the urge to snicker. Zhenhua scowled, clearly annoyed Kari had mastered the motion and on her first try, too.

"Like this," Kari said to Suying as she focused on maintaining her posture. "The trick is to find your center of balance before you attempt to lift your feet. Once you've done that, focus on maintaining a steady breath. As you sway from side to side, you'll need to adjust your weight accordingly."

Suying and the other two girls followed suit. After several failed attempts, Momiji was the first to successfully sit in her chair. It wobbled under her, but she maintained her balance. After falling off a dozen times, Suying was finally able to sit on the chair. Her body wiggled from side to side as she struggled to stay on top.

Kyoko, however, could not seem to find her balance. She kept falling off. The chair would wobble and top over. With each failed attempt, her legs shook more, her breathing becoming more frantic. At this rate, she had no hope of completing the task.

"Foolish girl," Zhenhua scolded. "Are you no lady? Your peers have successfully completed the task. Why can't you?"

Kari dropped from her pole chair, which caused it to crash to the floor, and rushed over to Kyoko.

"What are you doing?" Zhenhua stomped her feet.

"She needs help." Kari shot Zhenhua a scowl as she put her arms around Kyoko and helped the girl to her feet. "She's never going to get it with you belittling her like this."

"Your insolence will be beaten out of you!"

Kari rolled her eyes. Her actions were bound to have consequences, but after the day she was having, she'd quickly lost the ability to care.

"Take deep breaths. We'll get through this," Kari whispered to Kyoko.

Once Kari had Kyoko stabilized on the chair, at least to where she didn't look like she was just going to topple off, Kari returned to her own.

"No, for your actions, you must stand," Zhenhua demanded.

Kari shrugged her shoulders, insolently standing where she was.

"You will stand on the chair," Zhenhua added, pointing to the discarded pole.

"What?" Kari clenched her jaw, glaring at the matron.

"You heard my order. In fact, you will stand on the chair, balancing on one leg. The rest of you can get off and sit on the floor. If Kari fails to stand or falls, you will *all* be whipped and beaten."

Suying and the other girls turned wide eyes on Kari as they descended from their seats. Kari's nostrils flared. She wasn't about to give the matron the satisfaction of winning. Kari grabbed the pole, then set it upright. She needed to be quick or the pole would fall before she could get on top of it. She let go of the pole, leapt up, and landed on the red cushion with one leg. The other, she raised high into the air. The chair swayed from side to side, threatening to buck her off, but she readjusted her weight and stabilized herself.

"Know your place!" Zhenhua kicked the pole out from under Kari.

Her hands shot up to shield her face from the impact of the stone floor. She struck the ground with a thud as rage flared inside her. She wanted nothing more than to pop up to her feet and lay into Zhenhua, but logic seemed to dictate she should conceal her anger. Releasing her rancor would only exacerbate the situation.

Kari grunted as Zhenhua pressed her foot against the back of Kari's head, smashing her face into the floor. "You will stay here and be quiet until you are told otherwise, or else I will consider your life forfeit. If you do not care for your own life, then I will take hers."

She couldn't see who Zhenhua was talking about, but she knew it was Suying. Kari had overdone it. Her showboating and rebellious attitude were drawing too much attention to her. Anymore outbursts would be the end for her or Suying.

Kari zoned out as Zhenhua explained what was expected of the girls. She didn't care about their patriotic duties to the throne or the emperors. She just wanted to take Suying and go home.

"I am the head matron of this house," Zhenhua explained. "This is Matron Tama. She will oversee your hygiene and physical appearance. Together, we will ensure you meet the emperors' standards for cleanliness and beauty. We'll start with the basics. Quickly and concisely, tell me where you are from. Momiji, you will start."

"I grew up in Valceem's southern borough, Verzaku," Momiji said. "My family owns a rice farm there."

"Verzaku is a poor borough. Even a great city like Valceem has its uncivilized slums. At least you are here now. The decree of heaven has mandated you be elevated from a lowly peasant to that of a noble attendant serving the Sons of Heaven." Zhenhua wrote Momiji's details down in her book before turning her attention to Kyoko. "You... where are you from?"

"School." Kyoko's voice quivered, her eyes watering as she spoke. She must come from a wealthy family if they could still afford to send her to school. Most of the schools were shut down after the School of Enlightenment closed, and since the Imperial brothers took over, a lot of the students who remained in open schools were forced to find work. "Yesterday, a government official visited us. We lined up to greet him. He said I was his favorite, and he gave me a pendant to wear. Today, the guards showed up and asked for the girl with the royal insignia. The teacher pulled me out of class, then handed me over to the guards who brought me here."

"I don't care. Where are you from? Where is your school located?" Zhenhua crossed her arms, impatiently tapping her foot as she waited for a response.

"Da'lavoth," Kyoko whimpered. Kari was right—the girl did come from a wealthy family if she lived there.

"Stop crying. There is no need to be sad," Zhenhua demanded. "Anything worth knowing, you will learn here. As for your friends and family, they have already been informed of your service to the empire. They are rejoicing as we speak."

Kyoko's eyes swelled, tears pouring down her face. She cried in silence, not making a single sound. Was Zhenhua trying to be cruel or was she that daft to the feelings of others?

"Enough of this. You two, where are you from?" Zhenhua ignored the crying Kyoko, directing her attention to Kari and Suying.

"I'm from the district of Xiao'lavoth," Suying answered without hesitation. The coldness Zhenhua had shown Kyoko was already weakening her resolve. She was stronger than this. Kari just had to find a way to remind her. "Bandits raided my home and killed my family when I was eleven. I was on my own until I met Kari."

"No wonder you're so impudent." Zhenhua stared down her nose at her. "Any child growing up without a father figure to guide you through life is bound to turn out a deviant. Of course, only a coward would allow himself to be killed in such a shameful manner. At least you can redeem your family by loyally serving the throne now.

"And what of you?" Zhenhua asked, turning her attention toward Kari.

"I'm an orphan, too," Kari lied. If they knew who she really was, they would execute her without question. The Guardian of the Three Realms had criminalized the very existence of her people. "From Xiao'lavoth. My family was killed by raiders."

Zhenhua accepted Kari's story. It was rather typical after all, and not too dissimilar from Suying's. The guards of Valceem were more preoccupied with serving the emperors' backside than protecting the people of the city.

Once their backgrounds were recorded, Tama ordered the girls to undress down to their undergarments while she took their measurements. Tama called out each measurement for Zhenhua to record, all the while Zhenhua mumbled about various silks and colors that would accent each girl's look.

Tama was considerably younger than Zhenhua. She had her black hair tied in a bun with a red ribbon holding it in place. There was also a slight sadness to her face. When they were finished being measured, Tama led the girls to the bath and provided each girl with scented soaps and bath salts. Ten individual baths filled the room, each with folding wall panels that could be set up for privacy.

The bath was a pleasant change of pace. It had been years since Kari had taken a heated bath. The warm water felt amazing against her skin. Closing her eyes, she had to fight the urge to fall asleep.

Once they were finished bathing, Zhenhua returned with robes for each girl. They were rather plain, white with blue embroidery. Zhenhua explained they would have a whole new set of clothes, made from their measurements, if they were selected to join the palace harem. Tama remained silent as she helped them get dressed and brushed their hair. She had barely spoken a word to the girls since their meeting. Each had their hair brushed thoroughly before being tied into ponytails.

Tama led the group back to the sleeping quarters. "I will go prepare the artist for your official portraits. In the meantime, relax and get to know your fellow selected ladies."

Each of the four newcomers claimed a bed. Kari scoffed as she picked up the ceramic pillow from the head. She hated the pillows of Xiang. They were hard and cold, nothing like back home.

Kari slid the pillow underneath the bed. Collapsing on top of the sleeping mat, she draped her arms over her face. Damn this place. They were being treated like pets to be groomed and paraded around for the emperors. It was dehumanizing, worse than being treated like a prisoner. Anger, fear, passion, and whatever emotions she had experienced before faded away, leaving only a poignant dullness in their place.

"What do we do now?" Suying sat on the bed next to Kari's.

"I don't know." Kari sat up, taking in Suying's tear-stained face. There wasn't much they could do in their current situation but bide their time and find a way to escape.

"The best thing we can do is to simply go along with it," Momiji said. Kari cut her eyes to her. She didn't like anyone eavesdropping into her conversation, but with the close quarters, privacy would be scarce. "From what I hear, this life isn't all bad."

"How can you say that?" Kyoko asked. Kari clutched her thighs as Kyoko plopped down next to her. "My friends, they'll never know what happened to me. Or... what if they find out? What will they think?"

"But Kari, you have..." Suying started, but Kari held out a hand to stop her. She didn't want anyone to know about her magic. She couldn't risk the guards finding out about her abilities. If she were seen as a threat, there was no telling how they would react. Until she had a plan, she needed to be careful and hide, not just her powers, but also what she really was.

One slip up could be a death sentence.

Kari flopped onto her bed again while the other three girls crowded around, talking incessantly about home. Home had become just a strange word to Kari. It had been four years since she left hers, and she wanted nothing more than to return. She missed her mother and her friends, and she often dreamed about returning to the small island, but that was impossible. She was dead to that life. An exile from her own home, never able to return. But Kari missed the waves on the shore. And the weather. Unlike Xiang, where the weather changed, home was constant, not too warm and not too cold.

Kari shot to her feet as two guards approached their beds. The guards sniggered, eyeing all four girls up and down.

"What do you think?" one guard asked, stroking his chin as he circled the group of newcomers.

"This one is too skinny, not enough meat on her bones for my tastes," the other responded, referring to Momiji. "What about you?"

"I like the young one," he said, grabbing hold of Suying's arm.

Kari pulled Suying behind her, planting herself in front of the other girls. Whatever they were planning, Kari had spent too much of today sitting by and watching. No more.

Gritting her teeth, she pursed her lips together. No, she needed to restrain herself. She couldn't let her anger get the better of her or allow an erratic word to escape her lips. After what happened in the back room, she needed to keep a low profile and avoid making too much of a scene. At least with her hands unbound, she could defend herself if need be, but she didn't want to force a confrontation if she could help it. At least not yet.

"Are you that daft you can't see how gorgeous this one is?" Laughing, the guard motioned at Kari. She scowled in return. "Have you ever seen a woman look at you with eyes like that? And that color. I've never seen eyes that green before."

"You should be more hospitable." The second guard grabbed Kari's chin, then squeezed. She had to restrain from biting his hand. Kari jerked out of his grip, shooting daggers with her eyes.

"With an attitude like that, perhaps I should teach you some respect."

"So, which one do you want? The little one's mine." The guard shoved Kari aside as he seized Suying's shoulders, smirking.

Kari clenched her fists, focusing her energy into her hands. So much for avoiding a confrontation.

CHAPTER THREE

"I'll take this one." The guard grabbed Kyoko's arm, snatching her toward him. "Just look at her, so soft and submissive. She'll be their first pick for sure."

"She does have a lot of features the emperors like, but I have ten bits that says this one is chosen first." The guard shoved Suying away.

"Yeah, I can see that. Especially Jiaorong—he likes the young ones." The first guard released Kyoko, eying the girls up and down as he licked his lips. "I'll take that bet. Of course, if it's Jiaorong, I'm sure he'll take 'em all."

They were only betting on them? Kari breathed a sigh of relief as she relaxed her energy.

"Don't you two have something better to do?" Kari asked, annoyance dripping from her lips like venom. The plight of the girls was nothing more than a game to them. These guards didn't see people—they only saw playthings, toys for others to use, and from the sound of it, the emperors were worse. What did he mean by his comment that Jiaorong liked the young ones? This was fundamentally sick.

"You'll shut your mouth, girl, if you know what's good for you." The guard raised the back of his hand toward her.

Kari slumped down on her bed. It was useless. She wasn't a person to him, and there was no doubt he would act on his threat at the slightest inclination. People rarely liked to hurt others, but when they saw someone as subhuman, there was no telling what horrors they might inflict. Shagin, her people, knew all too well the atrocities humanity could wreak on itself when one group looked down upon another. She had no choice but to swallow her pride until she and Suying could escape from this nightmare.

With their bets placed, the guards left the girls alone. Kari fell backward, allowing her head to come crashing onto her bed. "Damn this place," she muttered under her breath.

"Don't let it get to you," a young woman with jet-black hair said, approaching the group. "They always place bets on who they think will be picked first from a new group. I'm Ina, by the way."

Kari and the other three girls took turns introducing themselves. Ina seemed rather pleased to meet them. She offered each a warm smile and a bow. Bowing was a foreign concept to Kari. The Xianese were the first people she had met who bowed for a greeting. It was a custom that took getting used to.

"Allow me to be the first to properly welcome you to the showroom. We sincerely hope you enjoy your stay in hell," Ina said with a flick of her sleeve. Kari smiled. Finally, someone who got it.

"Is this where all the attendants live?" Suying asked.

"No, only the ones awaiting placement into a permanent house." Ina sat next to Suying on her bed. "Occasionally, the emperors come by to choose from the girls within the main room. But, if you haven't been chosen after three months, you will be moved to the back room. Any noble is allowed to select from the girls in that group. Granted, they have to pay a dowry."

Kari's heart sank in her chest. Somehow, the thought of being bought seemed worse. There was no denying she'd truly be a slave then. *What must it be like to wait for some rich noble to buy you like a sword in a store?* She shook off the thought of girls lined in stalls as men browsed through and haggled over them like cheap wares.

The emperors had thousands of concubines. What kind of nagging thoughts must plague those not chosen when the emperors could take as many attendants as they wanted? It explained the glares the newcomers had received when they passed through. Even if a girl didn't want to be picked, there must be some small voice lingering in their minds wondering why they weren't good enough.

"At least they're closer to getting out," Ina said, noticing Kari staring at the back doors. "If you are sent to the back, you will only be there for three months at most. If no one buys you, you're released."

"Really? We can be set free?" Kyoko's eyes lit up.

"Do they just open the front door and let you walk out?" Kari asked in disbelief. It seemed too good to be true.

"Sort of..." Ina averted her gaze, fiddling with the silver necklace dangling around her neck. "But sometimes, that can be worse. Many of the girls here come from cities scattered throughout the empire. With no money, family, or friends, and nothing but the clothes they wore when they were taken, a lot of those released end up turning to brothels or falling into servitude in order to save up enough money to pay for return passage to their homes."

"That's awful," Suying added. Within Xiang, it was a sad fact of life that a woman without financial support from her family would struggle just to survive. The laws of the empire forbade women from working most jobs. Kari had gotten lucky to find a teahouse willing to hire her to perform and serve, but the pay was hardly enough to live on, especially for her and Suying.

"You know a lot about this place. You must have been here a while," Kari said, but Ina ignored her.

Smiling, Ina reached out to Kyoko and brushed her hair behind her ear. "You are very pretty. I heard Tama said they were getting ready to do your portraits."

"That's right," Kari said. Why would Ina change the subject like that?

"Those portraits are the equivalent of life and death. Once you become an attendant, the emperors use those portraits to pick out which girl will join him for the night. A good portrait will help you win favor with your emperor, but the artist usually demands some sort of bribe. If you don't have money, a pledge to pay him once you become an attendant is sufficient. I highly suggest you all take this offer if you want to live a comfortable life in the palace."

"Why would we want to do that?" Kyoko's brow furrowed. She had a point. They could improve their odds of not being selected to sleep with the emperors with a poor portrait.

"Right now, I know you don't want to be here, but it will get better one day. However, the only way it will is with the emperors' favor. The bribe is customary. Each girl here has to know her lot, and they must resign themselves to their fate early on because the comfort of their captivity depends on their representation to the emperors. The better your representation, the more often you will be visited by the emperors and the more favor you will earn. The more favor you earn, the more you are rewarded with money and freedom. Some girls even have their own homes within the palace, whereas they might not have one to return to." Ina unclenched her fingers from the necklace to place her hands to her hips. Kari didn't even have her own home outside of the palace walls, but she didn't want one inside them either. She had no intention of being trapped long enough to warrant making her stay more comfortable.

"How many girls are sent to the back?" If Kari was going to escape, she needed to know as much as possible about the storehouse. In her opinion, her new font of information had more knowledge for her to glean.

"Every month, they try to add twenty girls to the stock to replace the ones who become attendants. Out of each group of twenty, maybe four or five aren't picked," Ina said.

That didn't leave a lot of hope of things simply getting better. If Kari's situation was going to improve, it had to be done through her own fruition.

"How many girls are eventually released?" Suying asked. Was she picking up on Kari's train of thought or was she simply curious?

"That depends," Ina said, staring at the stone ceiling. "The dowry is one-thousand crowns per attendant, so usually only the wealthier nobles can afford one."

"A thousand crowns?" Momiji's eyebrows arched. "You could buy a mansion for that much."

"Sometimes, a commoner or soldier will save up their wages—or even sell their property—just to afford one. Unfortunately, they're not too strict about their policy of only nobles being allowed to purchase girls. And believe me, you don't want to be bought by someone with no property. That's a fate worse than death." Ina stood from the bed, then motioned for them to follow her. "Come on, I'll introduce you around."

With a wave of her hand, Kari declined. While she wanted to keep interrogating Ina, she needed to think through what she knew if she was going to escape. Besides, getting to know anyone else on a personal level would just make it harder to leave them behind.

Suying declined the invitation as well. Instead, she moved beside Kari while Ina led Momiji and Kyoko to meet some other girls.

"Did you hear that?" Suying asked, the innocence in her voice returning. "We just need to wait six months... then we can walk out free. All we have to do is to make ourselves less appealing. Don't bathe, cover ourselves in dirt, whatever it takes."

"I don't think that will work." Kari pursed her lips. "You heard Zhenhua explain the rules. It's just a hunch, but I don't think they would take too kindly to us sabotaging *their* property."

"So, what are we supposed to do then?"

"We have seven days before the emperors come. Based on what those two guards were saying, the emperor likes young girls. They seem to think you have a good chance of being picked quickly." The thought of the emperors liking children was troubling, and Kari convulsed at the thought of anyone younger than Suying being put through this ordeal. Kari shook her head, trying to dislodge the thought. "At any rate, I suggest we're not here when they arrive."

"How do we do that?"

"I'm getting ready to think of something." Kari winked. Suying's face lightened up as she smiled for the first time since early this morning.

Suying left to join the other girls, leaving Kari alone with her thoughts.

Kari scanned the room. Escaping wouldn't be easy. Two guards were stationed in the room with them. Not to mention the impenetrable vault door. It was too sturdy to break through, so any other option would require her to obtain the key or pick the lock, plus finding some way to get past the combination. Unfortunately, she missed the classes on lock picking in school. Sure, she could pick simple locks, but she struggled with standard door locks, and this was anything but standard.

Why did Suying have to be here? The weight of reality came crashing down on Kari's shoulders. Escaping with Suying would be far more difficult than finding a way out on her own. She would be a hindrance to her, no matter what plan Kari took.

She walked to the chest at the end of her bed, then rummaged through its contents. It was filled with make-up, soaps, lotions, and perfumes. Kari rolled her eyes. Of course it wasn't going to have anything useful in it.

Without a weapon or any viable escape route, there was little hope she would be able to plan an effective escape. As it stood, she might as well just be contemplating her navel.

"Kyoko, Momiji, Hikari, and Suying," Tama called from the doorway. "Follow me."

Grumbling, Kari stood from her bed and headed toward Tama with the other girls. Suying shot a worried glance at Kari. She smiled, trying to reassure her. There was nothing to be worried about yet.

"Good luck," Ina said as they gathered around Tama.

"I will take you to get your portraits done," Tama said, motioning for them to follow. She led them to the back where they were each placed in separate rooms before different artists.

The artist said nothing as Kari sat in front of him. He stared at her, jotting down notes and sketching a quick outline of her face on a piece of parchment. The room wasn't much bigger than a large closet, just enough space for her, the artist, and a small table topped with brushes, pigments, and parchments.

Kari gazed out of the large window behind the artist. The green grass of a beautiful courtyard beckoned. She would love to wiggle her toes in the grass, to feel the dirt and soil against her skin. She had only been here for a few hours, and she already missed the earth outside.

The artist ignored her longing eyes as he went about his work. He mumbled incoherently while he prepared his brushes and pigments.

"Aren't you a sight? Very lovely. Very lovely indeed. However, if you really want to grab the attention of the emperor, you'll need my help. Natural beauty can only carry you so far. However, I can make you a goddess. You'll be immortalized by my brush." The artist held out his hand, but Kari had no intention of paying the bribe.

After a few moments of silent glares, the artist dropped his hand and scowled. "I hold your future in a single brush stroke. A beautiful portrait will bring you riches while a poor one might leave you dissolute. Think on that for a moment, then realize a little incentive on my part to enhance your beauty might grant you a better future. If you cannot pay now, I will accept a pledge for a future payment."

"If you are after a bribe, then call it what it is. However, I have no intention of paying such a thing." Kari turned up her nose at the idea.

"You insolent little brat. Did you not hear what I said? I control your destiny." He slammed his brush onto the wooden table. The thud reverberated in the tiny room.

Kari's eyes narrowed. She would not let him intimidate her. "I am the maker of my own destiny. You simply seek to gain from the misfortunes and fears of others."

"As you wish."

Cursing her under his breath, he went back to work. He tossed the parchment from the table, then grabbed a piece of silk and began painting her official portrait. Kari became mesmerized by his meticulous brush work. He started with her outline, then layered colors one by one, switching between brushes to get the best strokes possible.

When he finished, he showed the final product to Kari.

"That looks nothing like me," she protested.

It wasn't a bad portrait by any means, but it wasn't remarkable either. All in all, it was a poor representation of her. Her hair was messy and unkempt; her eyes a dull blue, a far cry from their bright emerald green; her bone structure was different, more foreign; and he'd added a black mole underneath her right eye.

"Then perhaps you should have paid for a better portrait."

Disbelieving his audacity, Kari shook her head. Why was she getting so worked up over the painting? It wasn't like she had any intention of staying here. With any luck, she would be gone before the emperors even came for their inspection.

She forwent the gracious bow. Instead, stood and left the artist alone with his colors.

Tama escorted the four girls into the main room where trays of food waited. The food wasn't at all what Kari expected. She had anticipated high-quality food since they were now in service to the throne, but they were only served plain hot noodles with a single burnt piece of fish each. The poor food seemed to fit their desolate accommodations. Kari scarfed the noodles down as fast as she could. She was much hungrier than she realized, but even through her hunger pangs, she couldn't stomach eating the fish. It was far beyond simply blackened—it was inedible.

Once they finished eating, Tama escorted them to the baths to wash up. Kari didn't mind the mandatory baths. However, the inspection afterward was a bit humiliating. But at least it got her back into the warm water, and it was quite relaxing for a few minutes.

As Kari crashed into her bed, she stared at the ceiling. Cracks ran the course of the stone. Just how thick was it? Truthfully, it didn't matter. It was impossible for her to break through the walls. Even if she did, the noise would alert the guards and they would descend upon her. Stealth would be her key, which made Suying's presence even more unfortunate.

Kari's mind raced with various ideas and fantasies on how she would finally escape. Each seemed more impossible than the last. It wasn't long before her fatigue from the day caught up to her, and she drifted off to sleep.

Zhenhua woke the girls up before the sun had even risen. The guards led the girls through the back into the large courtyard, where they were made to stretch and run laps. The emperors had specific height and weight requirements, and they were eager to ensure each selected lady developed a regular exercise routine to maintain their figure.

Kari had to intentionally hold back to avoid outrunning everyone. She matched her pace to Suying's, even attempting to mimic her raspy breathing. The years of training Kari underwent were finally paying off.

Kari didn't want to stand out from the group too much. One of the first lessons Shagin taught was the ability to blend in with a crowd. Blending in, being ordinary, and being unremarkable was a powerful tool, especially when one needed to be invisible, and that was exactly what she needed to do. The less memorable she was, the longer it would take for them to notice she was missing when she finally made her move. At least, that was the idea.

However, she was already off to a poor start. Standing up to Zhenhua and making a spectacle the previous day would prove to have been counterintuitive.

After their exercise, Tama split the girls into groups and led them to the bathhouse. Kari enjoyed bathing in the warm water, and she couldn't wait to go back. She could see how submitting to the fate of a concubine could tempt girls simply to indulge in the luxuries the palace offered, but it wasn't a life she wanted. She would gladly trade luxuries for freedom any day.

Suying must not have slept much either, though, probably for different reasons. She had purple bags under her eyes, and she was being unusually quiet. Of course, she had been quiet the day before, too, so perhaps she hadn't adjusted to their unfamiliar environment. If everything went as planned, she wouldn't have to.

Kari sank into the warm water. The warmth caressed her skin as the steam from the water brushed against her face. She couldn't help it—since she was in the bath, all she wanted was to relax and let the water wash away her troubles, but she couldn't allow herself to enjoy a single moment.

She washed her hair and skin, then returned to her main goal. All the bathtubs lined the back wall. They needed some way to keep the water heated. This meant they had to have a boiler room behind one of the walls or under the floor. Wherever there was a boiler room, there had to be easy access to the outside to transport wood or whatever fuel used to the boiler. If she could figure out where they were located, she might be able to deduce how to gain access to it and make her escape that way.

Kari finished with her bath, got out, and toweled off. She shivered as the cool air met her still-wet skin. Tama took Kari aside, as she did with each girl, then brushed her hair and helped her put makeup on.

"I just love these baths." Tama pulled on the brush caught in Kari's tangled brown hair, making Kari wince. "It's been so long since I've had a hot bath."

"Only the finest," Tama said coldly. Getting her to talk would not be easy.

"How do you keep the water so warm? Do you use magic?"

Tama didn't reply. She just kept to her work as she styled Kari's hair. When she had finished, she sent Kari and the other girls back to the main room.

Kari couldn't give up, not after only one attempt. Trying to get information out of the guards might appear suspicious, but she still had one other person she could ask who might just have an answer.

"Do you know anything about the hot baths?" Kari asked, approaching Ina.

"I guess," Ina replied, squinting her eyes. "Why do you ask?"

"I just want to know how they work. What do they heat the water with?" Kari asked, feigning curiosity.

"They burn wood, I believe." Ina eyed her. "From what I hear, the baths in Guanwa Hall are even bigger than these."

"The boiler room... How would you get into it? Where's it located?"

"Why would you need to know that?" Kari knew she was being too inquisitive, but she couldn't focus on that. She needed the information.

"I'm just curious about how it works." She had to be careful. Ina may seem friendly and pleasant, but she had championed palace life by saying it wasn't all bad. There was no telling how she would react if she knew the truth.

"Please don't take me for a fool." Ina sat on her bed, serenely folding her hands in her lap. "You're planning on escaping, aren't you?"

Kari had said too much. What to do now? Could she trust Ina with the truth or was a lie a better option? From what she had gathered, Ina was a prisoner just like Kari, but there was always the possibility the girl was a spy for the empire. That would explain why she was so helpful and knew so much about the storehouse.

Kari rubbed her eyes. Paranoia was overtaking her. A spy? It was such an odd conclusion to jump to. Logically, she had no reason not to trust Ina. The girl had been nothing but helpful to her and Suying since they arrived, but something wasn't right.

Kari got a strange vibe from Ina. Still, she couldn't base her decisions on vibes. She had no reason to suspect her. The paranoia was merely the result of her own irrational fears of being caught, but, even still, it was best not to risk it.

"No, of course not," Kari said. "I'm simply curious about how it works. I've never seen anything like it before."

"You don't have to lie to me." Ina's smile was warm and inviting. It was almost like she wanted Kari to trust her and drop her guard. "I'm sure you're not the first to think of escaping. Heaven knows I would do anything to leave here, too."

"Then why don't you try to?" There was that vibe again. Ina was hiding something—Kari was sure of it. Ina's continued contradictions of detesting the harem and embracing it were too odd to ignore.

"I can't." Ina stared at her necklace as she fiddled with it. "There is nothing for me outside these walls. I have to stay."

"Why?" What was she hiding?

"I just do." Ina's smile faded. "I have to see this through to the end."

Kari sighed. "I don't understand. But maybe it's something I never can. If I have the opportunity to leave, I will take it in a single breath."

Ina placed her hand to her forehead. "You can't get to the boiler rooms. They built this place like a fortress so no one could escape. Do you honestly think they would leave an exit unguarded and open? Escaping is impossible. Even if you could get out of the storehouse, you are still locked behind the palace walls with nowhere to go. They will find you, and they will kill you. You should just accept where you are. Try to make the best of it."

Kari sighed. So much for that idea. The boiler room would have been a longshot anyway, but it was the only option she could see. She hung her head in defeat, realizing she would have to rethink her escape.

"I'm sorry," Ina said, clasping her hands. "I hate delivering bad news, but do take heart—your life will change soon. You will be an attendant. Once you are, you'll have free rein of the palace and your life will begin anew."

"Has anyone ever escaped?" Kari asked. If she couldn't escape the storehouse, she would try the next best thing.

"I don't know how they would." Pausing, Ina tiredly rubbed her eyes. "But I'm sure one or two have fled the palace over the years, so it's not impossible. But I don't think those who become attendants are willing to leave."

Kari's options were limited. On one hand, she could take her chances and wait this ordeal out. Maybe she and Suying wouldn't even be selected by the emperors. It was possible they would be released after six months, but that didn't seem likely. Perhaps a better opportunity would present itself later, but that would more than likely mean having to succumb to the desires of their captors, at least for a time. She had to get out before then. Kari wasn't going to risk becoming a conquest of the emperors. She would find a way to overcome and breathe the open air again.

Of course, that was it. She had been too busy trying to blend in to notice it. Why try to go through the walls when she could go *over* them?

The courtyard would be her best bet, though it presented a number of unique challenges. She would need to get there without being noticed while avoiding the guards who patrolled the walls and finding a way to scale their smooth surface.

Kari took a deep breath, cementing her plan in her mind. Those obstacles wouldn't be a problem. She knew how she would escape.

Kari enjoyed their time in the courtyard. She sat in the grass next to Suying and Ina, the warm sun bathing her in light while rejuvenating her. Kari toed off her shoes to wiggle her toes in the grass. She was connected with the earth again. Could feel the life of the planet rushing into her, filling her with a sense of calmness and determination.

She examined the stone courtyard walls. Guards patrolled the tops and looked down upon them. Just over those walls was freedom, or, more specifically, *access* to freedom. Once outside, she would still have to cross over the palace's outer wall and the Cerulean River. Alternatively, she could follow the Cerulean River around the palace to the Valceem River, then go around the walls to the city docks. That might be the better of the two options.

"Kari, you should try these sweet rolls," Suying said, handing her one and breaking Kari's concentration. "They are so yummy. Have you ever had anything that tasted this good?"

Kari took the sweet roll, bringing it to her mouth to bite into it. Its warm sugary goodness filled her mouth, washing over her tongue. Suying was right. It was extremely good. But the question remained, was the sweet roll actually this delicious or had the food they'd eaten over the past few days just been that bad?

"This might be one of the few good things about this." Ina took another bite of her roll. A smile creeped upon her face as she swallowed. "I hear the cooks in the palace are all experts. Supposedly, the attendants eat only the finest cuisine."

"How can you say that?" Kyoko asked, joining the group. She sat next to Suying. When she offered Kyoko a sweet roll, she ignored it. "Nothing is good about this place."

"I think she was just saying that not everything will be so bad." Suying recoiled her outstretched hand. "After all, outside of these walls, I couldn't afford anything half as good as this. Not being allowed to hold down a proper job meant we couldn't eat at all some days. On others, we became thieves just to survive. I was starting to understand how so many women ended up working in the brothels. Sometimes, there's no other choice."

Kari remembered those days all too well. Even with her job singing in the teahouse, neither was allowed to own property. Kari's pay had barely been enough for them to live on, but at least it had helped some.

"Not so bad?" Kyoko screamed, leaping to her feet. "They're going to rape us again and again until they grow tired of us and cast us out."

Kari averted her eyes as silence fell upon the group. She had spent so much time worried about herself and Suying that she'd nearly forgotten the other girls were going through the same ordeal. Leaving them behind would be that much harder, but it had to be done. As a captive herself,

Kari couldn't help them. If she escaped, she could petition someone for assistance. Surely, there was someone, somewhere, willing to help.

"I just want to go home to mama." Kyoko collapsed to her knees as tears streamed down her face. Kari knew that feeling all too well. Even she had to blink back tears.

"Please don't cry." Kari placed a hand on Kyoko's shoulder. The small act of kindness was to no avail. Kyoko buried her face in her hands, sobbing as if her heart were breaking. Her body spasmed, and her cries reverberated against the courtyard walls.

"What's going on?" Tama asked, rushing over. Her concern was surprising. It was the first time Kari had seen her show any emotion other than grief and disinterest.

"I want this to end." Kyoko gazed beseechingly at the matron, cheeks tearstained.

"We all do," Ina added, swallowing the last bite of her sweet roll.

"You poor thing." Tama helped Kyoko to her feet, then wrapped her arms around the girl. "You were taken from your school. I know what that's like. When I was chosen to be an attendant, I was taken from mine as well. I think it makes it harder. Try to remember your life will get better."

"I don't think she wants it to get better." Kari shot to her feet, grabbing Tama's arm. Tama jerked her head toward Kari, scowling, but Kari continued. "How can you be a part of this? If you've gone through this before, how can you condone this? If you care at all, then help us!"

Tama snatched her arm free, but she ignored Kari's plea. She offered a hand to Kyoko. "I'll see what I can do to make things easier for you. Come with me."

"Please, I want to go home," Kyoko said, wiping her tears away.

Tama led Kyoko to the courtyard door, but she stopped just shy of opening it. Turning toward Kari, she hung her head low. "I have no choice, and neither do you. Just accept it."

Kari dropped to her knees. So much for being connected to the earth. It never occurred to her the matrons were also prisoners. But why would they cooperate with their oppressors? They seemed so willfully submissive.

"Which one of you is Ina?" a guard asked as he approached the group.

"I am." Ina rose to address the guard.

"Come with me. Lady Zhenhua needs to have a word with you." Ina bowed to the group, then quickly followed the guard.

"What do you think that's about?" Suying asked.

"No idea." Huffing, Kari flopped on her back, staring up at the impossibly blue sky. A one-on-one meeting with the matron didn't sound overly pleasant, mostly because the matron wasn't a pleasant person. Since she'd been here, none of the matrons had ever called for a meeting with any of the girls, save for their initial arrival. She draped her arm over her face with a sigh. "Whatever it is, it can't be good. Nothing here is good."

"But it can be," Suying said. Kari gave her a puzzled look.

After she sat up, she leaned forward to speak more privately with her friend. "We need to get out of here. I'm starting to have the workings of a plan. Unfortunately, we must leave the others. It'll just be the two of us."

"I'm not going," Suying said, taking another bite of her sweet roll.

Suying's attachment to the other girls was understandable, but they could only focus on themselves if they wanted any hope of escape. "Now's not the time to get emotionally attached to anyone here. We have to look out for ourselves, first and foremost. Besides, maybe we can find someone who can help the others once we get out."

Kari ran her hand through her hair. Where to begin? It was unlikely anyone in Xiang would be able or even willing to help them. The Imperial brothers had a tight grip over the nation, one fueled by fear and retribution. Even those willing to help would be too afraid to oppose the empire or they'd lack the ability to do so. Anyone with the ability would no doubt be part of the upper class who would have enjoyed the corrupt fruits of the empire. They would have to find help from neighboring nations, but would anyone be willing to risk a confrontation with Xiang?

The Guardian was the only person with the power to save any of the girls now, but it was doubtful he didn't already know of the goings-on of Xiang.

Disgust sunk deep into her stomach at the mere thought of going to the Guardian for help. The Guardian of the

Three Realms had been the one to declare Shagin the enemies of humanity. He alone had ordered the Shagin Purge—declaring all Shagin were to be killed on sight. She couldn't risk entering territory controlled by him, even more so if anyone discovered who she was. Besides, following the betrayal of the Realm of Adgul, he was more preoccupied with winning his war than helping defend those he was sworn to protect. The harsh truth was Kari and Suying were on their own. Once they escaped, there would be no coming back for those they'd had to leave behind.

"No, it's not that." Suying put her dessert down, calmly wiping her hands. "I want to stay. I think it's better for me here."

"Do you even know what you are saying?" Kari could understand the temptation, but Suying wasn't thinking through the implications of what staying within the palace meant.

"I know what will happen if I stay, but look at the other concubines we've met. They seem happy to be part of the harem. I'm not saying I'm looking forward to any interactions with the emperors, or even assuming I'll be happy with my life here, but I don't want to die starving and begging on the streets."

"Suying, that's not going to happen." Had she not noticed Kari hadn't let that happen in the past, and she wouldn't let it in the future?

"You don't know that." Suying kept her eyes focused on the now-empty dessert tray.

"We'll find a way to survive, I promise you. What I do know is what will happen if you stay. That's not what you want." Kari reached out, gently brushing Suying's dark hair behind her dainty ear.

"It's not," Suying agreed.

"Then you'll come with me?" Kari clasped Suying's hands in hers, bringing them up to press them tightly against her lips.

"I don't know." Kari's heart sank, and she released Suying. How could the younger girl be this desolate? How had Kari not noticed it before? This fourteen-year-old girl was seriously considering staying and choosing a life of servitude. "I want to meet the emperors at least—just to see what they're like—before I make my decision. You understand, right?"

Kari lied, giving a short nod. But they couldn't wait. The emperors would be here tomorrow. They only had one chance to escape, and she had to take it.

"Time's up," a guard called. "Come on. Time to return to your quarters."

As Kari walked past the rose bushes under the entrance arch, she reached out and plucked the head off a flower. Glancing around to make sure no one was watching, she clenched her fist around the bud, pouring her spirit energy into it. In an instant, she could feel the petals transfigure. When the process completed, she opened her hand and looked down at the newly formed seed before slipping it in her pocket.

With her acquired treasure safely secured and out of sight, she rejoined the group and headed inside to her prison.

They returned to their sleeping quarters, then lined up in front of their bunks. Kari took her time, silently counting her steps from the back door to her bunk as she fell in line.

Zhenhua stood in the center of the room as guards handed out sheet music to each girl. Kari scoffed at the song title. It was called "Where I Belong." What a joke.

"Listen up, ladies," Zhenhua said. She cracked a leather-wrapped riding crop in her hands as she stalked up and down the room. "You have been chosen to serve the emperors. Tomorrow, they will come for the auditions. They will choose who among you will serve as royal attendants. Being chosen is an honor of the highest degree. You will be groomed and well cared for while living a life of luxury of the utmost standards. You should feel proud to be an attendant."

Ina rolled her eyes as Zhenhua went by. Kari grinned in response.

"But you must be perfect," Zhenhua continued. She pressed the tip of her crop under the chin of another girl, using it to lift her head. "Chin up, back straight. Nothing less than excellence will be accepted. Poise and dignity are the marks of a high-class lady."

"So now that we're in here, we're suddenly high class?" Suying whispered to Kari.

"Who's talking?" Zhenhua barked, spinning on her heel. She stormed down the rows of girls in search of the culprit. Each girl stood frozen and stared straight ahead, none daring to move. "I know someone said something. I want to know what was so important it was worth so rudely interrupting me for."

Suying closed her eyes. Her legs visibly trembled as Zhenhua came closer.

"I did it," Kari firmly stated.

Snapping her glare to Kari, Zhenhua clenched the crop in her hands.

"I was correcting her posture." Kari motioned to Suying. "Like you said, only excellence can be accepted, and I am her keeper, after all. I apologize. It will never happen again."

"See to it that it doesn't." Zhenhua pointed her crop at Kari. "For your insolence, you will not be allowed to eat dinner tonight. In fact, no one will. They have you to thank for that."

Kari wanted to protest, but it would be unwise to test Zhenhua. Judging from the dead silence in the room, the other girls knew it, too.

"Now, where was I?" Zhenhua continued to pace. "To celebrate this momentous occasion, let us sing a song."

She began swaying her arms around like a symphony conductor, demanding the girls to follow instructions. In a single voice, the girls began to sing from their sheets.

"Woman, wretched with broken soul,
Abandoned to death, could never be whole.

THE SONGSTRESS

Drowning in poverty, destined to die,
Without a savior, forever would cry.

"I am so joyous, singing my song.
This is my life now, where I belong.
Serving my emperor, relent to his way,
Abiding by him, never to stray.

"Wondrous salvation, finding the throne,
Joining his embrace, becoming his own.
Saved from damnation and certain death,
Made holy and pure, given new breath.

"I am so joyous, singing my song.
This is my life now, where I belong.
Serving my emperor, relent to his way,
Abiding by him, never to stray.

"Blissful submission, filled with his light,
Open to pleasure, all wrongs are made right.
Serve and praise him, be loyal and true,
And he will protect and give life anew.

"I am so joyous, singing my song.
This is my life now, where I belong.
Serving my emperor, relent to his way,
Abiding by him, never to stray."

"Again," Zhenhua demanded, and the girls repeated the song. She marched up and down the rows of girls, examining each as they sang. Some girls began to cry as they reached the third repeat.

This was cruel. It was nothing more than an attempt to break their wills. But there was nothing Kari could do. She had to go along with it.

They repeated the song one more time before Zhenhua released them. She left the girls alone with the guards, sealing the vault door behind her.

"Are you all right?" Kari asked. She shifted toward Suying, who had crumpled onto her bed, then sat beside her.

"It's all pointless. Escape is pointless," Suying morosely stated. "Maybe we should just accept it."

"Don't say that." Kari took hold of the younger girl's hands. "Look at me. We will get out of here. I promise you that."

"Nice going, bitch," a voice from behind her said.

Kari glanced up to see six girls advancing on her.

"Thanks to you, we've lost our dinner," the leader snarled. "You better have some sort of way to make it up to us."

"I don't want trouble," Kari said, rising to face them. "Listen, we're all in this together. Why don't we make the best of it?"

"Why don't you keep your mouth shut?" the leader snapped.

"Leave her alone," Ina said, running up to the group.

"What are you going to do if we don't? Are you going to stand with her?" The leader pointed her finger under Ina's nose.

"I am." Ina calmly moved the girl's hand away from her face. Kari tried to protest, but Ina raised a finger to stop her.

"Don't forget me," Momiji said, joining in.

"Fine. But you watch your back." With a scowl, the leader turned and left, her entourage following.

"Thanks," Kari said once the other girls had left. "I owe you one."

"Don't mention it." Momiji smiled. "Like you said, we're all in this together. Besides, you helped us when we first arrived. If it wasn't for you, I doubt any of us would have passed the silly chair test, remember? If we don't watch out for each other, who will?"

"Why don't you three come over to my bunk?" Ina whispered. "Don't tell anyone, but I've been hoarding food. I'm more than happy to share."

"You go ahead." Kari motioned to Suying. "I think I'm just going to stay here. Maybe rest for a bit."

Kari crawled into her bed, eyes on the ceiling as the others migrated to the offered treats. She really hated this place. Something about it wormed its way inside to corrupt and break. They tore girls down and rebuilt them in their image. Kari could already see it in Suying. The girl was beginning to doubt and lose hope. Was that what happened to the others? What had made them seem so submissive?

Rolling to her side, Kari shot up, her eyes wide, at the sight before her. This would be trouble. The leader of the group who had confronted her was talking to the guard. She gestured wildly to Ina and the others, who clearly had food. It wasn't hard to see. They weren't even hiding it. Kari had to think of something fast to avoid Suying from suffering any repercussions.

When the guard waved off the concern, the leader slunk to her bunk, sulking. Kari breathed a sigh of relief.

It was odd, though. Why hadn't the guard cared? On top of that, how did Ina have food in the first place, much less enough to spare? She could have been saving it like she'd said, but their meals were typically just enough food to keep them satisfied until the next. Ina must have either been saving food for quite some time or she never ate at all, but it didn't explain why the guards hadn't confiscated it. They could clearly see her and the other girls eating. In fact, everyone in the quarters could see them. The others appeared ready to pounce on them for it. Yet, the guards didn't seem to mind. Ina was flagrantly violating the matron's decree, and it was just being accepted.

Kari sighed. She was overthinking it. The guards just didn't care. They had shown nothing but apathy and disinterest so far, only grumbling and complaining whenever they were asked to do something.

The rest of the day was uneventful. Zhenhua instructed them on proper palace etiquette and what their expectations were when they were called to be with the emperor.

Kari ignored most of it. Once they finished their evening bath, they settled into their quarters, most with empty stomachs and sour expressions. Another day had passed. Soon, the emperors would be here for the auditions. Time was running out.

Kari took a deep breath as she pulled back her sheets. Most of the other girls were doing the same as they finished their nighttime routine, but something was off. Kari rubbed her eyes as she tried to figure out what was amiss. The filled-to-capacity room had one bed with a missing occupant.

Kari scanned for Kyoko, but didn't see the other girl anywhere. Come to think of it—Kari hadn't seen her since earlier in the courtyard. But surely she was okay, right? She had been with Tama, but why hadn't she been returned?

"Have you seen Kyoko since this afternoon?" Kari asked Suying.

"No, but Ina said she saw her in the bathroom a little while ago. She said she was crying," Suying answered as she crawled under her blankets.

"She was crying... and Ina left her alone?"

Suying shrugged, flopping onto her pillow. Kari winced as Suying's head hit the ceramic support.

Kari rose, motioning for the guard to take her to the bathroom. He grumbled as he stood from his chair, but led her through the back room and down the long hallway that led to the privies. When the guard opened the door and stepped inside, Kari refused to follow.

"I can't go if you're in there with me," Kari snapped. The guard frowned as he stepped back through the doorway, but he allowed her to enter alone.

Kari slammed the door behind her.

"Kyoko," she whispered. "Are you in here?"

The only response was a slight whimper from one of the far stalls. Kari hurried over and gently opened the door, not wanting to startle the girl.

Kyoko sat on the floor, curled up with her knees to her chest. Her face was wet from tears. After a quick scan, Kari noticed bruises on the girl's thighs. More were prominently featured on her arms and around her throat.

Gasping, Kari placed a hand over her mouth. "What the hell happened?"

"She said she'd take care of me. She *said*. Mommy... Mommy, why didn't you stop them?" Kyoko sobbed as tears fell like a torrential rainstorm down her flushed cheeks.

Kari reached out to put a hand on Kyoko's shoulder, but the upset girl withdrew in fear. *Those bastards!* Kari clenched her fists. Vengeance flooded her mind, but she tried to push her anger down. There would be time for fury later. Right now, she needed to focus on helping Kyoko.

"I'm sorry. I'm so sorry," Kari soothed. "It's over now."

"It's never over. It keeps happening again and again. He's so heavy. I can't get him off. I can't ever get him off." Kyoko wrapped her arms around her head to hide her face, turning away from Kari. Scooting in closer, Kari held Kyoko in her arms.

"It's going to be okay. It's going to be okay," Kari whispered. "Come on, let's get you cleaned up."

Kari tugged Kyoko up, then led her to the wash station. Taking one of the washcloths, Kari soaked it in the basin before cleaning the tears and dirt off Kyoko's face.

"It was one of the guards," Kyoko said, staring down at her feet. "He did this."

"I'm so sorry." Kari was at a loss for words. She wished she had some sage wisdom to make it all better—or at least something to contribute that would comfort Kyoko—but Kari's mind had become a pit, void of rational thought. "We'll make him pay for this. He will face justice."

"And Tama, too," Kyoko added. "Mostly the guard, I guess, but Tama locked me in a room. When she returned, the guard was with her. She told him to take care of me, then she left. He held me down. Put his hand around my throat. He said if I made a sound, he'd kill me."

"I promise they won't get away with this," Kari vowed, taking hold of Kyoko's hands.

"Don't tell anyone," Kyoko pleaded, shaking her head. "If anyone found out... I... my family would be dishonored."

"Kyoko, I have to. That's the only way he'll face justice," Kari said.

"No! No! Please," Kyoko begged.

Kari hesitated. There was nothing she could do if she didn't tell someone. The guard would be free to hurt the other girls, but she didn't want to cause Kyoko more pain.

No matter how much she hated it, Kari had to respect the girl's wishes. "I won't," she said reassuringly.

It was a promise she hated having to make. The bastard wouldn't face justice for his crimes, which meant balance would never be restored. At least it would be an easy promise to keep. Kari would be gone before the night ended.

CHAPTER FOUR

KARI DIDN'T SLEEP THAT night. Instead, she waited in her bed until everyone was asleep long enough she wouldn't fear waking them as she moved through the storehouse.

Kari rolled out of her bunk and onto the floor, staying hidden from the sight of the guards. She pulled out the clothing she had tucked under her bed, then rolled them under her sheets. Her makeshift dummy wasn't overly convincing, but, in the dark, it would at least buy her some time before anyone would notice she was gone.

Suying looked so peaceful asleep on her bed. It would be hard to leave her. She had been like a sister to her for the past three years. Kari brushed the hair from Suying's face, then bent to kiss her forehead.

"I'm sorry. I'm so sorry," she whispered. "But I can't stay here, and you've made your choice."

If Suying wouldn't come willingly, then there was no choice but to leave her. Time was against Kari, and she refused to become a concubine to the emperors. Perhaps one day, she could return for Suying, but if Kari didn't leave now, there would be no other opportunities to escape. She had to save herself if she wanted to have even the faintest chance of saving Suying.

Kari turned toward the guards, maintaining a low profile by crouching next to her bed. The two guards sat at their table. Even in the dark, they seemed tired, which was a good sign. Tired guards would be careless. Now was her chance, but she had to be quick and silent.

The path to the open doorway leading to the back room was clear. It was a straight shot. She could do this.

Kari despised her light cantrips. Using them filled her with disgust. They reminded her of what she truly was, but she couldn't deny their usefulness. Right now, that was more important.

Taking a deep breath, she focused her energy into the air around her, manipulating the light, bending it and refracting it around her body. The world around her faded and disappeared as her sight failed. She was now blind—the telltale sign she was also effectively invisible. The tradeoff was worth it. She just needed to take her time and keep true.

Her control was a bit clumsy at best, so the faster she moved, the harder it was to conceal herself. Not to mention the fact she couldn't see where she was going. Her movements needed to be slow and deliberate. It was exactly forty-eight paces from her bed to the back door. She carefully moved into the center of the room, counting each step. On the third pace, she turned to where the doorway was and inched toward it, counting her steps along the way.

She pawed at the air as she approached her count until she found the doorway. After taking hold of the frame to reorient herself, she darted into the room. Her vision rushed back to her as she became visible again. She crouched again, glancing through the door to make sure the guards hadn't spotted her. It was hard to tell in the darkness, but she didn't see any movement.

There was just one more guard station to go. Unfortunately, this one required her to actually open a door directly behind the table where the final two guards sat. Simple tricks were out of the question. They would hear her the moment she tried to open the door.

There was only one option to take. She just hoped it would work.

Kari placed the seed she had gotten from the courtyard under an empty bunk on the cold stone floor, then placed her hand on top of it as she cleared her mind. Kari needed perfect concentration if she were going to have any chance of success. Taking a deep breath, she opened her eyes.

As she transferred her energy into the seed, it morphed and transformed into a bundle of vines under her hand. They kept growing and stretching under the wooden bed, creeping their way under bed after bed, undetected by the guards. Once the vines had cleared the last bed, they grew up the far wall and over behind the guard post.

Kari smiled. The easy part was out of the way, but now she needed to be quick and accurate. She peeked out from her hiding spot to make sure she was lined up correctly. Kari visualized what she needed to do in her mind as she unleashed a surge of energy into the vines.

The vines on the wall shot out and took hold of the guards, wrapping around their arms, neck, and mouth. They struggled but couldn't break free. With their mouths covered, they weren't even able to call for help. Kari focused her spirit energy, causing the vines to tighten around their necks. The guards flailed about as their air was cut off, restricting the blood flow to their heads. After a few moments, they stopped struggling. Their bodies went limp, supported only by the strength of the vines.

Kari released the guards, and they crumbled to the floor. She poured her energy into the vines, having to concentrate and move quickly if she wanted to avoid detection. The vines rescinded, returning to their original seed form.

Kari took hold of it and darted for the door, running on the balls of her feet to avoid making too much noise. After she dashed through the door, she closed it behind her.

Speed was of the utmost importance now. It would only be a matter of time before the guards regained consciousness, then everyone would be searching for her.

Running through the dark hallways, she made her way to the courtyard. She crouched, easing her way into the cool night air. The fresh breeze was a welcome reprieve. She scanned the wall for any guards. Two guards patrolled the farthest wall. She hugged the side of the stone barrier, waiting for them to pass.

Once the guards were out of sight, she hurried along the edge of the nearest wall. She pressed her seed against it, then fed it with her spirit energy. Large vines covered the wall, stretching from the ground to the top. They were thicker than the ones she had created to neutralize the other guards. These would have to be. She needed them to support her weight.

Taking a strong grip with the vines, she began the climb to the top. Once she reached it, she cradled the vines, which quickly shrunk and reformed into the seed.

Kari sighed in relief. She'd made it. Against all hope, she was finally free.

"Halt!"

Kari turned on her heels as the two guards charged at her with their swords drawn.

She'd spoken too soon. Kari wasn't free yet.

Kari braced herself to fight as the first guard descended upon her. She jumped out of the way as he swung his sword at her neck. Clearly, they had no intention of taking prisoners.

"Surrender and come quietly," he barked.

"To my death?" Kari asked. "If I am to die, let it be here as a free woman."

The two guards stood side by side with their swords at the ready. She needed to end this before any other guards noticed, but all she had was her seed. She gritted her teeth as she readied herself for battle.

The guards rushed her, feeling confident since their prey had no weapon. Kari transferred her energy into the seed, then threw it at the nearest guard. The seed transformed in midair, becoming a cluster of vines and thorns. It collided against the guard's face, then wrapped around his head before twisting around his entire body. He convulsed as the thorns dug into his flesh, and he fell to the ground. He tried to scream, but the vines just used the opening to twist down into his throat.

"What the hell is this?" The other guard stared wide eyed at his companion, who gargled and choked on the plant. He whirled on Kari with fury in his eyes.

Kari focused her energy, spirit charging her muscles. She stepped to the side as he swung down at her. Without breaking her momentum, she closed the distance and collided her elbow into his face. His nose broke from the force. As he stumbled from the blow, she grabbed ahold of the handle of his sword and launched a back kick that sent him spiraling backward, releasing his grip on the weapon.

With the sword in hand, Kari rushed the guard and drove its blade upward into his chest. Her spirit aura charged the blade, allowing its point to effortlessly pierce through the guard's armor and into his body. He stared at her in disbelief before collapsing to the ground.

What had she done? She gazed at the fallen guards as their bodies laid prostrate on the floor. She had never killed before. It had felt so easy. Her training had just kicked in, then they were dead and she was alive.

Kari couldn't dwell on that now. She had to go. She'd crossed a line, and there was no going back. Kari rushed over to the plant-wrapped guard. With a single touch, the vine returned into a seed.

Freedom was just over the small retaining wall. The only thing in her way was a fifty-foot drop. She had done it.

Kari focused her spirit aura, then leapt over the side of the wall. She landed with barely a shockwave resonating in her legs from the fall's impact. With one last look around the perimeter to see if anyone else had seen or heard her, she dashed into the darkness and headed for the docks. All she had to do was to stick to the shadows and follow the Cerulean River to where it met the Valceem on the other side of the palace. It was only a few miles.

Kari breathed a sigh of relief when she reached the river docks. She had made it. It was over. At least for her. A part of her felt guilty for leaving Suying and the others behind, but she didn't owe them anything. She didn't know the other girls, not really. It wasn't her responsibility to take care of them. As for Suying, she'd made her choice.

No, leaving them behind was the right thing to do. Kari had to look out for herself. No one else would. She was alone.

But still, she couldn't shake this feeling of guilt.

The palace walls towered over the tops of the building she had passed through. A fortress in its own right, the palace watched over the city, oppressing her even now.

Kari couldn't think about that now. She needed to find a boat. There were plenty of ships coming and going from the docks. One would hire her, at least until she could get out of the empire.

Thoughts of the past flooded her mind. Memories of the cave and the rocks raining down all around her. She had been so scared, so sure she was about to die.

"Run, save yourself," the daughter of Alme cried out. A falling boulder crushed her leg, leaving a bloody mess and trapping her in the crumbling tunnel.

She looked so scared—the way Kari felt. She didn't want to die, but there was nothing left for her to do.

"Please, don't die with me."

Kari tried to shake the memories from her head. That was the past. It was different this time. This wasn't her fault. Besides, there was no turning back now. She had killed two guards. If she attempted to return, they would kill her.

But maybe not. No one knew she was gone, that she had been the one to kill them. If she could make it back to her bed before anyone noticed she was missing, there would be no reason to suspect her. But that was crazy. She would rather die than go back to that hell.

But Suying was the only reason Kari wasn't truly alone. Suying was her family now, her sister. How could Kari leave her?

Kari gritted her teeth as she squeezed her temples. She could at least return to see if the guards had noticed anything out of the ordinary. If they had, she would walk away, but if not... Kari didn't even want to entertain the idea of staying. It wasn't like there was anything she could do.

But then again, doing nothing simply because she thought it wouldn't help accomplished, less than nothing.

The whole idea was too dangerous and stupid. But what kind of person would she be if she left now?

Kari paced back and forth. This wasn't right. Nothing was right.

"Damn it."

Kari turned, heading back to the storehouse. The first step filled her heart with dread as the very thought of what might happen loomed over her like a shadow. Despite everything, Suying wasn't just like a sister to her—she had *become* her sister. Kari might return to her death or to a lifetime of slavery, but she couldn't leave another friend to suffer and die.

CHAPTER FIVE

"G̲ᴇᴛ ᴜᴘ! E̲ᴠᴇʀʏᴏɴᴇ, ɢᴇᴛ out of bed!"

Kari's eyes shot wide as a detachment of guards stormed into the storehouse. She had just fallen to sleep, too. At this rate, she would be lucky if she got even a solid hour of shuteye. It was her own fault for sneaking out in the middle of the night, then returning like a fool. The rush of adrenaline from her earlier activities had made falling asleep that much more difficult.

"Line up in front of your beds! Hurry up," the guard captain demanded.

What could this be about? Did they know someone tried to escape? That was a stupid question. Of course they did. She had left two bodies in her wake, and another two unconscious. This was expected.

Suying shot Kari a glance. Clearly, she was thinking the same thing.

Once the girls had appropriately lined up to the guard captain's desire, he began, "You are murderers. I don't know which of you did it, and I don't care. If I had my way, I'd kill the lot of you. Right here and now. Traitors don't deserve to live. Heaven has decreed that all who oppose the will of the throne must be eliminated."

"Now, now, Captain. Let's not go around making baseless accusations," a dark ghost of a man chided as he entered the storehouse. Kari had never seen another human being like him before. He was dressed in solid black, a stark contrast to his colorless pale face. The only color to him was a sky-blue sash, which was tucked away and obscured by his billowy coat. It was the blue sash that gave away what he was—a Kitsuno Kai, a wolf among men. As elite swordsmen, they acted outside of Imperial control. They could go anywhere and do anything they pleased to defend the empire. Only one thing was ever for sure about a Kitsuno Kai—wherever one went, death followed. If she were ever asked to describe an evil man, this would be him.

The man moved gracefully through the storehouse, each step echoing in the silence, his expression vacant. He moved around without a care in the world with this aloofness that made him seem uninterested in what was going on around him, but his eyes told a different story. They scanned everything—every person, every bed, every inch of the storehouse. Finally, he stopped near the guard captain.

"I must apologize for the captain's rudeness. It is awfully early in the morning, and he really did not want to be awake. For that, I share his sentiments. Where are the matrons?" He spoke without pause, without hesitation.

"I am head matron. I'm in charge here." The guards had lined Zhenhua up with the girls. Apparently, they considered all of them to be suspects.

"No, I don't believe so," the Kitsuno Kai said in a matter-of-fact tone. "I don't see anyone missing. How's your count?"

"They are all here," Zhenhua said.

"Count them again."

"But you just verified—" Zhenhua started, but the Kitsuno Kai held up a single finger to cut her off.

"Count them again." And with that order, she complied and began her count again. "Let me introduce myself. My name is irrelevant, and my position is meaningless to you. I'm sure you are wondering what is going on, but, then again, I'm guessing at least one of you already knows. Two guards were killed here tonight. One, at least, was killed by what I can only assume to be some kind of magic. On top of that, the two guards who were stationed in the very next room were attacked and rendered unconscious. My initial thought was someone had escaped, but everyone is here. Is that correct?"

Zhenhua nodded.

"In that case, what happened? Was something brought in? Are we communicating with individuals beyond our station? It is puzzling. Whatever the case may be, someone here heard something, saw something, or knows something. I need to know what that is. So, this is the deal I'm willing to make. Much like the captain expressed earlier, I do not wish to be awake right now either, so I'm looking to kill someone. Don't let that someone be you. You will tell me everything you know. If I discover you are lying or deceiving me in any way, I will kill you." The blue wolf bared his lips in a devilish grin. He seemed to enjoy the idea of murder. "Confiscate their belongings and prepare them for interrogation."

"But sir, the emperors will be here today for their auditions. These girls need to be preparing for them," the guard captain protested.

Sighing, the dark man placed a hand on the captain's shoulder. "Question my methods again, and you will find yourself in a pool of your own blood. Now do as I say."

"Y-yes sir."

In an instant, the guards leapt into action, stripping the beds down and packing the linen in each of the girls' chests, leaving only the bare wooden platform, which was then overturned and inspected for contraband. Once all the loose items were gathered up, the guards snatched up the chests and hauled them into the back.

"What did you do?" Suying asked once all the guards were out of earshot. "Did you kill those guards?"

"What do you mean?" Kari asked, trying to hide her guilt. It was better for Suying not to know any more than she had to, especially if they were to be interrogated.

"Don't lie to me," Suying said. "You tried to leave last night. You were going to leave me? After trying to talk me into going with you, you would leave me here? I don't understand you."

"I came back to help you, so we can escape together." She hoped Suying would understand and wouldn't be too upset with her. Kari couldn't blame Suying if she were, but surely Kari returning had to mean something.

"But I told you already... I want to stay here. If you want to leave so bad, then leave." Suying stomped her foot.

"I'm not leaving you here," Kari whispered. They were getting too loud. Someone was bound to overhear them.

"So, you're going to ruin my chance at a happy life?"

"Happy? What kind of life will you have being subservient to tyrants?" There was no denying Suying's life outside of the palace walls had been anything but happy, but there was no happiness to be found here, only complacency.

"What do you know about them anyway? It is only by the will of heaven they are able to rule." The will of heaven? Suying sounded like one of the emperors' lap dogs.

"Do you think the heavens really want you to lie with the emperors?"

"This is my one chance for a better life, one where I don't have to starve and struggle just to get by. No band of raiders is going to kill me or my family. Kari, I love you, but I won't let you ruin this for me."

Her sister was slipping away, using her fear as an excuse. Suying had every right to be afraid, to fear returning to their old lives. It didn't matter what it took. Kari would find a way to make things better. She just needed Suying to trust her again, to know how much she cared for her. "Suying, I want you to know I made it out. I was going to leave you here, but it was love that brought me back. I'm not leaving without you."

"I think you are confusing love with some delusion of heroism. There is no victim here other than you. I want to be here. Without hesitation, I would gladly choose this life. Why can't you understand that?" Suying's raised her eyebrows as she pleaded her case.

"What I understand is they've indoctrinated you into their twisted way of thinking. You deserve more than this." What would it take to make Suying understand? Maybe she just needed time. She must feel hurt and betrayed about Kari trying to leave without her. That was understandable. It must be what was exacerbating her fears of the real world.

"Indoctrinated? We've barely been here a week." Suying sighed as she studied Kari. "You're right. I do deserve more, but the only more to be had is here. Outside of the palace, life is fleeting, but if I stay here, I can live. It may not be the will of heaven, but it is a better life. It's what I want. Please understand that. I don't know if I can help you now, but if you get another chance to leave, take it. For your own sake."

"For your own sake, you two better talk more quietly," Ina said, approaching the pair. "I could hear what you were saying from across the room. Luckily, I think everyone else is too panicked to notice. And you better hope they were, too."

Kari gritted her teeth. She was being too careless. "What did you hear?"

"Just how you don't want to be here, and her saying you should leave."

If Ina overheard them, then someone else could have as well. Everyone appeared too worried to pay much attention to them, but there was no way to know for certain. All it would take is one person telling the Kitsuno Kai about Kari's dissention... and she could face death. He wouldn't even have to know she was the one responsible for the guards' death.

The guards' deaths.

The thought hadn't really struck her until now. Kari was responsible. She had killed two human beings. Had taken their lives, ended their hopes, their dreams, whatever plans for the future they might have had. Whatever family they had left would be devastated when they found out about their son's death. The death she caused. Would their mothers cry?

Life was fragile. It was so easy to extinguish it, like the flame of a dying candle. In the moment, she hadn't given them a second thought. She'd simply blown out the flame. They'd been her enemies, and they'd stood against her. She hated them. They'd been her captors, ready to kill or subjugate her, so she'd killed them.

And now she was hated.

Their mothers and fathers, sisters and brothers, their friends and comrades, they would all hate Kari for what she'd done. She had created an endless cycle of hatred and pain.

She could still see their faces, see the shock and fear in their eyes as she'd killed them. The sounds of a man dying, choking, struggling for life as her plant had twisted its way down his throat and into his body. That horrible gurgling reverberated in her head. The man's eyes had been wide with terror and fear as if he'd known the fate that had befallen him.

"Are you okay?" Ina asked, yanking Kari back to the present.

"I'm fine." Kari wiped at the tears forming in her eyes.

"You're trembling," Suying added.

"I said I'm fine. I just need a moment." Kari stumbled to her bare bed. Her knees buckled, threatening to give way with each step. She sat, pressing her palm against her forehead.

It was necessary. Her actions, their deaths—they were necessary for her survival. They were Imperial guards, loyal to a corrupt and unjust throne. Their actions had shown they were just as corrupt and vile as the masters they served.

It was what she had to tell herself.

"You there," a guard said, approaching Kari. "Come with me."

She was one of the first ones being called to the back. That wasn't a good sign. Had someone overheard? She needed to be calm. A calm person had nothing to hide. Kari stood, straightened her shoulders, and followed the guard.

The guard led her through the hallway. He opened a door, motioning for Kari to enter. She took a deep breath to steady her resolve before stepping into the bare room. The guard slammed and locked the door behind her.

The Kitsuno Kai sat in a chair at the center, reading a book. He didn't bother to look up as she entered. A lone chair was in front of him.

"Please, have a seat." The Kitsuno Kai motioned to the empty chair, still not raising his head.

Kari bowed gracefully before taking the offered seat.

"And what might your name be?" he asked, still avoiding her.

"What is yours?" Kari responded without hesitation. The Kitsuno Kai jerked his head up, his eyes filled with life as he shot arrows at her. Kari's heart jumped to her throat. If a look could kill, this one would be it.

"That's a rather impertinent question." His facial muscles relaxed into a more neutral expression, but the venom still dripped from his words.

"Not at all. Where I come from, it is quite rude to ask someone their name without first giving yours." She needed to avoid suspicion. Clearly, someone with nothing to hide would be brave and willing to confront her interrogator when he was out of line. At least, she hoped that was the case.

He leaned forward in his chair, his face coming within inches of hers. "I already have your name from the guards, but I would like for you to confirm it."

"Isn't *that* an impertinent statement to make?" Kari asked, turning his words against him. "I am at a disadvantage. You know who I am, but I do not even know how to address you."

He tossed his book behind him. The ruffling pages echoed in the mostly empty room before the whole thing crashed to the floor with a thud. Her heartbeat quickened at the sudden outburst. She needed to disarm him, turn the tables on him to avoid any troubling questions about her, but perhaps she had gone too far. After all, no one would question this man if he dared to cut her down here and now. If she were going to avoid suspicion, she needed to act as if she had nothing to hide. She needed to become less memorable. So far, she was failing. She would have to play the game a bit differently to avoid angering him further.

Smiling, he leaned back in his chair. "If manners so concern you, then you have violated your own etiquette by demanding my name without first offering yours."

"My lord speaks truly. I am remiss, and I've been rather discourteous. My name is Hikari. It is a pleasure to meet you." She gave him a coy smile.

"Likewise. And I suppose I should return the formality. You may call me Ronin."

"Ronin? Is that your name or what you are?"

"Perhaps it is both," Ronin answered with a smirk. "Now tell me, where are you from?"

"I'm from Xiao'lavoth," Kari answered in a matter-of-fact tone.

"No, no." Ronin held up a hand in protest. His sinister smile grew wider as if he were truly proud of himself. "I know that's what you've told these fools, but where are you really from?"

"I'm afraid I don't understand the question." Her eyes darted away from him as she tried to avoid his piercing stare.

"You are a foreigner of some sort." She recoiled as he reached out and stroked her face. How could he know that? Was it her eyes? *By the goddess, please don't let it be her eyes.*

"What do you mean? I'm Xianese." He could see her fully. There was no hiding from his perception. Her heart raced as sweat formed on her brow.

"Maybe on one side. While rural Xiang is homogeneous, Valceem has a plethora of ethnicities. Even still, there is something odd about you. Your accent is similar to someone from the southern nations. But then, there is your preference for the name Kari. Your features are similar to the Subarashii, yet different, but it is your eyes that give you away. Although blue and even green eyes are not uncommon in Valceem, no one who is a native to Xiang has eyes quite like that. I couldn't quite discern it earlier, but then you said it. Where you come from. So where would that be?" Damn her eyes. Did he know what she was? He couldn't. If he did, she would already be dead.

"I'm afraid you are mistaken." Who was this man? How was he drawing such accurate conclusions from such small subtleties? Was he merely making accusations to see how she would react?

"Is that so?" Ronin eyed her up and down. "I am rarely mistaken."

Clearly the former. He could discern the truth, at least parts of it, and he was bold about it. There was no telling what else he knew. Kari had to hide what she was. She had to hide the Seed.

"In this case, you are. I am not from the south, but from Friean far to the west." Kari told the half lie in a steady voice. She might not be able to hide the truth from him, but if she could mix enough truth with lies, maybe she could obscure his perception.

"Friean is on the other side of the continent. What are you doing here?" Ronin asked.

"My father is Xianese while my mother is Frieank, which is why I derive Kari from my given name. When they died, I wanted to travel to my father's homeland to serve as an Imperial concubine. I wanted a better life than that of a beggar. That's why I personally requested High Chancellor Cai Ren to allow me to serve the emperors." Hopefully, that was the official account Cai Ren had stated.

"The emperors are the physical embodiment of Xiang. Most would say serving them is a noble endeavor, but only a fool willingly submits themselves to the service of another. However, I think servitude for personal advancement is shrewd, if not downright conniving. What other schemes must you have?"

He'd called her a schemer as if he knew she was planning something. Her eyes burned as a wave of panic threatened to overtake her.

"My lord, I... I'm unsure how to respond. I swear to you I have no plans." That part was the truth.

Ronin held out a hand to stop her. "I digress. Tell me, Kari, what is your relationship to the girl? Name of Suying?"

"We are friends. I met her when I first arrived in the city."

"I see. Did she volunteer, too?" he asked.

"No, she was conscripted." Rubbing her eyes, she tried to calm herself. She didn't know how to respond anymore.

"And she was happy with this?"

"Not at first, but she understands her place now. She knows the emperors will provide her a better life." The thought of Suying saying those words sickened Kari.

Ronin paused, rubbing his chin. "Four guards were attacked, two ended up dead. One of the guards who was killed had the remains of some sort of plant growing down his throat. They pierced his organs, rupturing them from the inside. He died an excruciatingly painful death, unable to even scream for help. What do you make of this?"

"My lord, I am but a humble songstress. I do not know of such horrors."

"You are more educated than the other prattle here. That much is obvious, so don't play coy. You have a mind, so give an opinion." Venom once again coursed through his words.

"Sounds like witchcraft to me."

"Why witches?" He waved his hand as if to brush off the thought. "Never mind. It's magic, powerful magic. This magic could be used against the emperors, sure, who cares? But you're missing the big question. Two guards dead, two unconscious. Why? What does your education tell you?"

"I don't know," Kari whispered, breaking eye contact.

"Have an opinion!" He lunged at her, seizing hold of her shoulders, and forced her chair onto its hind legs to get in her face. Her heart nearly stopped as she instinctively grabbed at his wrists to keep from falling backward.

"I... maybe..." Kari stammered. She closed her eyes, frantically trying to think of a response. "Maybe the second pair saw them."

"The second pair saw them, yes." He released her, then leaned back in his chair. Kari frantically rubbed her shoulders where his fingers had dug into her skin only moments ago. Ronin chewed over the words as he thought through their implication. He motioned in the air with a single finger as if he were drawing a line between two points. "They made it past the first pair unseen, but the second pair saw them. But why? Were they already in the building? Did they bring something in and were leaving? No, they were trying to leave, trying to escape, but didn't. We've accounted for everyone."

Kari's heart pounded in her chest. He was piecing it together. When that happened, she would be as good as dead.

Ronin stared at Kari. No, he stared past her, through everything she was. "Unless they did escape but came back. But why? Was it a change of heart? A change of... *opinion?*"

"My lord, please, I..."

"But I've talked for too long. Don't worry," Ronin interrupted her. He stood from his chair, moving to retrieve his book. "I know what you fear—that I'll disclose your secret you are a mutt—but I will not bother the emperors with such frivolous nonsense. Now, return to your quarters and inform the guards I need to speak with Suying next."

CHAPTER SIX

KARI FIDDLED WITH THE tile in her hand. There were just no good moves to make. Ina was dominating the board. Every move Kari would make, Ina always seemed to have a counter. Ina had unbelievable luck, always drawing the right tile for the right situation, whereas Kari's luck seemed to have abandoned her.

Ina had suggested she and Kari play a game to help get their minds off Ronin's continued investigation, but it seemed like that was all she could focus on. Ina had no trouble concentrating on the game at hand. It was like she didn't have a care in the world about her impeding interrogation.

Suying's interrogation came and went with little fuss. All Ronin had asked her to do was verify her name and recorded history.

Kari clenched her jaw. The day would only get worse. Once Ronin was finished with his investigation, they still had the emperors' visit, and this damn fire tile she had just drawn seemed to have no useful moves on the board. She couldn't block Ina's next set, nor could she use it to add to any of hers.

"Giving up?" Ina asked.

"Of course not." Kari reluctantly placed the fire tile on an empty section of the board. She had no other choice than to try to start a new set.

"You're really bad at this. Are you sure you've played before?" Ina placed an earth tile, which completed another set, this one composed of earth, air, fire, and light. The completed set brought her score up five to Kari's one.

If Kari hadn't had so much on her mind, maybe she could have played competitively, but, as it stood, the game was just one more thing to overwhelm her already troubled mind. The morning was fading quickly. In a matter of hours, the path fate had set for them would be revealed. The thought filled her with dread.

Ina didn't seem to notice. The game was all she cared about. How did she even have an Aether board with her? None of the other girls in the storehouse had any personal possessions.

"Are you going to keep me waiting forever? It's your turn." Ina stared at Kari, clutching the pendant she wore around her neck.

Kari reached into her bag, then withdrew another tile. This one bore the symbol for light. Kari smiled. She was running out of tiles, which meant winning was out of the question, but she could still play on. Her new goal was to lessen her defeat, and her drawn tile gave her that opportunity.

She placed her light tile adjacent to Ina's white air tile, which served as a corner of her completed set. Ina's air tile was surrounded on both free sides by Kari's tiles, one light and one spirit. She had successfully countered Ina's set, reducing her score to four.

"Not bad. But don't think that will help you win," Ina said, drawing another tile from her bag. Sighing, Ina placed her tile on the table beside the board. "Are you still planning to try to escape?"

Kari was taken aback by her bluntness. "You shouldn't ask that. Someone might hear."

"But are you? The emperor will be here today, and you're still here. Is your plan to wait things out or have you given in to our fate?"

Kari leaned in closer so she could talk quietly, hopefully avoiding anyone overhearing. "I don't know. I would give anything not to be here, but, for now, I can't leave." Suying was here, and there was no leaving without her.

"Even if you could leave, you shouldn't." Ina placed her tile on the board.

"How can you say that?"

"I can understand why you would want to, I really do, but you have to decide which is more important—your dignity or your life. I know that might sound cruel, but those are our options. Take a look at what happened to Kyoko just for complaining too much. I'm warning you. You need to stay."

"How do you know about that?" Kari's brow furrowed.

"So, it's true. I suspected as much." Ina bit her thumb. "It wasn't hard to figure out. Just look at her. She's been near mute, just sitting with her legs pressed together and a blank expression. I wasn't sure what was wrong with her, but I figured you would."

She'd tricked her. "I don't like where this conversation is going."

"Don't end up like her," Ina said flatly.

"I'm done." Abruptly, Kari stood and walked away.

"Ina," a guard called as he appeared from the back room. "I need you to come with me."

"That won't be necessary," Zhenhua corrected the guard as she rushed over. "I will personally talk with Ina. There's no need to get the Kitsuno Kai involved." Ina bowed to Kari before following after Zhenhua.

"Dignity or death," Ina whispered as she brushed by Kari. "I'm sorry." She and Zhenhua disappeared into the back.

What was that about? Why would Zhenhua care about Ina? Something was wrong. Ina had food when no one else did, had personal belongings, private meetings with Zhenhua, and now Zhenhua was guarding her from Ronin. And to finish off the conspiracy, Ina had tricked her into confirming the incident with Kyoko.

Kari hurried over to her bed, flopping onto it. Time was running out. She needed to convince Suying to escape with her now. With the guards around, stealth would no longer be an option. They would have to fight their way out.

Could Kari do it—fight her way to the courtyard and kill anyone who got in her way?

She'd struggled against two guards last night. Now there were even more on duty and a Kitsuno Kai to make matters worse.

She needed to bide her time. Wait for another opening. It was the only way she could escape without being detected. That would give Suying more time to come to her senses anyway.

The vault door opened, interrupting Kari's thoughts. Cai Ren and a large number of guards poured into the room.

"Listen up, ladies," Cai Ren started. "We will be taking a little trip inside the palace to the courtyard of the Hall of Heaven and Earth. You will remain quiet at all times, and you'll march in a single-file line. Now, get ready to move out."

The guards ushered the girls into rank, then escorted them out of the storehouse and into carriages. More guards stood atop the palace walls, watching as the girls filed one by one into the convoy of horse-drawn carriages.

Without a word, the carriages headed for the Grand Entrance of the Palace. The massive wooden gates opened to allow them to pass through. Behind the wooden gate was a steel one that raised upward for the vehicles to pass. The long stone passageway forced any invading force into a bottleneck. Another series of double gates awaited at the end of the passageway to prevent entry into the palace. Retractable openings, protected by steel bars, ran alongside the stone walls. It allowed the palace soldiers to decimate anyone who tried to take the palace by force.

Once they were through the Grand Entrance, they entered the Imperial Way. This small district was filled with guard posts and stables and protected the Imperial District, which housed the Hall of Heaven and Earth. While every other district was connected to its adjacent districts through a series of moon gates, the Imperial Way was only connected to the Imperial District, though the latter was connected to every district.

The courtyard in the Imperial District was massive. A small stream ran from one side to the other with arched bridges allowing passage over the waterway. Legions could easily fit in the courtyard—could stand at attention in front of the gigantic structure designed to allow the emperors to speak on behalf of heaven.

The Hall of Heaven and Earth was the center point of the palace, and its monumental structure and three grand pagodas overlooked the entire palace. The massive pagodas rose to the sky and soared above the palace walls, serving as a constant reminder to the occupants of who their rulers were. The main tower housed the Imperial Throne Room and the Judgement Room, where matters of legal ambiguity were settled by trial by combat. The other towers consisted of courtrooms for the chancellors and royal ministers. The base of the hall housed a large formal dining area and plenty of quarters for private meetings and to conduct the state of affairs.

The walls of the palace were all painted a crimson red with gold, the color of heaven, decorating the roofs of all the buildings.

Once they had made it to the Hall of Heaven and Earth, they stopped in front of the fountain of Valceem. A statue of Valceem, the first emperor, stood in the center of the grand fountain. Even in stone, her beauty showed.

Valceem had been born into slavery in the nation of Shika. When she was Kari's age, she headed a slave revolt and led her free people to settle in Xiang—in the city renamed after her.

At the time, Xiang had been ripped apart in civil war, and the city was founded as a land of exiles, welcoming all who sought freedom and safety from the raging chaos. For centuries her city had stood rooted to those ideals as people migrated from the bordering nations to seek refuge behind her great walls.

The guards gathered the girls, then lined them up into rows.

"What do you think this is about?" Suying whispered, standing close to Kari.

"I don't know," Kari responded. A trio of guards appeared behind the ranks of girls, accompanied by Ina. They shoved her into the back row before stationing themselves at the entrance. Was this Ina's doing? "Stay close to me."

Cai Ren walked to the front of the group, scanning the girls.

"Welcome," he said, addressing the crowd. "As you know, the emperor will conduct his audition today. However, recent events have dictated a change in schedule. A pre-audition inspection if you will. Therefore, it is my pleasure to introduce His Most High Lord, joint ruler of Xiang, Emperor Jiaorong."

The girls kowtowed in reverence. Kari joined them, not wanting to draw attention to herself. A muscular man draped in a crimson red shenyi with gold embroidery and decorated with dragon motifs approached the girls. His black hair was trimmed close to his head. When he drew his sword, a hush fell over the group. Kari grabbed Suying's hand, yanking the girl behind her.

"Spread them out," Jiaorong ordered. In an instant, the guards leapt into action. They grabbed and shoved the girls, widening the space between the rows. Kari refused to let go of Suying's hand as she was pushed into position next to Kari.

"It has been brought to my attention that one of you is a traitor to my throne." Jiaorong stood, towering over everyone in attendance. He motioned to Cai Ren. "Bring her to me."

The girls stood in silence as Cai Ren weaved through the rows.

Kari squeezed Suying's hand. "Whatever happens, remain silent. If it gets bad, run," she whispered.

Each girl bowed their head as Cai Ren moved through the ranks, but Kari glared at him as he passed in front of her. It was odd how the sight of him could fill her with such rage.

"You still have fire in your eyes, I see." He stopped, raising an eyebrow at Kari. "Be as defiant as you want. In a battle of wills, mine is stronger, and you will submit."

He slapped her across the face. The blow took her by surprise, sending stinging pain through her cheek. She fought against her instincts to place her hand against her reddening face, simply scowling back at him. She would not give him the satisfaction of winning.

Cai Ren smiled at her resolve, but he did not waver in his either. "I see." This time, he struck Suying. She pulled away from Kari's grip as her hands shot to her face. "Do not think yourself my equal. You will not look me in the eyes. You will bow your head, or I will take hers."

Clenching her jaw, Kari closed her eyes in defeat, restraining herself from striking back. She wasn't his equal. He was beneath her. She couldn't wait to show him, but, for now, she relented and bowed her head. There was nothing she could do in this situation. Any action she took would only endanger Suying or get them both killed.

"You'll do wise to remember your place," Cai Ren said.

"I grow tired of waiting. Hurry and bring her to me," Jiaorong barked. "Do any of you know the penalty for treason? It is *death*."

Kari's heart jumped. Taking a deep breath, she prepared her body to fight. There were at least thirty guards stationed around the courtyard. Far too many to fight. Her only option was to run and escape, but that would prove problematic as there was nowhere to run to inside the palace.

Cai Ren cleared his throat. "An execution is in order. Let this be a lesson to you all. You belong to the emperors. You are their servants. Any dissent, any disorder, will be met with swift justice."

Kari closed her eyes and braced herself, but nothing happened. Not to her.

Cai Ren grabbed ahold of Kyoko, then dragged her out of line to the front where Jiaorong awaited. Screaming, Kyoko struggled fiercely as she tried to get away.

"Stop, you can't do this," Momiji screamed.

"Silence her," Jiaorong ordered. Two guards rushed over. After knocking Momiji to the ground, they beat her. "This whore dared betray her benefactors by sleeping with a guard."

"She was raped," Kari blurted out. She no longer cared about her promise to Kyoko. Saving her life was more important than saving her dignity.

Jiaorong motioned for the two guards who had attacked Momiji. They headed for Kari. She braced herself for their onslaught, focusing on her spirit aura. They knocked her to the ground, then began striking her again and again. For a moment, all she could see were fists and feet coming at her. Each blow sent shockwaves through her body. Just as quickly as their onslaught began, it ended.

Kari lay motionless on the ground. Luckily, their fists were a lot softer than they looked. Her aura ensured that whatever pain they inflicted on her, her body could easily take. She would quickly recover. Momiji wasn't so lucky.

She was balled up on the ground with her hands wrapped around her head. Her body spasmed as she sobbed. It was hard to tell from where Kari was, but it looked like drops of red blood had been spattered on the ground next to her.

"Any attendant who engages in consensual sex without approval from either emperor is guilty of treason. In the event of a legitimate rape within the city walls, it is reasonably inferred the woman would cry out for help. Since she did no such thing, she therefore consented and was not raped." Cai Ren led Kyoko to Jiaorong, who hit her across the face, knocking her to the ground.

"This slut couldn't keep her legs closed. If this sort of behavior goes unpunished, then it is only a matter of time before my palace is overrun with whores. She must die." Jiaorong grabbed Kyoko's hair, yanking her off the ground.

"No! Please no," Kyoko begged as tears poured down her face like waterfalls. "Mama, Mama, please!" But her cries did not soften Jiaorong or his bloodlust.

Jiaorong dragged her to the fountain before dunking her head under the water. Her arms flailed wildly as she struggled to free herself, but it was to no avail. Jiaorong held on tight. An eternity passed. Her arms grew weaker and dropped to the ground, but Jiaorong still did not let go.

He continued to hold her under the water for a few more minutes as the rest of the girls watched in stunned silence.

When he was finished, he grabbed her hair and snatched her out of the fountain before tossing her lifeless body to the ground.

Jiaorong breathed heavily, his eyes wide. "Here ends the lesson."

"Let's move. Back to the storehouse." Cai Ren motioned for the guards to escort the girls back.

"No," Jiaorong bellowed in the still-silent courtyard. "Give them a moment. Let this sink in. Once they fully understand who owns them, take them back and clean them up. I'm supposed to want to sleep with these women, remember? Right now, I wouldn't touch them. I want them ready for my audition."

Jiaorong, Cai Ren, and several guards left the courtyard, leaving the girls and only a handful of guards behind. The courtyard buzzed with murmurs and chattering. Some girls cried while others looked sick, all obviously terrified of what might happen to them if they ever acted out of line.

"Are you okay?" Suying asked, helping Kari to her feet.

Kari shook her head. The pain had subsided. Her body wouldn't bruise from such a weak attack, but so much more damage had been done. Part of her was relieved it wasn't her dead on the ground, discarded like a broken doll. She thought for sure Cai Ren was on to her. The relief she felt was mixed with grief and guilt. Grief over the loss of a friend, and guilt because she was glad she hadn't been the one who'd died.

"Momiji." Kari rushed over to her fallen friend.

"She's not good," Ina said, hunched over the still-whimpering Momiji.

Her face was bloody, her nose squeezed and twisted off to one side, clearly broken. Her soft features had been smashed, hiding her beauty.

"I think they broke a rib," Ina added.

"We need to get medical attention," Kari responded.

"One of the guards sent for a stretcher. Do you need help? How are you still standing?" Ina asked, her shock at seeing Kari relatively unharmed obvious.

"I'm fine," Kari responded. Without spirit charging the guards' attacks, there was little they could do against her aura. "I'm tougher than I look."

"Clearly."

They didn't have to wait long for the guards to return with a stretcher. They loaded Momiji onto the canvas before carrying her off.

Once Momiji was out of sight, Kari stumbled over to Kyoko and dropped to her knees next to her friend's body. Kyoko's lifeless eyes were frozen wide in terror. Kari ran her hand over Kyoko's face, closing her eyes. "She was so scared. She just wanted to go home. How could they do this? She was just so scared."

"Come on." Suying gripped Kari's shoulder. "Let's go. The guards are starting to take small groups back."

"Not yet." Kari stared at Zhenhua, who motioned for the girls to return to the carriages. Rising, Kari wiped the tears from her eyes.

She marched past Suying, stomping up to Zhenhua. "You have to do something," Kari demanded.

"Didn't they beat you?" Zhenhua asked, looking Kari up and down.

Kari ignored her. "One of your guards raped Kyoko."

"Tell me something I don't know," Zhenhua responded, dismissing Kari's concerns.

"If you knew, then why didn't you say something? Why didn't you save her?"

"It's a little thing called consent. You heard the law for yourself. She didn't scream, so she was just as guilty."

"Bullshit."

Zhenhua gasped. Obviously, she wasn't used to anyone standing up to her.

"It's no use. What do you want me to do? The guard has already been executed as well. The law is quite clear on the matter," Zhenhua said.

"What about Tama?" Kari interjected. "She's the one who let him do it. She locked Kyoko in a room with him for that purpose."

"Of course she did," Zhenhua curtly replied. "She always does that. It's her way to cull out the weak ones. Anyone who might not make it as an attendant."

"And you condone this?" Kari asked, stunned.

"No, but why stop it? Most girls she eliminates would probably kill themselves anyway. This life isn't for everyone, you know. Do you think we are blind? We know many initially resist, but most will adapt. However, there are those who don't have the stomach for this kind of life. For them, it is more merciful to end their suffering quickly. You should be careful, or I might just turn *you* over to Tama."

Kari had to hold her tongue. Her blood boiled at the thought of the matrons allowing girls to be raped. It was becoming increasingly clear Tama needed to die. Not just for vengeance, but to protect others from her sadism. But Kari couldn't just walk up and stab the awful woman in the heart. She needed to play this out more carefully.

"Consider this," Kari said. "When we arrived, the guards said Kyoko was the most likely to be selected from the four of us. How do you think the emperors will react if they find out that not only are you allowing their attendants to be violated and murdered, but it is also the ones they would most likely enjoy who are the ones being killed?"

"Are you threatening me?" Zhenhua demanded.

"No. I'm just saying when someone finds out—and the emperors will find out eventually—they might hold you accountable as well. How often is Tama visited by the emperors? It is obvious she is motivated by jealousy. How will a matron trying to regain lost favor by killing potential attendants look for you? I'm sure they'll believe you are plotting with her."

Zhenhua froze, clearly thinking about what Kari had just said. "What would you have me do?" she sulkily asked.

"Turn her in to the authorities. Let Jiaorong deal with her."

"Fine." Zhenhua nodded. "Now gather your friends. I don't have much time to get you presentable for your auditions."

The girls were returned to the storehouse where Zhenhua and a host of maidservants readied them for presentation. Each girl was dressed in a similar flowing silk ruqun comprised of a pink blouse tied around her chest and a light blue skirt. A crimson ribbon wrapped around the top of the skirt while a sky-blue scarf was draped around her arms. Some had small accessories that helped them stand apart—flowers, ribbons, and jewelry were the most common. The girls noisily talked amongst themselves as they were decorated with makeup and perfumes. While a few seemed excited for the opportunity to be selected for the Imperial harem, the rest were keyed up from fear-driven adrenaline.

Kari's heart raced. The past few hours had already been more eventful than a single day had any right to be, and her lack of sleep wasn't helping her anxiety. It was difficult to discern how Suying felt. She had acted eager to help the maidservant pick out which color eyeshadow would best suit her, but she now seemed apprehensive if her fidgeting was any indication. She was almost the opposite of Ina, who stood solemnly by herself, hands folded neatly in front of her.

"All right. It is time to begin," Zhenhua said, gathering up the first group of girls to be inspected by the emperor. "Listen up for a few late-minute words. Emperor Baoshun will not be here today. Matters of court have preoccupied him as of late, so I do not expect as many girls as usual to be selected. You will audition in groups of nine. While you are in the presence of the emperor, you will remain silent. You will be asked to present yourself to the emperor one at a time. Be cordial, be graceful, and be elegant. Attendants are companions for life. Present to him not as who you were, but who you have become."

Kari made sure she was close to Suying so they would go in together. When it was their turn, they followed the guards into the room the emperor waited in.

Jiaorong sat in a decorative wooden chair in front of a raised marble stage. He was a brawny, muscular man who seemed to envelop his entire chair. He was adorned in the royal crimson shenyi. Gold inlay decorated his chest and shoulders.

Guards lined the walls of the room. Off to the side of the emperor's sitting area was a lit furnace, which warmed the small room.

"Show me the next one," Jiaorong ordered, his gravelly voice booming throughout the area.

With no warning, a guard pushed Kari forward, making her stumble onto the marble platform.

"Introducing Lady Hikari of Xiao'Lavoth," Cai Ren declared as he read off Kari's measurements and background from Zhenhua's book. Strangely enough, being judged based on her appearance didn't infuriate her as much as Cai Ren announcing her as a lady. It was a patronizing title that only served to disguise how little they actually thought of the girls they put through this horror.

"Absolutely beautiful. One of the most exquisite girls I have ever seen. And I love those eyes," Jiaorong said. "Have you ever seen eyes that green before?"

"Just once." Kari's heart nearly leapt out of her chest at Cai Ren's reply. Shagin could easily blend into their paternal homeland, except for their eyes. Her people were known for their vibrantly colorful eyes. Could he know who she really was? No, he couldn't... or else she would already be dead.

"Let's have a look at her body," Jiaorong said, imperiously reclining in his chair.

Two guards quickly descended on Kari. Before she could even think to struggle, they'd stripped her clothes off, leaving her nude and on full display—an object to be gawked at. She tried to wrap her arms around her breasts and privates, but one guard grabbed her from behind and pinned her arms to her side. Kari instinctively fought against his grip, but she eventually succumbed to her fate and yielded, forcing her mind to go blank.

"Now that's a sight." Releasing a lusty sigh, Jiaorong bit his lip as he got up from his chair to approach Kari. She shivered as he ran his fingers along her shoulder. "So smooth.

So perfect. I wonder, beautiful one, just how many lovers have you had?"

Kari shuddered. Was it better to tell the truth or lie? Either way might pique his interests. After some thought, she decided to be honest. "None," she replied.

Smirking, Jiaorong leaned forward until his face was just inches from hers. Kari could smell his repugnant stale breath. "I could be your first."

Kari turned her head in response. She had anticipated her interactions with the emperors to serve as fuel for future nightmares, but this was visceral horror. The thought of this man raping her—just because he could—and the knowledge that countless other girls had been where she was and had been subjected to repeated nonconsensual sexual torture was maddening.

Jiaorong grabbed her chin, pulling her face close to his. "You will learn to love me." He forcefully slammed his mouth against hers. Kari's eyes grew wide, tears forming as his tongue penetrated her lips and slid into her mouth. His vile organ probed the inside of her cheeks, thrusting against her own. She stood frozen in place as he sucked on her lips.

And then it was over.

Jiaorong retook his chair. Kari's body went boneless, and she fell to her knees as the guard finally released his hold on her. Tears streamed down her cheeks. Through the blur of moisture, she stared at the ground, her chest heaving.

"She'll do." Jiaorong smiled, folding his hands in front of him. "Bring the next one."

Kari raised her head, fixing a glare on the emperor. The very sound of his voice filled her with a fiery rage that threatened to escape and consume her. She wanted nothing more than to welcome it.

"It's okay, dear. It's over," Zhenhua soothed. Her concern surprised Kari, who hadn't even noticed the woman had already draped a robe over her nudity. "Let's get you dressed."

Zhenhua helped Kari to her feet before assisting her with her clothes.

"Why are you being kind?" Kari asked more bluntly than she'd intended.

"This is always the hardest part to watch, but you no longer have anything to fear. He chose you. Tonight, you will start your life of luxury."

"Is that how you justify it?" Kari asked, but Zhenhua didn't respond.

Kari was led back to the lineup of the other girls, forced to watch as they were put under the same inspection she'd been subjected to. Each girl was the same. Cai Ren would read out each girl's stats from the book before the guards stripped them naked. Each time, it was a repeat. Jiaorong forced himself on each girl, some even more viciously attacked than she had been.

Kari wanted to have more sympathy for them, but she was hollow inside. She should have bit off that bastard's tongue when she'd had the chance. Should have fought back, done *something*, but logic told her any resistance would have only resulted in her death.

Breath catching in her throat, she watched as the guards marched Suying up onto the same platform to present her to the emperor. Kari wanted to be more concerned about the sister of her heart, but she was drained of all emotion and could only be relieved it was no longer her up there.

Kari had made a mistake in coming back. She should have escaped when she had the chance. Her empathy was gone, but she was glad at its loss. It was her empathy and compassion that had made her decide not to leave, which, in turn, had caused her to be violated.

From now on, Suying was on her own. All that mattered was protecting herself. Everyone else could fend for themselves

"I like this one. She's so fresh and nubile. I think I want her right now," Jiaorong declared, squeezing Suying's breasts.

Kari closed her eyes, attempting to convince herself it would all be over soon.

Kari remembered Zhenhua and Tama. Was this what had happened to them? Were they just as defeated as she felt?

"Strip her naked," Jiaorong demanded.

Stomach dropping, Kari squeezed her eyes, trying to keep them shut. Resolutely, she tried to ignore what the emperor said. If she didn't hear it, she could pretend it wasn't happening. Fists clenching, she breathed harder.

Was this weak girl who refused to help her sister who Kari really was?

Her eyes shot open, defiance blazing. "No," she screamed. "You can't do this! She's only fourteen!"

A hush fell over the room as all eyes turned toward Kari. Even Suying looked surprised over Kari speaking out so brazenly.

"Cut her tongue out," Jiaorong ordered without a second thought.

Before she could react, the guards descended upon her and threw her to the ground. When she tried to return to her feet, they kicked the backs of her knees, bringing her down again. A guard grabbed her head, holding it steady while another pulled her jaw open. Yet another took hold of her tongue, bringing a pair of sheers closer.

Kari's chest heaved as she struggled to free herself, but even with her spirit energy, they were too strong.

"Wait one moment," Cai Ren said, halting the guards' actions. "With all due respect, my lord, I beg you to reconsider. I don't presume to tell you how to govern your subjects, but this insolent girl is a songstress. I have heard her sing myself. She has such a lovely voice. It would be quite a shame for it to go to waste."

Why was the awful man helping her? She'd heard stories about the emperors' brutality. From what she'd heard, they didn't like being corrected.

"What would you have me do?" Jiaorong asked, annoyance dripping from his voice.

"I wouldn't presume to suggest any course of action. Nothing I say can compare to your wisdom, my lord. I merely wished to inform you of a detail I think was erroneously left out from her report. I just thought my lord might wish to preserve her talents." Apparently, even Cai Ren knew when to back down.

"A most wise counsel," Jiaorong agreed. "Fine, brand her."

The guard let go of her head as another appeared with a branding iron. Kari fought against the strength of the guards as they held out her arm. The red-hot iron inched its way closer and closer to her flesh. The hot air emanating from the glowing iron burned against her skin. It was inevitable. There was only one thing left to do.

Kari closed her eyes and focused her mind, bracing herself for the searing pain. Her spirit aura wouldn't be strong enough to protect her, but maybe it would lessen the damage.

A scream erupted from her throat as the branding iron contacted her inner bicep. She jerked and spasmed as her flesh sizzled, the metal scorching the Imperial seal into her body.

The guards removed the iron from her arm. Queasily, Kari swayed, cupping her hand over the burn and squeezing. The pain was worse than she thought it would be, but at least it was over. Eventually, it would heal.

"Let that be a lesson to hold your tongue when in the presence of your betters," Jiaorong commanded with a wave of his arm. "Get her out of here now. I want her and the other girls moved to the palace. Have them prepared for my return. Matron, bring me the next group for judgment."

The guards pulled Kari to her feet, shoving her over to the other eight girls. Suying rushed over to Kari.

"Thank you." Suying threw her arms around Kari. "Are you all right?"

Kari nodded. At least she had protected Suying. That monster hadn't had his way with her, and Kari had proven she was not defeated. Her Shagin spirit would never allow her to yield to tyranny. She and Suying were headed to the royal palace as official Imperial attendants. Life could only get more interesting from here.

CHAPTER SEVEN

Following Jiaorong's inspection, the Imperial guards escorted the chosen women through the Grand Entrance, past the massive inner walls, and into the Imperial Palace of Koryon. The guards kept a close eye on all the women within the palace.

But at least behind the inner walls, there was no fear of being raped—except by the emperors, of course—since all the Imperial guards were eunuchs. Some were volunteers while others were prisoners who had been given the choice of servitude or death. Why anyone would choose to faithfully serve those who had castrated them was a mystery to Kari. But, whatever their reasoning, the Imperial guards were considered to be the most loyal servants to the throne and the Sons of Heaven.

Besides the concubines and guards, the only other people allowed to live in the palace were the Imperial family, maidservants, and certain officials who had proven their loyalty to the throne. The ultimate test for any male, both official and guard alike, was castration. This proved their loyalty while protecting the purity of the Imperial line and harem.

The palace was a stark improvement over the storehouse. The cold stone walls were nowhere to be seen. Instead, these inner walls were warm, wooden, and painted red, decorated with elaborate designs and fanciful colors, then adorned with flowing tapestries. Purples and reds garnished the buildings, which were accented with gold, the color of the emperor. Gold tiles covered the roofs of every structure. The warm vivid colors were inviting, but they concealed the dangers lurking within the palace and its dark history. Just a few years ago, the Tian brothers had slaughtered hundreds of people, staining the white marble walkways the same crimson as the walls.

Once the Tian Brothers took control of Xiang, they solidified their rule with carnage until the nobility fell in line. The palace had been meticulously restored, any traces of the massacre that had occurred expunged from existence. Beneath the façade, however, there was still evidence of the brutal changes.

The School of Enlightenment, the central home of education and knowledge within the empire, was closed, and Guanwa Hall had been turned into the home of the Imperial harem. The hall used to house the various scholars and students of the School of Enlightenment, as well as commoners visiting the palace, but with the school closed and any commoner setting foot in the palace now illegal upon penalty of death, there was no need for the hall in its prior state. Instead, the entire district became the harem, dedicated to housing the innumerable concubines the emperors demanded.

There were nearly a thousand individual rooms, spread out over two immense pagodas. Kari was placed in the northern pagoda, the House of the Eternal Sun, along with the rest of Jiaorong's attendants. The southern pagoda, the House of the Ethereal Moon, was reserved for Baoshun's attendants. To ensure the women were never called on by the wrong master, it was forbidden to enter any house but the one they'd been assigned to. However, Guanwa Commons connected the two identical houses, and it contained the dining hall and communal area. In addition to the two main houses, higher-ranking attendants were given private homes, which dotted the landscape within Guanwa Hall.

Each new attendant was given a rank to signify their place within the palace hierarchy, along with spelling out the perks of their position. The guards' initial assessment of Suying had been correct—Jiaorong bestowed her with the rank of first attendant, which afforded her a private house and two maidservants.

Kari hated the guards for being right. The thought of a forty-year-old man lusting after a fourteen-year-old child was disgusting. Kari would need to move fast to protect Suying from Jiaorong's desires. If only Suying could understand the implications of her position, but she seemed far too excited about having a home again.

Jiaorong granted Ina the rank of second attendant, which came with her own private quarters within the House of the Eternal Sun. Despite Kari's apprehension and loathing for everything associated with Jiaorong, she couldn't help but feel envious of Ina and Suying. Kari's outburst in the audition had cemented her own position.

Kari had not been permitted a rank, which placed her at the bottom of the hierarchy and resulted in having to share quarters with three other attendants. Even if had just been her, the allotted room would have been small, but with three other beds crammed into the space, it was anxiety-producing confinement at its worst. It probably explained why her roommates were nowhere to be found.

Once left alone, Kari changed out of her plain robe and into a silk ruqun with a pink-and-blue skirt. The light fabric flowed around her body in an inquisitive dance. The sleeves on the pink-and-white blouse were loose and cascaded down from her arms.

As she lightly touched the burn on her bicep, Kari winced. Her spirit energy would accelerate the healing process, which would hopefully prevent any permanent scarring. The last thing she wanted was to be branded as the emperor's property forever. She'd found a basket of supplies on a table inside, overflowing with necessary odds and ends, and retrieved a bandage from it. When she wrapped it over the wound, the pressure helped relieve the pain. Defiantly, she placed a gold bangle on her arm to hide the injury. The sleeve of her ruqun would probably hide the wound well enough on its own, but the bangle provided her extra comfort. She didn't want to see anything that would remind her of Jiaorong—the thought of him made her stomach weak.

Once she finished her ministrations, she took off to meet Suying and Ina at the Commons for dinner. Both Ina and Suying waited outside the dining hall. They had each changed into more-fitting attire. Ina wore a ruqun consisting of a blue pleated skirt under a white cross-collar dress, wrapped loosely and decorated with blue flowers. Suying opted for a ruqun with a green-and-white blouse under a green pleated skirt. They were accompanied by a third woman Kari didn't recognize, but her white chang-ao worn over a grey skirt indicated she was a servant, one of Suying's no doubt.

"How's your cell?" Ina asked. Kari shot her a look as they joined the dinner line. She was in no mood for jokes, not after today.

"At least you two are in the same house. I feel all alone in mine." Suying's maidservant grabbed a tray for her as they approached the buffet. "But it is nice to have a home. How are your quarters?"

"They are not terrible." At least Kari wasn't confined to her personal living space. She was free to move about the palace as she pleased. The more Kari pondered the prospect, the more disconcerting it became. The emperors went to great lengths to keep the women from escaping the storehouse, but that didn't seem to be the case behind the palace walls. Either they were confident the attendants would become complacent with palace life and not wish to escape, or they believed it was impossible to do so. Sighing, Kari followed behind Ina, Suying, and the maidservant in the buffet line. She was too exhausted to think about escaping now. Today, she would relax with her friends. There was always tomorrow to worry about her plans to escape.

"If it would make my lady more comfortable, we are more than pleased to prepare food for you back at your manor. Only the lower-ranked attendants eat like commoners," the maidservant interjected, bowing her head out of fear of being reprimanded.

"No, I want to eat with my friends," Suying said, pointing out what she wanted loaded onto her tray. Her servants could probably prepare a meal with fresher food for all three girls, but Kari didn't mind the communal dining. She was too hungry to want to wait any longer to eat.

All sorts of delicacies and scrumptious goodies filled the buffet table, the aromas causing Kari's mouth to water and her stomach to growl. She grabbed a small bowl of soba noodles, then filled a plate with peach jelly, rice cakes bursting with sweet anko, and a variety of other confections. Her tray stood out compared to Suying's and Ina's, who had theirs loaded up with roast duck and various other types of meat.

"Good choice, fatty. I guess we know you won't be anyone's favorite," another woman scornfully said as she passed by. Kari glared. She wanted to throw her bowl of noodles right in the heckler's smug face, but it didn't seem worth it.

"Don't listen to her." Suying touched Kari's shoulder, her hands free to do so since her maidservant carried her food. "We all pig out occasionally."

"Thanks. You're a tremendous help," Kari said, letting the sarcasm pour from her lips. Angrily, she took the plate of sweets off her tray, leaving only the noodles. Suying apologized with a weak smile. She had meant nothing by it, but it still bothered Kari.

"Come on, let's find some seats," Ina said, leading the way through the crowd of tables. Kari averted her gaze from the other women in the room. It felt like everyone stopped to gawk at them. Did the attendants always react this way to new additions?

Shaking off her uneasiness, Kari sat next to Suying and Ina at a small square table not much different from those found at the teahouse. Except there, people didn't care if she only ate sweets. Her tray looked so bare now with only a cup of noodles left on it. Hopefully, it would be enough to satisfy her hunger until the morning. She had no intention of navigating the awkward vibe the other women were giving off just to make a return trip to the food line.

A woman wearing an elaborate phoenix crown and dressed in a pink-and-green shenyi, which was covered in ribbons and scarfs, rose from another table. Her tall fig-ure gracefully glided through the crowd until she reached

Kari's group. Haughtily, she stared at the trio. "You're in my seat."

"I'm sorry, my lady. We meant no offense." The maid-servant kowtowed as Suying and Ina quickly stood from their respective seats. This woman had to be important for Suying's maidservant to show that level of respect to someone other than her own mistress.

"Aren't you sitting over there?" Kari asked, refusing to budge. She was tired of being regarded as subhuman. Her people had a history of being treated no better than dirt, and acceptance of that treatment had ended in disaster for them. Besides, Kari was weary of everyone throwing their rank and position around to get their way. She had no cognitive thoughts about her actions—no intentions or plans. She just wanted to be left alone.

"Well, now I'm sitting here." Smirking, the woman crossed her arms. This was nothing but a show of superiority on her part. She didn't care about the seat.

"Come on, Kari. We can find somewhere else to sit." Suying grabbed Kari's arm, trying to pull her from the table, but she refused to move.

"I'm sorry, but we were here first," she said, ignoring Suying's attempts. Instead, Kari picked up her chopsticks, then began shoveling noodles into her mouth.

"Do you not know who I am?" The woman appeared legitimately offended at the open defiance. "I am Matron Mei. So long as you are a member of my house, you will show respect or face the consequences."

Frustrated, Kari tossed her chopsticks to the table. The matron? Goddess, she was tired of matrons. "If you are in charge, then you should have no problem making me move."

"What did you say? You need to learn your place, bitch." Two more women jumped up to join Mei. If they were trying to threaten Kari with numbers, it wasn't going to work. Today alone, she had watched a friend die, been beaten, branded, and publicly defiled and humiliated. There was nothing else these women could do to her.

"Kari, we don't need this," Ina said. Her eyes darted around the room. Everyone gaped at them, but Kari had come this far. What was a bit further?

"Listen to your friend." Mei stood inches away from Kari, a sneer twisting her lips. "You're new here, so I'll give you the opportunity to apologize."

"I'm growing exceptionally tired of everyone telling me what to do. You don't intimidate me," Kari firmly stated. Picking up her chopsticks, she returned to her noodles. The slurping sounds she made broke the stunned silence of the room.

Mei snatched the bowl from Kari's tray, then threw it across the room. It shattered as it struck the wall. "I can make your life a living hell."

Kari rose from her chair to face Mei. The matron was a good head taller, but she was no fighter. She was slender and pampered. Kari could easily take her in a fight, but the weight of the audience pressed upon her. Kari wasn't about to give them a show. There was no point.

"I'm done here." Kari casually walked away.

"Don't turn your back on me, you little bitch."

Kari ignored her, not even pausing.

"That's an order!"

Kari continued walking until she'd left the dining area. She had no intention of playing Mei's game. Ina and Suying rushed out behind her.

"You shouldn't have done that."

Suying spoke the truth. Kari had publicly defied and disrespected the matron of her house. There would be public consequences, but Kari didn't care at the moment. Nothing could be worse than what Jiaorong had done to her.

"You need to go back and eat," Kari said.

"You're not going to make a whole lot of allies with that attitude." Ina jabbed her finger in Kari's face. "What do you think you're doing? Mei is the head matron of our house. You will suffer lasting consequences for the way you disrespected her."

"I won't let anyone push me around." Kari's muscles tightened as rage filled her. How dare Ina scold her after everything that had happened?

"I thought you were going to start a fight," Suying murmured, looking concerned.

"We have to fit in with them." Ina took a step back, crossing her arms. "We've been over this. You don't want to become the next Kyoko, do you?"

Kari's rage boiled over. Seizing Ina by her collar, Kari slammed the girl into the wall. The heat from Kari's anger rushed to her face, making her feel even more out of control. "I'm not sure what your game is, but I'm tired of it."

"What are you talking about? Let go of me." Ina struggled, but Kari's spirit aura instinctively kicked in to enhance her strength. Ina wasn't going anywhere until Kari was done with her.

"I will only ask you once... Did you have anything to do with Kyoko's death?" Kari's question came out louder than she'd expected, echoing throughout the hall.

Ina gasped. "How could you ask that?"

"You've continuously been treated differently from everyone else. Why did Zhenhua call you into a meeting just before Kyoko died? Why are you so special?"

"Calm down, Kari. You're becoming paranoid." Suying placed a hand on Kari's forearm. Kari sighed. Her sister was right. This wasn't the way Kari normally acted.

Kari released her hold, her hands shaking uncontrollably as she inched away from Ina.

"Don't talk to me again. You don't know me. You're not my friend." Ina spat before pushing past Kari to storm up the stairs.

Kari buried her face in her hands. What was this place doing to them? Suying was lost to despair, and Kari to her anger. This wasn't like her.

"Are you all right?" Suying asked.

"I don't think so." Kari pinched her brow.

Without saying another word, Kari rushed past her friend and exploded out into the fresh air. The still-blue sky brought feelings of belonging and a simpler time. It was strange how, despite the goings-on of the world and the cruelty of man, the sky always stayed hopeful. The world never changed. She was small and insignificant. With all of her problems and the threats that came with palace life, the world went on all the same.

Maybe that was what Kari needed—the clarity of nature. She needed the openness. Longing to return to the forests, the open air, the sea breeze, even the caves of home filled her being. Her heart sank. There was no going home, but maybe she could find the peace she needed in the gardens.

She headed for the moon gate to leave the walled-off section of Guanwa Hall. The gates had an ever-present guard post stationed at each entrance, something the other districts lacked. Supposedly, it was to *protect* the attendants.

"Where are you going?" one eunuch asked as she approached the guard station.

Kari gritted her teeth. Everything about this place was so infuriating. "I wish to spend the evening in the gardens. I believe we are allowed to roam freely within the palace walls."

"Of course, my lady," the guard replied. "However, due to your rank, you must sign out at one of the guard stations before you leave. Upon your return, you must also sign back in."

With a huff, Kari reluctantly complied and signed her name across the parchment. Life would be so much easier with a higher rank, or, rather, *with* freedom. She preferred the latter, but she would settle for rank right about now.

"I will assign one of our guards to escort you."

"That won't be necessary," Kari objected. "I don't need to be escorted."

"My lady, with all due respect, non-ranking attendants are not permitted to leave the hall without an Imperial escort. It is for your protection."

Kari clenched her jaw in frustration. Because of her lower rank, she was seen as less loyal. They needed to keep a constant eye on her. It seemed her little trip to the gardens might be more trouble than she had originally thought. Still, her desire to reconnect and recharge her spirit quelled her objections. With her escort in tow, the gate guard allowed Kari to pass.

She eagerly made her way through the walled-off sections of the palace, the eunuch serving as her guard happily trotted alongside her. He smiled even as he struggled to keep her pace.

The garden was a magnificent sight to behold. There were rows and rows of flowers, bushes, and trees so thick she couldn't see the winding path that led through. Yet, everything was immaculately maintained. The vegetation filled her heart with joy. She felt like a little kid again, exploring the beautiful forests of Mystikos for the first time.

Making her way through the stone path, she eventually settled on a small clearing toward the center of the gardens. She plopped on the grass, crossing her legs. Folding her hands in her lap, she closed her eyes and focused on her breathing. She took long deliberate breaths through her nose before exhaling from her mouth. With each one, she felt rejuvenated, like a chisel was chipping away at her inner turmoil. Starting from her head, she focused on each individual muscle in her body and let it relax.

"Do you need anything, my lady?" the guard asked, breaking Kari's concentration.

"No, I'm fine," she curtly replied before returning to her meditation.

"Would my lady be more comfortable sitting on a bench or swing?"

"No, thanks." Her words were short, dripping with her annoyance. She needed peace and quiet if she were going to regain her inner composure. Closing her eyes again, she tried to block out his presence.

"If it is this spot you find preferable, I could bring you a bench to sit upon."

"You really don't have to stay. I am fine by myself." What was his deal? Why did he feel the need to continually pester her? Had he never seen someone trying to relax before?

"And what kind of guard would I be if I left you alone?" the eunuch asked. "I am here to protect you, and that is what I aim to do."

She was going to have to ignore him. He was just so blasted cheerful. It was infuriating. At this rate, her rancor would spill over and she would never relax again.

"And here she is," Mei said, rounding the corner. The two other women from before were with her as well as a handful of guards. Kari was done with this day. Why wouldn't anyone leave her be?

"Matron." The eunuch bowed out of respect. Kari glared, but she refused to stand. She would not give Mei respect simply because she demanded it.

"How dare you not show the proper greeting to your superiors?" one woman called.

"Now, now, Liling, let us not forget ourselves. We are, after all, the superior women here. It is our job to educate and train the newcomers," Mei said. "However, stubborn pride must be broken if a wild horse is to become a prized stallion. This marks the third time you have disrespected me. A punishment is in order. I believe five lashes will suffice."

"What?" Kari wasn't surprised so much as she was angry. This was how they operated. How they made people fall in line.

"Per each offense." Mei held up a single finger.

Kari shot to her feet as fury coursed through her body. Balling her fists out of frustration, she wanted nothing more than to strike out in anger. Mei smiled, noticing the rise she got out of Kari.

"In fact, you disrespected my other matrons just now as well. That's two more counts to your growing list of charges."

"That's twenty-five lashes." Liling laughed.

"Guards, you may take her," Mei said, her grin evil.

Kari could fight back or protest, but what would be the outcome if she did? The guards had already branded her. Had even tried to cut out her tongue. How could they treat other humans like this? Kari relented as the guards surrounded her and seized her arms.

Their tight grip dug into her skin, pressing against her burn. It sent a shock of pain through her body, but she did not resist.

Kari followed the guards as they led her out of the gardens to the military district of the palace. Soldiers, all eunuchs, filled the district and the barracks. They were busy training and sparring with each other.

The guards shoved her, face-first, against a wooden post before chaining her hands around the beam. Murmurs behind her and the sound of a cracking whip signaled what was to come. She closed her eyes in anticipation. Even with her spirit aura, this would hurt. She might be able to prevent long-term scarring, but there was no way she could prevent the whip from tearing into her flesh. Swallowing hard, Kari tried to suppress her fear and brace for the impact.

"What's going on here?" a male voice called as the sound of running feet echoed. Kari couldn't see who it was, but she recognized the voice.

"Lord Cai Ren, we were just about to punish this girl for disrespecting three matrons," a guard explained.

"I see. This 'girl' is an attendant. Did you actually think it would be a good idea to permanently scar her? Do you think the emperors will want to sleep with her after that? Release her," Cai Ren ordered.

She breathed a silent sigh of relief. Why was the high chancellor coming to her aid? He didn't seem to like her all that much. Nevertheless, Kari was grateful for his intervention. Although, she did wish he could be a less of a pig about it.

"But, my lord, Matron Mei ordered us to administer lashes," the guard said.

"How many?"

"Twenty-five, my lord."

"You will take them," Cai Ren ordered sharply. "For forgetting I am the high chancellor and not Matron Mei. As for the attendant, her punishment shall be a week in the dungeon. That will satisfy the matron."

Kari wanted to thank Cai Ren for his intervention, but by the time the guards had unchained her, he was already on his way out of the district. Why had he helped her? Surely he didn't do this for all the attendants. After all, the guards *had* seemed rather surprised at his ruling.

She didn't have long to consider his actions as the guards shoved her toward the dungeon. All the cells were housed behind a single iron door. Three guards sat watch over the prison. One rose and grabbed a lantern, then opened the iron door. A long hallway stretched into silent darkness. Thick metal lined the floor, walls, and ceiling. Along the length of the walls at constant intervals were metal door handles.

The guard escorted her down the narrow hallway before stopping. Even with the lantern's light, it was hard to tell where the wall ended and the door began. He unlocked the door, then swung it open.

"This will be your home until your sentence has been served," the guard said. He helped Kari into the cell. She had to bend down just to fit. It wasn't big enough to stand in—barely big enough for her to sit up. The guard slammed the door shut, sealing Kari inside the pitch-black hole.

She couldn't hear a single sound from outside. It was complete sensory deprivation.

Holding out her hand, she watched light erupt from her fingers. She formed it into a ball, then let it float to the top of her cell. As she stared at it, she grimaced at the reminder of her fate. The very sight of the light turned her stomach and made her heart heavy. But she needed it for now, so she gritted her teeth and tolerated its haunting shine that disguised the hidden darkness within her.

The cell itself was barely long enough for her to stretch out, and only about half as wide. Hay lined the ground, and a single bucket had been shoved in the corner.

Kari sighed. At least she could finally concentrate on her meditation in here. In fact, she would have a whole week to find her balance. No doubt the unrelenting darkness and the cramped confines were designed to break the spirits of prisoners, but Kari intended to use her time in isolation to restore hers.

She folded her legs as she sat upright in the cell, the top of her head brushing against the ceiling. It was a good thing she wasn't taller.

Once again, she focused on her breathing before relaxing each muscle in her body. She started from her head, slowly working her way to her feet. Serenity surrounded her as the cell faded away into a distant memory.

She hadn't realized how tired she was. Before she knew it, she had succumbed to her fatigue and fallen asleep. Her mother's words reverberated in her mind, echoing in her dreams.

The Fates have been cruel to you... They have taken you, and will carry you across the ocean... You are bound by destiny... A world of wonder awaits you... Wonder and fear will meet you... Follow the song in your heart... The tides are high... Farewell...

CHAPTER EIGHT

Chosen by destiny,
She makes her own path,
Guided by
The winds of change.

If love was a weapon,
None could surpass her.
Defying the Fates,
She descended into
The plane of mortals.

Life radiated from her,
Creating all living things.
Her task finished,
She ascended into
The heavens.

Her journey complete and Her quest fulfilled,
Her life faded.

The Fates arranged
Her passing,
But would not let her go.

Rewarded for her bravery,
She was reborn as
The stars.

The song of Nebura, the Eternal Goddess, filled Kari's mind. Was her path being guided as well? It was said the Fates placed Shagin on their path, but did not determine their destiny. Each Shagin had the ability to choose what to do once they were on their path, though the Fates maintained a watchful eye while never interfering. Would the Fates truly abandon her? Or would Nebura intervene on her behalf the way she did for humanity in its infancy?

The week in Kari's cell seemed to drag on for an eternity. She never once saw another living being. The guards would open a small slot in the bottom of the door to slide a tray of rice and a cup of water inside for every meal. She had to be careful to extinguish her floating light to not draw the ire of her guards.

The isolation gave her time to think. Kari had been foolish. If she were to survive long enough to escape, she had to play the game with subtlety and tact. She couldn't go around being so flippantly defiant.

The door to her cell sprang open as light from the guard's lantern filled her cell.

"My lady, I am pleased to announce your time is over. You may return to Guanwa Hall." The guard took Kari's hand, helping her crawl out of the darkness. "I truly hope my lady will not hold us in contempt for your imprisonment."

Kari shook her head. "Not at all." The truth was that she was grateful for the opportunity to clear her head—*not* that she ever wished to return.

A eunuch met her at the front of the dungeon. He led her back to Guanwa Hall, where he happily bowed and dismissed himself from her service.

Kari headed straight for the bathhouse, not wanting to waste a second in finding a warm bath. Washing off the seven days of grime she had built up in the dungeon was her only thought.

The warm water rejuvenated her skin as she washed away the dirt and fatigue. Her fingers grazed the side of her arm. The burn was healing nicely, though the area was still red and tender. But at least the impression of the seal had mostly faded. She had never been as grateful for Shagin's mastery of spirit energy as she was now. It didn't look like it would leave a lasting scar, but it was still probably better to keep the area covered even after it had fully healed. She didn't want anyone seeing her unbranded arm. They might become suspicious.

Once she had cleaned up, she returned to her room for a change of clothes. Her roommates were all sitting together when she entered. It was strange to call them roommates since she hadn't even met them until now, and this was hardly her room. She hadn't even slept in it, yet she had spent a full week in the palace already.

"Well, if it isn't the little rat," one girl said upon seeing her. "Did you enjoy your time in your nasty hole?"

Kari rolled her eyes, but she didn't respond. She didn't need more enemies. Even still, she had no desire to formally familiarize herself with her so-called roommates after that introduction. She ignored their snickering as she changed into a clean purple-and-blue ruqun, then quickly left the *comfort* of her shared room for the noisy bustle of the dining hall.

The one good thing about being an attendant was that the dining hall was always open. She loaded her tray with various meats, vegetables, and rice before finding an empty seat in the back corner. Her stomach roared at the sight of her plate, and her tongue was overjoyed as she took her first bite.

"There you are."

Kari looked up to see Suying next to her. Before Kari could respond, the girl threw her arms around her neck.

"I was so worried. When I heard they had put you in the dungeon, I didn't know what to think." Suying released her grip before sitting next to Kari.

"I'm all right," Kari reassured her. It was good to see Suying again. She had survived her first week in the palace and she was okay, at least from what Kari could tell. "I just need to be more careful. Has anything happened to you?"

Suying shook her head. "Not yet, but I think it'll be soon. The emperor has been calling a new girl to his bedchamber every night."

"We knew it was only a matter of time before this happened." Sighing, Kari pressed her fingers against the bridge of her nose. There had to be something she could do to protect Suying. "We should have escaped when we had the chance. I don't even know if that's an option now with how heavily guarded this place is."

"I'm not afraid. I'm ready to embrace the change."

Kari raised an eyebrow. "The change?"

"From a child to a woman." Now Suying wasn't making any sense.

"But you *are* a child."

Suying shot her nose up in derision. "I am not. I am an attendant and a servant of one of the Sons of Heaven. Being chosen to be the emperor's vessel is a blessing."

"Is that truly how you feel?" Kari had been gone too long. Suying was drifting farther and farther away. The nonsense they were filling her head with was slowly poisoning her reason.

"Well, that's how the matrons describe it." Suying's brow crinkled. "At any rate, if I please the emperor, he could bestow upon me his favor."

"And what does that entail?" Vague promises were easy to make, but they ultimately meant nothing, especially when considering the cost.

"I don't know," Suying said, shrugging her shoulders. "Gifts, treasures, prestige? Those in the emperor's favor live the best lives."

"That's garbage." Kari pushed her tray to the side. The young girl who sat beside her seemed so far away. Suying was being deceived with promises of gifts. The emperors had turned Suying's despair into hope, so now she was further rooted into their lie. It would now be even harder to convince Suying to flee from the dangers of the palace.

"You'll understand, eventually. I know you will." Suying's face lit up. "I know—you should talk to Matron Mei. She's really smart and knows all sorts of things. I'm sure if you apologize to her, she'll be glad to help you."

"I'd rather not, but speaking of which, where's Ina? I believe I owe *her* an apology." Kari still wasn't sure about Ina. Her intuition told her there was more to Ina than she was telling, but everyone had their secrets, even Kari, and she was not justified in how she'd lashed out against Ina.

"She's probably up in her room," Suying responded. "She's barely left it in the past few days."

"I'll head there when I finish. Will you accompany me?" The matrons were leading Suying astray, and Kari couldn't afford to leave her alone anymore.

"Sure," Suying responded. "I could use some time out of my house. My maidservants are starting to drive me crazy. They have been doing a poor job at keeping things as tidy as they should be. It upsets the balance of nature for things to be in disarray."

Kari scoffed at the thought of a fourteen-year-old girl telling off two grown women for upsetting the delicate balance of the cosmos for not adequately cleaning up *her* mess. Kari rubbed her eyes. She wasn't sure who Suying was turning into.

Kari quickly finished her meal before heading up to Ina's room with Suying

When she knocked on the door, there was no response.

"Maybe she's not here," Suying said, shrugging.

"Hello, Ina. It's me, Kari." She knocked again, but there was still no response. When she tried the handle to see if it was locked, the knob freely turned to her surprise. She pushed the door open.

"Go away," Ina cried out from inside the room. "I don't want to talk to you. I hate you!"

Kari stopped, pulling the door almost closed. She had that coming for how she'd acted, but at least she knew Ina was inside so Kari could apologize. "Ina, I'm sorry for how I treated you. I want you to know that."

"You accuse me of killing my friend... and now you apologize through a door and expect me to accept that? Leave my door. We are not friends."

Kari's heart sank. At least she'd tried.

"I think we should go." Suying grabbed Kari's hand, trying to pull her away. "We don't want another incident to occur."

Kari couldn't fault Ina for not wanting to speak to her. If their roles had been reversed, Kari might have felt the same way. She needed to give Ina some time. Maybe she would let Kari apologize in a few days.

"Come on," Kari said. There was nothing left for them to do but return to their quarters. The day was getting late, but maybe there was still enough time for Suying to help her with another problem. "I still haven't formally introduced myself to my roommates, and I'm fairly sure they already don't like me. Do you want to come and help me get to know them? Maybe you can smooth over the conversation for me."

Suying smiled. "Of course. What are friends for? Besides, they are probably just jealous. I don't know if you noticed, but you *were* the most beautiful woman in the dining hall the other day. That's why Matron Mei approached you—to see if your beauty matched your spirit."

It was kind of Suying to say that. Kari had always been complimented on her looks. She didn't mind. It made her feel confident about herself. The truth was, however, Mei had felt threatened. That was why she tried to get Kari to submit to her, not to test her character.

Kari and Suying headed back toward the stairs. As they approached, a familiar face emerged.

"What are you doing here?" Kari asked, spotting Zhenhua. Kari had half expected to never see her again. She supposed it made sense. Zhenhua was still an attendant and a matron even if her house was outside the inner wall.

"Is that how you greet your superiors? No wonder rumors of your impertinence have spread so far. Perhaps you could have used more time in the storehouse to learn proper etiquette." Zhenhua glared at Kari, the derision clearly mutual. Perhaps this was what Kari needed—a test of her new resolve.

"Forgive me, Matron." Kari tilted her head to the ground, avoiding eye contact, while Suying shot her a sideways look as if to beg her to be nice. However, Kari had already prepared for this moment or at least one like it. It was time to play the game. "Do not let my rudeness serve as a poor reflection of your instruction."

"I provided you perfect instructions on how to be a lady in the palace," Zhenhua said with a sneer.

"Of course, my lady. I had no intention of insinuating otherwise... or to imply your character is flawed and may have contributed to my unruly behavior. I want you to know I will never forget the experiences I had under your care."

Zhenhua stared at Kari as if to see her true intentions, but Kari just smiled coyly.

"I hope we can be friends through the coming years."

"You're infuriating." Zhenhua turned to stalk away.

"Ah, Zhenhua," Matron Mei said as she turned the corner. She was accompanied by a host of girls, including the two Kari had seen with her before. The matron must like traveling with an entourage. "So, they finally let you out of your slum house?"

Zhenhua ignored the insult. "As you know, I have full rights to travel to and from the palace. It's one benefit of running a house outside the main walls. I get to enjoy life in and out of the palace. The best of both worlds."

"And why would anyone want to experience the company of plebeians? They don't even properly bathe. How do you stand the stench? Of course, it does explain a lot." When Mei wiped the air in front of her nose, the women erupted in laughter.

Zhenhua closed her eyes, bowing her head.

Kari had seen enough. She might despise Zhenhua, but Kari couldn't stand anyone bullying another. Besides, she owed Mei from earlier. Kari took a step forward, but Suying grabbed her wrist to stop her.

"No, don't," Suying whispered. Kari obliged. Suying was right. Kari couldn't afford another incident. She needed to avoid confrontation if she were to survive the palace.

"So, what brings you here to my house?" Mei asked, placing her hands on her hips.

"I believe you know. You have something that doesn't belong to you." Zhenhua held her head high as she stepped closer to Mei. She wasn't intimated by her peer or the other women accompanying her. Her pride was her weapon.

Mei held up a finger to stop Zhenhua as she focused her attention on Kari. "Well, well, look who it is. Little Hikari. Did you enjoy your time in the dungeon?"

"As a matter of fact, I did," Kari replied with a smile. "It opened my eyes to my own shortcomings. I now believe I am all the better because of it. Thank you."

"Well... good," Mei said, taken aback.

Kari dropped to her knees, then pressed her forehead to the floor. "I wish to seek your forgiveness. I greatly offended you before by not rewarding you the proper respect. You are gracious and kind, and it is my humblest desire that you will accept my apology."

"And why would I want to accept?" Mei asked, tapping her foot.

"There is no reason I can give. Only someone with the mercy and graciousness of a saint would," Kari said, attempting to appeal to Mei's ego. If pride were Zhenhua's weapon, then cordiality would be Kari's. Hopefully, that would be enough to tear down Mei's ego. "But I know you have a vested interest in my well-being as I am a member of your house, and I do not wish my poor etiquette to publicly damage your reputation."

Mei looked at the host of women around her. "Very well, you may stand."

"Thank you, Matron," Kari replied, returning to her feet.

"As for you," Mei said, glaring at Zhenhua. "You might have the right to travel freely in the palace, but you have no authority here in my house. Leave."

"Not without the necklace," Zhenhua said. Her brow furrowed, and she balled her fists. She obviously had no intention of abiding by Mei's rule.

"But it looks so much better on me." Mei held up the pendant that was draped around her neck. Kari recognized it. It was the same one Ina had worn in the storehouse.

"You took a necklace from one of your charges because you liked the way it looked on you better?" Zhenhua's voice boomed, echoing in the empty hallway.

All this fuss over a necklace?

"Don't be silly." Mei dropped the necklace, allowing it to freely hang around her neck. "When the Matron Emiko died, she left a number of debts to the house. It is only fair her sister repays those debts."

Zhenhua swung her arm through the air. "This is nothing more than jealousy. You're envious of your predecessor—afraid Ina will surpass you in the emperor's favor."

Ina's sister was a former matron? That could explain the special treatment.

"That is a bold accusation, one which is unfounded. Now begone from my sight. I grow tired of your stench." Mei waved her hand, dismissing Zhenhua from her presence.

"I will buy it from you," Zhenhua protested, refusing to leave.

"I don't believe there is enough money to cover the cost of such an exquisite piece in your whole house, let alone what you personally own. That's what you get when you're nothing more than the leftovers from a forgotten era. You're barely above the peasants you mingle with. It's no wonder you act like them. An insignificant beetle upon a pile of dung, thinking yourself king of a mountain. Please, real royalty lives inside the walls."

The women laughed as Zhenhua hung her head.

"All of this fuss over a silver-coated copper necklace. Not even gold plated." Mei took the necklace off, holding it in the air by its chain. "However, if you were to show me proper respect and kowtow, I might consider allowing you to compensate me for this trinket."

It seemed cruelty was a prerequisite for a matron. Kari might not care for Zhenhua, but she couldn't stand by while someone was ridiculed.

"That is a lovely necklace, indeed." Kari stepped forward, pushing past Suying. "But I believe it would behoove you to return the necklace to its rightful owner."

"How dare you show such disrespect toward me! You have no right to tell me what to do with my belongings."

"I mean no disrespect by my actions. I merely wish to look out for your benefit. You have stated the necklace is worthless, at least in your eyes. It seems its only value is to Matron Zhenhua and Lady Ina. So clearly, the necklace cannot be used to cover whatever debts the former matron may have incurred. Since you have publicly stated this, I fear any further actions to seek compensation would only publicly damage your generosity." Each word needed to be carefully chosen, a pleasant affront. "I do not wish for that to happen."

"Its monetary value is irrelevant. Its value lies in what it represents." Mei wrapped her fist tight around the silver pendant.

"So it is sentimental to you? A necklace that belongs to someone else?" Kari asked, letting her doubt lace her words.

"Are you trying to shame me?" Mei asked.

"Why would I, who only moments ago publicly knelt before you in submission and begged for your forgiveness, be now seeking your subjugation? I only wish for your virtuousness to withstand a public presentation of what could be perceived as a petty squabble. Your beauty surpasses all in this room, but the claim has been made that you are jealous of your predecessor and of your current ward. We know this to be false, but you can demonstrate this by proving the superiority of your lineage and returning the lost necklace to its rightful owner."

Mei scowled at Kari, gritting her teeth. "Take it." She dropped the necklace on the floor. Her eyebrows curled inward as she narrowed her gaze. Kari did not relent. She stood firm in her resolve. Mei's face relaxed as a smile crept upon her face, and she offered out her hand. "Suying, come with me. I desire your company."

Kari's eyes widened, and Suying looked at her as if she were seeking permission. Kari had gone too far.

"Of course, Matron." Suying stepped forward to take Mei's hand. The two of them left with the group of women, leaving only Kari and Zhenhua in the hallway. Kari might have won the necklace, but Mei had taken something even more valuable from Kari.

She bent, picked up the trinket, and offered it to Zhenhua. "I believe this is what you wanted."

"Do you expect me to say, 'thank you?'" Zhenhua barked, refusing to take the necklace.

"I... I was just trying to help," Kari said.

"I didn't need your help." Zhenhua whirled and began to walk away.

"Don't you want this?" Kari called, still holding the necklace out for her to take.

"It's Ina's. You give it to her."

How was Kari supposed to do that when Ina wouldn't even talk to her? She stuffed the necklace in the sash around her waist before heading back to her room. Tomorrow, she would try to apologize to Ina again. This time, Kari could return the necklace.

Kari crashed in her bed. The evening was fading, but it was still light outside. Even still, the softness of her bed was comforting. It was a huge improvement over the straw-covered stone she had slept on for the past seven days. It felt like a cloud in comparison.

Her room might be cramped, but it was still nicer than anywhere she had lived since leaving Mystikos. While she hated to admit it, the palace was nicer than even her old home. The surviving Shagin, despite having lived on Mystikos for over a decade since the purge, only had limited resources, so the luxuries they enjoyed were quaint compared to the palace. Still, she would gladly return to her former life if she could. Not a day went by where she didn't miss her home, but she was an exile. It was forbidden for her to return.

Her bedroom door burst open. It collided with the wall, resonating with a loud thud that reverberated through the air. Kari leapt out of bed, nearly hitting her head on a lantern. She crouched like a tiger ready to pounce as a guard stood in her doorway. He smiled.

"Get dressed," he ordered. "Lord Jiaorong wishes to see you."

CHAPTER NINE

KARI'S HEART NEARLY STOPPED. It was only a matter of time before she or Suying were called to see Jiaorong, but the expectation of it didn't seem to ease the blow. Her mind raced as she tried to think of various excuses to avoid sleeping with her captor.

Kari tried to gather up her bath supplies, but the guard stopped her.

"That won't be necessary. The emperor is in a hurry, so let's make this quick. Just get dressed and come with me." There was no stalling. This was it. Adrenaline pumped through her veins as her chest tightened.

As the guard stepped outside the room, she closed her door and quickly got dressed. She put on a pink-and-blue flowing ruqun, then wrapped her brown hair into a bun before exiting into the hall. Two servants waited outside with a sedan chair draped in red silk curtains. They helped her inside before closing the curtains, lifting the litter, and carrying it to the Hall of Heaven and Earth.

"I thought I was going to see the emperor. Why am I being taken here?" Kari asked as the servants sat the chair down in front of the majestic hall. The guards pulled back the curtains and offered their hands, helping her dismount.

"I told you," the guard said, following behind. "The emperor is in a hurry today. He wants you to meet him at court." A public bedding—this couldn't get any worse. Even in a private room, the court would be filled with chancellors and officials. They would see her. Goddess, they would know.

The servants escorted her into the hall, then into an antechamber to the throne room. Jiaorong lounged on a chair sipping wine, a lone eunuch in the corner of the room. The emperor smiled upon seeing her. He was draped in a golden silk shenyi, signifying his ruling in court. The guards bowed their heads upon entering the room, shoving Kari inside before quickly backing out and leaving her alone with the emperor.

"Excellent. You're more beautiful than I remember," Jiaorong growled, finishing his cup. "You'll do fine."

"I'm on my cycle," Kari blurted out. Most men of Xiang wouldn't dare sleep with a woman while she was menstruating. It was part of their religion. Xiang, like most of the nations of Terra, worshipped the Triune Gods. Kari had studied their religion in school, and one of their commandments forbade them from sleeping with a menstruating woman. She didn't know how religious he was, but she hoped for the best. With any luck, he wouldn't want her to provide proof.

"Do you think I'm afraid of a little blood? Come closer," he said, waving her over.

So much for that idea.

Kari swallowed hard, slowly inching her way toward him. She didn't like he had been drinking. A drunkard with power seemed like a recipe for disaster, especially when rape was already one of the ingredients. She glanced over at the eunuch. Was he going to watch? Her blood froze at the thought of having her body stolen from her, but having an audience when it happened would just be cruelty of the highest degree.

"How's your arm?" Jiaorong sneered, noticing the golden bangle.

Kari clenched the bangle covering the bandage on her arm. Honestly, it probably didn't even need the wrap, but, for now, it was better to play the part of the scared, injured girl. Not that she had much issue with pretending to be scared.

"They say you can sing," Jiaorong said. "Is that true?"

"Yes," Kari responded. She tried to prevent her hands from shaking, but it was to no avail. Her plan was seeming increasingly foolhardy. She tried to push down her reservations. Drift out of her body. She had to be numb.

"Can you dance?"

"What?" Was he expecting a show?

"Can you sing and dance?"

"I suppose."

"Fine traits to have," Jiaorong replied. "I'm sure you could fetch a good profit in the markets. You are probably one of the most beautiful women I have ever seen, but your disrespectful attitude could use some work. First, you try to defend that traitorous bitch, and now I hear you've repeatedly disrespected your house matron. You are like a wild horse that needs to be tamed. I'm afraid you might be a little too mouthy for my tastes. I like my women to lie still and be quiet."

Kari took a step back, her weak legs buckling under her weight.

"Relax. I won't hurt you."

"What are you going to do with me?" Kari asked.

Jiaorong grunted at her. She wasn't supposed to talk out of turn.

"It's such a pity, really. Your looks have no rival. I think you would have been one of my new favorites. It pains me to do this, but you've left me with no other choice. If you will not learn respect, then there is no other way. Follow me."

Jiaorong rose, moving to the door connecting the anteroom with the Throne of Unity. He waited for her to step toward him, but she did not move. She couldn't. There was no telling what fate awaited her behind that door. Was she to be executed? She clenched her fists as she struggled to catch her breath. Jiaorong cleared his throat, his patience wearing thin. Mustering what courage she could find, she stepped forward.

The throne room was massive, spacious enough to allow for the hundreds of officials to convene at once. By the looks of it, they were all here this evening to watch her subjugation. Nine grand pillars supported the golden ceiling. In the center of the room was a raised platform, decorated in crimson and gold, that towered over any who would stand in the emperors' presence. Two golden dragons flanked either side of the platform. In the center were two golden thrones, one of which was occupied by the other emperor, Baoshun.

Her heart beat even faster. It felt like it might break through her chest at the realization she was standing before the two most powerful and dangerous men in the empire, the Tian brothers. They had built their throne on the blood and corpses of thousands, slaughtering their way to the Throne of Unity, the throne of heaven.

"Ah! Brother!" Baoshun stood from his throne, gesturing toward the pair. A host of advisors and guards parted, allowing for Jiaorong and Kari to pass through and greet his brother.

Cai Ren stood to the right of Baoshun. He quickly bowed upon seeing Jiaorong. Kari wasn't sure if she should hate him for forcing her here or thank him for saving her twice. Hate seemed appropriate, though. The bastard watched her closely as Jiaorong motioned for her to follow him up the steps to the top of the platform. Taking a deep breath, she trailed closely behind him.

Jiaorong hugged his brother. Despite wearing identical clothing, there was little similarity between their appearance. Jiaorong towered over his brother, dwarfing his frame. "How has court been?"

"Painfully dull," Baoshun replied. "If our advisors weren't so imbecilic, maybe we wouldn't have to waste our time with these bureaucratic fools."

"You've been spending so much time at court lately that you haven't had time to indulge in our usual luxuries. So, I brought you something that should improve your day—a present." Jiaorong said, motioning to Kari.

"She's for me? She's gorgeous." Baoshun reached out to stroke her face. "And her skin is like silk—soft and smooth."

Kari had to refrain from striking him out of reflex. To them, she was nothing more than an item to possess.

"She should be able to entertain you for some time. From what Cai Ren said, she is a gifted dancer and songstress. And check out those eyes. Have you ever seen such an emerald color like that before?" She was to be his entertainment, his plaything, his prized green-eyed possession.

"Brother, you shouldn't have."

"You deal with the court so I don't have to. Because of that, you have been unable to attend any of the auditions. Bringing you some of its bounties is the least I can do."

"You are too kind. I can't wait till we consummate our new union." Baoshun examined Kari. He felt up her figure and violated her body while his eyes pierced her core. She felt sick. "What is your name?"

"Hikari."

He slapped her. The sudden outburst took her by surprise, and she was unable to raise her spirit aura to protect herself. "Hikari what?" he demanded.

She placed her hand against her reddening face, almost stuttering. "J-just Hikari."

He balled up his fist, then struck her again.

"What did you say to me?"

Kari was tired of being treated like an animal. She focused on her aura. The radiating energy lessened the shooting pain in her face, and it would protect her from any other strikes. Let him try hitting her again. *Does hitting women make you feel powerful?* she wanted to shout, but Cai Ren cut her off as she opened her mouth.

"My lord... you will always address your betters as my lord," Cai Ren said, stepping beside Kari.

Kari sighed. Subtlety and tact. If she wanted to survive, she had to obey their rules. "Hikari, my lord," she said, giving in.

"Excellent!" Baoshun clasped his hands together, like a mother would when a child learned to talk. "Cai Ren, please be so kind as to escort her to her new living quarters. And make sure the storehouse is properly training the new attendants. We can't have them disrespecting the will of heaven with their rudeness."

"As you wish, my lord." Cai Ren bowed in reverence to the emperors. He motioned for Kari to follow, and she complied. She couldn't wait to leave the hall to escape the staring glares of the court officials.

Kari followed Cai Ren back to Guanwa Hall. Unlike the trip to the main hall, there was no sedan chair to pick them up. They were forced to walk.

"Aren't you going to thank me for helping you out back there?" Cai Ren asked. "In fact, I believe this makes the third time I've had to come to your rescue."

Thank him? Her face flashed red with anger, and she balled up her fists. The consequences be damned. "Help me out? You're the reason I'm here in the first place."

Cai Ren chuckled at her outburst. "I can see your time in the dungeon hasn't done a thing to curb your irreverence. Nonetheless, it would behoove you to remember your place within the palace walls. I can't always be there to save you."

Kari scoffed at his remarks. Her emotions were conflicted. On the one hand, she was truly thankful for the times he had interfered on her behalf. However, if it hadn't been for him, neither she nor Suying would have been forced into these situations. She hated him for that.

"So, is this all you do? Kidnap girls and drag them to their rapists?" Kari snarled, following behind Cai Ren. Their footsteps on the marble ground echoed in the evening air.

"It certainly seems that way," Cai Ren acquiesced. "Come, I want to show you something before I get you settled in."

Kari followed Cai Ren to the entrance of the palace. She remembered those gates all too well. If only she could freely walk through them and leave this hell.

"I believe this is your handiwork," Cai Ren said, motioning to a wall adjacent to the entrance.

Gasping, Kari covered her mouth. Her stomach lurched. Tama's body hung on display for anyone passing by to see. She was smashed and bloodied, and her face showed no resemblance to the beautiful woman she once was.

Kari knew this or something like it would happen. She just didn't think she would see it. It wasn't right. This wasn't what she'd wanted.

"A warning to anyone who would defy the emperors. I think she has you to thank for this?"

"She orchestrated the rape and murder of an innocent girl." Kari tried to justify her actions, but her words rang hollow in her head. Tama *had* deserved to be brought to justice for what she did to Kyoko, but this wasn't justice. This wasn't even vengeance. This was something far worse. This was barbarism.

"So, *you* orchestrated *her* death?" Cai Ren clicked his tongue. "Seems fitting."

Kari closed her eyes. The image of Tama's broken body refused to leave her mind. "Why did you take me here?"

"Don't tell me you didn't want to see this?" Kari stared at the ground. How could anyone want to see this? "At any rate, you needed to see this to fully understand the gravitas of your situation. Maybe now you will appreciate my help. For everything you've done so far, this could be you. I don't want that, and I'm sure, if you think really hard, you don't either."

Kari glared at Cai Ren. "What do you want from me?"

"Come, let me take you to your new quarters. We can talk then. There are eyes and ears everywhere in the palace."

Cai Ren led her into the House of the Ethereal Moon where Baoshun's attendants lived. She had hoped that since she was back from the dungeon, she, Suying, and Ina could help keep an eye on each other, but they were separated again.

Cai Ren escorted her through the hall to the third floor. The various women they passed on their way stopped to stare at Kari. She wasn't sure if they were simply trying to get a look at their new roommate, or if they were sizing up the new girl. Most were murmuring why the high chancellor was escorting her, which was sure to be a point of contention among her new housemates. Judging from her past experiences, Kari was ready to expect a certain level of resentment and unwelcomed feelings.

"This will be your room," Cai Ren said, opening a door on the third floor. "You'll find all of your belongings have already been moved over."

Kari entered without saying a word. Instead of a shared room, she was being given her own private accommodations. The room was long and narrow, and a single bed on a raised wooden platform had been placed at the far end with a little window overlooking the palace. A personal makeup table and chair lined one wall. Next to the table was a large dresser, and on the opposite wall were two armoires. Moving straight to the armoire, she opened the doors. Sure enough, the armoire was filled with her clothes. Hanging from a small hook was Ina's necklace. Kari sighed with relief. Without that, any apology to Ina would be hollow.

"Why am I being given my own room?" Kari asked, shutting the armoire. "I'm a bottom-ranked attendant. Shouldn't I have a shared room?"

"I thought you would be more comfortable with a little privacy," Cai Ren said, a wicked grin stretched across his face. "Besides, now we can get to the reason why I brought you here."

Kari cocked her head at Cai Ren. What was he planning? He had been a constant presence, always doing things for her. He had even been observing her in the teahouse before he'd abducted her. Why? What did he want from her?

Cai Ren sighed as he shut the door, then stepped closer to Kari. "Stories of your beauty and grace traveled from that loathsome teahouse to my ears, and you don't disappoint. I need you." She tried to back away from him, but he grabbed her arm. "I saved you—three times now. You should show more appreciation than that."

"Get off me," Kari screamed, twisting her arm free from his grasp. She tried to shove past him, but he threw her against the wall and entrapped her between his arms.

"I've been watching you for some time. Your songs were always so intoxicating. I knew I couldn't get you here by force. Those worms wouldn't have stood idly by if you had actively resisted me."

Rage flashed through her. He had planned it all. Without thinking, she kneed him in the gut and shoved him away from her.

"I can be a powerful ally for you, my little outcast."

Kari froze, her eyes wide. What had he said?

A guard threw open the door. "Is everything all right? I heard a commotion."

"Fine... I was just leaving." Cai Ren backed away from Kari. "I would carefully think over my request. When you are ready to be more than what you are, I'll be waiting."

When he left, Kari barricaded her door with the chair. She slouched onto the floor, hugging her knees to her chest. Cai Ren knew. He knew what she was. How?

The word *Shagin* meant *outcast*. It was the name given to the people who dared to be different, to the ones who were hated and despised among the other nations. What had she gotten into? She was surrounded by enemies on all sides. Did he know what she was before he had taken her? Of course he had. It was the reason she'd been taken. Why else single her out?

Cai Ren was right. He could be a powerful ally... or he could be her executioner. Kari had to escape. She wanted to be anywhere but here.

She missed her home with its rich forests and the waves that constantly beat against the island, crashing onto its beaches. Kari would do anything to return, but death would come for her before that ever happened.

Her mother's face flashed before Kari's eyes. The warm smile filled her with joy as she smiled in return. Kari held out her hand, staring as light emanated from her fingertips. It swirled with color, illuminating the room. The colors danced and swayed in the air. The gentle movements were mesmerizing, but Kari knew the truth.

She clenched her fist, stopping the light. The beauty was a lie. The light was a curse, one she couldn't escape. It infected every fiber of her being, infiltrating her very identity. It was a curse that not even death could cure.

Time escaped her. She wasn't sure how long she had sat there until a knock on her door was followed by a guard shouting, "Lord Baoshun is asking for you. You are to prepare yourself. A bath has already been readied. An Imperial escort waits for you at the gate when you are finished."

Kari couldn't believe it. He was calling for her already. He wasn't even giving her the night to settle in. She had to escape this life.

Kari bathed and changed into the clothes that had been picked out for her, a purple dudou that barely covered her front and left her midriff exposed. Kari hated it. She felt naked wearing the bodice. She might as well be for what it covered. It was a small piece of silk tied around her neck and back. A loose pink skirt hung from her hips. Long slits ran the length of its sides, exposing her legs.

Her heart pounded. What could she do? She was a doll to be dressed up for his amusement—a nightmare made real.

Once she was ready, much like before, servants carried her in the sedan chair, but to the emperors' mansion this time. The brothers shared a mansion together, but it was expansive enough to house multiple families, so space wasn't a problem. She was escorted up the stairs to the front door of the mansion. Two golden dragons flanked the entrance.

Kari kicked off her slippers upon entering, then followed the servants through the entry. Two stone lion statues guarded the inside, flanking a stone monument centered in the entryway with the names of the former emperors engraved in the stone.

Kari slowed her pace as they rounded past the monument and entered the first courtyard. She was in no hurry to rush to the emperor's bed. The servants escorted her through the main courtyard, past the second courtyard, and into the communal area of the main hall. The main hall of the mansion had been renovated just for the brothers. Two identical bedchambers were set opposite the communal area. The servants stopped at the leftmost door of the hall, motioning for her to enter Baoshun's bedchamber.

Kari's hand trembled as she slowly opened the door. He was already waiting for her. Another woman dressed in a similar outfit as Kari was inside, massaging his bare shoulders while he reclined on his bed. He wore only a pair of black pants. The woman looked up, her piercing blue eyes glaring at Kari as she entered. The servant closed the door.

"I'm sorry I took so long, my lord," Kari said, bowing her head in feigned reverence.

"Sometimes it is better to wait for the artist to finish before enjoying the piece," Baoshun said.

Great. He was trying to be poetic before he violated her.

"You are like rare jade lost in a sea of rocks. My brother was a fool to cast you aside, but his loss is my gain. Your beauty was evident to everyone in court. No one could ever challenge that. Tonight is special for you and me. Since this will be our first night together, Izumi will teach you the art of love. She will instruct you on the proper techniques and skills I require. Once she has trained you, you will be able to return to me, then we can fully enjoy each other's company."

Kari recognized the name Izumi. Unlike Jiaorong, Baoshun had taken a wife before ascending to the throne. Curious that not only did Izumi *not* object to her husband's extramarital affairs, but she actually partook in them.

"On your knees," Izumi demanded, slapping Kari.

Kari gritted her teeth and took the transgression, trying to repress her anger. What was it with these two and hitting her? She turned her attention to Baoshun. "My lord, I do not wish to make you unclean."

"What do you mean?" Baoshun asked.

"I am on my cycle," Kari lied. It might not have worked on his brother, but, with any luck, her ploy would buy her some time with him.

"Ah," Baoshun replied. "In that case, I will have to make you mine another night. Tell me, child, have you ever known a man?"

"No, my lord," Kari said honestly.

"In that case, tonight, you will learn how to please a man." Baoshun untied his pants. "While the gods might demand we cannot join together, there is nothing forbidding other pleasures."

"On your knees," Izumi ordered again. She kicked at the back of Kari's knees, causing her to buckle and fall to the floor.

"My lord," Kari pleaded, trying to stall. "May I sing for you first?"

"That won't be necessary," Baoshun replied. "As I have said, you are currently like a babe learning to walk for the first time. It is important you master these skills. When you return, all possibilities will be open."

"I have prepared a song just for you, my lord." Kari ignored what he was saying. Just hearing his words filled her with disgust. "As I am sure you are aware, I was a songstress before coming into your service. I think my lord will be quite pleased with my talents."

"Sounds like she is trying to get out of performing her duties. Sounds like treason to me," Izumi said, a wicked smile flashing upon her face.

"My lord, why would I not want to please you?" Kari asked, batting her eyelashes. "I have spent my whole life dreaming of serving you. I even volunteered to join your service. Lord Cai Ren can attest to that."

"Brother says you are ill tempered and resistant."

"My lord, I mean no offense, but I never wanted to serve him. He is far too brutish and foul mouthed. Nothing like you, my lord."

Baoshun laughed. "That he is."

"You are both handsome and sagacious. Ever since I was a little girl, I dreamt of nothing more than being in your company, my lord. To feel your hands caress my body. To make myself yours, both physically and spiritually. I couldn't stand being in his company, not when I knew you were within mere inches of me, my lord. I have heard stories of your prowess in both battle and in bed, and I wanted nothing more than to discover those myself." She had to be careful not to come across too strong. If she could play to his ego, maybe she could get out of this.

"There are stories?" Baoshun raised an eyebrow.

"Indeed, there are, my lord. I could not resist you, my lord. My love, since I was little, I perfected my songcraft so I could one day serenade my eternal love. Please, my lord, grant this poor girl her dream." Kari looked deep into his dark eyes before kowtowing before him. Eye contact conveyed emotion. Hopefully, her eyes could appeal to his. Her submissiveness should help put him at ease and make him feel empowered. With any luck, she would soften his position and not inflame his passions.

"Very well," Baoshun said, sitting on his bed. "Let us hear your song."

"You're not going to listen to this dribble? Can't you see what she is doing?" Izumi protested, but Baoshun raised a hand that silenced her protests.

Kari rose, eyeing Izumi. She would be a detriment to her plans. Izumi wasn't as easily swayed like her husband, but Kari couldn't focus on that now. It was time for her to do what she was best at.

Kari focused her aura, softening it, then infused her lungs and voice with spirit energy as she began her song. Her soft gentle voice radiated through the room. Baoshun closed his eyes, smiling as the melody caressed his ears.

> *"A thousand nights float by,*
> *And your form, divine.*
> *Haunts my memories,*
> *Their—"*

Kari stopped.

"Why did you stop? Keep going," Baoshun ordered.

"My lord," Kari said, cupping her hands over her heart. "My song is so personal it is meant only for you. It doesn't feel right to have someone else listen to the sounds of our hearts."

Izumi started to protest, but Baoshun cut her off. "Leave us."

"But..." Izumi protested.

"You won't be needed again tonight," he added motioning for her to leave.

Izumi stormed out of the room. Smiling, Kari resumed her song. As she sang, she let her feet carry her over the floor. She floated over to Baoshun, then let her fingers brush against his face.

> *"A thousand nights float by,*
> *And your form, divine.*
> *Haunts my memories,*
> *They're bittersweet.*
>
> *"You're all I need.*
> *Heaven indeed.*
> *Your sacred soul,*
> *It makes me whole.*
>
> *"Gleaming rays bring forth the day,*
> *Turning the dark into light.*
>
> *"Separated by time,*
> *But my heart still pines*
> *For your sacred touch.*
> *It heals me so much."*

"Amazing," Baoshun said as Kari finished. "Truly amazing. Where did you learn to sing like that?"

"I learned for you, my lord," Kari responded, draping her arms around his shoulders. "If it pleases you, my lord, I would like to compose a new song to celebrate our first night together."

"Yes, gods, yes."

"Since I am unable to join with you tonight, shall I go begin my masterpiece to attest our love?"

"When will it be done?"

"I shall return in seven days with a new ballad, my lord."

CHAPTER TEN

Kari's stomach growled. She had skipped breakfast, the stress from the night before making her stomach churn. Why had she only given herself seven days? In the moment, she was afraid to push her luck too far, and seven days seemed like a lifetime away, but today, it felt like a wild horse galloping toward her, ready to trample her under its feet.

There was nothing she could do about it now, though. Kari needed to eat something to recharge her mind. She had a week to come up with a new song to sing for Baoshun. She could either write her own song or come up with one she was confident he didn't know to pass off as a newly written song. Either way, it needed to impress. With a bit of luck, she might be able to stall for enough time for her to think of a new escape plan—not to mention, she still needed to convince Suying to escape with her.

At least they could discuss it over lunch. Suying sat under a cherry blossom tree in Guanwa Hall. She was flanked on either side by her maidservants, who held up a canopy shielding her from any rays of light that might break through the branches.

"Suying, would you care to join me for lunch?" Kari extended her hand for Suying to take.

"No, I think not," Suying replied, not even bothering to look at Kari.

Kari ignored her apparent disinterest. "Are you not hungry? I can wait for you if need be."

"No, I think it is best I'm not seen with you right now."

"What?" Kari was taken aback.

Suying stared up at Kari, her brown eyes revealing her youthful age. "It's nothing personal, Kari. This is just for a little while. After everything that has happened, you're making powerful enemies within the palace. I can't afford to share those enemies if I wish to actually enjoy this life. Things will change soon, I promise, but in the meantime, Mei thinks it's best if I avoid being seen with you. It's just until your reputation as a troublemaker abates."

"Are you serious?" How could Suying side with Mei after everything they'd been through together? They had been friends as close as sisters for years while Suying had only known Mei for a week.

"Mei says this happens whenever they bring new women into the palace. There is always one who has difficulty fitting in, but, given time, you'll adjust and be welcomed with open arms." Suying smiled reassuringly.

"I have no intention of fitting in," Kari blurted out.

"And that is your problem." Suying jumped to her feet. "You had the chance to leave, but you stayed. I don't know what you're here for, but it's not for me."

"It is for you," Kari interrupted. The two maidservants gasped at Kari's boldness. "Don't you see what this place is? What it's doing to you?"

Suying looked at her servants. "I don't think you see. I have a better life here than I would ever have outside these walls. This is my home, where I belong. Destiny has brought me to the house of heaven, and I will serve its sons faithfully."

"You're delusional." Kari shook her head, but she regretted the words as soon as she said them. They were much harsher than she intended, despite being true. But harsh words typically failed to change minds.

"You are dismissed." Suying waved her hand as if to motion Kari away.

"What is that supposed to mean? With a wave of your hand, I'm supposed to shut up and be quiet?" This wasn't Suying—this was a matron. Mei had gotten into Suying's head and had changed how she acted.

Suying motioned to one of her servants.

"My lady has expressed she is no longer interested in your presence. As a non-ranking attendant, I will notify the guards if you do not heed her words."

"So that's how it is?" Kari stared at Suying, who did not return her gaze. So even her sister would pull rank over her.

Kari stormed off to the dining hall. She was betrayed and hurt. Suying was her sister, at least, as close to a sister as she had. It seemed the longer she was here, the more Suying drifted away from Kari. What had happened to her friend? What happened to the little girl she would embrace just to stay warm in the frigid winter nights? It seemed like such a long time ago. When they'd been sleeping in alleyways, she would wrap Suying in her arms and hold her tight just to make sure she was warm enough. Suying would always fall asleep first, with Kari holding her. The younger girl looked so different back then.

Back then. It was funny that was just a few months ago. How had she lost her so fast?

Kari ignored the buffet when she entered the dining hall. On the far side of the room, Ina sat alone, but at least not behind a door this time. Kari placed her hand in her sash, the metal of the necklace feeling cool against her fingertips.

Kari was glad to see Ina at lunch. It was the first time she'd seen Ina in person since Kari had been released from the dungeon, and she could properly apologize at last.

"Ina, I'm so sorry," Kari said, taking a seat next to her. "I had no right to say what I did. You have been nothing but kind since I arrived. I had no reason to suspect otherwise."

"I guess I understand." Ina scrutinized Kari, but left her response at that.

"I have something of yours." Kari took the necklace out of her sash before handing it to Ina.

"How did you get this?" Ina gaped at the necklace. Her hand hovered over it as if she were afraid to touch it. "Did you steal it?"

"Of course not," Kari said. She placed the necklace in Ina's hand, then closed her fingers tight around it. "I just convinced Mei it was in her best interest to return it."

"I thought I would never see it again." Ina clutched at the silver pendant, then pressed it against her chest.

"I knew how much it meant to you, and I wanted to show you how much you mean to me. You've shown me nothing but kindness since I've met you, and I regret the way I behaved toward you."

"You must have gone through great trouble to get this." Ina didn't hesitate to drape the necklace around her neck. She smiled as the pendant fell into place.

"Like I said, you've been a good friend."

"Thank you. I am truly indebted to you. My betrothed gave me this." Ina closed her eyes, smiling as she placed her hand over the necklace. She looked truly at peace.

"Your betrothed? You were going to get married?" Kari could already imagine the reason Ina was here before she even said anything.

"Yes. My sister had been an attendant, one of the matrons and a favorite for Jiaorong. However, she grew sick and died a few months back. I guess Jiaorong wanted to replace her, so he sent his guards to collect me. It was my wedding day. When the guards told me I was to take my sister's place, Shinichi objected. They killed him for it. I will never see my betrothed again, but this amulet serves as a reminder of what could have been." Ina wiped at the tears streaming down her cheeks.

"I'm so sorry," Kari said. She placed her hand on top of Ina's. "I had no idea."

"Of course you didn't," Ina said. "Now all that is left of my life is to be filled by the emperors just like my sister until my death comes."

"Not necessarily," Kari said. Ina shot her a look of disbelief. "Last night, I was called to be with Baoshun."

"Are you all right? How did that even happen? You're an attendant of Jiaorong," Ina asked.

"I'm fine. Evidently, Jiaorong thought I would be too difficult to control, so he gave me to his brother as a present. I'm almost shocked they would treat anyone like an item to be traded back and forth."

"Really?" Ina asked. "They enslave and rape women. They have an entire district dedicated to that very cause, and you can't believe they would treat women as something other than human?"

"Anyway," Kari continued. "When Baoshun called me to his quarters, I told him I was on my cycle. That seemed to work okay, but then he wanted me to use my mouth. Instead, I tried to convince him to let me sing to him. When I had finished singing, he let me go."

"I don't understand. How does singing prevent you from sleeping with him?"

"I might have enchanted him." Kari smiled. She was quite proud of herself.

"What does that mean—you enchanted him?" Ina asked.

"I'm going to trust you with a secret you can't tell anybody." Ina had trusted her with her story, so it was only fair Kari trust Ina in return. Kari didn't have to tell her everything, just enough to repair their broken bond.

"You returned the last reminder of my beloved that I have left. You can trust me with your life," Ina replied. It was a welcome relief to finally have someone Kari could trust in the palace. They still didn't fully know each other, but trust was important for them to build their friendship. Kari leaned forward so she could whisper.

"I have magic. When I sing, I can infuse my voice with spirit energy, which I use to sway people. I can't control them, but I can influence their emotions and how they feel. Every song naturally elicits some emotion from its listeners, and I can intensify those feelings."

Magic had always been feared even though it was increasingly rare. With the Sovereign War, its place in society was coming into question again with some nations outright banning magic entirely. Luckily, Xiang wasn't one of them. At least not yet.

"At least that should help keep you safe," Ina said. "It's only a matter of time before I'm called. Jiaorong is already making his way through the group that came with us. He went through four girls last night alone."

"I wish I could help you more," Kari said. "I know Jiaorong isn't deterred by a cycle, so you won't be able to take that route. For now, try to fake an illness or something. If you have to, eat rotten food. Anything to make you sick. I don't think he would risk illness. You just have to find out what he is averse to and exploit it."

"That might buy us some time, but we couldn't keep that up for long," Ina said.

"I know," Kari said. "I'm working on a more permanent solution. For now, though, that's all we've got."

"You little slut!" Izumi busted into their conversation. Kari jumped from the table. She wasn't sure how much the other woman had heard. "You think he could ever love a whore like you? I'll kill you before I let you take him."

"Izumi! How long have you been there?" Kari wished she had chosen her words better.

"Long enough to grow tired of your voice." Izumi slammed her hand down on the table. "I want you to know just who you are. You are a whore, nothing more. I hope I'm there when he breaks you. I bet you're going to cry."

"My lady, what are you doing here?" Zhenhua asked, approaching the table. Great, it was all of Kari's favorite people coming together in one place. "I thought your days would be better spent by my lord's side just in case he had any scraps he wanted to give you."

"Remember your place, Zhenhua," Izumi threatened, but Zhenhua shrugged off the comment, unfazed.

"I meant no disrespect, my lady. I was merely suggesting that with so many women surrounding your husband, it might be beneficial to remain in his graces in case he forgets about you."

Izumi turned up her nose before storming off.

"Don't let her get to you," Zhenhua said, turning her attention to Kari and Ina. "Izumi is nothing but a paper tiger."

"I can't believe you said that to her," Kari said. And she thought her words to Suying were harsh. "Why would you help me?"

"You could try thanking me, little Hikari," Zhenhua reminded. "At any rate, I owed you from yesterday. I can't have you being the only troublemaker."

"Of course, thank you." Ina offered Zhenhua the seat next to her, but Kari glared at Zhenhua, silently warning her to stay away. Zhenhua obviously sensed the tension, so she declined the seat.

"I think I misjudged... or perhaps I judged you accurately after all," Zhenhua said to Kari.

"What do you mean?"

"Every now and then, a girl comes here who really doesn't want to be here. She's a troublemaker who will break just about every rule until drastic measures are taken. I thought you were going to be like that. I thought I needed to show my dominance early, but you did what I couldn't and stood up to another matron. You humiliated her in front of her peers just to help me get that back." Zhenhua pointed at the necklace around Ina's neck.

"By all rights, you should have been executed, but anyone who would risk that for another, I think I can learn to tolerate. Besides, Izumi is all bluster anyway. She's always giving the new girls a tough time, especially the pretty ones. She's just jealous, not that I blame her. Could you imagine your husband telling you he needed other women to sedate him? Doesn't change the fact she's a snake, though."

"I never thought about it like that," Kari said.

"I know you two don't want to be here, but there are many girls around this nation who would do anything to be where you are. It gets better, trust me. You just have to allow it." Zhenhua bowed before leaving Kari and Ina alone in the dining hall.

Kari missed the other side of Zhenhua, the mean-spirited matron, hell-bent on breaking the will of her charges. This human, caring side, made it difficult to hate her. Maybe that was the issue. She was just as lost as everyone else, trying to cope with a situation she was ill prepared for, merely trying to fit in and survive. Maybe hatred would only bring more hatred. It was a thought to ponder at least.

Days passed, and the allotted time of Kari's return to Baoshun quickly approached. Kari found she preferred to spend her days in the garden. She and Ina would explore the nearly two hundred acres of perfectly maintained vegetation and foliage, using it as a coping mechanism.

Kari loved finding new plants. Every new flower, bush, and tree, she would pluck a leave or petal and transform it into a seed, which she kept in a small pouch tied securely to the waist of her skirt. When she finally left the palace for good, she would have a marvelous garden of her own.

Ina was astonished the first time Kari showed off her plant magic. For Shagin, magic was an everyday phenomenon, and it always surprised Kari how little of it existed on the mainland.

Kari and Ina took to eating their meals in the garden. It was quite the trip from the dining hall to the other side of the palace, but it was well worth it to eat away from the commotion of Guanwa Hall. If anything, the long walk just made them appreciate their food even more.

Kari was thankful for Ina's presence. Suying was still in avoidance mode, so it was nice to have a friend to talk to. Not to mention, with Ina's rank, they didn't need an escort to leave Guanwa Hall. They could roam the palace in peace.

All things considered, palace life was rather uneventful, especially when compared to their time in the storehouse. The former prison was structured and rigid, but, in the palace, they were free to pass the time however they saw fit, and there were plenty of options to choose from, whether it was swinging in the gardens, practicing calligraphy, learning art from master artists, reading from the vast collection of books available, or simply admiring the intricate architecture around them.

The women who had been in the palace the longest seemed bored with all the activities, more preoccupied with the appearance of politeness as they schemed and gossiped behind each other's backs, a not-so-subtle attempt to sway the emperors' favor from one woman to the next.

They could have it for all Kari cared. She wanted nothing more to do with the emperors, which was ironic seeing as she was the only one with a set date to meet with one.

Escaping from the palace would be no easy task. Nearly ten thousand eunuchs guarded the palace, and all the perimeter walls were heavily guarded with watch towers strategically dispersed along them. There was no way to sneak past without raising an alarm. Not to mention the hundreds of officials and thousands of attendants who lived within the palace walls who might notice any escape attempt.

Finding a way out wasn't her only concern anymore. She still needed to convince Suying to go with her, a task that was becoming increasingly more difficult. And then there was Ina.

"If I found a way out, if we could escape, would you come with me?" Kari asked her.

"I don't have a life to return to," Ina replied.

"We can make a new life."

Ina didn't respond. She never responded when Kari pressed her about leaving. Had the emperors taken away all Ina's hope? Or did she merely know the truth? The truth that loomed over Kari as high as the hundred-foot walls. The truth she was becoming increasingly aware of the closer she looked at her options.

There was no escaping the palace.

Kari spent all day preparing for her visit with Baoshun, with the bulk of her preparations spent bathing in rose petals and perfume while servants combed her hair. They used different brushes for various parts of her hair and scalp to ensure the precise sheen and softness.

They dressed her in fine silks, tying a pleated blue-and-purple skirt around her waist and a blue blouse around her chest. They draped a blue, sheer daxiushan gown around her, tying it in the middle. The sleeves of the gown were long and flowy, perfect for dancing.

When the time had come, a litter took her to the emperors' mansion just as before. Kari slowly stepped out of the chair. The stairs leading to the door of the mansion seemed ominous and high. She took a deep breath. Kari could do this. She had practiced for this.

Kari followed a guard, and they weaved their way through the mansion and its two large courtyards. The architecture of Xiang seemed to be the opposite of Shagin. Instead of a yard surrounding a house, the houses surrounded the yards. Kari stopped at the door to the main hall. The full moon of the night sky radiated down upon her, a normal sky on an abnormal night. Kari followed the guard as he opened the door, entering the communal area. Lady Izumi sat in a chair at the entrance.

"Another conquest, I see," she said as Kari stepped forward.

Kari ignored her. Instead, she headed to the door leading to Baoshun's quarters. The guard stopped just shy of the door, motioning for Kari to continue.

"This is as far as I can go, my lady," the guard said, bowing in respect.

Kari took another deep breath before slowly sliding the door open. Baoshun lounged on his bed, a translucent crimson canopy surrounding him.

"It is good to see you again." Baoshun's attention piqued as Kari slid the door closed behind her. "I have dreamt of our reunion ever since I first heard your beautiful voice."

"It is a pleasure to be in your company again, my lord." Kari bowed graciously.

"Before we begin, there is one matter we need to attend to."

"What is that, my lord?"

"The eunuchs have informed me that Cai Ren provided you with your own private quarters." Baoshun paused as if he were waiting for Kari to acknowledge this claim.

"Yes, my lord, he did."

"That is not fitting of an attendant of your rank. Those quarters are for second-rank attendants only. Per your rank, you must share your quarters with other non-ranking attendants. It is our law and custom. Are you aware of this?"

"Yes, my lord. I apologize, I meant no offense." Kari bowed her head in submission. She needed to play the part of the loyal concubine if her plan were to work.

"However, you are not suited to those quarters," Baoshun said, clearing his throat. "You will be moved immediately into your own house and given the rank of first attendant."

"Thank you, my lord." Kari dropped to her knees, kowtowing before the emperor. That was unexpected but welcomed.

"There is no need for that." Baoshun opened the canopy to his bed. "Tonight is a night of celebration. We shall celebrate our union."

"Yes, my lord." Kari stood to her feet. She took a bottle of wine from the end table, then poured a glass for Baoshun. "As promised, I have prepared a song especially for tonight. A song to show my devotion to you."

Baoshun leaned back against his cushions as Kari began.

"You left me alone behind.
Deep in the silence of night,
Forever I'll be consigned.
The love in my heart shines bright.

"My solemn heart pines for your touch,
Stronger than a lover's heartbeat
"Find and caress me again,
Cry out in the forlorn dawn.
My love will always extend,
Chasing a virginal fawn.

"Crystallize the love we share.
It will not lead you astray.

"Like a leaf in the breeze,
Guiding you back to passionate means.
Our yearnings will never ease,
Embrace me in your dreams.

"Your sacred heart longs for the world,
Breaking like the waves on a shore.

"Eternally intertwined,
Together in the silence of night.
Forever we'll be consigned,
The love in our hearts shines bright."

"That was exquisite," Baoshun said once Kari had finished. "You have made love to my soul with your heavenly voice. Now, let us make love with our bodies."

Kari smiled coyly. "My lord, this song is merely the beginning of what I have prepared for you tonight."

"I cannot wait any longer. I have thought of nothing else since I last saw you."

Kari poured him another glass of wine. "My lord must be patient. I would be remiss if I could not illustrate to you the depth of my feelings."

Kari danced. Every step, every movement, she had carefully planned out. Graceful and light, she moved in small circles across the floor, her skirt and gown spinning and twirling with her. Leaping through the air, she landed like a cat.

She danced and danced, sometimes with song and sometimes without, but she did not stop. As Baoshun's attention waned or his eagerness spiked, Kari would change dances or let her voice enchant him through song. With his hunger temporarily abated, she would pour another glass of wine as he became entranced in her performance again.

She danced and sang for hours. Her muscles ached as they grew fatigued. This was the most extreme exercise she had experienced since her childhood on Mystikos. She wouldn't be able to continue much longer, but as she became tired, so did he. With each passing glass of wine, he became more sedated, and his eyes grew heavier.

Kari stopped her dance, moving to embrace the emperor. She had one more song for him. Focusing the last of her spirit energy into her voice once more, she began a lullaby her mother used to sing to her as a child.

"Time to dream, my little one.

Fall asleep, my love.

Time to rest your weary head,

Lay your cares to sleep.

Time to close your heavy eyes,

The day has flown away.

Fall asleep,

Fall asleep,

And then wake up and sing."

Baoshun laid his head in Kari's lap, and she gently stroked his hair. She hated this. It was almost sickening to pretend to care for this man, to lovingly care for him just so he wouldn't rape her. Her rage boiled over inside like a kettle waiting to erupt.

Now wasn't the time for anger. She had accomplished her goal. He was asleep, and she was free to leave his presence.

Kari gently laid his head down before tiptoeing out of his bedchamber.

It would be a long walk back to Guanwa Hall. There was no carriage waiting to bring her back. After all, she wasn't expected to return until the morning, but she refused to spend the night in the emperors' mansion.

Guards rushed by her, carrying a royal sedan chair as they headed for the Imperial mansion. The silk curtains concealed the occupant, an attendant for Jiaorong, no doubt.

Poor girl. Kari could manipulate her way through an evening with the emperor without having to sacrifice her body. Yet, the other women couldn't do the same. She was a fool. She hadn't been thinking of anyone but Suying and herself.

The truth was she didn't have a plan. She didn't even have the beginnings of a plan. All she wanted to do was escape since the moment she'd arrived, but she couldn't leave Suying. And it was clear Suying would never come with her. Everyone else in the palace seemed to be just like the eunuchs rushing, resigned to their fate. They had accepted it.

But it wasn't her fate. She wouldn't let it be.

The hands of fate were rushing toward her, though, and she was lost just like everyone else.

Kari crashed in a chair in the communal area of Guanwa Hall. It was late, so the room was empty. It was the perfect place for her to be alone with her thoughts.

Had she really been that selfish? The poor girl in the chair being taken to Jiaorong was now destined to be stripped bare—everything she was to be laid out and fully given to the emperor whether she wanted it or not.

There would be no escaping from the palace. Escape had seemed so easy, but things had changed. Kari didn't want to escape the palace anymore. She didn't want to run away. If she did, the palace would still be inside her psyche, taunting her, a reminder of her cowardice.

She had left her childhood friend to die in the caves of Mystikos. Panic and fear had gripped her as the cave crumbled. The daughter of Alme had been so brave. She'd never once thought about herself. Even when the boulder fell on her, she'd been more concerned with ensuring Kari's safety. Her body betrayed her, though. She had told Kari to run, but she'd reached out to Kari for help. Help that Kari could not provide. No, that wasn't right. Kari *could* have helped—she *could* have saved her—but she didn't.

The blood and bone of what had once been the daughter of Alme's leg, along with the look of pain on her face, had sent a cold fear penetrating through Kari's very essence. Kari didn't want that to be her, so she'd ran. She'd sprinted deeper into the cave system as the tunnel collapsed.

The daughter of Alme had died, nameless and alone.

Now fear was trying to drive Kari to flee again, to leave behind the countless women who were victims to the emperors and the societal constructs that ensured their perpetual subjugation.

Kari wouldn't leave them.

"Hikari, have you seen Ina?" Zhenhua asked, entering the common room and breaking Kari's train of thought.

"No," Kari replied. "So, is this your daily please-for-give-my-sadism visit?"

"You really hate me, don't you?" Zhenhua scoffed.

"I really do," Kari snapped, startling herself with her bluntness.

"You're just as black bellied as everyone else, so don't you dare judge me," Zhenhua snarled.

"People have died because of you." Kari narrowed her eyes.

"You act righteous, but you're the one who forced me to betray Tama to Lord Jiaorong. She was a good friend, and her death is on your hands." Zhenhua spoke the truth Kari already knew all too well.

"Just like Kyoko's is on yours," Kari replied. Was that the truth of the world? One person killed, and another killed, and they blamed and hated each other for eterni-ty? "How many others did you let die?"

"Their deaths were a mercy."

"It's your job to protect them. To ensure they are taken care of—that they can thrive in the palace—and you let them be murdered."

"You really are a naïve girl," Zhenhua said with a sneer. "We were saving them from hell."

"What is that supposed to mean?" How could someone think like that?

"This life can be miserable, even at the best of times. I've seen women wait their whole lives just for a single visit from the emperor that never comes. It is a lonely life filled with enemies and rivals. Everyone behind these walls will gladly stab you in the back if they think it will benefit them."

"Not everyone is like you." Kari said the words, but they still sent a cold sweat down her spine. It was odd. She was afraid of her own words. It wasn't the words per se, but the implication. She wasn't like Zhenhua—yet, she was. Kari was one step away from being just like Zhenhua, from not caring about the suffering of others. Kari had tried to leave. If she continued to stay, what would keep her from taking that last step?

"Don't act like you know me. I've served the throne since before the Tian dynasty. I know more about palace life than you ever will."

"I thought the Tian brothers had all the former attendants killed?"

"I was one of the unlucky ones." Zhenhua averted her eyes. She turned to walk away. "I should go."

"Wait," Kari called, stopping Zhenhua in her tracks. Zhenhua was a horrible monster—at least that was what Kari thought—but she had been wrong about so many things up to this point. Kari wanted Zhenhua to prove her wrong again. "What do you mean, 'one of the unlucky ones'?"

"You wouldn't understand."

"Then help me to." Kari needed to understand. It was the only way to ensure hatred and despair didn't overtake her heart. At least that was what it felt like.

"I won't entertain you, Hikari," Zhenhua said, but Kari only raised an eyebrow, silently pleading with her to talk. Kari wasn't sure if she really wanted to know or not, but it felt necessary. Sighing, Zhenhua took the seat across from Kari. "If you must know, I was eighteen when the Tian usurped the throne, just a year older than you. I was a consort to Emperor Weijin Kong-Ce."

"A consort?" Kari asked. The consorts carried a ranking above the attendants. They surpassed even the matrons. There was just one requirement to become a consort. "You have children?"

"I *had* children. Two boys, heirs to the Weijin dynasty. They are gone now."

"I'm sorry," Kari muttered.

"I didn't know them, not really. They were just babes when they were killed. Even when they were alive, they weren't truly my children. Since I was a consort, they were taken from me after birth and given to the empress to raise."

"I suspect that doesn't make it any easier."

"No, it doesn't." Zhenhua stared at the ground, unable to look up at Kari. "I thought if I humbled myself before the Tian brothers, if I showed them I could be loyal to them, they might spare my sons and me. I was wrong. I was spared, but they were put to the sword. I allowed the Tian brothers to humiliate me, and it was for nothing. And now, as repayment, I get to oversee the transition of all the new attendants."

"That can't be easy for you, but it doesn't excuse what you've done."

"I did nothing," Zhenhua snapped.

"And that is the problem. It's your house. You knew what Tama was doing, and you did nothing to stop her. You let her do it. That makes you just as guilty."

Zhenhua waved her arm as if to push the thought away. "What Tama did was merciful. She exposed those girls to a single fleeting moment of pain to prevent them from experiencing elongated suffering."

"If you truly cared about the girls in your charge, you would have found another way."

"I don't see *you* finding another way. I wonder how many bodies you'll rack up within these walls. You already have one."

That wasn't true. Kari had more than one. Her heart sank at the realization.

A loud crash echoed through the room as the door was thrown open. Ina ran into the common room, then stopped and stared at Kari and Zhenhua.

"I might have a problem." Her face was bloody and bruised, her clothes ripped.

"What the hell happened to you?" Zhenhua jumped up from her chair, rushing over to Ina.

"Jiaorong caught me lying about being sick."

Kari's heart skipped a beat.

"What did he do?" Kari asked. This was not good. Jiaorong didn't seem like the kind of person to take being lied to lightly. This was Kari's fault. She had told Ina to fake an illness, and now Ina would face the consequences of Kari's game.

"He threw me down on his bed, beat me, and tried to rape me. I kicked him in the groin and ran."

"By the gods, they'll kill you for that," Zhenhua whispered, helping Ina to sit in one of the cushioned chairs.

"I know," Ina said calmly. "I don't know what to do. I don't think the guards are far behind. I don't want to die. Not by him."

Were the Fates testing Kari? Were they testing her resolve? Kari exhaled. There was only one thing left to do. She wasn't going to let another friend die.

"Zhenhua, can you take Ina to the storehouse?" It was time to act. No more fear. No more doubt. No more.

"What?" Zhenhua responded, shooting Kari a perplexed look.

"Keep her hidden for now. I'll deal with Jiaorong, but I need Ina somewhere safe," Kari explained. "Please, keep her safe."

"Of course." Zhenhua didn't hesitate. "I know a few places we could go, but we need to hurry."

Zhenhua grabbed Ina by the hand, yanking her toward the door.

"What are you going to do?" Ina asked, glancing back at Kari.

"I'm getting ready to think of something." Kari smiled reassuringly at Ina as Zhenhua hurried her out the door. Kari didn't have to wait long before four guards poured into the room.

"Where's the little slut?" one demanded.

Kari ignored his question. "I need to see Lord Jiaorong."

"Get out of the way," the guard barked, shoving Kari aside.

"She's under my protection," Kari boasted. There would be no turning back now.

"What?"

"You should take me to Lord Jiaorong," Kari added.

"Or I can execute you now for treason."

"I have committed no such act, but if I am to stand accused, then take me before the emperor and let him decide my fate." Kari raised her chin, holding her head high.

"Take her to the emperor." The guard motioned to another. "Come on. The bitch couldn't have gotten far."

Kari swallowed her fear as she followed the guard to her fate.

CHAPTER ELEVEN

"WHAT DO YOU WANT? I didn't call for Hikari. Where is the whore who struck me?" Jiaorong growled as Kari and the guardsman entered the room. She must have left an impression for him to remember her name. Hopefully, that would benefit her.

"This girl claims to be hiding her," the guard explained.

"Is that true?" Jiaorong asked. At least she had piqued his interests.

"You should leave us," Kari told the guard. He hesitated until Jiaorong motioned for him to leave.

"You have courage to stand against me," Jiaorong said once they were alone. He approached Kari, then placed his hand around her throat, but he didn't squeeze. Kari lifted her head, meeting Jiaorong's dark eyes.

"Quite the opposite actually." Kari's legs trembled and threatened to give way with her, but she had to be brave. She swallowed hard against his grasp, feeling her pulse beat under his grip. "On both counts. I have very little courage, and I do not wish to stand against you. I only wish to better serve my lord. I am not hiding Ina. I merely asked

Matron Zhenhua to take her to the storehouse so I may humbly beg an audience with you. If you desire to punish her, there is nothing I can do to stop you from seeking justice when she returns. I am merely here to show you that her punishment is futile, my lord. You need not waste your energy on her. You have no need for a woman who cannot see your greatness."

"Is that so?" Jiaorong released his hold on her. "Go on."

Kari breathed a sigh of relief, fighting the urge to place her own hand at her throat for protection. "Of course, my lord. Ina was a fool not to embrace you."

"And you're no fool?" Jiaorong cocked his head to the side to better examine her. "I seem to remember having to brand you for speaking out of turn."

"I spoke up not in defiance of you, but out of compassion. There was no need to kill Kyoko when the only woman you ever need is standing right before you. When I heard Ina had no desire to faithfully serve you, it was I who instructed her to feign illnesses, and the cause is simple. No one else is worthy of you. No one but me." With any luck, her natural beauty and charm would help win him over to her side.

"And what makes you so worthy?" Jiaorong asked.

"For years, I have yearned to be with you. I learned to sing and perfect my craft so I could impress you, my lord. I worked hard to make a name for myself in the hope I could be by your side. And then, one day, a miracle happened. Lord Cai Ren came by the teahouse in which I was perform-ing in search of women to audition before you. While he did not choose me, I knew this was my only opportunity to be with you. So, I chased him down and faced the wrath of his guards, pleading my case to him. Begged him to take me until he finally relented." A half-truth was always more convincing than a full lie. Hopefully, Jiaorong was at least passingly familiar with the events of her abduction. He needed to trust her, to believe she would do anything for him.

"And yet, this is the second time you have stood against me."

"My lord, don't you see?" Kari stepped forward and embraced him, placing her head on his chest. She fought back a smile as he wrapped his arms around her. He was softening. "All of my actions have been for you. I was ignorant. I believed you did not truly know the nature of Kyoko's treachery. However, I was wrong to question you. My lord's wisdom is unequaled. I believed I could prevent you from committing an unjust deed, but it was I who was uninformed of her treachery. The true nature of you, a Son of Heaven, is that you are just. Your decrees are intrinsically just, and it was I who was unjust. I made a grievous mistake, and I gladly accepted my punishment."

He grabbed her shoulders, holding her at arm's length. "And what of this whore you shield from me tonight? Would you dare question my honor again? My justice knows no bounds."

"It is not your honor or your justice I am questioning." Kari took hold of his hands, placing them on her face.

Closing her eyes, she made his hands caress her cheek. He needed to believe she was melting at his touch, when, in fact, it was quite the opposite. His calloused palms scratched her smooth soft skin. She hated him with every fiber of her being, but she had to suppress her anger and pretend to love him. "I believe my lord is too close to the offense to make the appropriate decision. Killing her would be quick. Instead, if a more permanent punishment could be found, she would suffer for her offense for the rest of her life."

"And what do you think would be appropriate?"

"I would not presume to make such a decree, my lord." Kari lightly kissed the back of his hand, the act making her queasy. She hated this. It was agony acting loving and tender to her captor, but she had to protect Ina, no matter the cost.

"No, please, by all means. You've come this far. Enlighten me as to what your justice looks like." Her plan was working. He was trusting her and listening to her suggestions.

Kari mulled over this. She needed to think of a punishment that was severe enough to satisfy Jiaorong, but soft enough to save Ina. Too soft, and Jiaorong would outright dismiss Kari and all of her suggestions. "She struck you, my lord. She insulted the Imperial throne, so she should be stripped of all titles and honors and made to serve the throne for the rest of her life as penance."

"It's a start, but as she struck me, I shall also strike her. An additional fifty lashes will be added to her punishment.

Do you have any objection to that?" He was testing to see if she would continue to object to his justice, to see if her true goal was to protect Ina or to serve him.

"It is as you say, my lord. Your justice is truly divine." Kari bowed her head in respect to the emperor. He reached out, then lifted her chin until their eyes met. She clenched her jaw to keep from trembling at his touch. It was time for him to dismiss her. At least, she hoped it was. For speaking out against him, he could punish her, execute her, or worse. A cold sweat sent chills down her spine as the possibility donned on her.

"The question now becomes what I should do with you? It is treason to enter the emperor's house uninvited. On top of that, you've entered my bedchamber while in the service of my brother. By all accounts, you should be forced to kill yourself."

Kari had to choose her words carefully. She was navigating treacherous waters. Every word, every movement could betray her. "My lord, my actions were driven not by treasonous intent, but for the utmost love for you. However, if my life is required to satisfy your law and aid your honor, I will do as you command."

"Why are you so quick to die without a struggle, when you fight so hard for others?"

Kari grimaced as Jiaorong seized her shoulders, his fingers digging into her.

"As I have said, it is not for their sake I risk my life, but for yours. My life is in your hands. You have but to will it, and I will give it to you. I will die for your sake, my lord."

"That's all well and good, but I don't know if I trust you."

Kari pulled free from his grip. "If you do not trust me, then trust in this. The god Talus declared he was incapable of hurting the one he loved. And you have not hurt me."

He might not care to follow the commandments of his own religion, but he had to be aware of the stories. Kari lifted the sleeve of her arm, removed the gold bangle, and untied the bandage, revealing the place where she had been branded. Unmarred skin showed where her charred, burned flesh should have been, courtesy of her spirit energy. Her spirit aura had completely healed the area, leaving no trace of the wound behind. "I hid my arm in fear of what it could mean when there was no mark to be found, but now I've realized the meaning. The gods are watching over us. You are Talus, unable to hurt your love. We are destined to be together. However, if you do not desire this, I will gladly take my life and free you of this burden."

The emperors took great care not to cross paths with the other's concubines. She prayed that would be the case with her, despite her allure. It was time for him to dismiss her. She clenched her fists. Their discussion was over. He'd gotten what he wanted—punishment for Ina. Now, if he'd only let her leave.

He grabbed Kari's waist, yanking her to him. She let out a whimper as her heart pounded in her heaving chest. When he stroked her face, she closed her eyes. *Please let this nightmare end.*

"You are incredibly beautiful, and I must admit I was very hesitant to give you to my brother. It was only after the incessant pestering of Cai Ren about your untamable attitude that made me finally relent, but I am to love you? What could you, a slave girl, offer me that I don't already have?"

"My beloved." Kari tried to pull free, but his embrace was too strong. There was no way out. If she turned back now, she would surely die. It wasn't how she wanted this to happen, but she desperately wanted to live. She gritted her teeth. He wouldn't dare betray his brother and act on his desires. She had to continue to fully gain his confidence, so she could leave with her life. "You carry such a heavy burden. I wish only to be by your side. Let me be your constant companion. In return, you can pour out your troubles onto me." She instantly regretted her words.

Kari shuddered as Jiaorong fully enveloped her in his arms. He kissed her neck. His warm breath and wet saliva against her skin mirrored the tears that fell from her emerald eyes.

Her life was in his hands, in more ways than one. Was there a way out of this? Death or submission? Dignity or life?

"It is odd," he said between kisses. "I have never want-ed anyone like I want you."

In one swift move, he picked her up and threw her onto his bed. He climbed on top of her, pulling at her clothes. Every instinct in her body told her to fight back, to resist, but she was frozen. Fear took what little strength she had, leaving her vulnerable as he stripped her bare. She was naked, devoid of any defense or protection. In the moment, Kari's mind went blessedly blank. She faded from her body as he proceeded to pierce her to her core.

An eternity of hell passed before the ordeal was over. After he finished with her, he rolled his weight off and laid beside her.

"That was truly amazing," Jiaorong said, panting.

Bare and motionless upon his bed, Kari clutched at the bedding beneath her. She gazed unseeingly at the ceiling. Her world had just changed—suddenly and violently. What had just happened?

"We have committed a sin." Jiaorong smiled. Pain like lightning struck her heart at the inclusion of the word *we*. Had she done this? "My brother would be very cross if he ever knew about our transgression. You should go. I'm afraid I can't have the guards escort you back. If I did, word might spread about what we've done. Don't fret, however, we will be together again, even if I have to kill the gods to do so."

Kari said nothing in response as she redressed. She had played a dangerous game and lost. What had she done?

She quickly found herself alone in the dark night, standing outside the emperors' mansion. The dim light of lanterns was scattered along the barren road. The guard who accompanied her had already left, leaving her alone to make her way back to her room.

She stumbled down the road. Her legs were weak and wobbly, and her whole body ached. It felt like her insides had been torn up and ripped out of her. She tripped as she reached the first moon gate leading to the Hall of Heaven and Earth. A guard ran over to help, but she jerked away out of reflex, losing one of her shoes in the process. Kari didn't even care. She hurried past the guards at the gate, not stopping to search around in the dim light for her missing shoe. Instead, she merely kicked off the other one and continued on her way.

She was supposed to return to her room. It was expected of her to be a good little girl and shrink away when she wasn't wanted, but if she returned now, her body would surely cave in on her. Bereft, she continued walking without purpose.

She walked for hours in the chilly night. None of the guards dared to stop her now that she was a first attendant. Of course, as long as she remained inside the walls, there was nowhere she could go and no need to stop her. She was a prisoner.

She wandered through the gardens. Flowers always found a way to bring new life to her, but the ones of the Imperial garden had no effect on her hollow heart. Kari reached out to touch the pink petals of a lily, but her hand stopped just shy. It was so beautiful and vivid. Why was it so pretty? Kari collapsed to her knees. Her body quivered as her gentle sobs echoed in the night. She wrapped her arms around her chest, but she couldn't stop her hands from shaking or her tears from falling.

It was useless. The flowers mocked her pain. Kari rose, hurrying onward, as she tried to process what had happened just a few hours earlier. No matter how much she tried to think on it, her mind was cloudy as if some force were keeping her from seeing what she had done. Unfortunately, that couldn't change what she had to do.

She had sacrificed her body to save her friend. There was no going back now. Jiaorong expected her to return to him, to be his lover. To confess her undying love for him. The very thought pressed against her head, threatening to break through to her skull. There was no way out of that. If she tried to back out, not only would Ina be executed, but Kari would also.

Pausing, Kari stared as she reached the statue of Valceem. She didn't even remember leaving the gardens. The irony of seeing a statue of Valceem was not lost on Kari. Valceem had fought against oppression and slavery. Now her kingdom and her throne were the oppressors, enslaving and abusing members of Valceem's own gender.

Kari gazed into the pool of water surrounding the statue. Kyoko had died in this very water. The thought of drowning seemed horrific, but so was having to return to Jiaorong. How many other girls had died here? Kari ran her fingers through the water, its bitter cold freezing her bones. The water was so calm and still, perfectly reflecting the night sky. The full moon stared at her through its reflection. She reached into the water, but the moon disappeared at her touch.

Ripples formed as she sloshed her hand through the water, the sound of droplets hitting Valceem resonating in the empty night. She studied the chilly water. What had it been like to die here? The ripples formed mesmerizing circles, beckoning her forward. Expanding circles spread from one end of the fountain to the other.

A welcomed silent embrace was what she craved.

The world went quiet as a blast of freezing water struck her face. She'd tumbled into the fountain. Kari wasn't sure if she had slipped or dove, but it didn't matter. Her body longed for the water to wash over her—to take her. This was all she wanted.

Kari exhaled, sending bubbles scampering to the surface while allowing her body to slowly submerge and sink to the bottom. The burning sensation in her chest, along with the coldness of the water and the roughness of the stone, was an odd sensation.

His fingers had been rough like stone.

Kari's chest convulsed as her lungs demanded air—air she didn't deserve. This was how Kyoko had died. She had struggled so much to breathe before her life had left her.

Kari thrashed in the water, breaking through the surface and gulping in much-needed oxygen. She shivered in the cool air before climbing out. Her bare feet struck the rough stone ground. Not even bothering to wring her clothes out, she made her way back to her room, leaving behind puddles wherever she went.

When Kari slipped inside her quarters, she stopped and examined herself in the mirror. The girl with the green eyes and brown hair who stared back at her was no longer her. Kari didn't know who she was.

"Never again," she vowed.

CHAPTER TWELVE

"Kari." Ina threw open Kari's door, sprinting into the room.

"Ina, is everything all right?" Kari sat up, but she didn't get out of her bed.

"You look like death! What happened to you?" Ina blurted out upon seeing the state Kari was in. Kari hadn't bothered changing from the night before. Her clothes were still wet, which had soaked her bed. "Are you okay?"

It was an odd question coming from Ina. Her face was bruised and purple, with cuts dotting her cheeks and lips.

"I think so. I confronted Jiaorong. But I..." Kari's words faded away. She didn't feel like talking. The act of telling Ina what happened would make it real. Averting her eyes, she clenched her fists. Why was she hesitating? She wanted to tell Ina what transpired, but the words would not come. How could Kari begin to describe it? How could she adequately explain her feelings and emotions? They were too complex for mere words.

"What did he do?" Ina asked. She sat on the bed, then placed her hand over Kari's clenched fist. Kari gritted her teeth.

Ina needed to know. Kari didn't have to go into detail—partially to save her dignity and partially because a substantial portion of what took place was still a blur. "Jiaorong forced me to sleep with him."

Ina's gaze fell as her hand tightened around Kari's. "I'm so sorry," she muttered. "This is all my fault."

"No." Kari lifted Ina's head until their eyes met. "This is his doing and his alone. If I hadn't gone through with this, then he would have killed you."

"Thank you," Ina whispered, eyes going misty. "I don't think I can ever repay you for what you've done."

"I'm sorry I couldn't do more." Kari brushed Ina's hair behind her ear. Her porcelain skin had been bruised and blemished with purples and blues. One glance at her face showed Jiaorong had already gotten his revenge, yet he demanded more pain be inflicted on Ina. Kari sighed. "Jiaorong has agreed to spare you, but you will still have to face punishment. Fifty lashes, and you'll be enslaved as a servant for the rest of your life."

"I'm already a slave." Ina threw her arms around Kari to embrace her. "We're both alive. For that, I owe you everything."

Kari breathed a sigh of relief. If Ina were grateful, it would make what was to come easier.

"I think it is time I tell you who I really am." Kari focused on her friend. She wasn't sure if this was the right thing to do, but it needed to be said. She had the whole night to think this through. It went against every fiber of her being, every ounce of her spirit, but her brain told her it was necessary. She needed Ina to fully trust her, and for Ina to know the trust was mutual. "I am Shagin."

Ina's brow furrowed as she silently gaped at her in disbelief. Was it fear or disgust that kept her quiet?

Kari's hand brushed against Ina's, but she recoiled and scrambled away from her. Her eyes were still fixated on Kari.

What had she done? Her people were hated and feared, and it was fear that showed in Ina's blackened eyes. Kari wanted nothing more than to retract her words. She could claim she was merely teasing.

Kari swallowed hard, ignoring the desire. It would take time for Ina to adjust. Kari had anticipated that. She needed to continue. Ina needed to know the truth.

"More specifically." Kari kept her gaze on her bed. Her eyes watered and burned as she forced out the words to her confession and disgrace. "I was banished. I'm a Shagin exile. I think I can trust you with my truth."

"So, you mean to say you're entrusting me with your life?" Ina's eyes widened as the severity of Kari's confession settled in. The Guardian's law was quite clear on the matter. Any Shagin was to be executed immediately. They were enemies of humanity—an all-female race known to the world as seductresses, baby stealers, and monsters.

Kari clasped her hands. Ina said nothing in response, her mouth agape. This had been a mistake.

"I shouldn't have said anything." Kari clenched her jaw. If Ina told anyone, if anyone found out, Kari would die. She turned her head away, tightly shutting her eyes. Why couldn't this just be over?

Ina reached out, gently turning Kari's head back toward her. "Of course you can trust me." Ina smiled reassuringly. "You've done so much for me; I would take your secret to my grave. I just can't believe any Shagins survived the Purge. But if any are like you, they can't all be bad. But why tell me this?"

Kari ignored the backhanded compliment. She was sure Ina didn't mean it the way it sounded. "I'm telling you this so when I tell you the next part, you will fully understand what I'm saying."

Kari paused, inhaling a deep breath. She had risked being seen as a monster with the first half of her story, but it was the second half that risked her being seen as insane.

"Following my exile, I came to Xiang in search of my birth father. What I found instead was a land overcome with tyranny. Two tyrants have taken hold of this nation, and you know firsthand how disgusting they can be. I am going to save Xiang from their tyranny."

Ina rubbed her face in contemplation. "I don't understand. How would you even go about doing that?"

"I don't have a plan," Kari admitted. It was ludicrous to make such a bold statement without one, but if she were correct, she didn't need her own plan. "At least not yet, but

I think I know someone who does. We need to go see Cai Ren."

Ina's expression went skeptical, but she did not object. Kari hoped she was right in her assumptions. He said he needed her for something. At the time, she had felt threatened and interpreted his behavior and actions as that of a sexual nature, but he was high chancellor living in the Imperial palace. Like all men living there, he was a eunuch. Any behavior she interpreted as sexual was obviously misplaced. At least, she hoped it was.

The only question remaining was why had he brought her to the palace? He had been watching her. Had known who she was the moment his soldiers entered the tea-house. He knew she was Shagin, and he hadn't killed her for it. Why would anyone in his position want to bring a Shagin into the Imperial harem?

Judging on the conversation she'd had with him, Cai Ren didn't seem fond of his current role. Perhaps he desired more for either himself or the land. Whether ambition or justice motivated him, she was unsure. Seeking his aid would be a significant risk without knowing his true intentions, but after last night, any risk seemed negligible.

Kari would have to be careful to discern his true motives. If she revealed her intentions and ended up wrong about his, her pain would be for naught.

"You know you can't go outside like that, right?" Ina asked, referencing Kari's disheveled look. "I'm still a little confused. At what point did you decide to take a bath in your clothes?"

Ina helped Kari change and detangle her hair. Kari forwent her usual ponytail. Instead, she tied her hair in two loops, adorned with ornaments, gems, and pink-and-white flowers. Once Kari was adorned with the fine silk garments and makeup of an Imperial attendant, the pair set off to see the chancellor.

The day was as beautiful as any other. It almost seemed the events of the night before hadn't even occurred. Kari wasn't sure what she expected. Nature cared little of the comings and goings of humanity. There were various superstitions of the local populace about how the cosmos or whatever would react to the dealings of people. A howling dog at night meant someone had died. The alignment of the stars would dictate future events. A raging wind was an omen of things to come.

The truth was simpler. Nature simply behaved the way it did regardless of human events. The sky didn't care what horrors were inflicted on others. It existed constantly. Humanity was a small insignificant bit of stardust in the universe. Life was short, fleeting, and relatively unimportant in comparison to the stars, moons, and distant planets that dotted the night sky.

That made it precious.

Life was unique. It was fragile, and it must be protected. The sky did not dream. It was life's dreams that set it apart, that made it vastly more valuable in the grand scheme of the cosmos.

Kari honestly believed that.

She had spent far too long thinking of only herself. She had left her childhood friend to die in the caves of Mystikos and she had been willing to leave Suying behind, but not anymore. It wasn't just herself or Suying or Ina she wanted to protect. It was everyone. No one should ever have to experience the pain she went through last night. Never again. That was her dream.

They left Guanwa Hall to enter the residential quarters. Being high chancellor, Cai Ren lived in one of the largest manors in the palace, located in the center of the quarters, just south of the emperors' mansion. It would take them about half an hour to walk from Guanwa Hall to Cai Ren's home, but Kari didn't mind.

Kari enjoyed the chirping birds and the cool morning air. She almost wanted to forget about the marble roads, throw off her shoes, and stick to walking in the grass. It wouldn't be becoming of an attendant, but the children playing in the meadows didn't seem to mind.

Kari stopped, clutching the sides of her skirt. Her raspy breathing caught Ina's attention, causing the other girl to regard her curiously. Why hadn't Kari noticed the children before? She hadn't thought. She never did.

The residential quarters was where the consorts lived, the concubines who had given birth to the emperors' children. These were the children of Jiaorong and Baoshun.

Kari shut her eyes, not wanting to see their faces. They were all young and innocent, and she was plotting to kill their fathers. Her actions would bring indescribable pain to these children, and they would forever hate her. It would beget an endless cycle of hatred that would only result in more death and pain.

The Tian brothers had murdered the children of the former emperor when they usurped the throne. Was it done to break the cycle before it could start? Was that the only option in life? To end it? To kill?

"Kari, is everything all right?" Ina held out her hand for Kari to take, but she shook her head and refused.

Why had she chosen her name? Kari hated herself—her very nature demanded she walk in blood and death. Hatred and darkness would be the only thing she could bring to the world. She bore the Shagin curse, one that filled her with the darkest light.

Whatever action she took, these children would see her as the monster who ruined their lives.

Kari took a deep breath. It had to be done. The Tian brothers had to die.

Three consorts stood watch over the playing children. They didn't acknowledge Kari and Ina's presence, but merely talked among themselves.

Had the consorts asked for this life? Had the life that grew from them asked for it? Had she?

Kari hugged her stomach, dropping to her knees.

Would this be her fate, too? Would it be another curse to befall upon her for her to bear? She had slept with the emperor, and he hadn't held back.

Motherhood was a spiritual journey for Shagin, a sacred duty needed to preserve their race. Would this be how she reached it?

"Goddess, help me." Kari squeezed her eyes shut as tears welled.

Ina knelt to embrace Kari. "I'm sorry. We don't have to do this, but we do need to go. The consorts are watching."

"I can't bear his child. I can't do it." Kari stared up at her friend.

"It was just one time. Most concubines never become pregnant," Ina said, helping Kari to her feet.

She was right. It was just one time, and there wouldn't be a second.

Kari glanced at the consorts. They'd gone back to ignoring them. Would this be her in nine months? She gazed into the blue sky.

"I can't worry about what may happen," she said, mostly to herself.

"That's right," Ina replied. "Only focus on what has happened and what you know *will* happen."

Kari smiled. It was nice to have a friend to lean on again.

"We don't have to do this today," Ina said.

"No, we need to see this through before I lose my resolve." Kari stepped forward, the first step of a thousand, and continued her walk to see Cai Ren.

They stopped at the entrance of Cai Ren's residence. Kari banged the iron knocker on the front door, then waited for a response.

Cai Ren opened the door, taking in the two women at his threshold with wide eyes. Kari was surprised he'd opened the door himself instead of one of his servants. It wasn't suited for someone of his station, and it didn't fit what she knew about him. But perhaps she had been wrong. She hoped so.

"What are you doing here?" he asked.

"We need to talk," Kari replied.

"Indeed we do. Hurry, before someone sees you." Cai Ren motioned Kari and Ina inside his house. After gaining entry, they kicked off their shoes, then followed him through the first courtyard of his manor and into the great room. He gestured toward a knee-high square table in the center. They each knelt on the red cushions surrounding it, Kari and Ina on one side and Cai Ren on the other. "And what is the nature of this visit? Why have two attendants come to see me?"

"There have been some changes since last night," Kari started.

"So I've been told." He poured each a cup of tea. Kari graciously bowed as she accepted hers. Cai Ren regarded Ina as he handed her a cup. "So, this must be Inahime then."

"Yes," Kari responded. He was the high chancellor, so it was no surprise he would be well informed. She took a sip of the tea, its warm goodness flowing into her empty stomach. It growled in return. She had yet to have breakfast, a decision that was not aiding her growing anxiety.

"I'm afraid there is nothing I can do, if that is what you're seeking. Lord Jiaorong is already showing more mercy than is usual for him. I fear any meddling from my part would snap him back to his old self."

"That isn't why we are here." Ina carefully placed her cup on the table, then met his gaze. Interlacing her fingers, she twiddled her thumbs. "My fate is set. I am aware of that."

"We're here to discuss something else," Kari added. This was the moment of truth. What could she say and what did she need to hide? The man who sat before her was the catalyst of her pain. She had hated him for that, yet he had protected her more than once. He was a snake, willing to manipulate and use others for his gain—that much was certain—but now was not the time for hatred. She would have to put aside her resentment if she were going to save the kingdom. Kari needed a powerful ally, which he could be. "I'm not sure if I trust you."

"This is an odd way of displaying distrust, showing up at my door like this." Cai Ren gestured to the surrounding room. "You can speak freely here. We are alone. I dismissed all my servants some time ago. Too many eyes in a palace that sees all."

That was good. It made things easier, knowing no one else would overhear. It didn't change the fact she still needed to be careful around Cai Ren. She only suspected he knew what she was. Even if she were right, there was no telling if her assessment of his plans for her were. "If I am correct and you know what I am, then I have no choice but to trust you. So, do you? Do you know my secret?"

"Do you go around announcing yourself to the world?" Cai Ren shook his head, rubbing his eyes. "Yes, I know. You are Shagin. It is the eyes that give you away. Never will you see such vivid eyes except on a Shagin."

"You said I can help you get what you want. I thought due to your aggressive approach in my room you might assault me—that it was your whole plan for having me brought to the harem—but you're a eunuch, just like all the men in the palace. Is that correct?" She was right, at least about part of her theory. Now, she needed to know what his true intentions were.

"That is true," Cai Ren answered. He took a drink from his tea, then set his cup in front of him. "So, you misconstrued my intentions, and now you are here to see why I am interested in you. Is that so?"

"Yes." Kari looked at Ina, who was intently listening to them speak. She hoped she was right about him, or else she had little hope of providing meaning to their sacrifices.

"My intentions are complicated to say the least." Cai Ren clicked his tongue as he thought through his response. "To tell you the truth, I couldn't stand by and watch the empire crumble, so I voluntarily castrated myself to prove my loyalty to the Tian. Now I am high chancellor to a degrading throne."

"What do you think I can do?" Kari asked.

"You are Shagin. It only took ten thousand Shagin to bring the world to its knees. I thought for sure it would only take one to topple an empire."

"You thought I could be an assassin?" Kari asked. Her heart felt weak. The Shagin would only ever be remembered for the actions of a few renegades. They would forever be thought of as vile murderers, child stealers, and criminals. That was what he wanted of her—to kill. There was more to Shagin than being simply warriors and killers, but there was no changing the legacy of those who forever changed the face of the world, who fought in the Sovereign War.

"Why not? You wouldn't be the first assassin I've used against the Tian. This nation used to be unrivaled under heaven, but with those fools running it, it will slowly die. The only remedy is their deaths." Cai Ren stood from his cushion to begin pacing around the room. "The issue is, they share a peerless might and are always within a stone's throw of each other. I have seen the most skilled assassins be rendered useless against them. I thought you might fare better, that you might be a dragon in hiding, but I see I was wrong. You are not one of the warriors of myth the world has come to expect from Shagin. You are nothing more than a scared girl. For that, I am sorry, for both our sakes."

She was more than that. Shagin was more than that. But would the world ever see it? Kari sighed. "I have had a lot of time to think this through. The emperors have destroyed many lives, and they will destroy many more. I will play my part in bringing them to justice."

"And what part is that?" he asked. "The role of an assassin?"

"No, I am not a killer," Kari said. Was that true anymore? The light within her hinted at her true nature, and she had already taken life. She refused, however, to let that be her defining trait. "I will not be an assassin, but I can drive them apart so they can be challenged."

"That is what you can do? Drive them apart?" Cai Ren raised an eyebrow in disbelief.

"Yes," Kari said confidently. "Men can often be distracted by a beautiful woman. Once they lose focus, your assassins can strike."

"That's a little vain, don't you think? That you're so beautiful you can cause two of the most powerful men in the world to lose focus?" Smiling, Cai Ren took his seat. "Why wouldn't I just give you a dagger and let you slit their throats in their sleep?"

He already had the answer. She was sure of it by the way he smirked.

"If it were that easy, you wouldn't need me," Kari replied. "Any attendant would suffice."

"Good, you're not as empty-headed as I feared."

Kari gritted her teeth at the insult.

"With the way you have been acting since you've arrived at the storehouse, I feared you were lacking as you showed no sense of self-preservation. You wouldn't have lasted this long without my interference. No, I have no intention of sending you in there with a dagger. I've already attempted that route four times, all failures. The Tian are tough bastards. The last attendant attempted to stab Jiaorong in the throat and heart, but she didn't even leave a scratch. No, any more attempts of that nature might tip the emperors off to my plans. We need tact."

"I assume you already have a plan," Ina said.

Cai Ren grinned. "You have magic. I've seen what you are capable of. Get close to them, use your magic, and kill them."

"No," Kari shook her head. "I will help however I can, but I will not kill."

"Foolish girl!" Cai Ren clenched his jaw. "Do you really want half the results for twice the effort? You have magic and the element of surprise. Use it and kill these traitors!"

"I can't. I'm sorry." Kari closed her eyes. Was she being selfish? She had already killed before, and she had no qualms with bringing about their deaths, so long as her hands were free of their blood. She was a hypocrite.

"You damned fool. Think of Suying—the only way to protect her is to kill the Tian."

"Is that why you brought her with me?" Kari's voice quivered.

"I needed some way to control you."

"You got her involved just for that?" Kari jumped to her feet, glaring at Cai Ren. Her spirit energy flared with her fury.

"Enough!" Ina slammed her hands on the table, rattling the teacups. "The both of you. You've already stated Kari is nothing more than a scared girl in your eyes. You said it yourself. Sending her to assassinate the emperors who have survived similar attacks would be foolish. You recruited her after all. If she fails, the Tian will descend upon you. And Kari, what's done is done. We have to move forward now. Agreed?"

Gritting her teeth, Kari dropped back to her knees. "Agreed."

"What alternative do you suggest?" Cai Ren asked.

Kari took a deep breath. Ina was right. They needed to focus on the problem at hand. "If I can get close to each, I think I might be able to slowly plant seeds of doubt in their minds against the other."

"Would that even work?" Ina asked.

"I believe so," Kari said. Ina and Cai Ren seemed skeptical. "That's the best I can offer."

Cai Ren scoffed. "That's good," he said, clicking his tongue.

"It's all I've got," Kari replied. Her idea seemed so much more solid in her head last night. Speaking it aloud just seemed like foolish nonsense.

"No, that's good," Cai Ren corrected, stroking his goatee. "I believe your stratagem is wiser than you realize. First, if you can seduce both and effectively distract them, you can make them more negligent. Then, if we can leak your affair to each, we create discord and jealousy. With their tempers, the aggression that will arise between them will be palpable. Then we strike. They might even kill each other for us. Either way, we'll require assassins, good ones."

"Not Kari," Ina reminded.

Cai Ren groaned. "There is a resistance movement in Valceem. I have used them for assassins in the past. I'm sure we can find help there, but we'll need more than just assassins. If we succeed, we will have cut off the head from the body, but the body cannot survive without it. We will need to control both the military and any opportunists who might arise in such chaos. We'll need an army to maintain order."

"Where will we get an army?" Kari asked.

"Leave that to me," Cai Ren said. His smarmy smirk stretched across his face. "I trust you not to fail in your assignment."

Kari nodded. "I won't fail."

"Doesn't this put you in the most danger?" Ina interjected.

"Possibly, but I think it's going to be our best chance at ending their tyranny. Hopefully, as I'm acting as a dividing blade, we can avoid any more surprises like last night." Kari scrutinized Ina. Her beauty shone through despite her bruises and cuts—unlike Tama, who had been disfigured in death. Kari couldn't bear to see her friends meet a similar fate. "There is another thing I need. I want Suying and Ina kept safe. It is the least you can do after what you've done to me."

Cai Ren sighed, his smile fading. "I will do what I can."

"If you are to be the dividing blade, then let me be your sheath," Ina argued. "It is the least I can do."

"No," Kari replied. She didn't want Ina to be put in more danger. Once their plan was in full motion, Kari wouldn't be able to protect her.

"You might as well go along with her," Cai Ren added. "Suying is an attendant, so I can try to shield her as best as I can, but there is little I can do for Ina."

"If we are together, we can help keep each other safe," Ina pleaded.

She was right, but there was no way to stay together with Ina now in the servant class. "How would we even manage that?"

"You're high chancellor." Ina turned her attention to Cai Ren. "If I am to be a servant in the palace, let it be to Kari. You can make it so."

"I could, but I won't." Cai Ren shook his head. "Manipulating your sentence could jeopardize our cause. I won't risk it."

"You just said I should allow Ina to help me," Kari argued. "You owe me."

Cai Ren paused, rubbing his chin. "Fine, I'll make it happen, but I trust you to fulfill your duties. Once I have heard from the resistance, I'll let you know. In the meantime, sever the Tian in two. And your plan better work."

"It will," Kari said, solidifying her resolve.

Goddess, please let it work.

CHAPTER THIRTEEN

"WHAT ARE YOU DOING here?" Suying asked when she saw Kari.

"I received an invitation this morning," Kari responded. The emperors were having a feast, and they had invited some of their new attendants, along with some old favorites, to attend. The guards had arrived earlier to inform Kari of her invite. She hadn't wanted to go, though. She liked her new house too much to want to leave. In fact, she had barely left it since moving in. She had lived on her own for four years, but she'd never had her own house before. It was exciting, all things considered.

She wished she could stay there all day without having to see the emperors again. It was a small house with only one courtyard, a common room, servant's quarters, her room, and a bathroom. It even came with a servant—Ina. Cai Ren had come through on his word to ensure she was assigned to Kari. Even though Ina was technically a servant, Kari had no intention of treating her friend as such. So far, Kari had waited on her more than the other way around.

It seemed only right, after all, Cai Ren wasn't the only person to keep his word. Jiaorong ordered the guards to punish Ina, and they'd obliged. When she returned from the military district, the guards had dragged her into her quarters and left her on the floor in a pool of her own blood. She'd been a mess, her body limp and weak. Someone had attempted to bandage her back, but it was clear they hadn't really cared. The bandages had been loosely tied, and they hadn't even covered all the wounds.

Kari had cleaned and rebandaged her wounds. Over the next few days, she'd waited on Ina. If the roles had been reversed, Kari was sure Ina would do the same for her. Maybe, once Ina healed, Kari could teach her some energy manipulation. She wouldn't have to teach her anything fancy, just enough for her to form an aura and accelerate healing. It was too late to prevent scarring, but it might help them fade with time.

Shagin had strict rules on teaching outsiders their techniques. Kari would be labeled a traitor, but none of that mattered now. She was the Bearer of the Seed and already an exile. What were they going to do, exile her again?

Suying's eyebrows scrunched as they stood outside the banquet hall. "But you're not even ranked. Why would they invite you to their banquet?"

"I guess you haven't heard. Baoshun promoted me. I'm a first attendant now."

Suying's mouth fell open. "Lord Baoshun favors you? I had heard he called upon you. You are so lucky."

Lucky... it was an odd choice of words. Kari felt anything but lucky. If she truly were, then none of this would have happened. Then again, maybe it was fate that put her on this path and luck that was getting her through it.

"My lord." Suying folded her hands in front of her, bowing as Baoshun approached. He was accompanied by a man Kari could never forget, the Kitsuno Kai, Ronin. Kari hesitated before remembering she was supposed to bow as well. Quickly, she imitated Suying.

"Lady Hikari, it is good to see you again," Baoshun said. "Allow me to escort the pair of you the rest of the way."

"It would be an honor, my lord," Kari said. She stood upright, smiling at the emperor. "It is a pleasure to see you again, Master Ronin."

"Is it?" Ronin asked. His ghostly skin coupled with his dark eyes sent goose bumps all over her body. "I suppose it would be. Though I cannot say the same."

"Ronin," the emperor rebuked.

"I meant no disrespect to you," Ronin added as he waved off the emperor. "I just cannot abide useless people whose only function in life is to look pretty and occasionally lie down. I guess some might find that taxing, though it is a waste of good potential. Besides, it sounds rather boring."

Baoshun said nothing. He merely scowled at the Kitsuno Kai. Ronin was bold to openly mock the emperors and the harem, and to do it in front of them no less. Just what were the Kitsuno Kai that gave them such tenacity?

"I heard a most distressing rumor from some of the guards," Baoshun said, taking back the conversation. "The other night, when you left my side, they said you visited my brother, uninvited."

"I'm sorry, but I have to make a couple of corrections here," Ronin interrupted, leaning forward with a smile. "You see, Baoshun is avoiding the direct approach. When he says guards, he means me. And when he says rumors, he means what I saw and the information I obtained by interrogating the guards who aided you."

"Ronin, that is enough," Baoshun said, stepping in between Kari and the Kitsuno Kai. "Hikari, can you explain this? I do not understand why you would visit my brother's bedchamber after everything we shared."

She'd thought this might happen. Cai Ren had told her nothing was ever truly private within the palace. Luckily, she was already prepared for such a question. "As you are aware one of Lord Jiaorong's attendants defied him? I discovered this and knew where she was hiding, so I sought out Lord Jiaorong. I believed aiding the throne to be my duty. So, I told him what I knew."

"Yes, I am aware of this," Baoshun said. He rubbed his chin as if to mull over the information. "I believe he showed mercy with a minimal punishment to the traitor."

"That doesn't sound like him," Ronin added. He tapped his chin with his finger. "I wonder what could have softened his resolve?"

"I did," Kari said bluntly. There was no point in lying now. Ronin knew more than he was saying. She would have to be careful. Every word she said could potentially betray her.

She would have to weave truths with deception, a tactic she was becoming all too familiar with, if she were going to succeed. "Ina was a friend. She still is. While I have my duty to the throne, to the empire, and to heaven, which cannot be forsworn, I didn't want to see my friend die. My lord, I committed a sin. I begged your brother to abstain from the will of heaven, and to spare her life."

"And he willingly agreed?" Baoshun asked. Clearly, he expected there to be something more to the story. Something that played right into Kari's plan, and she was more than willing to provide.

"He did," She widened her eyes as she tried to force herself to cry. Luckily, all she had to do was to think back on the events of that night for her eyes to tear up. "But he grew jealous. He is jealous of you and me. He had heard about me, about my songs. He stated he regretted giving me to you, and he embraced me. I tried to fight him, but I couldn't."

"I had no idea." Baoshun wrapped his arms around Kari. "Everything will be all right now. I will not let him harm you."

"I think he means to take me from you." It was sooner than she expected, but she knew she would eventually have to lay the groundwork for their jealousy.

"That will never happen."

"Perhaps we should follow up on this new information," Ronin said. He didn't believe her. The Kitsuno Kai seemed to perceive the truth no matter what. He was dangerous.

There was no doubt he wouldn't cease his suspicions of her. He'd try to foil her plans.

"I will handle my brother," Baoshun replied, waving off Ronin's concerns. "You have done enough today. Leave us."

"As you wish." Ronin slunk away without so much as a bow, which was odd behavior from someone in the presence of an emperor.

"That man, why do you let him disrespect you like so?" Suying asked. The trio watched as the Kitsuno Kai disappeared beyond a moon gate.

"He is a Kitsuno Kai. They're useful attack dogs, though their loyalty is hard to ascertain at times, but so long as they support the throne, the people will never think about rebellion. They are far too respected and feared. The Kitsuno Kai have saved the city of Valceem on more than one occasion, even preventing a fire attack in the early days of its founding, before the walls were built. Despite their ruthless and violent reputation, most people still hold them in high esteem, not that it quells their fear of the blue wolfs."

"He seems evil," Suying said. She wasn't wrong. The very sight of the man gave Kari shivers. He would have no hesitation in killing her, even within the palace walls if he ever thought she was truly a threat. The fact he hadn't yet either meant he hadn't gathered enough evidence to meet his needs or he simply didn't see her as an opponent worthy of killing.

"Don't mind him. Though he seems awfully preoccupied with you, my dear," Baoshun said, addressing Kari. "He won't tell me why."

"Do you listen to him?" Kari asked. If Ronin had the ear of the emperor, her plan might be more difficult than she initially thought.

"Not if I can help it," Baoshun replied. "Come, we have a feast to attend."

Kari, Suying, and Baoshun walked together as they made their way into the banquet hall. Jiaorong and several other women, including Izumi, were already there around a large round table.

"Brother, it is so good of you to show up, and with such a lovely entourage no less," Jiaorong bellowed.

"I would appreciate it if you didn't comment on the appearance of my attendants," Baoshun rebuked.

"Of course, brother," Jiaorong said, his smile fading. It seemed, even though Suying was invited, neither brother knew who she was or else they would have known she was Jiaorong's attendant. Kari breathed a sigh of relief. Suying hadn't been called yet, but if they were inviting her to a banquet, Jiaorong must intend to call upon her soon.

Based on their interaction, the brothers were already pulling apart from each other. It was something to be pleased with. All Kari had to do was to continue playing on their natural jealousy of one another.

"Everyone, be seated so the feast can begin," Jiaorong said, motioning for the guests to take their seats.

"Lady Hikari, I have a place for you here to my left," Baoshun said, pulling out the cushioned chair next to him.

"My lord, are you sure?" Izumi's voiced cracked.

"Fear not," Baoshun replied. He motioned to the next empty seat. "You may sit to Hikari's left."

"Brother, do not dare tempt fate," Jiaorong said, feigning concern. "It would not be proper to place an attendant over your consorts, let alone your wife."

"It is most appropriate," Baoshun retorted. His hands balled into tight fists as he faced his brother. "She is to be my honored guest; therefore, she must sit to my left."

"My right is free, as I do not have a wife. Let her sit beside me if she is to be our honored guest and allow the empress to sit to your left. Will this not satisfy your honor and the will of heaven?"

"But it would not satisfy *me.*" Baoshun stepped within inches of his brother, scowling at him. Jiaorong stood a good head taller than him, but neither backed down.

"You would place your own satisfaction over the will of heaven?" Jiaorong placed a hand on his brother's shoulder, forcing him back to arm's distance.

Baoshun sighed in defeat, averting his gaze to the floor. "I will not challenge the mandate of heaven. Lady Hikari may sit at your right."

Kari bowed in reverence as Jioarong pulled the chair out for her to sit in as she slowly approached the dining table. The stares of the other guests bore into her. Their silent glares felt like prickles on her skin. She took a deep breath to clear her mind of their judgment, then quietly sat next to Jiaorong.

It was a rare sight to see the Imperial brothers fight, much less over a woman. The other attendants must wonder what she was doing to cause such friction between them and why she was being honored as such.

Kari said nothing as the feast began. She had no intention of causing a scene any further than what had already transpired. The emperors' hostile politeness illustrated the seeds of discontent she had already begun to sow between them. Still, it would be better not to rush things too quickly or else she could tip her hand of her true intentions. It was a relief to see them fighting, if not disconcerting for the public attention it was bringing her. She didn't want any further altercations with the other attendants.

Kari had never seen such an extravagant arrangement of food. Dishes of food were piled on the round table, leaving none of its surface bare. In front of each chair was a small placemat with an individual bowl of steamed rice, along with three glasses filled to the brim with beer, wine, and some sort of incredibly strong alcoholic drink Kari couldn't even bring herself to sip. The Imperial brothers had their seats adorned in gold-and-red cushions. They were seated side by side at the far end of the round table, facing into the room and toward the main door.

The group went about the meal, all the while discussing diverse topics from politics to fashion. The emperors railed on about how tremendous their reign was compared to the emperors who came before them. It seemed their only judge of success for the kingdom was the quality of the luxuries they partook in. They seemed to know or care little about the lives of the people outside the palace walls. Koryon was its own world, completely isolated from the rest of the kingdom and the troubles of reality.

"I wonder," Izumi said, turning the conversation back to Kari. "What must a new attendant do to be granted such favor as you, much less be honored above her superiors?"

"I do not understand your question," Kari said. She would have much preferred for the feast to have quietly ended without her being brought to the center of attention again. "There is at least one other attendant here who is just as new as me, and all the blessings that have been bestowed upon me have come from the emperors. If you perceive some injustice has occurred, perhaps your question is better suited for them."

Izumi turned her nose up in disgust as she went back to the feast. Even she would not question the judgement of the emperors at their own table.

Kari had never seen so much food. Just when she was sure the feast was ending, servants would come and change out the serving dishes with freshly prepared meals. She had eaten her fill early on during the first course alone, and hadn't expected the eight other courses that followed. The rest of the guests seemed to have no problem keeping up with the seemingly never-ending supply of food. Jiaorong kept passing more morsels to her, which she piled in her bowl and played with as everyone around her ate more and more. By the end of the last course, she had built up quite the mountain of uneaten food. She hated wasting so much food, especially knowing how little others in the rest of the city had to eat, but it was simply too much for her.

"And now on to the entertainment," Jiaorong said as servants came and took the remaining dishes away. "Brother, I believe you said you had something special planned."

"Of course." Baoshun motioned to Kari. "Lady Hikari, if you would do us the honors."

"My lord?" Kari asked, unsure of what he intended.

"She has such a lovely singing voice. Plus, the way she dances with such grace and beauty... She has written songs to attest her devotion to me. They are exquisite."

"My lord, are you sure?" Kari asked. She needed to think. She couldn't have Jiaorong thinking she was composing songs dedicated solely to Baoshun, yet Baoshun needed to believe that was exactly what she was doing. "Any words that may have been written were not intended to be heard by others."

"Go on. They were written for me after all, and I want them to be heard."

"Very well, my lord." Kari stood from her seat, then bowed graciously to the emperors. Her eyes met Jiaorong. She allowed her fingers to gently brush against his shoulder as she passed behind him to make her way to the front of the room. "I wrote this song to illustrate my true feelings for my beloved."

Kari danced as she sang. Each step was made with precision and grace. She swayed her arms through the air, allowing the sleeves of her ruqun to flow freely as she moved like a gentle breeze through the leaves of a tall oak tree.

"I see you so far away.
Forbidden desires,
Swimming in ethereal skies.
My heart aches to be with you.

"The two of us, hands never touching,
Swirl around in eternal waves.
Torn apart by circumstance,
May the night forever hide our embrace.

"Grasping out to be with you,
Tell me all of your mystery.
And I will sing for you,
A prelude of eternity.

"The two of us, hands never touching,
Swirl around in eternal waves.
Torn apart by circumstance,
May the night forever hide our embrace.

"Hush my love, fear not the dawn,
Keep me safe, deep in your heart,
Believe in me as I dream of you.

Follow the song, sail along, sail along.

"The two of us, hands never touching,
Swirl around in eternal waves.
Torn apart by circumstance,
May the night forever hide our embrace."

When she had finished, she spun in a circle and dropped to her knees. With her arms outstretched against the ground, she bent forward and bowed in respect to the emperors.

"Marvelous," Baoshun cried. "Wouldn't you agree, brother?"

"Yes, it was quite telling," Jiaorong replied. Kari sank in her chair next to the older brother. The rest of the guests simply glared at her.

As the night went on, other entertainers entered the dining hall and beguiled the emperors' guests with dances and songs as the emperors drank from a seemingly never-ending source of wine.

With the feast winding down, Baoshun stood to his feet and motioned for silence in the hall. He swayed back and forth, the evening's drinks clearly taking its toll on him. "I have a request I would like to make in the presence of all here to see. We have all seen the testament of Lady Hikari's love for me. There can be no denying it now." Baoshun shot Jiaorong a glance. "I now ask for Lady Hikari to join me in my bedchambers for the remainder of the evening."

Kari's heart jumped. She could feel the stares of the rest of the women in attendance as they burned into her. She glanced at Jiaorong, who clenched his jaw and turned his head away.

"My lord, I humbly request you to rescind your generous offer," Kari said.

"What?" Baoshun asked in disbelief.

Kari had to choose her words carefully. She was committing a sin in the eyes of the emperors to turn down his request. To say the least, it was an embarrassment for her to reject Baoshun in his dining hall in front of his guests. Not to mention that any wrong word at this point could derail her entire plan. "If you would have me, my lord, I ask for you to extend your offer for tomorrow eve. I am taxed and fatigued from the festivities. However, if you so desire for us to be together tonight, I will gladly join you, my beloved."

"No, no. You may rest for the evening," Baoshun said, slumping back down in his chair.

"I will join you my lord," Suying spoke up. Kari's eyes widened. What was Suying doing?

"Very well, prepare yourself. I will have the guards pick you up and deliver you to my estate." Suying bowed as she left the table.

There had to be something Kari could do to save Suying, even if only to save her from herself. Kari departed with the rest of the attendants, rushing after Suying.

"Suying, wait up," Kari called as she ran up to her on the walk back to their quarters. "What are you doing?"

"What do you think I'm doing?" Suying snapped, jerking away from Kari. "I'm taking the only opportunity I've been given. Unlike you, I haven't had the world handed to me. I guess you have to be a sing-song girl to get anywhere."

"I know it doesn't seem like it, but I'm doing this for you, to help you."

"I have eyes that see. You're in there flirting with both emperors. Are you trying to see which one you can manipulate the most? The person I just saw wasn't you, so don't even pretend. You can lie to everyone else, but you can't lie to me."

"I've never lied to you," Kari said. "I'm still your sister."

"No, we were never sisters. After everything we've been through, I can't believe you would treat me like this. First, you try to persuade me into leaving with you. You acted like you hated the very idea of being here, and now you're trying to bed both emperors? What, were you just jealous of me? Were you afraid they would like me better?"

Kari was perplexed. There was truly little she could say to help Suying understand her motives. "Please, you're only fourteen. You're just a child. Don't go through with this."

"I'm not a child. And you're nothing but a damned hypocrite. This is what I want. I will earn the emperor's favor, and I'll prove I am worthy of my rank."

"I won't let you do this."

"You can't stop me," Suying spat back. Turning her back on Kari, she began the walk back to her estate.

Kari watched her friend walk alone down the path back to Guanwa Hall. Kari took a deep breath. She could stop her, but the consequences of doing so were uncertain, but there was little time to think them through. Time was against her. She had to move quickly if she were going to succeed.

"Please remember I tried to stop you," Kari whispered as Suying disappeared beyond a moon gate.

Kari ran back down the path she had come from to the emperors' mansion. She was stopped by a guard at the entrance.

"What are you doing here?" the guard demanded. "The emperors are not expecting you."

"I need to see Lord Jiaorong," Kari said. "It is urgent I see him."

"Lord Jiaorong hasn't returned. And before you ask, no, I don't know where he is. And no, you can't see Lord Baoshun either."

Kari gritted her teeth. Damn. There was only one other option. Kari spun on her heel, then sprinted toward Cai Ren's house. It wasn't a wise idea to constantly be seen around Cai Ren. Eventually, someone would get suspicious, but she didn't have time to wait around for the emperors to return.

She ran up to Cai Ren's house, frantically banging on his door. "Cai Ren, are you here?"

Cai Ren slid the door open. "Keep your voice down. No one should see you here with me, but since you are, I have valuable information I need to give you. Come inside so we can talk in private."

"I don't have time. Suying is on her way to see Baoshun."

Sighing, Cai Ren stroked his goatee. "That was always a possibility. There's nothing that can be done. If you want to help her, come inside and we can discuss our plans, but make peace with what will transpire tonight. It is done."

"No, you know I can't accept that. I can prevent this, but I need Jiaorong. You either help me, or I won't help you."

"Damn it, girl. You would doom an entire nation so one little girl doesn't have sex?" Cai Ren huffed, then grabbed a small satchel as he headed out of his house. "You are just stubborn enough to do it, too. Jiaorong is most likely at the Hall of Heaven and Earth. The guards won't let you see him, so I must come with you. We can talk on the way."

Cai Ren led the way through the night to the Hall of Heaven and Earth.

"I want you to take this." Cai Ren handed Kari the satchel.

"What is this?" she asked.

"Inside are documents you will need. Tomorrow, you will need to leave the palace and go into the city. Our allies wish to meet you."

"Why do they want to meet with me?"

"They are putting their trust in you. It is only natural they would want to know who they are trusting. Tomorrow, go into the city, then head out the western gate and venture into the Dragon Wilds. There's a map that will lead you to the rendezvous point. Everything you need to know is written down in the bag along with a few marks if you need them. There is a hidden entrance in the School of Enlightenment you can use to sneak out of the palace. The location is written down. I will cover for you while you are gone. There is also a gate pass that will grant you passage through the boroughs of Valceem. Try not to lose it. We shouldn't say more in the open. I can't go with you, so you'll be on your own. Just follow the instructions I have prepared for you. Don't mess this up."

The guards approached them as they entered the hall. With a single wave of his hand, the guards stopped and allowed the pair to pass.

"Cai Ren, what is the meaning of this?" Jiaorong asked as he saw them approach.

"This insolent pest came demanding she see you right away," Cai Ren said. "She wouldn't say what for."

Jiaorong snarled. "You are making a habit of barging in to see me, Hikari. What do you want?"

"I wish to speak to you in private."

"Leave us." Cai Ren and the guards all left, leaving Kari alone with Jiaorong. "I must say, I am perplexed by your actions. Was your song meant for me or my brother?"

"Everything I am is for you."

"And yet, you write him songs."

Kari dropped to the floor and kowtowed before the emperor, pressing her forehead firmly to the ground. "You are my beloved. I rejected his advances this very evening, and here I am coming to you."

"So I see." He reached out, then lifted up her face to meet his.

"Your brother is jealous of you. Even as we speak, he plots against you. He knows my heart belongs to you. Therefore, he is trying to take from you in other ways. The attendant he invited to his chambers is your attendant." She feared how Jiaorong would react, but only he had the power to stop Suying.

"Is she? Sometimes I forget, since there are so many. I will not stand for this injustice. I will put a stop to this." Jiaorong opened the door to the hallway outside.

"You must hurry," Kari said, following behind him. "She prepares for him even as we speak."

"Guards!" The guards came to their master's call. Jiaorong turned back to Kari. "This attendant, does she have a name?"

"Suying," Kari replied.

"Tell my brother my attendant will not be joining him this night. As for Suying, find her and execute her."

Kari nearly fainted. What had she done? "Suying..." Kari muttered. "My lord... I..."

"What is it?" Jiaorong asked. He steadied her as she swayed from the shock.

"My lord, please don't kill her," Kari begged. She instinctively grabbed his hands for support, and Jiaorong kissed her forehead in return.

"Suying, is this the same girl you spoke up for at the auditions?"

"Yes."

"You care for her?"

"Yes, like a sister."

"Hold that command," Jiaorong barked at his guards. "Don't kill her. I am feeling generous tonight. Suying has committed treason. She has conspired to defy the natural order of heaven to seduce a man she does not belong to. She is to be stripped of her rank and given twenty lashes. Now go."

Kari wiped at the tears forming in her eyes. "Thank you, my lord."

"Your dance was exquisite tonight." Jiaorong placed his meaty hands on Kari's shoulder, bending to kiss her neck. "Tonight, you have blessed me with your beautiful song, honored me by refusing my brother, respected me by maintaining the order of my house, and loved me by only coming to me. Now allow me to return the favor by filling you with my holiness, my beloved."

Closing her eyes, Kari gritted her teeth. Her whole body shivered with dread as he threw off her blouse and untied her skirt. It would be over soon. Her body went numb, and she forced her mind to go blank as he pressed himself upon her.

Hell repeated, it seemed.

CHAPTER FOURTEEN

KARI WAS GLAD TO leave the palace to return to the real world even if it were just for a day. The stark contrast between the lavish palace life and the rundown streets of Ashyakko was unsettling. Empty streets with abandoned market stalls and boarded-up buildings were a common sight within the old city.

Signs of what the city used to be were still visible despite the new grim.

Kari ignored the beggars who kept coming up to her as she made her way through what used to be a bustling market district.

Kari regretted wearing a silk ruqun. She should have changed into more common clothing or at least something made out of ramie. The fine silks made her an easy mark for beggars and criminals. Once she had snuck out of the palace, she had taken a carriage to the markets in Ashyakko and had spent nearly a full hour wandering through the market streets looking for an open store. When she finally found a vendor, she used the money she had gotten from Cai Ren to buy a large blue ribbon and some cloth straps.

Now all she needed to do was find a blacksmith, then she could go meet with Cai Ren's contacts. She jingled the remaining marks and bits she had left over in her hand. It wasn't much. Hopefully, though, it would be enough. Kari had never bought a sword before. She had trained with one as a child, but after leaving Mystikos, she didn't have a need for one.

This would be so much easier if she could just go to the storehouse to buy a weapon there. She actually knew where that was located, but she couldn't risk someone seeing her purchasing a weapon and being able to identify her. Besides, the rendezvous point was outside the Western Gate of Ashyakko anyway.

After some searching, Kari found a cart of wares outside of a smithy. The blacksmith smiled as she approached. "What are you buying?" he asked.

Kari eyed his products. This was no good. A small display of cooking knifes was all he had out. "Do you have anything else? I'm looking for a sword."

"Of course I have swords, but I don't have time to entertain beggars or thieves. You won't be running me through with my own steel."

"I'm not here to rob you. I'm looking to buy a sword for protection. I have money, and I can pay." She held up the coin purse for him to see.

The blacksmith stared at Kari. "Well you've certainly got the look. Don't blame me. People can't be too careful these days. Come inside, and I'll show you what I've got."

Kari followed him inside. Various kinds of swords, pole arms, and shields lined the walls and cabinets of his shop. Kari browsed his wares before stopping at a pair of ko-dachis. Picking up one of the short swords, she unsheathed its curved blade. The blade had a good weight, and the grip was comfortable in her hands. It felt familiar. She gave the sword a couple of quick swings. With each, the blade cut through the air with an audible whoosh. They were sharp, just what she needed. It was better to rely on an actual weapon than her magic. Her magic had limits and wore her out too quickly, but she could reliably use a sword in a fight if it came to that.

"How much for the pair?" Kari asked, sheathing the blade.

"And what does a girl like you need a sword for?" the blacksmith asked, eyeing her up and down.

Kari rolled her eyes. "Does it really matter what my intent is? I have money, and that should be enough."

"All right, all right. I was just asking. Let me see. If you're taking both, I guess I can cut you a deal." The blacksmith scratched his chin as he considered a price. "Forty-seven marks should do it."

"Forty-seven?" Kari took out the remaining coins from her pocket and jingled them in her hand. Only five marks and twelve bits. "I can give you six now and the remaining forty-one later."

"Six? I thought you said you had money?"

"I promise you I'm good for it," Kari said. If she could tell him she was from the palace, he would probably agree to her terms, but she couldn't risk anyone finding out what she was doing.

"Maybe, but I don't know you," the blacksmith said. "You might take my swords and never come back. That's a risk I can't take. I've got a family to feed. With the economy the way it is, I can't afford to accept anything other than what I'm asking."

"How much does she need?" a familiar voice asked. Kari turned to see a ghostly pale figure dressed in all black. The light blue sash of the Kitsuno Kai draped around his chest, visible under his long black coat. Ronin, the blue wolf, was here.

How? Was he following her? He couldn't be. She snuck out of the palace through a hidden entrance, and she was careful to make sure no one was following her. It had to be a coincidence. But what was he doing here? Out of all the shops in Valceem, there was no way this was a coincidence. This was bad.

Not only did he still look like a ghost, but Kari also hadn't even heard him enter. His movements were that of a specter.

"Where the devil did you come from?" the blacksmith asked. He shook his head as if to move on from the thought. "It's forty-seven marks for the two kodachis, but she only has six."

"Is that inflation or exploitation?" Ronin shoved his hand into his coat, then pulled out a single coin—a crown worth one hundred marks. "This should cover her end. And throw in that dagger for me. I could always use a good murder knife," he said, pointing to a small concealable blade on the counter. It was more than enough to cover it. Ronin was practically paying twice what the smith was asking. The value meant nothing to him.

The blacksmith took the money before handing Ronin his dagger. Kari took her swords, then added them to her satchel before thanking Ronin and quickly leaving the shop. "You seem to be in a hurry," Ronin said, following behind her.

"I have places to be," Kari said, trying to brush him off, but he kept following her. She stopped as three other Kitsuno Kai approached. They were wearing the traditional light blue and white of their order. Ronin must indeed be someone important to differentiate from their standard colors. "If it is money you want, I can pay you back."

"That won't be necessary," Ronin said, holding out his hand as the other three surrounded Kari. What could she do? It was forbidden for an attendant to leave Koryon unless the emperor willed it. She needed to find some excuse, something to appease them with. "I'm curious, though, what use do you have for two swords? An attendant has no need for a weapon. Someone might think it is suspicious when a young lady of such stature travels into the slums to buy two swords. Especially after just acquiring her rank. To make matters worse, the same young lady was just a suspect in a plot that left two men dead. It certainly raises questions."

"If you think I might have had a part in that, why wouldn't you follow up on your investigation?" Kari tried to take a step back, but the other three wolves closed in, limiting her movements. Was this what he had been waiting for? For her to leave the safety of the palace to confront her? It didn't make any sense. He could kill her wherever he liked with little fuss. Maybe all he waited for was for her to confirm his suspicions, something she had no doubt accomplished by sneaking out of Koryon, an act in itself that could warrant death.

"Oh, I have. I've been watching you for some time now... and then you leave the palace. Where would you go? I just had to find out."

How long had he watched her? Had he seen her sneak out or had he merely spotted her in the city?

"I have permission to leave." That much was true. Well, sort of.

"I'm sure you do," Ronin said. "But from whom? Are you serving Baoshun or Jiaorong? It is a head scratcher. It's getting so hard to tell."

"These swords, they're not for me," Kari lied, trying to change the subject. "They're for my brother. He is an expert swordsman. I'm on my way to see him now."

"I was unaware you had a brother. It's not mentioned in your profile."

"Does my profile contain everything about me? Or just what you think you know?" Kari gripped the satchel close to her body as if holding it tighter would allow the contents to protect her.

"A fine point. But this brother, why does he need swords?"

"Self-defense," Kari replied instinctively.

Ronin smiled at her retort. "Why not rely on the guards?"

"Would you rely on the guards?" Kari asked in response. "People have to fend for themselves."

"Very well," he said, motioning to the other Kitsuno Kai. "I'm more than happy to help supply you and your brother with better protection. There is no need to repay me. It is an honor to aid an attendant. I would be remiss not to escort you to your brother. Imagine the controversy if the emperor found out I let his favorite attendant traverse the city without protection, especially considering you cannot rely on the guards."

"That won't be necessary. My brother is not far from here, and I find the thrill of traveling without an entourage to be freeing."

"In that case, I will respect your wishes, my lady. For your sake, I hope you stay safe and out of trouble." It was a ruse—it had to be. From the start, he'd known more than he admitted. This was a game to him. He was a wolf hunting his prey, but she wouldn't give him the satisfaction of beating her.

He waved, signaling he was done with her. Kari quickly headed down the road, hurrying away from the den of wolves behind her. Once she was out of sight of the Kitsuno

Kai, she darted in and out of alleyways and down random roads, trying to make sure she wasn't being followed. Once she had covered enough distance, she stopped in an alley to catch her breath.

Peering into the road, she squinted as sunlight glistened off the green tile roofs of the wooden buildings. She wasn't being followed, not as far as she could tell. Kari rubbed her eyes, sighing. She couldn't delay any longer. She returned to the main road before heading for the Western Gate.

The guards took one look at her papers, then let her through. She had half expected more resistance to get through the gate, but she was glad for the relief. Cai Ren had come through on his end.

Once she was far enough out of view of the guard tower, she made sure no one was around and darted into the forest of the Dragon Wilds. Kari moved through the forest until no signs of the road or civilization could be seen before stopping and taking out her kodachis. She took her skirt off, then tied the strap against her abdomen. Once it was in place, she unsheathed a sword and cut two slits in the sides of her skirt. Sheathing the kodachi, she slid her swords into place, one on each side of her hip. She tied the skirt high around her chest. Once she was happy the print of the swords wasn't showing, she tied the blue ribbon into a bow around her waist, concealing the fresh slits in the fabric.

She continued through the forest, following the directions Cai Ren had given her. After a few hours of walking, she finally came to a small cabin in the woods. Kari hid in the trees as she examined the structure. From the outside, it looked like it was not bigger than one or two rooms with only one door and no windows, so there was no telling who was inside. There was no movement in the surrounding trees, nor were there any signs of anyone waiting in ambush.

Once Kari was satisfied it was relatively safe, she cautiously made her way to the door and knocked five times as instructed.

A young man slowly opened the door to a crack. He raised an eyebrow at Kari. "Why have you knocked on my door?"

Kari paused, trying to remember the passphrase Cai Ren had given her. "I offer a humble genuflection with my sincere apologies for I do not wish to disturb you, but I beseech you to provide aid to a tiresome traveler."

"How can I turn down such a request?" The young man stepped aside, motioning for Kari to enter. As she did, she was greeted by a scarred man with a crossbow. He aimed the tip of the bolt at her head.

"Never trust the empire." Smiling, he pointed to the scars running along his face. "That's how I got these."

"What is this?" Kari asked as the man secured the door behind her.

"You must be the assassin," the scarred man said.

"I'm not an assassin," Kari said defensively. Her hands moved slowly to the swords hidden at her side.

"No? Then what are you doing here then?" When he lowered his crossbow, Kari's muscles relaxed at the gesture.

"Follow me," the younger man said, leading her into a back room where an old man with a long gray beard sat at a small wooden table with a maidservant standing behind him.

"You must be Kari. I am Shenrong. Please, have a seat," he said, gesturing to a chair opposite him. "May I offer you a drink? Sake, perhaps?"

"Tea will be fine," Kari said, noticing the teapot on a table in the corner. She took the seat opposite Shenrong.

"You can tell a lot about a person simply by the drink they choose," Shenrong said. He motioned for the maidservant to fetch the refreshments. "For instance, I can already tell you do not wish to follow, but instead demand respect. You value equality, and you carry a certain spirituality and peace of mind. Maybe you are a bit rebellious at times, but you tend to seek tranquility and calmness."

"You can tell all that from my drink?" Kari skeptically asked. She didn't believe it. It sounded like vague nonsense coming from a superstitious mind.

"And much more. For your inner self picks the drink that most reflects your soul."

"I just like the taste," Kari said.

"Quite right you are." Shenrong chuckled. "It is a fine taste, perfectly refined for a more sophisticated beauty."

The maidservant brought over a cup of tea for Kari and a ceramic bottle of sake for Shenrong.

"Onto more pressing matters," Shenrong said in between sips of his drinks. "I would like to ask you a few questions."

"I will answer anything. Within reason, of course," Kari said. That was the reason she was here, to belay their doubts, but the more questions she could avoid about herself, the better.

"Of course." Shenrong placed a small bag on the table. "The first question—who are you?"

"I am Kari."

Shenrong held out his hand to silence her. Reaching into the bag, he pulled out a handful of decorative tiles, which he then lined on the table. "Use these and tell me—who are you?"

Kari inspected the tiles closely. There were eight tiles, each with a different symbol etched onto it. There was a parasol, a conch shell, two fish, a lotus blossom, some sort of banner, a vase, a wheel with eight spokes, and an image of an interwoven knot.

"How am I supposed to choose?"

"Which one speaks to your inner self?"

Kari rubbed her chin, trying to see if any spoke to her like Shenrong claimed, but no matter how long she stared at the tiles, they all seemed the same. How was she supposed to figure out which one spoke to her? She had studied the various religions and superstitions of the mainland, but she didn't understand them.

Kari picked up the lotus blossom. If she had to be compared to one of the images, might as well make it a flower. It seemed fitting considering her plant magic.

"The lotus is a fine choice," Shenrong said. He took the tile from her to examine it closely. "But I wonder... what color are your petals?"

Kari shrugged. "White," she said, hoping for the best.

"The white lotus is a powerful symbol for one's soul, but answer me this. How does the lotus bloom?"

Kari carefully considered his question, trying to think back to her study of plants. It had been a while since she had seen a lotus blossom, but even knowing what they looked like didn't provide much clues as to what he was in search of.

"With a leaf and bud," she answered to the best of her ability.

"Interesting. For my next question, what is your intent?" Shenrong motioned for Kari to choose another tile.

How was she supposed to choose intent from the tiles? None had any action to them. Again, all she could do was pick one and hope for the best. Kari closed her eyes as she gestured to a tile.

"Ah, the eternal knot," Shenrong said, taking the tile from under her finger. "Like the knot, all of time and space are interwoven. Everything is connected within the eternal union of compassion and wisdom. A fine choice. You have chosen wisely, and you have passed my tests."

"Then you will help us?" Kari asked. It didn't make sense to her, but if it eased his doubts and convinced him to join their cause, she wasn't going to argue.

"Just because you passed the tests does not mean we will follow you. You have merely proven your intent, not your cause," Shenrong explained, holding up a finger. "I am still curious... You are an attendant, are you not?"

"I am," Kari replied.

"Why would you care about politics?"

"I don't," Kari truthfully said. "I care about people. Right now, there are people suffering whom I can help."

"And you think a whore is an adequate threat to the reign of tyrants?"

Kari clenched her jaw as she tried to ignore the *whore* comment. Was that all anyone would ever see her as now? "Yes, because I am more than that. I have seen the pain they inflict on others. I know their tyranny firsthand."

"I still don't know why my men and I should join you. You are asking a lot of us. If you are truly sincere in your quest to fight against them, then you should submit to me instead."

"This isn't about submission to anyone," Kari said. "I am not asking you to pledge yourself to me, just to my cause. You have been fighting for how long? And what progress have you made? I believe I can change that."

Shenrong sighed. "You are very stupid indeed. Even if you could do the impossible and defeat them, the power vacuum that would follow any coup could be disastrous."

"Then why do you fight?"

"Because, I am also a stupid fool. But still, you have proven your desire, but, as I stated, it is not your intent lacking, but your ability." Shenrong clapped his hands. "Yamato, get in here!" The scarred man with the crossbow entered the room, then immediately sat next to Shenrong.

"This is Yamato the Deadshot."

"My lady," Yamato said, shooting her a grin.

"You are not the first assassin Cai Ren has hired to kill the Tian. You are not even the first attendant."

"I am aware of that." Cai Ren had already told her he had tried before, even conscripting four attendants to his cause.

"Thirty-seven assassination attempts that I know of. Six of which have been orchestrated by Cai Ren. Believe me, intent is not enough."

"That's how I got these scars," Yamato added. "The Tian brothers are a tough pair of bastards. Their might is peerless. I wouldn't mind another shot at them myself, but unless you can get me in the palace, I have no intention of aiding you."

"The problem is..." Shenrong continued. "Individually, they are a force to be reckoned with. They are two peerless warriors of our age. Unfortunately, paranoia has driven them even closer together. It is a fool's errand."

"If you thought it was so hopeless, then why even meet with me at all?"

"I was hoping against hope Cai Ren had finally found a worthy adversary for the Tian. He claimed you could lead us to victory, but when I look at you, all I see is a girl. A child playing pretend in a man's world."

"The best thing a girl like you can do is to run," Yamato added. "Escape from their tyranny. There are plenty of countries willing to accept refugees."

"I can't," Kari said. "We've moved beyond that."

"Haven't we all?" Yamato laughed. "I have killed many men. I have faced legions of warriors and swordsmen. I have fought the best, and I've killed the best, but the Tian are in a completely different class. When I fought them, I had the element of surprise, plus superior numbers, and I still barely escaped with my life. Now you are asking me to try again, and your whole plan is to sleep with them until they don't get along? That's laughable. Unless you can also give me the favor of the gods, you will merely be planning our deaths, and your head will end up decorating a spike."

There had to be some way to inspire them again, to give them the hope to try one last time. She knew the answer to her own question before she even asked it, but the ramifications could be disastrous. If she were to give them hope, she had to prove it wasn't a lost cause. She would have to gamble with her life.

"I may not be able to give you the favor of the gods, but I can provide you with something even better. I come from an extensive line of great warriors." Kari took a deep breath. A whore or a monster, it seemed that was all she could ever be seen as. "My people are feared for their prowess in battle. That same blood, that same heritage, runs in my veins. I am Shagin, and I can stop the emperors, but we need help for one last try."

"What?" Shenrong exclaimed, shooting up from the table. "I thought they were all dead."

"A fucking Shagin." Yamato went for his crossbow.

Kari jumped to her feet as he took aim at her.

"What are you doing?" Shenrong demanded, placing his hand on Yamato's crossbow. "This could be the opportunity we needed."

"She might have what it takes to end their reign, but what then? The Shagin are evil. The gods themselves have cursed them. If I don't kill her, she'll bring this world to its knees. And this time, they might just destroy it."

"Yamato, think this through," Shenrong pleaded. "She is a weapon."

"She's a monster who deserves to die!"

"Please," Kari begged. This was a mistake. It took every effort not to give into instinct and run away. "All I want is to help my friends. If I truly had ill intentions, I would have kept my heritage hidden, but we need to trust each other, and it was imperative you know why we will succeed."

"She is just one Shagin," Shenrong said. "Once this is over, if we believe she is a threat, we can notify the Guardian, but until then, we have a trump card."

Kari wasn't overly reassured by the possibility of them turning her in when all was said and done, but it did cause Yamato to lower his crossbow.

"Fine," Yamato said. "I can agree to that."

"Very well," Shenrong said. He regarded Kari. "Notify Cai Ren of our joining. Tell him to signal us when he is ready to discuss stratagem."

Kari breathed a sigh of relief. She had succeeded—the beginning of their revolution was at hand.

She left the cabin, then headed back the way she came. The sun was getting high in the afternoon sky. Its light broke through the treetop canopy. She was in no hurry to return to the palace. Returning would just mean more time trying to avoid the emperors. It was ironic how much she never wanted to see them again. Yet, she'd willingly agreed to be with them to drive them apart.

The hike through the forest was relaxing. It reminded her of Mystikos. The birds serenaded her with their songs as she made her way to the stifling city. It was a shame she couldn't enjoy the hike more, but she couldn't waste time on her trip to Koryon. If the emperors discovered she was missing, her schemes would be ruined and she could be labeled a traitor.

Cai Ren had come through with the gate passes. Surely he would be able to conceal her absence. It was only for a day.

"Look at what we have here." One of the Kitsuno Kai stepped out from behind a tree as another descended from the treetops. The crunch of twigs on the ground alerted her to the third approaching from behind. "What do you think? Spy or fool?"

"And what would an attendant be doing all the way out here? Were you meeting your brother for tea?"

Damn. If she tried to run, even if she could get away, they would only have to report her and a whole squad would take her out. There was no getting around it. She had no choice about returning to the palace. Her life was forfeit.

Her hand twitched as she remembered her two kodachis.

"Lord Cai Ren sent me out here on official business." It was one last gambit to avoid having to fight for her life.

"Oh, is he a spy, too?"

"Don't be afraid," one said, drawing his katana. "I'll give you a quick death."

Kari threw her satchel at the Kitsuno Kai, then dove to the side, trying to create distance between her and her attackers. She drew her weapons and faced the Kitsuno Kai. The weights of the swords felt strange in her hands. It had been a long time since she had held a weapon, and even then, it had only been in training.

The three warriors were undaunted by her pose, quickly approaching her from the front. Parrying one attack, she leapt backward. She needed to keep as much distance between herself and them as possible so she could adjust her positioning to keep them from surrounding her.

She parried another sword swing, then another. Her two short swords allowed her to quickly change and alternate between opponents, but that didn't change the fact it was still three against one. Their full-length swords gave them an advantage with reach. Since she was intentionally trying to keep her distance, she could only defend against their attacks. If she wanted to go on the offensive, she would need to get closer, but, at close range, there was no way she could attack and defend against three opponents simultaneously.

She had to run.

Kari darted from the battle in a full-out run through the woods. She went as fast as she could, leaves and branches swiping at her face and leaving behind small cuts and scratches. Even flinching with each small cut, she did not break her stride. She had to create as much distance as she could. Only then could she fight.

She whirled to face her pursuers. Her plan worked. The difference in running speed had separated the Kitsuno Kai, at least for a moment. The fastest runner had stayed close to Kari while the other two dragged behind. It only gave her a few moments to make her move, but that was all she needed. If she could take him out quickly, before the others caught up, then she could even the field.

Kari darted forward at the Kitsuno Kai, taking him by surprise as he had not expected her to turn and attack. She let forth with a quick series of slashes, but he blocked each one. She put all of her might into each attack, dancing and twirling and hacking and slashing her way through the foliage, but each was met with his sword, the very thought of which was unthinkable.

Shagin typically didn't bother with defense, allowing their spirit aura to protect them instead. Their fighting style was pure offense. The purpose of the double swords was to keep an opponent off balance and to make it harder to defend against the onslaught of Shagin. The Shagin-sword style was often thought of as impossible to guard against, yet the Kitsuno Kai negated its advantage with sheer skill and precision.

She switched her left hand to a reverse grip, hoping the change of style would confuse him, but it seemed to have no effect, only limiting her leverage. She attacked with a backhanded slash followed by a backhanded stab, but he dodged both. Kari leapt forward with a downward slash, thinking for sure it would hit, but he stepped aside, leaving her open for attack.

With his opening, he countered with his own downward strike, which she blocked with her left-handed sword and struck at with her right, parrying his sword and leaving him open. Using her momentum, she spun on the ball of her right foot, allowing her left sword to take advantage of his opening and attack with a stab, but once again, he dodged the attack.

Using both swords, she launched forward with a double downward slash, but he blocked both blades. Using the power and leverage of his full-length sword, he parried her attack and struck her in the gut with a forward kick, which caused her to stumble backward.

Kari jumped out of the way as the sword of the second Kitsuno Kai slashed at her, barely missing her neck. She had

before thrusting her shoulder into his chest, the blow sending him to the ground.

The third Kitsuno Kai had finally rejoined the fray. Kari wasn't sure how much longer she could keep up the fighting. She was exhausted. With each breath, she struggled to fill her lungs with oxygen. She needed to end the fight now. She still had one more move left, though she hated using it.

The Kitsuno Kai charged at Kari with his sword raised, ready for a thrusting attack, but he never made it close enough to attack. Kari held out her hand, focusing her energy. A blast of light shot forth from her palm, blinding her attacker. He screamed out in pain as the light ripped and tore at his flesh. Once the light had subsided, Kari rushed the Kitsuno Kai before he could regain his composure. She slashed at his neck, the tip of her sword cutting through his flesh and releasing a spray of blood. Not breaking her momentum, she followed up her attack with a thrust that impaled him through his chest.

She ripped her sword free from the fallen warrior as she struggled to stay on her feet. The power of her attacks had taken too much out of her. Her body was on the verge of collapse, but she could not rest yet. She stared down the Kitsuno Kai whom she had toppled to the ground earlier.

Kari's eyes widened as a hand took hold of her sword arm, and a blade of a katana struck against the side of her neck. She winced as pain radiated through her, the cold steel digging deeper into her flesh.

When had he freed himself from the trees?

Kari screamed out in agony as the Kitsuno Kai slashed at her neck. The force of the attack sent her spiraling to the ground. Blood gushed forward like a fountain, painting the forest floor red. She knew it before she had even hit the ground, she had felt it. He had severed her carotid artery. She would be dead in seconds.

Acting on instinct, she dove her fingertips into the wound on her neck. She no longer felt pain, barely noticed her own fingers rummaging inside her neck. Once she had found her artery, she pinched it closed, trying to stop the bleeding. It was only a stall tactic. She was going to pass out, then die in the forest.

Death was assured.

The Kitsuno Kai who had killed her raised his sword to finish her off before she lost consciousness. Kari could let go of the vein and bleed out before he struck. She would rather die by her own hands than his blade. Glaring at her, he moved in for the kill.

A sword tore through his chest, entering at his shoulder and cutting down to his diaphragm.

Ronin appeared. He bared his fangs at his own men, saving her from the sword. When he pulled his sword out, blood sprayed through the air as the body of the Kitsuno Kai crumpled to the ground. The last of the Kitsuno Kai that Kari had fought mouthed something to Ronin, but Kari could not make out the words. Her entire world had become mute. The Kitsuno Kai rushed him, but Ronin parried the attack and slashed at his aggressor. Blood sprayed the trees as he slayed the last of the warriors.

Ronin sheathed his sword before rushing toward Kari. Her world dimmed. Blood gushed freely from her neck as her life painted the forest floor, and her consciousness faded away.

CHAPTER FIFTEEN

The Past

"THIS WILL BE THE start of your trial," elder Nina told the girls. "Make your way through the tunnels to the sacred forest. I will meet you at the edge of the forest where the obelisk overlooks the river in one month's time, on the morning following the full moon. Look after each other, and may you find what you seek."

The daughters of Eanna and Alme stepped into the darkness as Nina sealed the door behind them.

"Come on." The daughter of Alme pulled her glowstone out of her pocket, motioning for the daughter of Eanna to follow. "We don't have time to dally. Who knows how long it will take us to make it to the surface?"

The daughter of Eanna sighed as she took her own glowstone out. "This is pointless."

"This is tradition," the daughter of Alme corrected. "Every Shagin undergoes the trial."

"That was before," the daughter of Eanna corrected, following behind her friend. Their words echoed through the rocky belly of the earth. In front of them was nothing but a vast empty darkness, the only light the soft yellow from their enchanted glowstones. "There is no need to test our survival skills now. We are never leaving this island."

"You're missing the point," the daughter of Alme said. "Survival is secondary to the trial. Even before the Purge, no one ever died on their trial. The point is self-discovery—to find out who you really are."

"A name." The daughter of Eanna rolled her eyes. The pair stopped as they came to a split in the tunnel. The daughter of Alme paused to pull out a folded map. The daughter of Eanna scoffed as she took the left tunnel. "I already have a name picked out, so why do I have to do this?"

"You're doing it wrong. It's not merely about picking out a name." The daughter of Alme rushed to catch up to her friend. "A name is symbolic of who you are. It is your identity. You can only fully know yourself by searching deep inside of your soul, connected to the earth and away from distractions."

"And how are we supposed to connect to the earth when there is no grass here? No wind, no trees. Just stone and darkness."

"We are closer to the earth than anyone. We are a part of it." The daughter of Alme stopped, fumbling with her map. "Are you sure this is the right way? I think we should have reached another split by now."

"You remember the lectures." The daughter of Eanna didn't slow her pace. "All of these tunnels will come out somewhere. It's impossible to get lost."

The daughter of Alme ran to catch up with her. "Yes, but they specifically told us which path to take."

"And that's probably the hardest path," the daughter of Eanna said. "This is just another test. All the training, the sword play, the survival techniques, energy manipulation—it has all been to prepare us for a day that will never come."

"You don't know that," the daughter of Alme said. "We could still go on pilgrimage."

The daughter of Eanna stopped, impatiently flopping on a boulder. "Shagin have been on Mystikos our whole lives. In thirteen years, not a single person has left this island. We are the last generation. Shagin dies with us." Sighing, the daughter of Eanna dropped her pack to the rocky ground. "I'm tired. Let's set up camp here."

The daughter of Eanna took out a pair of seeds from a pouch tied to her belt. She placed them on the stone ground. With a single touch, the seeds blossomed and two tree trunks embedded themselves into the stone. With the trees in place, the daughter of Alme took out two mesh nets and tied them into hammocks between the trunks, with one hanging above the other.

There wasn't much food to find in the tunnels, only what they could bring, so the daughter of Eanna had brought seeds to produce papayas and mangos, which helped to cut down on their carry weight. They were easy enough to grow with her powers.

The daughter of Alme broke off pieces of wood from the trees, then used them to start a fire. A single flick of her fingers was enough to ignite the wood pieces. The warmth of the crackling fire was a nice reprieve from the cool stone.

The daughter of Alme spent the evening meditating while the daughter of Eanna watched from her hammock. The daughter of Eanna ran her hands through her brown hair. This was so stupid. She just wanted to go home. Shagin were trapped in their traditions, too afraid to move forward. Their race would die because they refused to adapt. Forget the trials, forget the pilgrimages, and forget trying to find a mate—survival should be their only focus. Shagin were a group of people dedicated to magic and perfecting various survival skills. Ironic then, that their desire to hold onto tradition would be their demise.

The daughter of Eanna dreaded the day when it would just be her and the handful of other girls of her generation left. An all-female race, isolated from the rest of the world, there wouldn't be any other Shagin born. She and the Daughter of Alme were the second youngest, born just before the Purge. Only the daughters of Ninti and Zarya were younger than they were.

The daughter of Eanna rolled over onto her side. The hammock folded her around, making laying on her side that much more uncomfortable. Huffing, she closed her eyes, accepting her position for the night.

Days passed in the tunnels. At least the daughter of Eanna thought they were days. Without being able to see the sky, it was difficult to tell the passage of time. They walked until they were tired, stopped when they were hungry, and set up camp when they grew sleepy. At every break, the daughter of Alme would go off just beyond the edge of the glowstone's light and meditate. When they were rested, they continued on their journey through the tunnels, searching for the surface.

"That's not what we are looking for," the daughter of Alme said. "We are searching for our true selves."

The daughter of Eanna rolled her eyes as she finished tying off her hammock. Another camp and another day had finished. "I told you I already have a name picked out. I am Fujiko."

"Fujiko?" The daughter of Alme raised an eyebrow.

"It's a name taken from my father's homeland. It's pretty, don't you think?"

"What does it mean?" the daughter of Alme asked.

"I don't know," the daughter of Eanna said, sitting next to her friend. "I think it means child."

"Child of what?" the daughter of Alme asked. "Your name should fit you. It should be who you are or what you do."

"So, what, plant girl?"

"No, but maybe if you meditate, you can find your inner self, then combine those ideas together."

"What about you? Do you have a name picked out?"

"I think I'm starting to understand my role, and yes, I have an idea."

"What is it?"

"I can't tell you. It would be improper to tell you before my introduction."

The daughter of Eanna left the daughter of Alme to meditate while she climbed into her hammock. She'd grown tired of sleeping in a folded position. She missed her hay bed. Leaping out of her hammock, she stared at the tree trunks anchored into the walls of the tunnel. If she could reposition them, maybe she could make the hammocks tauter. Give them more support. The daughter of Eanna placed her hand against the rough tree bark.

She poured her energy into the wood. It grew and moved through the stone, breaking off rocks in the process. The trees moved into position, tearing through the stone and pulling the hammocks further apart, making the mesh tighter.

The daughter of Eanna climbed into her hammock, then closed her eyes. In just a few more weeks, this would all be over. She could go back to her everyday life.

The hammock snapped free. Her heart skipped as she fell. The tree she had moved broke loose from the stone, and she and it came crashing to the ground with a thud. Rocks rained down upon her, covering her in debris.

"Are you all right?" The daughter of Alme ran over to her, then helped her to stand from the rubble.

"I think so." The daughter of Eanna dusted herself off. "What happened?"

"The tree came loose from the rock." The daughter of Eanna stared at the gaping hole in the stone. She was lucky. The whole tunnel could have come down on her.

A low rumbling noise echoed in the darkness.

The pair looked at each other as small stones tumbled from the tunnel's ceiling.

"Run!"

The two Shagin darted away from the camp as boulders and rocks rained down around them in a thunderous cacophony. A large boulder smashed down behind the daughter of Eanna, slamming her into the stone wall. Smoke and dust filled the tunnel as the chaos subsided.

The daughter of Eanna rubbed her eyes. The faint glimmer of the glowstones was still visible through the smoke.

"Help me!" The daughter of Alme's screams pierced the silence.

She laid face-down in front of the collapsed tunnel. A pool of blood oozed out from under the rubble. The daughter of Alme's leg had been crushed by the falling stone.

"Help me! Get this off me," the daughter of Alme cried out as tears streamed down her face.

The daughter of Eanna tugged on the stone, but it was too heavy to move. She had to find a way to help her friend. She could go back and get help, but she didn't even know which way back was, and even if she could find her way to

Shi Zinni, she wouldn't know how to find the daughter of Alme again.

The tunnel rumbled to life as small rocks and pebbles fell again.

"By the goddess, it's going to collapse again."

"You have to get me out of here." The daughter of Alme stared at her with wide eyes. "Cut my leg off. Just do something."

Cut the girl's leg off? Could she do that? The rumbling was getting louder. Whatever she was going to do, she had to do it fast.

The daughter of Eanna took out her knife, then grabbed hold of the daughter of Alme's leg. Warm blood seeped in between her fingers. She stumbled backward. She couldn't do this. Her grip loosened on the knife, and it tumbled to the stone floor.

"I can't. I'm sorry." The daughter of Eanna retreated into the darkness.

The daughter of Alme tugged at her leg. It wouldn't budge. Her body trembled as she stared at the daughter of Eanna. She looked so scared—the way the daughter of Eanna felt. The daughter of Eanna didn't want to die, but there was nothing left for her to do. The stone shifted, and larger rocks fell once more.

The trapped girl reached out to the daughter of Eanna, clutching at the air. "Run, save yourself!" Stone crashed and smashed into the ground as more rocks plummeted. "Please don't die with me."

The daughter of Eanna pivoted, then ran into the darkness. The daughter of Alme screamed, and the daughter of Eanna spun on her heel toward her childhood friend. All she could see was dust and debris as the tunnel collapsed, enveloping her sister.

The chaos was over. Silence and darkness fell all around her. Clasping her hand over her mouth, the daughter of Eanna wept. She could taste the lingering blood on her fingers. Wrapping her arms around herself, she collapsed to her knees. Her body violently spasmed as she cried in the darkness.

She'd run away, and her friend had died. She was alone in the darkness with no light, no food, no supplies, and no hope.

She groped her way through the tunnel, slowly inching along. It was impossible. Hours passed, and there was no way she could find an exit to the surface in the dark. They wouldn't come looking for her for weeks. By then, she would be dead, too.

There was only one thing left to do. She steadied herself in the darkness, sitting on the ground. Crossing her legs, she focused on her breathing. The daughter of Alme had relied on meditation to find her purpose. She said she had found it. Perhaps the daughter of Eanna could do the same. Maybe, deep inside of herself, the Fates would show her the path to survive.

She relaxed her muscles, starting from her head down to her feet. Mindful meditation was a period of relaxation and self-reflection. Who was she? She was a coward. She'd run when her friend had needed her most. There was so few of them left on Mystikos. Every last one was precious, a friend. Her best friend, her sister, was dead because of her.

The daughter of Eanna longed for the goddess's intervention. How she wished there were a heaven. If the goddess could hear her now, she just wished to have some sign her friend was happy. That the daughter of Alme was safe and protected and loved.

Warm tears streaked down her face, and she wiped them away with her bloodstained hands. "I'm so sorry."

The daughter of Eanna held out her hands in front of her. In the pitch-black darkness, she couldn't even see them.

What?

The shape of her hands came into focus. A brilliant flash of light erupted from her fingertips to tear through the shadows. It illuminated the underground.

"The daughter of Alme," she whispered. "Thank you. I'll see you again, someday."

The daughter of Eanna used the light to navigate the tunnels, eventually finding her way to the surface. The fresh air and green lush landscape were a welcomed companion. Alme needed to know what happened to her daughter, but the daughter of Eanna knew better. She wasn't allowed to make contact, even for that. How would she tell Alme about her death? It was a conversation she dreaded.

Loneliness made the next three weeks rather difficult. She greatly missed having her friend to talk to, often finding herself weeping and mourning the loss of her sister. It seemed every night, she would cry until she fell asleep. All that was left was to wait for her time to be over, so she could return home.

She meditated just as she had been taught, just as the daughter of Alme had done. She would ensure the daughter of Alme lived on in her memories and deeds.

Raindrops disrupted her thoughts as they fell upon her cheek.

The daughter of Eanna retreated into her makeshift hut as she took shelter from the rain. She had used her magic to manipulate and control the plants, forming them into a primitive hut she had used since coming up from the tunnels. As she'd been in the wilderness for a month now, it was hard to believe it was almost over. Tomorrow, she would go home.

The light that emitted from her hands and illuminated the darkness didn't just show her the way out of the tunnels. It showed her true self. She finally knew who she was, and she couldn't wait to stand before the village and finally introduce herself to her friends and family.

However, she was a little surprised. She was unaware of anyone developing new cantrips. Shagin made sure each girl knew how to utilize and control their energy enough to manipulate it into their cantrips before their trial. She had never heard of anyone discovering another cantrip later in life, so she was a trailblazer in that regard. A true sign Nebura was watching her.

With her head racing with thoughts of home, the daughter of Eanna drifted asleep.

After she woke up the next morning, she packed up her camp. She dismantled her hut, putting away the tools and supplies she had made on her trial. When she had finished, she headed for the edge of the forest where she was greeted by the Shagin elders.

"Welcome home, daughter of Eanna," elder Nina said. "Have you found the inner you?"

"I have," the daughter of Eanna replied.

"Excellent," she said. "In that case, it is time to introduce you as Shagin. Where is the other? Where is the daughter of Alme?"

"Elder..." the daughter of Eanna started. She didn't know how to finish the sentence or even how to start it, but they had to know. "There was a cave-in. She... she didn't make it."

"I see." Nina rubbed her eyes. "The poor child. I will inform Alme. No need to make you do so."

"Thank you, Elder."

"Come on, let us return to the village. Tomorrow, we will mourn our lost child. Today, however, we will celebrate our discovered sister."

The elders escorted the daughter of Eanna back to the village, which had been decorated and prepared for the feast to welcome her back. It was always a joyous celebration whenever a girl returned from her trial.

Upon seeing her, Eanna ran up and embraced her in a hug.

"My daughter, I am so glad to see you again. I've missed you so much."

"I've missed you, too," the daughter of Eanna replied.

"So, you have it? You have found your name?"

"I have, Mother." She smiled as Eanna kissed her forehead.

"I can't wait to hear it at your introduction."

That night, the whole village gathered together to welcome the daughter of Eanna into adulthood. They feasted on fish, beef, and veggies. Songs were sung in her honor. It was bittersweet her friend could not be here.

When it was finally time to introduce her, the elder stood on a platform at the village center. She called for silence before beckoning the daughter of Eanna to take the stage with her.

"One moon ago, the daughter of Eanna ventured into the deep to face the trials of adulthood. Today, she returns to her home. She is no longer simply the daughter of Eanna. Today, she is Shagin and a sister to all." The crowd cheered in response. The elder held out a hand to her. "Daughter of Eanna, tell us who you are."

The daughter of Eanna took the elder's hand, moving to center stage. She had spent the past weeks dreaming of how she would introduce herself. It was surreal to finally be living out this moment.

"I have faced the loneliness of the deep. I have faced the darkness, and I've discovered my inner self. I am Hikari."

The crowd cheered even louder as some chanted out her name in response. A smile took over Hikari's face as she held out her hands.

"And I bring light to the world!" Hikari shone forth light from her palms.

The crowd's response died, falling into silence as they gaped at her. Hikari's smile faded as she looked at her mother. Eanna clasped her hand over her mouth, tears streaming down her cheeks.

"You need to come with me," the elder said, taking hold of Hikari's arm. She didn't resist.

"It's not true. You don't know it is," Eanna protested, following behind them.

"We won't know for sure until we do the tests," the elder replied.

Nina placed Hikari in a room within Bitabame, the house of elders. "Hold out your hand, child," Nina said, taking out a ceremonial dagger.

Hikari did as she was told, and the elder used the tip of the blade to prick Hikari's finger. She winced as the point drew blood. The elder squeezed out a few drops into a ceramic bowl.

"Wait here, child. I must consult the seers." Nina took the bowl of blood, leaving Hikari and Eanna alone. Eanna embraced her daughter, wrapping her tight in her arms.

"Mother, what's happening?" Hikari asked.

"You have a new cantrip, which doesn't happen often," Eanna explained. "It could be nothing. Or it could be the Seed."

"The Seed? I thought the curse was just a myth."

Eanna shook her head as her tears flowed freely.

"What's going to happen to me?" Hikari asked.

"I don't know, little one."

After a few hours, the elder returned.

"I'm so sorry, my child. You are the Bearer of the Seed," Nina said.

"But that can't be," Eanna protested. "When did the last bearer die?"

"We don't know," the elder replied before turning her attention to Hikari. "But that's the whole point. We can never know. It appears the Fates must be cruel. We cannot watch you grow. From this point forward, you are dead to us."

"Don't say that," Eanna demanded.

"You know it must be done," the elder replied.

"What will happen to me now?" Hikari asked.

"A boat is being prepared for you. Our warriors will see you make it back to the mainland. From there, you are on your own. You can never return, and we can never have any contact with you. We will make sure you have plenty of supplies to last you a while. I am sorry, child, but every moment you are here, you risk bringing grave danger and destruction to our home. You should head to the pier now."

"Do I have time to fix a few things for her?" Eanna asked.

"Be quick," Nina replied.

Hikari was escorted to the pier. The village looked deserted now. The celebrations were replaced by a solemn quiet as Shagin returned and shut themselves inside their homes. The stark contrast was eerie.

This was punishment. Her actions had killed the daughter of Alme, and now the Fates had stricken her with the Seed. She was cursed. It seemed it was her destiny to forever bring ruin and destruction to those around her, for that was the curse of the Seed.

The Seed was ancient, older than written history. Through its power, the Three Realms were held apart. Its creation had ended the old world, nearly wiping out all life. Shagin had borne it in secret throughout the ages, with a single Shagin chosen by fate to carry the curse inside of her until her death, when another would be chosen.

It was feared, if the Seed was ever discovered, it could be used to snap the Three Realms together again, causing a second apocalyptic cataclysm. It was why the Bearer was always banished. If anyone ever came to Shagin looking for the Bearer, no one would ever know her whereabouts.

Her light was a lie. It was darkness that dwelled inside of her. The death of her friend, the death of countless victims of the Seed—they were only just the beginning. She was a threat to all life.

She never wanted to see that light again.

Now even her name would remind her of her true nature. She had chosen it based on the father she had never met.

Like most Shagin, she spent a great deal of time studying and learning about her paternal culture and heritage. In the ancient tongue of her father's homeland, hikari meant light. Just yesterday, she was so proud of that fact. She'd wanted to bring light to the world, but she never would. Her true nature had seen to that, and now her home and her mother were being stripped from her forever.

She never wanted to hear her name again. It was who she was. There was no changing that. But it wasn't who she wanted to be.

Hikari waited at the pier next to a small boat. A single Shagin warrior would escort her on the long, dangerous voyage to the mainland. It would take them weeks just to reach the shore.

Eanna ran up to Hikari with a bag in tow.

"Take these," she said, handing Hikari the bag. "I hope they aid you in your life."

"Thank you."

"My daughter," Eanna said, placing her hand against Hikari's face. "My little one, my Hikari. When I finally know what to call you, I have to lose you."

"I hate my name," Hikari grumbled. "I'll never use it again. I just want to forget it."

Eanna placed a tender kiss on Hikari's forehead. "I love it as I love you. It is who you are. I love you so much, and I will never forget you. You will always be Shagin. As far as I'm concerned, you will always have a home here."

"I could never forget you," Hikari replied, wiping tears from her eyes. "I love you."

CHAPTER SIXTEEN

KARI WAS SURPRISED TO be able to open her eyes. Considering her wound, she had rather thought she wouldn't wake up at all. She might be alive, but she felt like death. Her whole body ached and spasmed as she tried to move. Blinking as her eyes adjusted to the light, she realized she was back in her bed. Both her arms and her neck were bandaged.

"You fight well, little one," Ronin said. He sat in a chair on the other side of her bed. She was stunned she hadn't noticed him right off.

"Am I..." Her voice sounded distant and weak.

"You're safe, for now. It seems you stumbled upon a plot to assassinate the emperors, and you were attacked for your troubles. At least, that is what the emperors believe. The three traitorous Kitsuno Kai who attacked you have been killed, their bodies dismembered and burned."

"What?" Kari rubbed her face as she tried to process what was going on.

"That is the official story," Ronin replied. "That is what I told the emperors. Should I go tell them the truth? Would that satisfy you?"

"You killed your own men."

"I warned them not to confront you, but they disobeyed, fearing you were a greater threat than I realized."

"I don't understand, why help me?"

Ronin smirked. "We'll get to that, but first... what is a Shagin doing here in Xiang?"

Kari stammered. "I–I'm not..."

"Don't lie to me," Ronin screamed, jumping to his feet and pressing his face within inches of hers. With a scary smile, he slowly returned to his chair. "You are only alive because I will it. However, if you don't tell me what I want to know, I can easily arrange for your execution."

Kari sighed. There was no escaping this. Ronin was clearly deranged and ruthless. He'd demonstrated that by killing his own men. If she tried to deny what she was, if she tried to hide, he wouldn't hesitate to kill her. There was nothing left to do but to take her chances with the truth. Or at least a part of it.

"How do you know?" Kari asked. She struggled to sit up in her bed. Her head ached, spinning at the effort. She had lost a lot of blood. Ronin had to be skilled if he'd been able to keep her alive after a wound like that.

Ronin drew his two kodachis from their sheaths. "They do have a certain feel for home, don't they? Of course, I would take a jhuma any day, but it's more than that. It's the way you move, the way you fight. Shagin rely primarily on their spirit auras for defense while utilizing a relentless attack. You don't see such offense from the other cultures.

It's usually a decent balance of offense and defense with a sword, not so from Shagin. And then there are those eyes. Your vivid emerald eyes are a dead giveaway. I suspected you of being Shagin from the moment I saw you, but I didn't know for sure until I witnessed you fight."

"How do you know any of this?" Kari asked. He looked too young to have fought in the Sovereign War.

"Because Shagin raised me. My father fell in love with a Shagin woman. She basically raised me, but then she abandoned us."

"We were hunted down and exterminated. I would hardly call that abandonment." Kari tried to hide the anger in her voice. The Purge was a sore topic for Shagin, even for someone like Kari who hadn't lived through it.

"She was the closest thing I had to a mother, and she left out of fear. She could have taken me with her like she took my sister, but no. I wasn't Shagin. I would call that abandonment." He was acting like his mother had a choice, like she was a coward for fleeing. Shagin had been hunted down and killed. Still, Kari could sympathize. A child having to say goodbye to their mother was always devastating.

"I'm sorry," Kari said. "I've never even heard of Shagin who would live away from her sisters. We are hated outside of our homeland. Even before the Purge, being an open Shagin could be a death sentence."

"So why are you here? Shouldn't you be in hiding? Or do you have a death wish?"

How much should she tell him? While it was nice to finally meet someone who knew about Shagin and didn't see only a killer, this man was dangerous. She had no idea what his true intentions were, much less if he would suddenly snap and kill her like he had his men. "I was born here after the Purge. I've been hiding ever since."

"You're lying," Ronin said, stone faced. If only she could know what he knew, then maybe she would have some success with her lies. "Perhaps I should just kill you and be done with it."

"Maybe you're not as perceptive as you think."

"You were clearly raised by Shagin. You know how they fight and what weapons best complement their style. Your spirit aura matches theirs. There can be no mistake. But if you were raised by Shagin, they would have taken you to Mystikos. It would be the only place where you could truly be safe."

"How do you know about Mystikos?" The island was home to the Shagin trials, and it was one of their closest guarded secrets, especially now that their homeland lay in ruin.

"I told you, my adopted mother was Shagin. That's where she fled with the rest who were smart enough to escape."

"Do you ever wander what happened to her?" Kari asked, trying to change the subject. If he knew about Mystikos, then he might know about the greatest Shagin secret. He might know about the Seed. She could hardly think about the possibility without her chest tightening up. If he knew that, he could figure out why she was here, then all hope would be lost.

Her heart raced as she tried to shake the thought from her mind. Her chest tightened and hurt from the pressure. She could feel every beat of her heart as it pumped adrenaline through her body, preparing her to fight. She wanted to move toward the door, but how would he react? Would he kill her? Judging by how effortlessly he dealt with the other two Kitsuno Kai, she couldn't beat him in a fight. If it came down to it, she would have to run. But in the condition she was in, she struggled just to sit upright.

"I've wondered quite a bit what might have happened to her." He stared at the ceiling. "I often wonder if she made it. If she's still alive. How many survived? How many made it to Mystikos?"

"Not many. I think there were just over five thousand of us left." Kari relaxed a bit. So long as he didn't press her about why she was here, she could hide the Seed. She had spent many nights wandering what she would do, what she was prepared to do, if someone discovered she was the Bearer. At first, she had kept a dagger by her side if that moment ever came, but the thought of cutting into her own flesh, of ending her life, sent shivers down her spine so she discarded it. Now, facing the possibility of being discovered, she longed for that option.

Ronin squinted his eyes. "If there is that few of you left, then maybe you would know her. Her name was Eanna."

Kari's heart nearly jumped out of her chest. It felt like someone had just stabbed her in the heart with a knife. "No," she stammered. "No, no, no... That's not right."

"What's wrong?"

"That can't be right. This is some sort of trick." Kari tried to stand, but her legs buckled under her weight and she crashed to the bed. "This is just a sick trick. That's all it is."

"I truly don't understand."

"Eanna is my mother."

How could this be? It had to be a trick. But how would he know her name? Could he read her mind?

"Now I agree with you there. That's not right." Ronin rubbed his chin. "If you are really Eanna's daughter, why are you here?"

"Before I left, Mother gave me a bag. Inside that bag was a note about my father, about where he lived. He was a man from Valceem named Okawa Nobuhiro, so I came here with only a name."

Ronin stuck out his tongue, curling it upward. "That's my father's name. Could you really be her? My sister. I always imagined what I would say to you if we ever met. I thought I would despise you. Once you were born, she took you and fled, leaving me behind. But it wasn't your fault. You were just a newborn. But why would she send you away from Mystikos? Unless... the Shagin curse."

He knew. The man before her knew. He knew the most guarded Shagin secrets, and he knew her mother's name. Was this really her brother? Could she trust him? She had no choice now. Her life was already in his hands, but the truth was worth more than merely her life. Why hadn't he let her die?

If he knew, would he kill her or protect her? Maybe there was more to him than she realized.

"Unfortunately, yes," Kari said, lamenting her very nature. "I am the Bearer of the Seed."

"I thought it was just a legend."

Kari shook her head. "I found out during my trials. I didn't know what it was at the time or else I wouldn't have announced it during the celebration. They exiled me that night, put me on a boat to the mainland, because I'm a monster."

"Do you really think that?" Ronin asked. "You're not a monster, but unless you accept what you are, you will never find peace."

She didn't want to hear what he had to say. What did he know anyway? He wasn't Shagin, nor the Bearer. "Knowing what city my father was from, I came here looking for the last of my family."

"You found it," Ronin said, standing. "Father died some time ago. How long have you been searching?"

"Four years," Kari replied. It had been four long years of hunger and strife, and now it was all for nothing. "There is so much I could have used his help with."

"If I were him, what would you have asked for?"

Was he really willing to help her? He had saved her life. Maybe she could try. Besides, if he wanted to kill her, he had more than enough reason to already.

"As you are aware, I am currently serving as an Imperial attendant," Kari said. Ronin's brow furrowed. "This country is in chaos. The Tian Dynasty will leave this land in tatters. I believe I am in a position to save many lives, to end this chaos, but to do so, I need to find a way to end the reign of the Tians."

"Consider it done," Ronin replied, gripping his swords.

"I don't think it is that simple," Kari said, taken aback by his sudden agreement.

"Is it not? You met with known assassins in the forest. While I could not hear the details, I assume you have a plan. Now you can add me to it."

"Why are you so eager to join me?"

"After I stopped your 'assassination,' Baoshun has asked me to be your personal bodyguard. I would be remiss if I did not aid you in your quest. If this is the path you have chosen to walk, then I will walk beside you."

Kari wasn't sure what to say. The man before her might be her brother, yet the last time she saw him, he had cut down his own men, men he had led to capture her. But if he were going to kill her, she wouldn't be lying in her bed now. She needed to trust him. A strong sword and a capable assassin were what she needed if she were to see this to the end.

Kari sighed. Were the Fates finally lending her a hand? "Thank you for your aid. I need to speak with Cai Ren to discuss our future plans. Would you be able to accompany me?"

"No," Ronin said coldly. "You need your rest. I shall bring him here."

Without saying another word, he gracefully glided out of the room.

Kari breathed a sigh of relief. He was a dark man, just as brutal as the stories said.

She placed a hand on her neck. Goddess, that was close. She should have died. There weren't many people who could treat such a wound, even less who could claim to have had their throat sliced open and still be alive to tell the tale. Even with her spirit energy, it would take a while for her wounds to heal.

Kari jumped as her door was thrown open. Ina ran toward her, scrambled up beside her, and threw her arms around her neck.

"I thought you were going to die," she said. "How do you feel?"

"I've been better." Kari winced as Ina brushed against the wound on her neck.

"No doubt. You've been out for six days. What happened?" Ina asked. "They're saying some of the Kitsuno Kai had been plotting to assassinate the emperors, and they captured you and dragged you out of the city. I know you left to meet with Cai Ren's contact, but did that man really save you?"

"Yes, the Kitsuno Kai who attacked me—they were his men, and he just killed them. There was no hesitation at all. They almost killed me, but he slaughtered them to save me." The turn of events still seemed too bizarre for her to fully comprehend, and they sounded even stranger spoken aloud.

"He killed his own men?" Ina asked. "Why would he do that? I didn't think the Kitsuno Kai were all that loyal to the throne."

"I don't know," Kari replied honestly. Surely there was a better way to save her than to murder his friends. After all, he was their leader. He could have stopped them another way. His plan, if he even had one, involved killing those who trusted him, all to protect her secret. It was absurd, but not more than the revelation he provided. "I think Ronin might be my brother."

"I think you need to lie down." Ina moved to the floor, placed her hands on Kari's shoulders, and then pushed her into a prostrate position. Shaking her head, Kari sprang up.

"I don't know how to explain it. It doesn't even make sense." What were the odds of finding her lost brother? Her mother had told her to come to Valceem to find her father, but she'd never mentioned Kari had a brother. "He says he's the son of the father I never met, and my mother raised him as her own."

"He's lying," Ina said, scowling. "It's some sort of Kitsuno Kai trick."

Kari shook her head. "He knew my mother's name before I ever said it."

"He found out somehow. That's what they do. They're dangerous wolves who like to play with their prey." Ina sat at the foot of Kari's bed, appraising her. "Do you believe him?"

"I don't know," Kari said honestly. "I don't see how he could have known her name. There are no records, and most people on the mainland are content to think we all died. But he knew more than just that. He knew Shagin secrets. Things we would never tell an outsider. Most alarmingly, he knew why I was exiled."

"You never told me." Ina placed a hand on Kari's.

Kari closed her eyes. "I can't. It's the most shameful thing."

"You can trust me."

It went beyond trust. Shagin were taught from an early age that the secret of the Seed was to be guarded until death. The Seed was a curse, a power created by the Cataclysm of the Three Realms, the event that split the world into three pocket dimensions. As the Bearer, she could draw on the power of the Seed in the form of her light magic, but at a heavy cost. The Cataclysm destroyed the old world to create the new. Countless lives gone in an instant, and it was their lives that gave Kari her power.

Such destructive power, if misused, could undue the severance of the Three Realms, resulting in a second Cataclysm. It was for this reason the Bearer's identity must remain hidden and her location unknown from her sisters.

Shagin were always hated and feared, and it was believed if anyone ever discovered the truth of the Seed, it would bring destruction to Shagin. The world would use the knowledge of its existence to justify further hatred of Shagin.

For Ronin to know of its existence, he would have to be raised as Shagin. It was the only way a Shagin would trust someone with their greatest secret and greatest shame.

"He's my brother." Kari's brow furrowed. "I don't understand. Why wouldn't my mother tell me about him? Why would she keep this a secret?"

"Maybe it was too painful to tell," Ina said. "It sounds like shame is a large factor in Shagin secrets. I can only imagine how difficult it would be to leave behind a child you raised in order to save your life and the life of a second child. Maybe she didn't want you to think less of her for doing so."

Kari nodded, but she wasn't sure what to believe. It was possible her mother was afraid of what Kari would think, but their entire race was being exterminated. Following what few survivors were left to safety wasn't cowardly. Kari would like to think the thought of leaving her adopted son was simply too much for her mother to admit to. She hoped that was the truth.

The two girls watched quietly as the door slid open.

"What is the meaning of this?" Cai Ren demanded as he entered the room, escorted by Ronin. "What happened? Why has *he* brought me here?"

"He's our new ally," Kari said. She didn't want to reveal too much about her relationship with Ronin to Cai Ren. It was probably better to keep some of her secrets to herself—at least until she could work out her own feelings of the matter.

"Are you sure he can be trusted?" Cai Ren asked.

"Don't talk about me like I'm not here," Ronin said.

Honestly, Kari wasn't sure. He was so quick to agree to help her, but then again, they were family. Well, sort of. The truth was that trust was the one luxury she didn't have in the palace. She would face the might of the emperors, two peerless warriors who had ruthlessly thwarted every attempt to remove them from power, and if she were to succeed, she would have to put her trust in untried hands.

"Make no mistake," Ronin said. "My loyalty to her is unquestionable."

"Fair enough." Cai Ren responded. While Ronin's loyalty *was* debatable, he had protected her so far. Maybe blood meant something to him. He knew she was Shagin and the Bearer of the Seed, and he still hadn't killed her. At any rate, she had no choice but to fully trust him now.

"The meeting with Shenrong didn't go as smoothly as I had hoped," Kari explained. "They were downtrodden, hopeless, and wouldn't help. At least not until I told them what I am. We're not alone anymore. Once I'm healed, I can continue working to drive a wedge between the emperors."

"How is that not good?" Cai Ren asked. "They've agreed to help us, which should be all that matters."

"Because now they know she's Shagin, you twit," Ronin shook his head in disbelief. "That was a reckless thing you did. We don't need you in any unnecessary danger."

"I know," Kari replied. Was that genuine concern in his voice? It was hard to tell. It might have just been wishful thinking on her part.

"You're already playing a dangerous game," Ronin said. He scowled at Cai Ren. "Or has the fool failed to see the folly in his ploy?"

"What are you on about?" Cai Ren demanded.

"Who will be the first to see it?" Ronin smiled as his eyes bounced between them. "Kari is Shagin. Jiaorong is emperor. Before that, the Grand General. And before that, he was what?"

Ina gasped. "A war hero! He could recognize her!"

Ronin pointed his finger at her. "Very good."

"I don't understand," Kari said. "How could he recognize me?"

"How much did they teach you about the Shagin War?" Ronin asked.

"A little," Kari responded. "I know it wasn't the Shagin War. It was the Sovereign War. Shagin stayed out of it."

"We all know that's not true," Cai Ren added.

"The Renegades went against the decree of the elders," Kari said, rage flaring inside her. Like so many times before, Shagin were the outcasts, blamed for any troubles the world faced. And they were murdered when their allies accused Shagin of bewitching them to fight—all so the other nations could avoid the consequences of their actions. "The Renegades might have been Shagin, but they weren't Shagin."

"I fail to see the distinction," Cai Ren said.

"Despite their small size, they were the most dominant fighting force the Sovereign Alliance had," Ronin said with a gleam in his eye. "It was dominance that ensured the momentum of the war stayed with the Alliance, despite being outnumbered. Shagin played a critical role in every major Alliance victory, and only suffered two defeats through the course of the war—at the Battle Akashvani and the Siege of Valceem.

"Jiaorong led a number of raids against the Alliance encampment during the siege. He ignored the protection of the wall, staying on the offensive. His actions slowed their progress. By the time they breached the outer wall, it was too late. The bulk of the Coalition forces were advancing, and they had to end the siege to meet them. The point is Jiaorong has seen Shagin."

"It's a calculated risk," Cai Ren protested. "Just because he has meet Shagin doesn't mean he can identify them."

"Strange you're not at risk." Ronin crossed his arms, glaring at Cai Ren.

"He hasn't figured it out yet," Kari said. "If he had, I wouldn't be alive. Besides, the only physical trait Shagin share is our eyes. If it were that easy to discover who we are, Shagin would never go on pilgrimage."

Kari hoped she was right.

Sighing, Ronin rolled his eyes. "He either doesn't know, he does and he's too enamored with you to care, or he doesn't view you as a threat. The later thought is disconcerting."

"But don't the other options work in our favor?" Ina asked.

"There is no point in dwelling on what-ifs. The fact is the emperors do not suspect our intent, and now we have our assassin." Cai Ren stroked his chin as he thought. "We are one step closer to our goal, and we cannot falter now. The four of us need to begin making our final preparations."

"The three of us," Ronin corrected, pointing to Ina. "I'm not counting her."

"What's that supposed to mean?" Ina countered, placing her hands on her hips. She was quite brave to confront him so brashly.

"You're an untrained child we cannot afford to babysit. What are you going to do? Bleed on them to death?"

"Enough," Kari interrupted. "Ina is my friend."

"A friend?" Ronin asked. His inflection made the word seem as if it were foreign to him. "Is your friend worth your life?"

"I said she's staying," Kari said.

"Of course, my mistake." Ronin rolled his wrist, bearing his teeth at Ina. "I don't see why we don't just skip all the talking and go kill the emperors right now."

"Maybe it's because we want to continue breathing," Ina said. Ronin's hand twitched as he continued to glare at her. The veins in his neck pulsed. Kari recognized that look. It was the look of a wild beast ready to strike, but he never did. This was him showing restraint. Kari would hate to see what would happen if he didn't.

"Because an emotionally compromised fighter is a distracted fighter. There have been thirty-seven assassination attempts on the emperors, and only one person has ever survived. That tells me that they are terrifyingly strong. We have to find a way to weaken them first. If we can break the bonds between them, we can demoralize them, then we strike," Kari said. She gently placed her hand on Ina's, a subtle reminder to all in the room Kari would always support her friend.

"There's more to it than that," Cai Ren added. "The real fight occurs after they are gone. If we remove them from power, there will be a vacuum. Xiang will fall into chaos and civil war, unless we have the strength to control both the throne and the nation."

"That's why we need an army?" Kari asked.

"Partially, but we also need a strong leader and the support of the populace."

"The Kitsuno Kai," Ronin said.

"How does that get the people on our side?" Kari asked. "Aren't they loyal to the emperors?"

"The Kitsuno Kai are independent from the throne," Ronin explained. "We are loyal only to the people. If the well-being of the people is threatened by the throne, we will take up arms against it."

"Then we need to show them that is the case," Cai Ren added, stroking his goatee. "Can you arrange a meeting with Master Okita and me?"

"No." Ronin smiled. "But Kari and Master Okita? Consider it done."

Cai Ren scoffed. "I will ignore that insult, for now. Anyway, I know a few administrators who share no love for the emperors. I will also arrange a meeting with them. There is a chance they will want to meet you as well."

It was weird. They had the makings of an army, with her as the dividing blade, upon which their entire endeavor rested. She hated that idea. But for them to succeed, she would have to accept the role for now. "It's settled then. I will continue working on the emperors. Ina will continue aiding me, and Ronin and Cai Ren will forge our army."

Once they had all agreed on their current course of action, they left Kari alone in her room. She struggled out of bed, her whole body felt like it had been broken, but at least she could stand.

Her spirit energy would speed up the process, but with her body already weak, the daunting task of healing her wounds would take time. She would need her rest. It was her spirit aura that protected her. Without that, she would not have survived the assault.

Ronin was an enigma. He didn't seem loyal to anyone other than himself. There was no telling what his true goals were. He had been so quick to join her, and there was no way of knowing if he was truly sincere or if he had some dark scheme. His name seemed fitting. Ronin, a warrior with no master.

She placed her hand to her neck. Her survival was due to him. Her wounds were beyond the care of any doctor she was aware of, but Shagin with spirit energy could have helped her heal and seal the wound shut. She owed him her life, and now he knew her darkest secret. Once again, her life was in his hands, not to mention the fate of the Three Realms. Loyalty might not be his strongest aspect, but she had no choice but to trust him now.

Kari jumped as her bedroom door opened again. The figure of a man she cared not to see entered her room.

"I did not mean to frighten you," Jiaorong said. He held out a hand to her. "Please, there is no need to bow. You are too injured."

That was good to know because she hadn't planned to bow anyway. Not out of intentional defiance, but fatigue had caught up to her. Protocol and etiquette were the furthest things from her mind. She collapsed on her bed, and he sat beside her.

"Brother told me you were attacked." Jiaorong wrapped his arm around Kari's waist, and she had to fight the urge to recoil. "I am glad you are still alive. What happened?"

Kari needed to be careful what she said. Ronin had already started the lie, but she wasn't sure what was already conveyed. She needed to be light on details, so she could try to get Jiaorong to provide what information he knew. "I overheard them plotting something. I feared for your safety, so I followed them. I couldn't hear what all was being said, but they discussed assassinating you. I tried to flee, to come and warn you, but they saw me. I don't really remember what happened after that."

"They abducted you," Jiaorong said, filling in the details. "They took you just outside of Valceem, then tried to murder you. Luckily, a Kitsuno Kai loyal to the throne was tracking you. He killed them and saved you, though by the looks of it, he was almost too late."

Kari winced as he stroked her face.

"You truly are a remarkable woman. You almost died to protect me. I've had other women, other attendants, confess love to me, but no one has ever shown it like you have. Thank you."

"I would do anything for you, my love."

"Please, do not put yourself in harm's way. Let the bastards try to kill me. They will cower before my might." Jiaorong stared at Kari's neck. "You need your rest, and you should get those bandages looked at. I'll send a doctor by here to tend to you. Do you need anything? Where are your servants? Has my brother not given you any?"

"I just have the one, but I do not know where she is at the moment." With any luck, Ina was off hiding. She wasn't sure if Jiaorong knew Ina now served her, but she was sure them seeing each other would only elicit strong and painful emotions for both.

Jiaorong kissed Kari's forehead before leaving her alone. Kari didn't need a doctor. She could heal the wounds herself, but the doctor came and went. He had been a bit surprised to see her neck had completely closed. He merely surmised the initial attack wasn't as bad as suspected. Still, he instructed her to spend the next couple of weeks in bed, just to be on the safe side.

She actually enjoyed the time she spent recovering. Being injured meant she had a few days to not think or worry about the state of the world. She wouldn't have to see Baoshun and sing for him, nor would she have to join Jiaorong in his bed. She could just lay in hers and read the many books on her shelves, none of which appeared to have ever been read. Their spines were rigid and firm, and their binding was immaculate.

Ina played the role of servant, tending to Kari and ensuring she was taken care of while she healed. They would often leave and spend time in the gardens. There was plenty of peace and quiet to be found there.

The red wooden swings were a particular favorite of theirs. They were scattered throughout the gardens, usually located in secluded clearings. The swinging chairs made for a wonderful place to relax and pass the time.

Ronin shadowed Kari everywhere she went. She wasn't sure if he was merely acting the role of a bodyguard, or if he was genuinely concerned for her safety. Either way, he was never far from her, but he did not impose upon her either. He maintained his distance, merely staying within eyesight. When she would return to her home, he would stand guard outside of her door. Ronin never left, even at night. He would merely sleep on the ground outside of her house. It made her feel safer, knowing she had a strong sword watching over her.

In the evenings, she would settle in bed and read by candlelight. She had started a book about a young woman who was cursed to turn into a bird during the day. Kari liked all animals, but she'd always had a fondness for birds.

A knock on her door tore her away from her story.

Kari answered her door. Izumi stood on the other side with a tray and tea.

"I wanted to apologize for my behavior the other day," she said. "Please, let me serve you tea."

Kari hesitated before stepping aside. If she had learned anything from her time in the palace, it was that everyone deserved a second chance. "Of course."

They sat on Kari's bed, the tray of tea between them. Izumi poured two cups, then handed one to Kari. "Your bodyguard is quite protective of you. He had to inspect my teapot and cups before he would let me see you."

"I'm sorry if he offended you." The aroma of the tea was inviting and heavenly. Kari took a sip. The warm liquid bathed her tongue, dancing with her taste buds. "That's really good."

"Thank you," Izumi said. "Are you feeling any better?"

"A little," Kari replied.

"I suppose I should thank you. They tell me the men who attacked you were planning a coup. Your abduction saved my husband. I know it wasn't planned, but that is the way it turned out."

"I would do anything to better serve the empire."

Izumi sighed. "I am sorry for the way I've acted toward you. It wasn't always like this. Everything used to be so much better."

"What do you mean?" Kari asked.

"Before Baoshun ascended the throne, he was quite loving. I think I was his only one. But with the throne came power and women. I was cast to the side in favor of his concubines. He rarely even talks to me anymore. The only time he even touches me is when he has a new woman. He says no one else knows him better than I do, so he forces me to teach the new women the proper way to love him. It's degrading."

"I'm so sorry," Kari said. "I had no idea."

"Save your pity for yourself," Izumi replied. "I know it is only a matter of time before he leaves me. Part of me wants it. I'll finally be free, but I still love him. I'll fight for him if need be."

"Have you not talked to him about this? If he still cares for you, then I'm sure he'll listen." Kari took another drink from her cup.

"I can't." Izumi placed her cup back on the tray without taking a sip. "I should go. This isn't right."

"No, please stay."

"Enjoy your tea," Izumi said, rising and hurrying to the door. She gently closed it behind her, leaving Kari alone in the room.

Kari couldn't help but feel sorry for Izumi, but it didn't excuse her actions. Regardless, she was allowing someone she loved to commit horrible crimes. Kari couldn't fathom how anyone could love someone or even stay with them after all the things Baoshun had done.

Kari finished her tea before returning to her book. She continued to read, but her thoughts were not on the book but on Izumi. Kari wiped at the sweat running down her face. The brush of her fingers against her skin caused her face and hands to burn.

What was this? Staring at her cup, she placed the tip of her finger in the remaining liquid. Her vision grew blurry as her eyes watered. Without warning, vomit erupted from her mouth and coated her bedsheets.

She'd been poisoned.

CHAPTER SEVENTEEN

Izumi had poisoned her. Kari gripped at the pain in her chest as the room spun. She didn't have much time.

What were her symptoms? Burning sensation in her face and arms, vomiting, pain in her chest and abdomen, dizziness, and watery eyes. That didn't tell her much. She placed two fingers to her throat, noting her pulse was weak and slow. What had caused this?

She'd studied poisons, but for the life of her, she couldn't even think about what was ailing her.

She vomited again as she tried to stand to her feet, the taste of bile filling her mouth.

Ronin—she had to get to Ronin. He was right outside, and he could save her. Kari tried to scream, but only a tiny squeak came out. She didn't have the strength to reach him. She could barely stand as it was.

Kari had to think. She might not know what she'd been poisoned with, but she had to find a way to counteract it. Whatever it was, it was slowing her heartbeat down. That was her priority.

She stumbled over to her armoire. When she reached for the handle, she lost all strength in her arm. It fell limply to her side. Damn it! She was fading quickly, already struggling to catch her breath.

Her arm convulsed and shook as she slowly raised it. She groaned with every inch she managed until she was slowly able to open the armoire door. Her arm collapsed to her side again as she gasped for breath.

She couldn't rest yet. Sweat poured down her face as she took hold of her seed bag. Collapsing to the floor, she emptied the seeds in front of her.

Kari sifted through the scattered seeds until she found the tiny one she was looking for. She grasped it between two fingers and unloaded her spirit energy upon it, but nothing happened.

"Come on," she pleaded as she focused harder.

The seed glowed and the shape of the purple-shaped Gufang flower formed in her hands. She picked the leaves off the plant, then held them in her hand. The Gufang produced a toxin that drastically increased one's heart rate. It was a plant that could be just as deadly as whatever was killing her. Hopefully, there would be just enough poison in the leaves to help keep her heart rate up and not simply kill her faster.

She swallowed the leaves as she fought poison with poison.

Kari violently vomited in response. The leaves of the Gufang were covered in chunks of bile. That was no good.

She needed to regrow the leaves. The toxin in the rest of the plant would be too potent for her to take.

She grabbed the remainder of the plant, sending her energy into it. It did nothing. She was spent. Kari focused with all of her might on the flower between her fingers. She breathed a sigh of relief as it glowed, but then it exploded in a puff of smoke to leave no trace behind.

Fuck!

Her energy had become too unstable and weak. She was running out of options. Kari picked the leaves out of her own sickness, the smell of her stomach bile causing her to retch. It was her final option. She stuffed the vomit-soaked leaves into her mouth, the act of which nearly ended with a repeat of before.

She held her hand over her mouth, forcing herself to swallow. Her body instinctively tried to expel the leaves again, but she forced them down.

She collapsed motionless on the floor. Her prostrate body blankly faced the ceiling. She didn't have any strength left in her. All that was left now was to wait and hope for the best. In the morning, she would be found and either taken to a doctor or the undertaker.

Time became meaningless. She didn't remember falling asleep, only opening her eyes to see Ronin rushing in along with the morning light.

"What happened? Are you all right?" He helped her sit up.

Her chest was still tight and her stomach ached, but she was definitely better. "Izumi tried to poison me, but I counteracted the poison with Gufang."

Ronin dipped his finger in the teacup, then sniffed the remains. "Nisidu," he muttered. That was it. She had known that, but, in the moment, she hadn't been able to decipher the poison. "How did I not notice it? I'll kill her for this."

"No," Kari said. She was covered in dried vomit, and the smell of herself and the room was making her nauseous again. Of course, that could have just been the aftereffects of the poison. "I need to do this the right way. Help me clean up."

Ronin helped her to the bath. "I'll be right out here if you need anything," Ronin reassured her before he closed the door. The water soothed her as she washed the stink off her skin. Exhausted, she had to fight the urge to fall asleep. Once she was clean and dressed, she grabbed the teapot and headed out to see Baoshun.

"Let me summon a chair," Ronin said.

"That won't be necessary. I think it will be better if I walk. I need the fresh air." Kari stumbled out of her front door. She didn't want anyone seeing her so weak and frail. "If you don't mind, I think I would prefer to go alone."

She left Ronin behind as she headed for the emperors' mansion. Each step felt like an earthquake as she struggled to maintain her balance. She wasn't even halfway there before she had to stop for a break. Perhaps she should have called a sedan chair after all. It was too late to worry about that now. Kari leaned against a tree, examining the teapot. Her breathing was heavy and fast. She was exhausted after only having walked such a short way.

The teapot's elegant design juxtaposed the deadly poison it had contained. Izumi had known what she was doing. After all, she had managed to sneak her poison past Ronin. She had put on a convincing charade. It was as if she had done it before. After a few minutes, Kari finally caught her breath and headed off to meet with Baoshun.

Baoshun sat with Izumi in his study. Kari suppressed her anger at seeing the poisoner sitting with the emperor as if she hadn't tried killing her the night before, but Kari couldn't afford to let her emotions get the best of her. At least Jiaorong was nowhere to be seen. She wasn't interested in seeing him.

"My lord," Kari said, approaching Baoshun. Izumi gawked at her in wild disbelief.

"Hikari, what a pleasure to see you. I am glad you are feeling well enough to walk about. You had us all worried for you," he said.

"My injuries are doing much better. Thank you, my lord. I wish I were here to exchange pleasantries, but that is not the case." Izumi watched Kari with wide eyes, but she remained silent. They both knew the consequences of what was to come if Kari revealed Izumi's plot and Baoshun believed Kari. There was no going back. It was exactly what Kari had come here to do.

"What's wrong?" Baoshun tilted his head as he examined her.

Why was Kari hesitating? Izumi had tried to kill Kari. She'd nearly succeeded. If Kari didn't deal with this situation now, she might not survive the next time. "Lady Izumi made an attempt on my life. Last night, she tried to poison me."

"That cannot be," Baoshun replied.

"I did no such thing." Izumi jumped up to confront her. Rage flared inside Kari like an out-of-control fire at Izumi's denial. "If you were poisoned, then how are you still alive? If you were poisoned, then how do you know it wasn't the traitors who had already made an attempt on your life?"

"She brought me tea that was laced with Nisidu poison," Kari said, handing the teapot to Baoshun. Izumi would pay for her ploy. There was no more patience or mercy to be had. Kari had come this far. It was time to seal Izumi's fate and bring an end to her cruelty. Past time to ensure Kari's own survival through this horrible ordeal. "This was the teapot she served me with. I thought nothing of it at the time, but she drank none of the tea herself, which leads me to believe she knew it was laced with poison. I know it is difficult to grasp, but I guarantee it's true. I'm sure a doctor could examine me and confirm my story. It was only by the favors of the gods I survived."

"This is an outrage," Baoshun shouted. He shot up, towering over his wife with a livid expression.

"My lord," Izumi spoke up. "I refuse to allow this girl into our household. She is a harpy, and she cannot be trusted."

"Hold your tongue, wench," Baoshun demanded. He placed a hand on her shoulder, forcing her to sit. "Is that the reason you tried to murder her?"

Izumi bowed her head. He'd seen through her lies, so it seemed the woman's goal would be to simply appeal to his compassion for her. Ultimately, it didn't matter what he did to her, so long as she was no longer a threat to Kari.

"I will not be disgraced within these halls. I demand what has been promised me."

"My lord," Izumi started. She grabbed his hands. "My husband, if you have any love left for me, you cannot take this girl's side."

"I have *no* love left for you," Baoshun said coldly. He pulled away from her grip. "Hikari, return to your house. The guards will be there shortly to pack your things. You will be moving into this house. Clearly, the safest place for you is in these halls."

"Yes, my lord," Kari meekly said. She would hardly call living with her oppressors "safe," but it might make things easier for driving the brothers apart. Still, the thought of living with them sent shivers down her spine, but it did bring her one step closer to her goal. She would replace Izumi in Baoshun's heart, and she would use that to bring about his downfall.

She left Baoshun and Izumi to head to her house. Her strength was slowly returning to her, courtesy of her anger.

However, she still called for a servant to bring her a chair. She didn't want to risk collapsing on the walk back.

It didn't take long for the guards to clear out her house. They were probably getting annoyed at having to move her around so often. She would miss her house. In all the palace, it was the one place she'd felt safe, and now she would have to leave it behind to live with the emperors in their nightmare-filled mansion.

Then there was Ina. The guards gathered her possessions as well. There was no doubt returning to the mansion would be a disaster for her.

"We shouldn't be moving there," Ina said. "If Jiaorong sees me again, he might have a change of heart and kill me."

"Then perhaps you should stay here." Ronin suddenly appeared from behind them. Ina screamed, then placed her hand on her heart. He was like a phantom, just appearing out of sight.

"Where did you come from?" Kari asked.

"Window." Ronin pointed to the nearby open window. "If I were you, I would just stay here. You know it's vacant now, so you shouldn't have to worry about being discovered. At least for some time. Besides, I don't think Kari will send the guards out looking for you."

"That's not a bad idea," Kari agreed. "We could still spend time together throughout the day, and you could avoid the emperors."

"But that won't help you," Ina interjected. Her expression of concern was appreciated, but Kari didn't want to put her friend in harm's way.

"I'll be safe enough," Kari said. She hoped she was right. With Baoshun dealing with Izumi, she should be safe from any threats on her life. Now all she would have to deal with was avoiding the emperors' bedchambers.

"Good, since that's settled, I have received permission to escort you to the Mitokhan, the home of the Kitsuno Kai," Ronin said. "There you can speak with Master Okita about the traitors who attacked you and other matters surrounding that event."

Kari nodded. It was time for them to solidify their alliances, to move forward with their plans. "I'm ready."

The Mitokhan was located between the outer and inner walls of the palace. The headquarters of the Kitsuno Kai was where they lived and trained. It was a den of wolves, a place for the most ruthless and feared swordsmen in the empire to perfect their craft of death.

The Mitokhan itself was a massive building with a large dojo comprising the bulk of the bottom floor. Kitsuno Kai trained and sparred night and day. They were clearly mentally deranged since they used live blades in their sparring sessions. It was a testament to their skill and mastery of their weapons that they could be so precise as to not wound or kill each other in their training sessions. The soft blues decorating the dojo contrasted with the crimson red of the empire, a reminder they saw themselves as different, as separate to the throne.

Ronin took Kari into a back room filled with a sizeable rectangular table, a strategy room for their leaders.

"We'll wait here," Ronin said. "Master Okita will join us shortly."

Ronin paced around the room with his arms folded behind his back as they waited. Kari wanted to know more about him. Supposedly, this was her brother. A brother she had never met, and she hadn't even known about. Mother never mentioned him, but, then again, all Kari had known while growing up was where her father was from. Kari hadn't even learned his name until she had read the letter her mother wrote her when she'd been exiled.

Her mother had trusted them. She had lived with them for some time, evidently, and even trusted them enough to share Shagin's most closely guarded secrets. She must have trained Ronin for him to have some degree of energy manipulation. Her mother had loved them at one point, that much was clear, but why hadn't she mentioned them?

"What was Father like?" Kari asked. It wasn't necessarily the question she wanted to ask in the moment, but it was a start to learn more about her brother.

"What was he like?" Ronin licked his lips as he thought. "He was a general with a short patience for nonsense. He traveled a lot, even after Eanna left with you. He would travel with the army and leave me in the care of our servants, but he would always return with sweets and gifts from his travels. He was a good father."

"Did they love each other?" It was something she had feared growing up. Usually, early in adulthood, Shagin would go on pilgrimage in search of a mate. The goal was not to find love, but to find survival for their people by returning home and giving birth to a Shagin daughter. It wasn't unusual for Shagin to undergo multiple pilgrimages, but the intention was always the same—to become pregnant and return home. Kari had feared the time when she would be expected to go on her pilgrimage, if such a thing had ever been allowed again. She hadn't understood how she'd been expected to procreate without actually caring for her partner, but then there was her mother, who must have had the same fear. Her mother had stayed with her lover for some time. Had it truly been love?

"I suppose. Judging by your initial shock of our familial bonds, I take it Eanna did not speak of us."

"No, she didn't." If she had loved them, why hadn't she?

"It's funny." Ronin collapsed into a chair. He leaned back, letting his hand drape over the top. "My mother died when I was born, so Eanna was the only mother I ever knew. She would enthrall me with stories of Shagin, and I worshipped them. I wasn't born with the name Ronin. When I came of age, I ran away from home to undertake my own personal trial. That's when I realized I didn't belong anywhere. Eanna abandoned me, the same way I had abandoned my mother and the heritage she left for me."

"I'm so sorry." Kari couldn't believe it. To her, the man before her was death personified, yet deep beneath the surface, he was a child longing for the love of a mother he could never have, clinging to whatever scraps he could find. In a way, he mirrored her. She had spent her childhood fascinated by the culture of her father, a man she would never know.

An old, grizzled man with stringy grey hair entered the room, shutting the door behind him. "So, this is the young lady I've heard so much about."

"Master Okita." Ronin stood from his chair, then bowed toward the old veteran. "Allow me to introduce you to Kari."

Okita bowed his head in respect to her, and she returned the gesture. "It is a pleasure to make your acquaintance."

"Likewise." They all took their seat around the table.

"I do hope you are worth the sacrifice we have paid," Okita said. "Ronin told me the true nature of the events that led to the death of three of our own, but I believe it was necessary to protect you. The less people who know you are Shagin, the better."

Kari's heart jumped in her chest. She glared at Ronin. He had betrayed her. Did he not understand the severity of her secret or did he simply not care?

Ronin shrugged. "He is my master. We can trust him. After all, you told the resistance leaders of your true nature to ensure their cooperation, I required the same level of proof to provide to my master."

This was his way of making a point. He was teaching her a lesson for divulging her secrets to Shenrong and Yamato.

"Take a moment to consider what you are asking of us," Okita said, trying to reassure her. "You want us to follow you in a quest that may lead to our deaths and throw the empire into chaos. I required some assurance you would be able to succeed, before I could commit my order to your cause."

"I understand." Kari rubbed her brow. "I was just taken aback is all."

"Good, then we may continue," Okita said, folding his hands together. "Let us not dally around the issue. Why should the Kitsuno Kai join in your crusade? What benefit would we reap? Our forces are dedicated to maintaining order and peace in the empire whereas your plan would disrupt that order and could lead to the suffering of innocents. Why should we not stop you?"

She had expected an audition, to have to convince him to join them, but not to have to convince him to not fight against them. It didn't matter, her argument would be the same either way.

"I remember reading stories of the Kitsuno Kai," Kari started. "Ever since your founding, there have been stories of your deeds. Every time, the stories are the same—the Kitsuno Kai are ruthless and will slaughter any who oppose them, but there is more to the stories. You prevented a rebel fire attack from burning the city, you've provided shelter and protection for the poor during times of famine and war. The Kitsuno Kai protect the people of Xiang. Those living in Valceem can sleep at peace knowing the Kitsuno Kai are in the city and will not stop protecting them."

"Yes, these are things I already know," Okita interrupted. "But keep in mind, your plan will put those people at risk."

"If you truly believed I was a greater threat to the people than the Tian, I don't think we would be having this conversation." She hoped she was right. He knew she was Shagin, and he still agreed to meet with her. Ronin must have already laid the groundwork for their conversation today for him to ignore the propaganda of the Guardian and not see her as a monster, set out to destroy the world. Okita trusted and respected Ronin to even listen to him knowing he killed three of his own men. Okita knew the truth, she wasn't here to convince him of that, but to relieve his hesitations and doubts for going to war against the throne. "I know you've seen it. The empire is in disarray. Soon, the land will fall into chaos as hunger spreads. You know this to be true."

"What I know is irrelevant," Okita said. "It is true the empire is weak and faltering, at a time when it needs to be strong. War with Adgul looms like a vulture circling ahead. What reassurances do you have this coup will not impact the people?"

"I don't think I can guarantee that," Kari said honestly. "I believe it won't, but I have no evidence to provide to support that. What I can guarantee is the people's suffering will only worsen under the Tian, but if you join with me, we can give them hope."

Okita stroked his beard. "I believe I have heard all I need to hear. Thank you for meeting with me."

That was it? He had made his decision after such a short conversation? Kari stood, then bowed to the master. "Then you will join me?"

"I am uncertain," Okita said. "But I will not stop you."

"Master." Ronin clasped his hands together as he pleaded. "We could desperately use your sword in this endeavor. Fights like this are the reason we exist."

"Go with her." Okita extended his hand toward Kari. "Aid her as best as you can. I will think through your proposal. If I deem revolution is necessary, I will join you in your quest."

Kari and Ronin departed from Mitokhan, returning to the palace. "It wasn't a no," Ronin said reassuringly.

"It's something for now at least," Kari agreed. At least the Kitsuno Kai wouldn't be actively trying to stop them, despite knowing of their plan. That meant Okita agreed with their actions even if he was still hesitant to join.

CHAPTER EIGHTEEN

WHEN THEY LEFT THE Mitokhan, Ronin escorted Kari to her house before departing. "I have to check on a few things," he said. "I won't be long."

Wooden boxes filled the main room of her house. The servants had finished packing her belongings, but they hadn't begun to relocate them yet.

"How did it go?" Ina asked.

Kari shook her head. "I don't know." She had to be careful with what she said. There was no telling if anyone were in earshot, and she couldn't risk speaking openly about their ploys.

Baoshun appeared in her doorway, flanked by several servants. He looked at the wooden boxes, motioning for the servants to get to work.

"They will move your things," he said. He extended a hand for Kari to take. "But first, I want to show you something."

Baoshun and Kari boarded a sedan chair draped in red silk. They were carried through the palace walls to the Hall of Heaven and Earth. Kari gasped. She saw it before he even pointed it out to her. Izumi's body had been tied to a cross around the statue of Valceem. Her neck was purple, a sign she had been strangled.

"This is for you," Baoshun said, pointing to Izumi's corpse. "Now we can be together forever. Isn't that great?"

She tried to fight the emotions, covering her sorrow-filled eyes as tears poured down her face.

"What's wrong? I thought you'd be happy."

"I am," Kari lied, wiping her eyes. "These are tears of joy."

"I'm sorry," she whispered. "I'm so sorry."

She had known Izumi would be killed if Baoshun believed Kari's story, but seeing the woman's body made it real. Kari had wanted it at the time. Another victim had died due to her. Izumi tried to kill her, that was certain, and Kari had to deal with her or face the possibility of another attempt on her life. But was this justice or vengeance? It was rage and hatred that had fueled her decision, not a desire for balance.

It was done, and there was no going back on the decision now. Izumi was dead, Kari was alive, and she was glad.

"Come on," Baoshun said, taking hold of Kari's arm. "Let's go home."

Home. The word made her sick. Her home was now with the very people she was opposing, and if she succeeded, they would die, too—not that they didn't deserve it. Death was truly all she was good for, the only thing she could bring about.

The servants were busy moving Kari's belongings into the emperors' mansion when they returned to the emperors' residence.

"All of Izumi's belongings are yours," Baoshun declared. "You may go through them and dispose of anything that does not suit you."

Kari's stomach turned. "Thank you, my lord."

The door to Jiaorong's bedchamber slid open. "Off you go. I had my fill of you last night," Jiaorong told an attendant as they entered the main hall. He paused as he spotted Kari. His eyes dropped to the floor, seeming almost shamed. Kari averted her gaze as well. The very sight of him made her already weak stomach wretch. "Return to Guanwa Hall."

The attendant bid them a farewell before being escorted away by a guard.

"Brother," Baoshun said. "I would like you to meet my wife-to-be."

Kari's heart skipped a beat. When had this been decided?

"I must thank you, brother, for giving her to me. She is by far my favorite. With her, I have no need for the harem. If you like, after our wedding, you can have my attendants."

"She must be good in bed." A crooked smile stretched across Jiaorong's face.

"Um, well, actually we have not consecrated our union yet, but we will tonight."

"What a shame... she looks like she would be fun."

Kari was sure the vomit was about to return.

Baoshun's face reddened as he grew flustered. "If you'll excuse me, brother, I have to make preparations for our wedding."

And with that, Baoshun stormed off, leaving Kari alone with Jiaorong.

"So, you and my brother are to be married?"

Now was her chance.

"My lord," Kari said, throwing her arms around Jiaorong. His face lightened, his eyes gleamed, and his lips curled into a smile at her embrace. "You must save me. Take me back into your care. I believe he knows about us and our eternal bond. That is why he has moved me in with you and why he is forcing me to marry him. I have no desire to be with him. Only you, my lord."

"You know I cannot intervene," Jiaorong replied. "I would dare not go against the mandate of heaven and steal you from my brother."

"There is no need for you to steal me. Lord Baoshun has already promised you his entire house."

"Only after you are wed, and that won't include you."

Kari stared up at Jiaorong. "You can petition your brother for an early release. After all, you gave him one of your attendants, and another one of yours plotted with him to transgress against you. If you bring up these points, I'm sure he will grant you this gift."

Jiaorong shook his head. "He might, but recent events have made me question his loyalty. I believe he would send me someone out of spite, but even if he granted my request, he would not willingly part with you."

Kari couldn't contain her joy. They were already questioning each other. Her plan was working. "Request a new attendant from him and let him send the girl of his choosing. If you have him pick from the Imperial portraits, he would not be able to recognize me."

"Why is that?"

"Take a look." Kari pointed to the shelf of portrait scrolls on the nearby wall.

Jiaorong took out the scrolls, opening them until he found Kari's. He smiled upon seeing it. "How did your portrait turn out so hideous?"

"I refused to bribe the artist." Kari smiled as she looked at the mole that was added under her eye. It seemed the artist was right after all. He had held her future in a brush stroke. "You should take my portrait to Lord Baoshun, along with that of four other women. Make sure they are beautifully drawn. Cover the names on the back, then let him choose which one to send. If you are correct, and he chooses the least appealing portrait, he will send me to you. Then he could not fault you for my transfer."

"That is clever," Jiaorong said. "Very well, I shall speak with him at once."

"My lord," Kari interjected. "That woman you were with last night, does she mean anything to you?"

"Compared to you, she is a dying blossom."

"Excuse my impertinence, but then why spend the night with her?"

"You were injured and unavailable. I did not wish to disturb the rest you needed."

Kari bowed her head toward the emperor. This was the opportunity she needed to finally save Suying. "My beloved, you could never disturb me, but I must wonder, I desire nothing more but to spend my life with you. Do you not want the same?"

"I do, very much so. And I will let nothing stand in the way of that."

"Except for the attendants." Kari cut her eyes at Jiaorong.

"What would you have me do? Release them all? Every emperor since the Jine Dynasty has always had a harem. I cannot break tradition."

"My beloved, will you let tradition rule you?"

"No," Jiaorong said. He straightened his back. "I am the emperor, and I will do what I please."

Jiaorong left to find Baoshun, leaving Kari to settle into her new room. She laughed. Her plan was working better than expected.

Kari lounged in a cushioned chair. She had no desire to rummage through Izumi's belongings. It didn't feel right to do so after everything that had transpired. Her eyes flicked to a decorated ivory box that was placed on a nearby shelf. Its intricate designs beckoned to her, and she couldn't resist opening it. The box was filled with letters and poems

from Baoshun to Izumi back before he became the emper-
or. Her hands trembled as she read them.

My dearest love,

It has been a fortnight since I last saw your glimmering smile. The current assignment from the emperor has dragged on far too long. I fear at this rate, I will not return for another month. Brother, in his boorish ways, has been successful in finding ways to motivate the prefect. Still, fear will only get us so far, and I believe he lacks the tact to ensure any long-term change.

Brother believes we are owed greater positions for our work, and I believe he will petition the emperor for a promotion for the two of us. His military actions certainly warrant a higher rank, though I don't know the likelihood of him being made a Tiger General. I am already a chancellor. I do not know what position could even be given to me. Though I do not desire more power, I would like to be able to stay with you in the city without having to constantly travel.

I desire nothing more than to be back by your side. When we are together, my world is complete. The palace, in all of its glory, is the only place fitting for someone as radiant as you. But with you by my side, I do not pine for the palace. I do not envy the emperor or his riches. If given a harem of a hundred women, I would still choose you every time.

Stay safe, and I will see you upon my return. I will write again when I know when that will be.

Love forever,

Baoshun

Kari couldn't help but feel sad for her. Izumi had genuinely loved him, yet he'd continually betrayed her love until death. His love for her must not have exceeded the hundreds of women within Guanwa Hall.

Kari tossed the letter into the box. Closing her eyes, she covered her face with her hand. This was never ending. Every day was another challenge, another obstacle to overcome. What was she becoming? She was a songstress, but that had seemed so long ago. Now she was a manipulator, a conspirator, and soon-to-be bride. She hated every moment of it. All she wanted to do was to return to her old life, to be the songstress in the teahouse, but that person was gone. She could never return to that life, not now.

"It looks like you're going back to Jiaorong," Cai Ren said, breaking her thoughts as he entered the room. "I don't know what you did, but I can bet Baoshun will be furious. He just announced his betrothal to you to the court. He'll be made the fool when he then announces your reassignment to Jiaorong. But what happens when Baoshun goes to present you to him? Do you think he'll just let you go that easily?"

"That's the idea," Kari said. "It ultimately doesn't matter. Either way, tensions will greatly increase between them. Of course, if he publicly makes the announcement, I don't see him going back on his word."

"And this has nothing to do with your impending marriage?"

"It might have a little." Kari smiled.

"Come with me. I am to bring the selected attendant to court to be presented to Lord Jiaorong."

Once they had made it to court, Cai Ren motioned for Kari to stand away from him so as to not tip off Baoshun as to who he had selected too early. Approaching Baoshun, he whispered something into his ear. Baoshun clapped his hands together as he stood.

"Brother," Baoshun announced to the great hall. "After careful consideration, I have found a new attendant who will serve you faithfully."

Baoshun presented the portrait of Kari for evidence to the chancellors before handing it to Jiaorong. He motioned for Cai Ren to summon his chosen tribute. Cai Ren waved Kari over. Trying to hide her glee, she proceeded up to the royal thrones.

"Cai Ren, where is my tribute?" Baoshun demanded, looking nervous. "Do not keep us waiting."

"I'm not, my lord," Cai Ren said. "This is she."

"What are you talking about?" Baoshun demanded.

"Is there a problem, brother?" Jiaorong asked, a wicked grin on his face.

"Of course not, but this is not the girl I selected."

"I'm afraid it is, my lord," Cai Ren said. "If you do not believe me, check the name on the back of the portrait."

Baoshun snatched the portrait from Jiaorong, then turned it over.

"What is the meaning of this?" he shouted.

"My lord," Kari said. "The artist demanded I pay a bribe to him. When I refused, he intentionally painted the portrait to mislead you."

The anger showed on Baoshun's reddening face. "Take her back and bring me another."

"Are you going back on your word?" Jiaorong jumped to his feet to face his brother.

"Of course not, but you cannot have this one. She is betrothed to me."

"Have the bridal gifts been exchanged? I don't understand, brother. I graciously offered her to you before this very court, and I received nothing in return. And now you promise her to me, then insist she is to remain with you. Is this your way to humiliate me before the court? To degrade me, your own brother? Did you not tell me that you had not joined with her? What is so special about this girl that you would betray your blood, betray your throne, to have her?"

Baoshun remained silent.

Jiaorong faced the assembly. "Clearly the gods desire she and I be together. Who are we to deny the gods?"

"Lord Baoshun," Cai Ren said. "If I may, appeasing your brother and maintaining your standing is perhaps more important than a single attendant. The strength of your reign depends on your union."

"Fine." Baoshun huffed, gritting his teeth. "I will yield her to you, but I demand all artists within the city to be brought to the palace and executed."

Kari wanted to protest. She had never intended for anyone to be killed due to her plan, but Cai Ren must have sensed her intention because he placed a hand on her shoulder. He shook his head as if to tell her to remain quiet.

Jiaorong bellowed, "Very well, brother. Cai Ren, escort Lady Hikari to my manor and ensure she is settled in appropriately. She is to be given the rank of noble lady and all honors associated with the title."

Cai Ren bowed to the emperors before walking over to Kari. He took her by the hand, then led her out of the throne room. Baoshun's fiery stare followed them as they exited.

They left the Hall of Heaven and Earth before heading for the emperors' mansion. "Well done," Cai Ren said. "They are publicly fighting. It appears your plan is coming to fruition. We are just about ready then."

Kari nodded. She wanted nothing more than for this nightmare to be over. She hated playing the seductress. Hated being paraded in front of the hordes of ministers and nobles as a prized possession of the emperors. Worst of all, Suying had noticed the change in Kari and had seen her intentions to play both emperors. Surely, Suying wasn't the only one. Kari was reinforcing Shagin stereotypes in the minds of all who knew her plans.

"My child, give some time for these old bones to catch up," an elderly woman cried out, following closely behind Kari and Cai Ren.

"I'm sorry, who are you?" Kari turned toward the woman. Grunting, Cai Ren buried his face in his hands.

The old woman smiled, waving off the offense. "It is all right. We have not yet met. You must excuse my sons' bickering in the court. They are quite taken with you, and I can see why."

Her sons? Jiaorong and Baoshun? This was the Empress Dowager Xiaoxianhua.

Kari threw her head down, bowing toward the empress dowager. "My lady, I apologize. I meant no disrespect."

"I have heard so much about you, yet we have not had a chance to chat." Xiaoxianhua lifted Kari's head with a gentle touch of her hand. "Your eyes really *are* something."

Kari's face reddened as she tried to look away.

"I am sorry my sons have dragged you into their petty squabbles. They have grown into fine men, saviors of our land, but they are still boys at heart."

"No, it is I who should apologize."

Cai Ren placed a hand on Kari's shoulder, shooting her a look out of the corner of his eyes.

"I had heard Baoshun was seeking your hand to replace Izumi as his empress consort. Now that you have returned to Jiaorong's side, I am afraid Baoshun will be without a wife. Losing Izumi is a shame, but I am forever indebted to you for discovering the plot to harm my boys and risking your life to protect them. I believe Jiaorong intends to marry you, and he has never shown such commitment. Either way, you will make one of my sons a fine wife. I just wish the gods had brought us two of you."

"You speak so delicately about your sons." Kari shook her head in confusion.

"You mean to say how can I still see them as boys? They have been stern and harsh, but such is necessary to secure the mandate of heaven. A strong leader is needed to restore balance and peace to the land. Before we came to the palace, I saw the state of our nation. It was in tatters. Now look around and see what my sons have done."

"Have you been out of the palace much?" There was a stark contrast between the palace dream and the real world outside of Koryon. It was plain for anyone to see once they stepped outside of the red-and-gold walls.

"Not since my sons' coronation, but I have heard of the tremendous accomplishments they have achieved. Surely you, being relatively fresh from the outside world, have seen these accomplishments for yourself."

"Oh yes, they've been a roaring success." Cai Ren pinched Kari's arm. "I'm afraid I must get the young lady settled in before nightfall."

"We have time yet." Xiaoxianhua held up a hand. "Have you met any of your children?"

"My children?" Kari's heart sank in her chest. She wrapped her arms around her stomach as the world spun around her. Cai Ren squeezed her shoulder, anchoring her in place.

"Without an empress consort, a noble lady is the mother of the emperor's children. My, my, what are they teaching the selected ladies at the auditions? At any rate, would you care to meet them?"

"She's not feeling well." Cai Ren seized Kari's hand, starting her on their path.

"I'm sorry, my lady," Kari whispered. "My injuries have taken their toll on my body."

"Of course, another time then, when you are well."

Cai Ren left Kari at the emperors' mansion without so much as another word. He merely scowled at her before leaving. Even with Cai Ren's quick departure, she didn't have much time to enjoy her solitude before Jiaorong returned.

He pulled into his bedchamber, insisting they celebrate their victory by laying together despite the fact Kari was still recovering from both her wounds and from being poisoned. Kari relented. Any resistance now would only be counterproductive.

Every time he touched her, it was like he was slowly ripping a piece of her away. Kari couldn't keep this up. She would rather die than to endure him even one more time.

When he was done, he rolled off her and pulled her close to him. She tried to inch away, but when she did, he would merely pull her closer. She was trapped with her only option to wait until he was asleep.

She had more work to do. After witnessing the animosity between the brothers in court, she couldn't waste this opportunity to seal their jealousy and resentment of each other. She needed to see Baoshun.

Once Jiaorong had fallen asleep, Kari slowly eased out of his bed and crept to Baoshun's bedchamber. She slid his door open, then stepped inside.

"What are you doing here?" Baoshun asked as she entered his room. He rose from his bed to approach her. "You don't belong to me. You are my brother's, and as evident from the sounds through the wall, he has already made you his."

The reminder of her time with her rapist tore at her very core, and a tear slid down Kari's face.

"What's wrong?" Baoshun asked.

"I'm sorry, my lord," she said. "Just trying to forget."

"What is so horrible you want to forget?" he asked, embracing her in his arms.

"My time with your brother," Kari said flatly. She laid her head against his chest. "He was aware of my feelings for you, and he made me pay for them. He forced himself upon me. His violent temper knows no bounds. He even tried to brand me when we first met."

"That fiend!" His grip on her shoulders tightened.

"He's jealous of you." Kari pulled away from his tight grip. "He never wanted me to return to you. It's why he fought so hard to keep me."

"That explains the portrait and why he was so adamant about taking you," he said, stroking his chin. "Damn it! How could he betray me like that?"

"Please, my lord," Kari begged, staring into his eyes. "I love you. Please save me."

"Don't worry, my love," Baoshun said. He gazed into her emerald eyes, then clasped her hands in his. "I will see that he pays for his crimes. For now, you should return to him. We don't want him to know we are plotting behind his back."

Kari nodded, standing on tiptoe to kiss him on the cheek. It made her sick. She made herself sick. But it was necessary.

She bowed to him and stepped out of the bedchamber, closing the door as quietly as she could. Slowly, she made her way back to Jiaorong's bedchamber. She slid open Jiaorong's door, then crept inside.

Her heart jumped, her eyes growing wide. Jiaorong stood before her with his dao drawn.

"You returned to his side." Jiaorong pointed his sword at Kari. His gravelly voice shook. "Why?"

Kari hesitated, very carefully trying to think of her next words. "It was not by choice, I assure you. Your brother is trying to reclaim me. He wants me to betray you and return to him."

"And yet, you did."

"No, my beloved. I met with him only so I could learn what he is planning."

"Which is?" He did not lower the point of his blade, but his face softened as she explained.

"I do not know. He would not tell me. I do know he is considering a coup and framing you for abuse against me. I believe he was the one who orchestrated my abduction—the one who sent Lady Izumi to poison me, though she failed and was subsequently killed for that failure. I believe he will make another attempt at my life in order to subvert power from you."

"Why didn't you come to me with this before?" He lowered his sword, then reached out toward her with his free hand.

"I did not have evidence against him. My love, I would dare not commit heresy against the throne. While I still do not have evidence to support my accusations, the Kitsuno Kai who attacked me had ties to Lord Baoshun, his wife tried to have me killed, and, when he discovered I was still alive, he killed her for failing. He will try to kill me again to get to you." Kari took his hand, placing it against her cheek. "Please, my beloved. I love you. Please save me."

"If what you're saying is true, then we can take no chances," Jiaorong said. After he sheathed his sword, he placed a gentle kiss on Kari's forehead. "Come with me. We will sleep in the safety of the Hall of Heaven and Earth tonight."

CHAPTER NINETEEN

"I can't believe this is happening," Kari said. Kari and Ina stood outside Guanwa Hall, watching in disbelief as the guards helped the newly freed women gather up their belongings and load them into carriages to be taken back to the city. "We did it."

"Not yet." Ina shook her head. "This is only one house. There are still two more. Even though Baoshun has also agreed to release his attendants, now that your wedding has been called off, I'm unsure if that will ever happen. As for those being dismissed, I wonder where they will go."

Kari's smile faded. "But we have done something worth celebrating. Finally, we're seeing our work pay off." There was no harm reveling in their first victory. Besides, Suying would now be safe. Kari would no longer have to worry about her sister being called to be with Jiaorong. It was over for her.

Kari had accomplished what she set out to do. It was bittersweet, however. Many people had died to get here, and they died due to her actions. Their deaths would forever be with her. There was no escaping that, and Kari didn't want to escape from it. The truth was, everyone who'd died, they'd died because of her. Their memories would live on with Kari, and she would find a way to honor them.

"Kari," Suying said, approaching from behind.

"Isn't this great, Suying?" Kari proclaimed.

"Great? I refuse to go back to what I was. Your delusion has ruined all our lives," Suying screamed, pointing a finger at Kari.

"I don't know what you mean." Kari feigned ignorance.

"Don't play games with me. We both know you've wanted this since day one. Now look at what is happening! I have worked my whole life to get to this point, and I'm not having some spoiled girl take away what is rightfully mine. You're not even from here. Look at all these women. How many of them have bled and clawed their way to get to where we're at?"

"And how many were taken against their will?" Kari responded with fire in her eyes. She no longer cared about being harsh with Suying. The world was harsh. "How many have spent years being raped while a select few grew in power? Can't you see I did this for you, to protect you?"

Suying spat in Kari's face. Grimacing, she wiped the spittle away. How could her sister do such a thing?

"You don't know what you're talking about." Suying balled up her fists like a petulant child throwing a tantrum. "You don't know what it's like to be alone on the streets with no money, not knowing if you'll ever eat again."

"I'm sorry Suying. The price was too high." Kari wiped her hands on her skirt before turning to walk away. There was nothing more for them to say to each other. Suying was too far gone to be reached through reason, at least for now. Sisters fought. But when tempers cooled, they reconciled as well.

"I know what you're planning. Change it back or gods help me, I will expose you. I will tell them what you are, and they will have your head on a platter!"

Kari froze. What had Suying said? Her own sister was threatening to end her life? Kari took a deep breath and continued walking. "I haven't the faintest idea what you're talking about. Unless you have proof, I wouldn't make false allegations against a noble lady."

Suying grabbed Ina from behind, wrapping her arm around her throat, a dagger pressed firmly against her back. "Don't you walk away from me. I will kill her. This is your last chance, Kari. Go ahead and tell the entire world what you are. Fix this! Or I swear to the gods, I will put a knife in her back."

Kari turned, gaping at Suying. What had she become? Was this the matron's doing or hers? Suying wouldn't do this. Not the sweet Suying she knew.

The guards circled the area with their swords drawn. They shouted commands to Suying, but neither she nor Kari listened. They were too focused on each other.

"She's Shagin," Suying screamed to the guards, but they did not move. They were focused entirely on Suying. "Go ahead, tell them. Tell them what you are!"

"She's delusional and crazy," Ina cried. She tried to pull away, but Suying just dug the dagger deeper into her flesh as she tightened her grip.

Kari loved Suying. She would do anything for her, but there was nothing she could do now. This had grown far larger than either of them. People depended on Kari succeeding, and people had died so she could.

Ina screamed as Suying dug the blade into her back. "We're waiting. Tell everyone the truth. Tell them you're Shagin."

A crowd of women and guards had gathered around. The guards all stood with their swords ready, waiting for an opportunity to strike. There was no telling if anyone believed Suying, or if they thought she was just throwing out wild accusations to get her way. It wouldn't be the first time in history someone had ever claimed a rival was Shagin just to have them eliminated.

Tears fell down Kari's face as she realized the truth. Someone was going to die today. She had to stop this. She had to confess, only then would Suying release Ina.

Ina shook her head.

"Suying, I love you. I..."

"No," Ina screamed, grabbing ahold of Suying's wrist and driving the dagger deep into her own back. Ina immediately collapsed to the ground, the knife protruding from her. Suying's mouth dropped as she stared at Ina.

"No, wait," Kari screamed as the guards rushed forward with their swords. "I'm sorry, Suying." Kari closed her eyes as the guards descended upon Suying. For a moment, all Kari could hear were Suying's screams as the blades of the guards tore into her body... then, nothing but silence.

Kari dropped to her knees as tears flooded down her face. She sobbed as the guards carried Ina to the doctor and Suying to the undertaker. Kari had failed her sister. Suying was only a child. Her whole life had vanished in an instant. The body they carried away was cut and slashed until it didn't even resemble the child she was.

Kari didn't stop crying even as the guards helped her up and escorted her to the emperors' mansion. She couldn't do this anymore. She had sacrificed so much. How much more did she have left to give?

"What happened?" Ronin rushed toward Kari, then took her from the guards. He examined her for injuries before leading her inside.

"Where were you when I needed you?" Kari sobbed. Tears fell like rain from her face, dripping onto her blouse and skirt.

"I had important business to attend to. We are just ready." Ronin helped her sit. "What happened? Are you injured?"

"Suying confronted me. She tried to get me to confess to being Shagin. She stabbed Ina, then the guards killed her."

Kari buried her face in her hands. Why? Why did Suying have to die? Kari's whole body shook as she cried.

"That's unexpected," Ronin said. Kari glared at him. Ronin glanced around the room as if to find the appropriate response. "And... sad?"

He didn't have a heart.

"Look, there's no time to dwell on the past," Ronin said. The past? It had *just* happened. "We are almost ready, but first, you need to gather yourself. Our allies are here, and they've requested to speak with you."

Kari wiped away the tears, fighting to keep her body from spasming. "You shouldn't speak of these things here."

"Don't worry. We are alone. No one else is here. Now are you ready to end this?"

Kari nodded. She wanted everything to end, to go back to being a songstress, to a simpler life. Swallowing her sorrow, she pressed the image of Suying's body from her mind. "Are we really ready?"

"Almost. Our allies are lined up. The administrators Cai Ren spoke of are willing to hear us out, and I've already taken the liberty of talking to both."

"I'm sensing there is more to it," Kari said.

"They don't trust Cai Ren or me," Ronin said. "I think the only reason they are even willing to hear us out is because I infiltrated their inner circle and didn't kill everyone."

"What do we need to do to gain their trust?" They were fools to place their trust in her. Everyone who did died.

"You," Ronin said, smiling. "They want to meet with our leader before they'll join. I've arranged a meeting for you today."

"Wait, why am I the leader?" Kari said.

"Because you are," Ronin said in a matter-of-fact tone.

"I'm really not."

"You're the one who has brought us together, and you're the one who gives us hope. You're the one we turn to. Even that snake Cai Ren is taking orders from you. If you show these people your heart, they'll turn to you. They'll trust you just as much as I do." He was talking her up, trying to boost her confidence. She wasn't a leader, but if what they needed was motivation and hope, she could provide that.

"So, my role is more of an inspirational leader?"

Ronin nodded. "This will be the most important meeting of our coup. All of our allies will be there. Cai Ren's administrators, who might just be joining us to gain power, but we can work with that. They are undecided, but I'm sure after speaking with you, their hesitations will be resolved. Then there are the rebels led by Shenrong. With the rebels joining us, we have a rather large force on our side. And I've heard from Master Okita that the Kitsuno Kai will be joining the field on our side. All we have to do is have you meet with and astound them. Once we've done that, they'll be ready to mobilize at your command," Ronin said. The field? He spoke like it was a game.

"My command? I thought we just established I was just the inspirational leader? I'm no general," Kari protested.

He seemed insistent to push her to be the leader of their group. That might have been a vote of confidence on his part, or fear of what Cai Ren would do in the role.

"Leave that to me," Ronin said. "I'll manage your army and take care of the strategies, but if they are to truly respect you and fight for our cause, they need to believe you have the ability to command and lead them."

"My army," Kari repeated. The phrase seemed foreign rolling off her tongue. She'd never wanted an army, but an army meant the power of life and death was truly in her hands. People depended on her to succeed. No matter what happened, people would die. The thought made her sick to her stomach. "Just how many people do we have on our side?"

"There are three hundred Kitsuno Kai. The bulk of the order is ready to fight. Both administrators are sending around two hundred and fifty each. That's about all they can send without suspicion. The rebels make up the largest part of our numbers. They are contributing nearly twenty-four hundred men to our cause."

"That's about thirty-two hundred soldiers," Kari said. Thirty-two hundred people who were putting their trust in her. They would fight and die for her. It was maddening. Their leaders were volunteering their lives to her cause, but how many would willingly make the sacrifice on their own?

"The Kitsuno Kai should really count as three fighters each," Ronin said. "The emperors have approximately ten thousand soldiers in the palace and another forty thousand in the city. Our forces cannot engage with any hope to win; therefore, we need to rely on our ability to quickly take out the emperors. Hopefully, we can end the fight before the forces in the city are able to mobilize. The administrators will use their remaining numbers to help us maintain control after we've seized the capital. What about you? Are you ready?"

"I believe so," Kari said. "The emperors think they were betrayed by the other. Now is probably the best moment to make our move before they discover my ruse."

"I'll send word to our allies," Ronin said. "You'll need a speech."

"Why do I need a speech?" Kari asked.

"All great leaders give speeches to their men before asking them to put their lives on the line. It can be a great morale boost."

She didn't want to be the leader, not even a puppet leader put in place to boost morale. She wanted no one dying for or because of her. Too many people had already done that. Her hands were covered in their blood. How could humanity live like this?

Fighting, death, chaos.

Was this humanity's true nature, to be at constant war with itself? Nobody wanted to die, to have their life ended and their dreams cut short, but killing—was that easier than dying? To take a life, to end someone's dreams and future, was that what humanity desired?

Ronin seemed to have no hesitation with murder. In fact, Kari had met very few who did. The emperors killed to secure their power, and she had killed to threaten it. Even someone as sweet and young as Suying had no trouble drawing a knife to kill in order to protect what she held dear. She had died for that.

Kari had killed her for that.

There had to be more to life than to simply kill those who stood against them. The guards they would face in battle were no different from them. They had their own dreams and ambitions, their own families and friends, their own ideals and beliefs, and they would kill for those. They had their duty to protect the throne, and they would kill and be killed to fulfill their responsibilities and to defend their ideals.

She was expected to give a speech to motivate her side to fight harder and kill better. The truth was the speech was needed to end the violence before it began, to reason with both sides to find a better way to solve their differences. It was just a fantasy, though. The real world was not kind and reasonable. When ideals clash like lightning, chaos was the resulting thunder.

To protect the nation, to secure their freedom for future generations, the actions they were about to take were necessary. They had moved beyond the point of words. Only the edge of a blade could turn the tide of chaos and put an end to the tyranny of the Tian.

Tomorrow, countless dreams would end.

Kari wiped the tears from her eyes as she stared at the ceiling. She didn't have much time to prepare.

The few short hours before the meeting flew by. Before she knew it, Ronin was escorting her into Cai Ren's mansion. Cai Ren sat at a rectangular table with five other men, three of whom Kari recognized. Shenrong and Yamato looked ready for action, as did Okita.

"Meet your generals," Ronin said, motioning to the men. "Master Okita and Shenrong you know. Then there's Administrator Yoon and Administrator Zhouren, who preside over some stuff. It's not important. Nobody really cares."

"I'll have you know I control the Sui Han Commandery," Yoon spoke out. Ronin just glared at the administrator, who gritted his teeth and averted his gaze.

"Thank you all for coming," Kari said, trying to guide the meeting away from the confrontation. "Lord Shenrong, Lord Yamato, I am delighted to see you again."

"This is no time for personal vendettas or petty squabbles," Yamato said. "You say you can finally end the tyranny of the Tian, then I will lend you my aid. I do not do this because of any admiration for you, but merely because I believe you possess the strength necessary to do what others have not." Shenrong nodded.

"That remains to be seen," Yoon added. His voice indicated he was clearly still agitated from the insult hurled at him by Ronin. "You are asking a lot from us. You want us to place our lives in your hands."

Kari was prepared to defend her position, but the best defense wouldn't come from her. She would have to turn to Okita for that. "Master Okita, what reason does the Kitsuno Kai have for challenging the throne?"

The old man sighed as he gathered his words. "It is quite simple, really. The Kitsuno Kai are not loyal to the throne or the ass that sits upon it. The Kitsuno Kai serve and protect the people of Xiang. Under the current regime, this nation has weakened, and, if our path isn't changed, we will falter and fall. When that happens, chaos will erupt anew, and the people will suffer. Action now is the only course available. If we wait any longer, there will not be an empire to save."

"We have all seen the oppression of the Tian." Kari stood, addressing the men. It was time to step up and be the leader Ronin was pushing for. "Master Okita is correct. The people of this nation cannot thrive in this atmosphere. The task we are about to undertake will forever change the course of history. Together, we can forge a new empire, a better empire. Our actions and sacrifices within the coming days will determine the fate of millions. We cannot fail them. We *won't* fail them. We will usher in a golden age for Xiang. With any revolution, someone has to take the first step, the hardest step, the step that requires the most courage and strength. Thank you for taking that step with me."

"Here, here," Zhouren cheered. At least one of the administrators was unfazed by Ronin's irreverence enough to understand the severity of their undertaking.

"I trust you have a plan to go with that bravado?" Yoon said. He might not have been fully past the insult, but he appeared to be onboard with what needed to be done.

"Make no mistake," Ronin said. She was glad he'd stepped in to answer Yoon's question. While she had a general idea of what they needed to do, she was no tactician. Kari wasn't really even a warrior. She wouldn't be the one fighting, and, for that, she was relieved, if not abashed, for having others kill and die for her. "This won't be easy. We are outnumbered three to one—and that's just counting the soldiers within the palace—but we have the advantage. We have Lady Kari, who has proven again and again that she can make the impossible *possible*."

Why was he holding her up as their bastion of hope? She understood his intentions to use her as a tool to motivate and inspire, but she wasn't anything other than a concubine. Whatever hope they placed in her would be false. She couldn't provide victory or even increase their chances of success. There was nothing she could do.

"We will kill them with borrowed knives." Ronin spread a map of the palace and its surrounding area on the table. "The palace is designed to be nearly impenetrable. That's our advantage. If we attack the front gate during the early morning hours before the sun is up, while the emperors are still asleep and the guards are changing shifts, we should be able to draw most soldiers away from the rear of the complex, leaving the Tian vulnerable."

"And just how do you plan on taking the front gate?" Shenrong asked.

Okita grunted as he leaned forward and slammed his hand on the map on top of the Mitokhan. "The Kitsuno Kai are already stationed inside the outer palace walls, and we are able to come and go as we please. We will have no problem securing the gate."

"But that still leaves the bulk of our forces outside the palace," Shenrong said, stroking his silvery beard.

Ronin pointed to the map. "The Kitsuno Kai will capture the two front gates. Once your men have made it through the second gate, we will reseal it and use its defenses against the onslaught of the army. Our forces will be surrounded and attacked on four sides. The soldiers inside the palace will attempt to retake the gate. They'll strike from both the rear and from the adjacent walls. The walls are narrow. Therefore, their numbers will be meaningless as they are forced into a bottleneck. The area around the front gate is designed to limit the number of troops able to enter the palace, it will work the same way for the soldiers who attack our rear, however, this will be the bulk of their attack.

"To counter these areas, Administrator Zhouren will defend from attacks on the western wall and Administrator Yoon will take the eastern wall. It is imperative your men hold those walls to keep archers from raining down on our men."

"Understood," Yoon said.

Kari's heart felt heavy. Their men were a shield to take the brunt of an attack. They would die, and she would simply sit in her room and hide until it was over.

"Master," Ronin continued, turning his attention to Okita. "I'll need you and the Kitsuno Kai to defend against the attack from the front."

"We'll tear out their spines," Okita replied.

Was this the way the world worked? The words sounded casual. Okita was proud of his statement. He was proud of the deaths they would cause. Was it all bravado or did he really enjoy carnage?

"What do I do?" Shenrong asked.

"It is vital you maintain a strong presence at the gate. As soon as the fighting starts, the remaining forces in the city will mobilize and attack. That's forty thousand additional soldiers. When they enter the fray, the odds drastically change. We'll be outnumbered fifteen to one. It is imperative they are held at bay. They will try to attack the gate. With it sealed, that should prove problematic, but that doesn't mean they can't break through. With enough time, they will. Your job is to keep that from happening as long as you can.

"They might also send naval forces from the north. Our bottlenecks should play to our advantage, but you'll need to reposition your troops accordingly in order to reinforce the other three units.

"While we are fighting for our lives, Cai Ren will provide intel and orders to the enemy. With any luck, he can slow down their reaction and disrupt their strategies, giving us more time to hold that gate."

"This sounds like a suicide mission," Zhouren said. It truly did. Kari had started this. Was she now sending those who trusted her to their deaths? "Your plan is to simply take the main gate and hold on for dear life. How can we expect to win against such odds?"

"Our goal is not to win by military might," Cai Ren said. "We will simply provide a distraction and an opportunity for the Tian to be attacked. If we attempted to attack the emperors, and failed to kill them immediately, we don't want to have to fight the two strongest warriors in the land and all of their guards, do we? Once they are dead, I will become the supreme commander of the military. My first order will be to stand down, which will end the battle."

"So, who will kill the emperors?" Okita asked as one might ask another to serve tea. Was this what battle does to people? Killing and death had become meaningless to them. This was how Ronin could murder his own men, how Okita could accept it. It was all necessary in their eyes. She didn't want any to die, but so long as the Tian were alive, people would suffer and perish under their rule. They needed to die. Would she die inside as well?

"That is where I will come in," Yamato added. A wicked grin spread across his face. "I will lead a squad against Baoshun and loose an arrow through his eye."

"It will behoove us to take them both out quickly," Ronin said. "The sooner they are killed, the sooner the battle can come to an end, and we wouldn't want one being notified of our attempts. Therefore, I will be the one to slay Jiaorong."

"Young lady," Okita said, the whole room focusing on Kari. "And what will you be doing while the men are out dying?"

It was a fair question. Her role was finished. Now others would fight and die on her behalf while she could avoid the carnage. She couldn't do that. The longer the fight went on, the more people would die, on both sides. If she could help, she would. "I can help assist Ronin and Yamato. I know the palace and the habits of the emperors."

"She will help indirectly, of course," Ronin added. He was trying to take her out of the fight. She was glad he wanted to protect her, but she couldn't hide now. "It is more important for her to remain safe throughout the fighting. She has risked enough already, and she still hasn't fully recovered from two attempts on her life."

"Very well," Okita said.

"Sounds like a decent plan," Yoon said.

"It will work," Ronin replied. "But it all hinges on misdirection and taking out the emperors quickly."

"We can do this. We can save Xiang," Kari said, rising. It was time to test out her speech. She wished it were a song, instead. She could do songs. "We stand upon the shoulders of giants. Empress Valceem stood against the tide of tyranny. She faced impossible odds, and she overcame them, and so will we. Like the legendary empress, we are forging a new chapter in history. We will save the people of this nation from tyranny and oppression. Future generations will sing songs about our triumph. Today, we are nothing more than visionaries, but tomorrow, we will be legends."

"Then we are in agreement?" Ronin asked.

"Yes," they all said in unison.

"Good. Then prepare your men for battle. Tomorrow, before the break of dawn, we go to war."

CHAPTER TWENTY

Kari couldn't sleep that night. She tossed and turned in her bed, her heart racing with anticipation. She sent Ina into the city for the night so she wouldn't be caught up in the fighting. Ina had argued the need to stay, but with her injury, she relented. At least one of them would be kept from the chaos.

Ina wanted this day to come more than anyone else, so much she was willing to give her life just to get there. Even though she was back on her feet already, she was still in bad shape.

How many more would be hurt in the ensuing battle?

There was no telling just how much damage would occur to the palace and its inhabitants. The thought of having thousands of people depending on her made Kari queasy. So many lives rode on her success. The fate of Xiang would be determined in a few hours.

She had managed to sneak away from the emperors' mansion and sleep in her house. It wasn't hers anymore. Her home was with the emperors. The thought made her weak. Ronin had suggested she sleep away from the emperors tonight. They would undoubtedly have questions about her whereabouts, but, if everything went according to plan, they would be dead before they could ask them.

Her job was mostly done. Ronin and Yamato would see the deaths of the emperors, not her. Still, when the fighting started, it would be her role to help locate the emperors and guide the assassins to them, if needed. For that, she required her rest, as much as she could get anyway, but despite how much she tried, she couldn't go to sleep. The more she tried, the more restless she became.

She was leading thousands to an unknown fate. So many people had died because of her, and her heart was heavy with their pain and loss. Many more would die and risk death for her and her cause.

A lot had happened to get her to this point. Every time she tried to help someone, every time she tried to do anything, someone died. Kyoko was the first. The poor girl was so frightened. Kari would never forget her face. Tama was next, killed for killing Kyoko. Izumi died after she tried to murder Kari. It was what Kari had wanted at the time, though now she wasn't so sure, but it happened regardless. All the artists in the city were executed because of her. She had no idea how many that was, but it didn't matter. Their deaths were hers to carry. Her scheme had killed them. *She* had killed them. Then there were the people she'd directly had a hand in their deaths, two guards and three Kitsuno Kai.

And there was Suying. Kari had wanted nothing more than to protect her. It was her goal from the beginning, and she had failed. Not even Ina was safe, having been whipped and stabbed for her.

Now thousands of people and the fate of an entire kingdom rested in Kari's hands. Like all of her other plans, people would die, and it would be her fault.

The sounds of whistles and men yelling pierced through the early morning silence. The allotted time had come faster than she'd expected. She quickly got dressed, then sheathed her swords within the sash around her waist. Kari opened her door, staring into the darkness. What future would the rising sun bring?

Kari sighed. Better to wait a few minutes before heading to the emperors' mansion. It would give the guards enough time to thin out.

The path to the mansion was just as nerve wrecking as ever before. Soldiers scurried around as they tried to ascertain the nature of the attack. The entire trek to the mansion was met with guards and servants running around trying to figure out what needed to be done to protect the palace. It was chaos.

The hallways of the mansion were empty. Kari entered the emperor's room, only to find it empty as well.

"Lady Hikari," a soldier called from behind her. "The palace is under attack. I've been instructed to escort you to safety. Lord Baoshun is awaiting your arrival at the gardens."

"Take me to him," Kari said. It was fortuitous the guard came upon her. With the current pandemonium, finding the emperors quickly would prove to be difficult and the faster they could find them, the faster the battle would be over.

Kari followed the soldier as he led her to the gardens. The noise from the battle at the gate echoed against the red walls. The distant sounds of screams and yells signaled the death and chaos that occurred at the front gate. Smoke rose over the tall buildings just as the rising sun shone on the golden roofs. The smell of burning flesh assaulted her nose.

Each scream pierced her heart. People were dying because of her. They were dying *for* her. How could a world of peace be made with bloodstained hands?

Baoshun stood amongst the flowers. He smiled when he saw her.

"I am so glad you are safe," he said. "Rebels have infiltrated the palace. They are attempting a coup."

"My lord, we should go somewhere safer." Kari slowly made her way to Baoshun. Yamato would have headed for the mansion. He would be waiting for him there. That was where she needed to get Baoshun to. "We are too exposed here."

Baoshun held out a hand for Kari to stop. "Where did you get those swords?"

"I had my bodyguard buy them for me," Kari said, gritting her teeth. She should have hidden them. Why hadn't she thought about that? She couldn't afford to raise his suspicions now. Any hesitation to trust her and their plan would be for naught.

"Is that why you're carrying them now?" Baoshun asked. "Do you not trust in the skills of my guards?"

"As you said, my lord, we are under attack," Kari said, inching toward him. "The last time there was a coup, everyone even remotely associated with the throne was hunted down and killed. It would be unwise for me not to take precautions. Besides, there has already been two attempts on my life."

"Are you afraid your soldiers will not recognize you?" he asked. Her heart jumped in her chest.

"What do you mean?" Kari asked. Her brow furrowed, and she took a step back.

"The rebels attacked from inside the palace. They must have had help from someone within the walls, then there's the fact that while they could have attempted to go straight for the throne, they attack a gate. Sounds like a distraction to me. And now here you are with weapons, coming to greet me. I never thought you could be an assassin."

"I am no assassin," Kari protested. That part was true enough.

"I beg to differ," a voice said.

Yamato and five other men stepped out of the foliage where they were hidden.

"I'm sorry, my love." Baoshun drew his jian, a straight-edged sword. "Imagine my shock when a former assassin returns to me and warns me of a current one. And better yet, he tells me this new assassin is not only my betrothed, but is also Shagin. I scarcely believed it until the attack, but here you are. I loved you. Was that all part of your plan? Did Izumi discover the truth? Did I kill her for that?"

"My lord, I would never..." Kari was at a loss for words. There was nothing she could say to get out of this one.

"It's quite a shame really. I very much did enjoy your songs. Kill her."

Kari drew her kodachis as she prepared for the on-slaught. The soldier who had escorted her was the first to engage her blades. She parried his attack, but before she could counter, Baoshun was already upon her. She dove out of the way of his sword, then slashed widely, trying to disrupt his follow through.

Backing her against a tree, he swung for her head. She ducked out of the way of the blade. It struck the tree trunk with a loud thunk, sinking deep into the wood. She raised her sword, poised to strike the emperor, but before she could, an arrow whizzed past her face, missing her by mere inches.

One of Yamato's men had a bow trained on her. She jumped back as he released another arrow. She blocked a series of attacks by Yamato. His single blade forced her to retreat as she struggled to match his speed and skill.

"Out of the way," Baoshun screamed, charging for-ward.

Yamato jumped to the side, allowing Baoshun an open attack. Kari raised her sword and blocked his blade, but the force of the blow knocked her back and dislodged her sword from her hand, sending it careening into the bushes. Kari blocked blow after blow with her remaining sword, but each attack was executed with such force the impact of their swords kept knocking her off balance.

Baoshun yelled, and he swung with all his might. Kari blocked the attack, but she was knocked into the stone wall.

The other seven men had taken positions to completely surround her.

"It's over," Baoshun said, raising his sword. "The rebellion will fail, and you will die."

It wasn't over yet. She couldn't fail. Too many people were depending on her. Too many people had died for this chance. There was still hope. She needed to find Ronin.

Kari was surrounded. She held out her hands, releasing a blinding flash of light that illuminated brighter than the early morning sun. The armed men cried out as they shielded their eyes from the brightness. Kari focused her mind, reflecting and bending the surrounding light, causing her world to turn black as she became invisible and blind.

"Where did she go?" one man asked.

They couldn't see her, but neither could she see them. With any luck, they would think she escaped in the flash and would run off to look for her.

"She disappeared."

"Where could she have gone? We were right here."

"Find her."

She waited until she could no longer hear the soldiers before reappearing. Once her vision had returned to her, she ran with all of her might through the garden and headed for the Hall of Heaven and Earth. She had to find Ronin. He would have dealt with Jiaorong by now. He might be tired, but hopefully they could take on Baoshun together.

She ran up the steps to the Hall of Heaven and Earth, nearly ripping the door apart as she rushed inside. She ran to the throne room. The doors were already open, torn off the hinges, clearly the work of Ronin.

Kari rushed forward, but then stopped and stared in horror at the sight before her. Jiaorong had his hand around Ronin's neck and was holding him off the ground. Ronin's body was limp and covered in blood, which dripped into a red puddle underneath his dangling feet.

"This is no place for you," Jiaorong said upon seeing Kari. "But then again, the safest place will be right here by my side."

"My lord," a guard said, entering the throne room. "We have routed the rebels at the gate. Several have been captured, and the rest are fleeing or are dead. We believe Lord Cai Ren was aiding them. He was seen giving the rebels instructions."

Kari felt like throwing up. How had it come to this? For their plan to fail so utterly, were the Tian really that strong?

"I want him arrested and interrogated," Jiaorong ordered. "Find out who else was aiding this farce of a rebellion, then execute them. Take this trash with you. Find out what he knows. Make sure it's painful, then kill him."

Jiaorong tossed Ronin's unconscious body, which flailed like a rag doll in the air before crashing to the ground next to the guard. The guard lifted Ronin, then carried him out of the throne room.

"My love, I am glad to see you unharmed, but you shouldn't be here. A woman shouldn't be witness to such brutality," Jiaorong said.

"My lord," Kari said, wrapping her arms around him. Death was coming for her. Baoshun and Yamato would eventually catch up to her. They would reveal her involvement, and she would die. She didn't want to die. Jiaorong was her only hope for survival now. He returned her embrace. "Something terrible has happened."

"Do not worry," Jiaorong said. "I won't let anyone harm you."

"Even your brother?"

"What do you mean?"

"Lord Baoshun has labeled me a traitor. He says I am responsible for the uprising. He and a number of men entered my room. They tried to kill me. I barely escaped. An assassin named Yamato was with him."

"Yamato? It can't be the same man," Jiaorong mumbled. She was glad he remembered. After thirty-seven attempts, it might be hard to keep up with each assassin, but one would always remember the one who got away.

"I think he is jealous of my love for you," Kari added. "I have spurned his advances time and again. I think he wants to dispose of me in order to get to you."

The door to the antechamber was flung open, the clash of which echoed in the throne room. Baoshun, Yamato, and a host of other men entered the chamber. Jiaorong grabbed Kari's arm, yanking her behind him.

"What is the meaning of this?" Jiaorong asked.

"Brother, that woman is a traitor. Now stand aside so we may kill her." Baoshun pointed the tip of his sword at Kari.

"The only traitor I see is you." Jiaorong drew his curved dao. "I had always wondered how an assassin was able to enter the throne room undetected and escape with his life. Every other one, I had killed with little effort, all but one. One lived. Now I see the same assassin *you* failed to kill allied with you. I seem to recall when he tried to take my head. Yet, here you are with him and nearly thirty soldiers."

"Brother, do not listen to the lies of that vile woman," Baoshun pleaded. "The assassin came to me to warn us about her plot. He is the only reason I survived."

Jiaorong lowered his sword, pivoting toward Kari. He stared down at her, not making a move. "Do you love me?"

"I do," she responded.

"Will you marry me?"

Kari bowed her head. "Of course, my love."

"Do not fall for her tricks," Baoshun screamed. "If you are unsure of who to trust, trust in me. I am your brother."

"Not anymore."

Jiaorong let out a soul-shattering roar that echoed in the expansive room. He charged forward at the host of men. His sword clashed with the soldiers, but he showed no hesitation, no resistance to killing either Yamato's men or the Imperial guards. Blood sprayed through the air as he ripped through them. His sword slashed through flesh and bone, bodies and severed limbs falling to the floor. He never broke his stride as he effortlessly glided through the gaggle of soldiers.

Yamato tried to halt his slaughter, but Jiaorong parried his sword and lobbed off his head, cutting through bone like straw. Jiaorong didn't even slow down when he reached his brother. Baoshun tried to meet Jiaorong's attack, but Jiaorong struck at his hand, severing his fingers and disarming his sword.

"Brother, please," Baoshun begged, dropping to his knees.

Jiaorong was unmoved, swiftly driving the tip of his sword through his brother's skull. He withdrew his blade, spraying a mist of blood and brain matter into the air. Within a matter of moments, Baoshun and his men were all dead. The floor of the throne room had been turned into a pool of blood and body parts. Jiaorong had made quick work of the soldiers. They weren't even able to slow him down.

Kari could do nothing but stand in wide-eyed horror as she watched the carnage unfold. She had never seen anything so terrifying in her life. The level of mayhem and destruction Jiaorong caused was breathtaking. He truly was invincible.

"I cannot rule this nation alone," Jiaorong said, cleaning the blood off his sword. "Baoshun might not have been much of a warrior, but he knew how to rule. I have no interest in petty politics, so I will need a partner, someone to rule with me, by my side. I would like you to be my wife, my queen, the Empress of Xiang."

Kari didn't say a word. She just gaped, fixated on the winged tiger before her.

CHAPTER TWENTY-ONE

"Wʜᴀᴛ ᴀʀᴇ ʏᴏᴜ sᴛɪʟʟ doing here?" Ina asked. It had been two days since the failed coup. Ina's wounds were healing nicely, but her body was scarred, and they wouldn't fade. Kari's injuries wouldn't scar, one benefit of her spirit energy. Kari felt guilty for that. Only one would bear their wounds forever.

"I've been wondering that myself." Kari stopped, hopping down from the red swing. A bird fluttered from the branch of a nearby tree, soaring over the walls of the garden. She could escape, too. She could easily take Ina and use the hidden entrance in the School of Enlightenment to flee. It would be extremely easy, but she couldn't.

"We have to use this time to leave while we can." Ina took Kari's hands, holding them in her own.

"How can we?" Kari shook her head. "Over seven hundred dead, another thirteen hundred captured. How can we leave them to suffer and die while we run?"

"Because if we don't, we'll join them," Ina said. Kari didn't want to hear it. Pulling away, she averted her gaze from Ina. "I think we need to face the fact we failed."

"It's not over yet," Kari said. Ina was right. Kari knew it. There was no victory to be had here, but still, something drove her to stay. "If we ran now, it would never be over for the people we are abandoning. There is still hope. Tomorrow, after the wedding, I will be crowned Empress Regnant and take Baoshun's place. I can use that to strike back. We can still make a difference."

"I can't tell if you have gone insane or actually think you can still save the kingdom," Ina said.

"Maybe a bit of both." Kari smiled. She was delusional. There was no hope for them here. That was what her logic told her, but her heart told her she had to try. She might fail, she might die, everyone might die, but if there were a chance she could possibly help, she had to try. "We've come so far and accomplished so much, I can't run away now after all of this. So many people have died to get us this far, and many more will die if we run. I won't leave them. I might not be able to save the kingdom, but I have to save those who trusted in us. I know I can't ask you to stay with me. You'll be safer if you don't. We could very well all die here tomorrow, but I will need help."

Ina sighed. "I guess I can't be the only sane person. I'm staying, too."

"Thank you." Kari smiled at her friend. "First thing we must do is to make sure we live to see tomorrow. I need to talk to Ronin."

"He's in the dungeon. How are you going to get in there?

"I plan on walking through the front door."

Kari headed for the Military District. The guards didn't stop her. She was a noble lady who would soon be empress. She didn't expect any issue walking through the district. It would be getting in the dungeon that would cause her problems.

She opened the door. The guards stationed at the gate stared at her as she entered.

"My lady," one guard said, bowing. "Lord Jiaorong has forbidden anyone entry to the dungeon. Even someone of your rank isn't allowed in. I'm afraid I will have to report your visit to the emperor."

"Do you think that will be necessary?" Kari dropped five crowns onto the guard's table. Izumi had a wardrobe filled with money, bribes Kari could use to her advantage now. She held out a purse filled with even more coins. "These men have made multiple attempts on my life, and they've threatened the very security of our nation. I have to find out why. I have to hear it for myself. I have fifty-nine crowns with me. I will give them to you to share amongst yourselves if you allow me entry without disclosure to my betrothed."

The guard eagerly accepted the purse from Kari. In exchange, he handed her his keys. "Take as much time as you want. You were never here."

Kari bowed graciously before heading into the dungeon. She peeked through the slots of each cell door, looking for Ronin. When she finally found him, she opened his door with the guard's keys.

Ronin laid on the stone floor. His wounds had been bandaged, and he had regained consciousness.

"What are you doing here?" he asked. His voice was weak and faint, and Kari had to lean forward to hear him. "You need to leave Xiang, or you'll die with us."

"Why does everyone keep telling me that?" Kari asked, annoyed. "I can't leave just yet."

"Our men are already being tortured for information. Someone will tell them about your involvement. Even if they don't, I was your bodyguard. Someone is bound to connect you to us," Ronin said.

"I know. That's why I need your help. I need you to buy me another day. I have a contingency plan to free everyone."

"You'll be courting death. Jiaorong is too strong to confront. It was a fool's errand."

"I know, but I have to try. Tomorrow, I am to be married to him. Following the ceremony, there will be a coronation where I will be crowned as the joint Empress of Xiang. I think I can use that power to free you."

"You're an idiot," Ronin scolded. "Run while you can."

"I'm not leaving you," Kari said. "Please, I need you to tell as many people as you can to stay quiet about me for another day. Give me the chance to save you."

"I'm not going to help you kill yourself."

"You can either help me or watch me die. Either way, I won't abandon you."

"Fine," Ronin said, wiping at his eyes. "I'll see what I can do."

"Thank you," Kari said. "I promise, I will save you all."

After she left the dungeon, she suffered through until the following day when the hands of fate would either guide her on her path or leave her desolate and lost. Her wedding day had come like so many other days before. The sun rose in the morning, and time sprinted by as she prepared herself.

She was dressed in a ruqun with a red-and-gold blouse and a pleated skirt. A crimson red daxiushan gown wrapped over the ruqun. A golden phoenix embroidered the sides of the gown. Silk scarves were draped across her arms.

Kari stared into the mirror. The woman with the green eyes who stared back seemed foreign to her. She ran her fingers against the golden phoenix on her gown. It wasn't exactly her ideal wedding.

It was rare for Shagin to marry. It was highly unusual for any outsider to be permitted within the Shagin nation. That made marriage rather difficult for Shagin. However, occasionally, two Shagin would wed.

After her banishment, she had thought about one day getting married, but being bound to someone for life was frightening. Not to mention that marriage was often used to subjugate women. She had no intention of being traded for a goat. But there were those who married for love, and she envied that kind of love. Love that was so eternal it brought two people together to become one.

Now she was getting ready to marry, not for love or wealth or subjugation, but for survival. Her marriage would hopefully aid her in ending the tyranny of the Tian. Weddings were supposed to be a period of joy and celebration, but not for her. How many other women were forced to marry their rapists?

"Are you all right?" Ina asked.

Kari's thoughts were broken, and she realized she had been crying. "I'm fine," she said, wiping the tears away.

"It's hard to believe it's come to this," Ina said.

"I know what you mean." Kari sighed. There was just a little further to go. "I need you to do something for me."

"Of course," Ina said.

Kari handed Ina a coin pouch. "I need a sword. Two kodachis. I seem to keep losing mine."

"I'll see that it's done." Ina clutched the coin pouch tightly in her hand as if to keep it from disappearing.

"After that, I need you to take this." Kari handed her a pouch full of seeds. "I need you to set a trap for me."

Ina left with Kari's instructions, leaving Kari alone in her house. It was customary for the bride to prepare away from the groom, and she had chosen to make her preparations in the only safe place in the palace.

How had it come to this?

She missed her mother. Kari wanted her here more than anything. She always had the right thing to say to make Kari feel better. And, right now, she could use some words of encouragement. What would her mother think, if she ever saw Kari again, and she found out what Kari had gone through?

She had become the very thing the world feared about Shagin. That they will infiltrate, seduce, and destroy the world of men. Kari had given up her body to this man. He had violated her, and now she was marrying him, all to remove him from power.

Light emitted from her fingertips.

Kari wasn't the monster the world would label her. She was Shagin, the Bearer of the Seed, a concubine to a tyrant... These things were forced upon her. She had no choice in what she was, only what she would become. The Seed was a curse, but it didn't make her a monster. It was simply a part of who she was.

Just like the curse, she had been thrust into this situation against her will. She was a victim, but she had refused to remain one. She had fought back, and now the fate of an entire nation rested on her shoulders.

Jiaorong was a tyrant. He used his power to abduct and abuse women. He had taken Ina on her wedding day, killing her betrothed in the process. He'd murdered Kyoko. His throne was built on blood and ashes. His desire to tend to his own pleasures over the needs of the people was tearing the land apart. For the sake of Xiang, he had to be defeated.

One would die today.

Kari had no misconceptions. Most likely, she would be dead in a few hours. The strength of Jiaorong, the carnage he had caused, it petrified her. He was like a tiger with wings, fearsome and swift. She wasn't much of a fighter. Her magic gave her an advantage, but fighting had never been her strength. She had struggled against lesser foes than him, and he'd slaughtered a large group of seasoned warriors in a matter of seconds. This wouldn't be a fight. It would be a massacre.

Still, she had to try. She couldn't give up hope, just because she had none. If she couldn't match his strength, she would have to outsmart him. Her magic would aid in that. He had no idea what she truly was or what power she possessed. He would underestimate her. That would be his undoing. So many people had trusted her. She wasn't about to betray their trust now.

"My lady, are you ready?" a maid servant asked upon entering Kari's chamber. "Your procession is waiting to escort you to the emperors' mansion."

"I am," Kari said. She stood from her dressing chair, then followed the maidservant.

Outside, she was greeted by a large procession comprising a band, dancers, servants, and royal guards. The maidservant helped Kari into her covered sedan chair, which was carried by four servants. As they marched through the streets, the band played loud and joyous music as the performers danced along beside Kari's chair. Servants lit firecrackers. Launched them high into the air. A crowd of nobles and chancellors had formed and kowtowed in respect as the procession slowly made its way to the mansion. Kari could make out their outlines through the silk curtains.

The procession stopped, then they set the carriage down in front of Jiaorong's mansion. A red mat led from the carriage up to the front door where Jiaorong waited for her. Another maidservant was there to help Kari out of the small carriage. The crowd cheered loudly upon seeing her, and more firecrackers were set off.

The maidservant escorted Kari to the stairs of the mansion where a stove had been set on the ground and lit. Kari carefully stepped over the stove, then made her way to Jiaorong. Turning toward each other, they bowed.

"You look magnificent," Jiaorong said, holding out his hand. He was wearing red formal attire with a black sleeveless coat that flowed to the ground. A gold dragon embroidered the coat.

"Thank you." Kari took his hand as he led her inside to his bedchamber. She was numb. Her wedding, surreal. This was worse than what was to come. Pain and death were easier than living knowing she had married her rapist. A man whose very presence filled her with burning rage. At least, either way, it was a pain she wouldn't have to live with for long.

Jiaorong shut the door, motioning for Kari to sit on the bed. He took two goblets that were linked by a red thread before handing one to Kari as he sat next to her.

Kari glanced into the cup. Its red liquid smelled sweet. They both drank from their respective goblets before exchanging cups and drinking the rest. It was an odd concoction that was sweet with a bitter aftertaste.

Jiaorong offered Kari his hand to lead her back outside. Empress Xiaoxianhua met them in the inner courtyard. Kari bowed before her new mother-in-law.

Xiaoxianhua took Kari's hands, clasping them together. "The past few months have seen drastic changes occur in our lives. I have lost one daughter and now my son, but I now have a new daughter. One who loves my son as much as I. Noble Lady Hikari, may the gods bless you as I do now. I bestow upon you the name Empress Consort Xiaoxiannu."

Kari bowed a second time as tears streamed down her face.

"Come," Jiaorong ordered. "Now for your coronation."

The crowd cheered and applauded as the newly wedded couple exited the mansion. A larger sedan chair now awaited them at the bottom of the stairs. Once they had entered the chair, the servants carried them to the Hall of Heaven and Earth for Kari's coronation. The crowd followed as the band continued to play.

They headed to the throne room where they took their seats on the two thrones overlooking the crowd in attendance, blood from the gruesome slaughter still staining the floor. A minister bowed before them, before taking a crown and placing it on Kari's head. Once he had finished, he rang a gong and the members of the Imperial Court entered one at a time, each stopping to bow before Jiaorong and Kari and pledging their loyalty to both.

Once everyone had taken their places, Jiaorong stood to address the crowd.

"Today marks a tremendous occasion. Not only is it my wedding day, but we also have a new empress to replace the fallen traitor who once resided over half the empire."

The crowd chanted in unison, "May the mandate of heaven shine upon you."

Jiaorong motioned to Kari. "I present to you, Lady Hikari, Empress Regnant Xiaoxiannu of Xiang."

"My lords and ladies, it is an honor to serve you as empress." Kari addressed the court. "As each of the members of court have pledged their loyalty to me, I, too, pledge my loyalty to each of you. I will do my best to serve you so that, together, we can make this kingdom stronger and preserve this land for future generations to come."

The crowd cheered in response, "Xiaoxiannu, Xiaoxiannu."

"My lady," Jiaorong said. "It is time to address your adoring public."

Jiaorong led Kari to the steps of the hall where wealthier citizens of the city had gathered in anticipation, hoping they might catch a glimpse of their new empress. It was a rare occasion for commoners to be allowed in the palace, but for the coronation, certain wealthy citizens were granted permission to enter the courtyard of the Hall of Heaven and Earth, provided they pay a substantial fee. The crowd roared as the two appeared before them.

"Silence," Jiaorong said, holding out his hands. The crowd quickly went dead. A rare sight indeed for commoners to see the emperor. "To commemorate this day, as chosen by heaven, I present to you, your new ruler, my queen, and dual emperor of Xiang, Empress Xiaoxiannu!"

Kari took a deep breath before stepping forward.

"I am the new empress and joint ruler of Xiang, and my first act as empress..." Kari took a deep breath, facing her husband, "is to challenge you to a duel for total control of the empire."

Jiaorong laughed. "What?"

"I'm challenging you for sovereign rule," Kari repeated. The words felt silly coming out of her mouth. He would have no reason to accept, other than pride. Hopefully, he would underestimate her and try to kill her himself and not have the guards do it.

"This is quickly losing its humor," Jiaorong said. "What is the meaning behind this?"

"Your tyranny has gone on for too long, and I intend to end it," Kari stated.

"Cease this charade," Jiaorong demanded, stepping closer to her.

"I am the leader of the rebellion against you," Kari said, fighting the urge to step backward.

"That was you?" Jiaorong's eyes burned with rage. "I'll have your head."

"Then come and take it," Kari threatened, bracing herself for him to pounce. She regretted the words. She didn't have a weapon to defend herself with, and he could strike her down now, but he stood where he was, merely content to fume and glare at her. Xiaoxianhua stood behind her son, her eyes narrow and her mouth agape. Kari took a deep breath, filling her lungs with air. Another person would hate her forever for her actions, yet it had to be done. "I propose a duel to settle this dispute once and for all."

"To the death?" Jiaorong asked, gripping the hilt of his sword.

"To the death," Kari repeated. Hopefully, he would have the patience for her to find a weapon and not just attack here and now. "If you are confident in your strength, you should have no problem defeating me."

"Do you think you can honestly challenge me?" Jiaorong asked. "A girl like you? I will break you in half. If you thought you could beat me, I have to wonder why you didn't try all the nights I bedded you, and why you fled from my brother. The truth is you're as weak as a dry reed. I'll accept your challenge. My reward will be death, and, if you win, you can have the empire. Prepare yourself, then head to the Judgement Room at the top of the centermost tower."

Kari nodded. Jiaorong stormed off with a small crowd of loyalist in tow.

Ina and Zhenhua rushed up toward Kari with her swords in hand.

"Here goes nothing," Kari said, taking the swords from Ina.

"You're a fool," Zhenhua said. Kari was surprised to see her here, but she supposed they all had their reasons. Zhenhua, too. "But a brave fool, if that's any consolation."

"You'll need a second," Ina said.

"What does a second do?" Kari fixed the swords to her side.

"The duel is to the death," Zhenhua said. "Imperial law dictates that when a duel is to the death, the second fulfills the obligations of the fallen combatant. In this case, Jiaorong wants life. If you lose, the second will be executed."

"Oh." Kari's eyes widened. Someone else would have to put their life in Kari's hands.

"That's my job," Ina said. "I'll be your second."

"No," Zhenhua said, placing a hand on Ina's shoulder. "I won't let you, Ina. I'll be Kari's second."

"You're only saying that because you think Kari will lose. I will second her, because I think she will win. This is for Emiko, for Shinichi, for Kyoko. I will second Kari in memory and honor of those I have lost."

"Are you sure?" Kari didn't want anyone to risk their life on her, but she felt more confident knowing Ina believed in her, if not a bit more apprehensive as well. She couldn't let her down.

Ina nodded. "If you're going to put your life on the line, after everything you've done for me, I can do the same. I believe in you."

"Thank you," Kari said.

"You have shamed me." Zhenhua smiled at the pair. "You both have. For the things I have done, I have many regrets. Kari, you follow your heart. You do what is decent and right. For that, you have my eternal gratitude. My empress."

Zhenhua dropped to her knees, kowtowing before Kari. It was an unusual sight. Kari dropped to one knee to help Zhenhua up.

"Thank you," Kari said, returning a bow. "My opinion of you has changed for the better. I think *you* have changed for the better."

Ina hugged Zhenhua. "Goodbye, Zhenhua."

Kari and Ina entered the hall together, then headed up the stairs to the top floor, to the Judgement Room, to face their fate.

CHAPTER TWENTY-TWO

"Are you prepared?" Jiaorong asked.

"Yes," Kari replied.

"I trust you have a second. Is she prepared as well?"

"I'm ready." Ina stepped forward, and Jiaorong's eyes narrowed upon seeing her.

"Where's your second?" Kari asked.

"I won't need one," Jiaorong declared, smiling.

"Humor me," Kari said. In essence, Jiaorong was right. He wouldn't need a second. She wasn't demanding to take a life if she won. She just wanted those in attendance to know she was confident in her ability to win.

"I'll be his second." Xiaoxianhua stepped within inches of Kari. Kari averted her eyes, but the old gray woman's piercing glare did not waver. "You have killed my son, and now you threaten my other. I trusted you. What kind of mother would I be to allow my son to fight for his life without my support? If he dies, my world is gone and my life is forfeit, but I will forever haunt you to your grave. My son, give her a dog's death."

"The rules are simple." A chancellor stepped forward. "Both parties will enter the dueling chamber armed with whatever weapons they choose. The doors will be sealed from the inside. Both combatants will fight to the death. Whoever is alive at the end, wins. Once the doors are closed, anything goes, but the fight must be one on one. No one else can interfere or the match is forfeit. The winner will take the life of the fallen's second and full sovereignty of the empire will be given to him. May the mandate of heaven fall to the victor."

"After you." Jiaorong motioned to the door.

"Good luck," Ina called to Kari as she headed into the Judgement Room.

"I look forward to killing you soon," Jiaorong called back to Ina as he followed Kari. Once he had entered, he shut and locked himself in with Kari. Glaring at her, he drew his sword. "Have you prepared yourself?"

Kari unsheathed both of her swords, then dropped the scabbards to the floor. She raised her weapons, poising herself for his onslaught. "I'm ready. Let's begin."

Jiaorong let out a deafening roar before charging forward.

Kari dove out of the way of his attack. She had seen the way he charged forward before, and was expecting a similar opening attack, but before she could get back to her feet to retaliate, he launched a kick that struck her in the face, sending her rolling on the floor.

"You move like that Kitsuno Kai," Jiaorong said. "If I can beat him, I can beat you."

"But I don't think he could do this!" Kari blasted him with a burst of light. Screaming, he covered his eyes. The light energy ripped his clothes and knocked him off balance, but it didn't seem to do any damage. With him temporarily off balance, Kari lunged forward with her swords, but he parried both blows, causing her to stumble backward. Her legs felt wobbly after the attack. She wouldn't be able to use her light powers too often in the fight, or she would be too weak to continue.

"Impressive," Jiaorong said. "So, you have some fight in you after all. And here I thought you were just another wannabe Shagin whore."

"You knew?" Kari's heart skipped. He'd never seen her as a threat. He still didn't.

"Or course." Jiaorong smiled. "I know a whore when I see one."

Kari crossed the blades of her swords and charged forward again, attacking both sides of his neck at once. Jiaorong swung his sword upward, deflecting her attack. With her attack broken, he struck her in the gut with the hilt of his sword. Kari hunched over from the impact, stumbling out of his reach.

He could have easily impaled her, but he chose not to. He was toying with her.

"Of course, the question now becomes—should I rape you and kill you or simply lop that pretty head off and adorn it to my throne?" Jiaorong said.

Kari clenched the grips of her swords, turning her knuckles white. She knew he was just trying to goad her into making a mistake, but she couldn't help but be rattled by his words. She had to find a way to defeat him.

Jiaorong rushed forward. Kari tried to block his attack, but he knocked her swords to the side, throwing her off balance, then sliced at her arm. The steel of his blade easily slid into her flesh, spilling her blood.

She cried out at the pain as she jumped out of his reach. His sword pierced her defense way too easily. Something wasn't right. An attack like that shouldn't have cut her that easily. Her aura should have blocked it.

"I believe I branded you on that arm before." He licked her blood off his blade. "Think of this as simply returning a mark that was supposed to be permanent."

"Do you think that bothers me?" Kari asked. "After what you put me through, what you did to me, this pain is nothing."

"I believe you enjoyed it." Jiaorong snickered.

"Shut up." Kari charged forward. She struck at his sword with one hand, trying to keep his sword arm busy, and lashed out against his chest with her offhand. He blocked her one attack, then stepped out of the way of the other. Using his non-sword hand, he struck the back of her neck with the flat of his hand, causing her to topple forward.

Before she could regain her composure, he nicked her side with the edge of his blade.

Kari winced at the pain as blood trickled from the wound.

"I believe I owe you pain," Jiaorong said. "After all, you caused me to kill my brother."

Jiaorong lunged forward with his sword grazing her forehead above her left eye. She wiped the blood from the wound with the back of her hand. It didn't make sense. He was intentionally causing shallow wounds, yet her spirit aura should be strong enough to protect her from simple worrying cuts like this. The only way he could bypass her defense would be if he were spirit charging his attacks. But that would be impossible.

"I guess I should thank you really," Jiaorong said. "With my brother out of the way, I have the whole kingdom to myself. Can you imagine all the women I'll get to have?"

"You'll have to deal with me first," Kari said, backing away from him.

"And yet, you back away in fear." Jiaorong stalked toward her.

"Who said I'm afraid?" Kari dropped to the ground. She placed her hands to the floor, sending her energy into the floorboards. Vines grew and shot up, wrapping around Jiaorong, curtesy of Ina and the seeds Kari had her place there earlier. The thorns of the vines cut into his skin. Immobilized him. "This is called composure."

"What the hell is this?" Jiaorong said. His sword arm was wrapped in the vines, unable to move.

Kari dove forward with her swords, unleashing a flurry of slashes against her opponent. Jiaorong groaned from the onslaught before collapsing to the ground.

"Bitch," he screamed. He swung his sword wildly, but she jumped out of his reach.

Kari stared in disbelief as he rose to his feet. All of her blows amounted to nothing more than mere scratches and shallow cuts. That proved it—he was spirit charging.

"Don't look so shocked." Jiaorong grinned, towering over her. "I learned a few tricks while fighting your kind in the war."

This guy was unbelievable. This was why no one could beat him. How could he learn spirit charge techniques like that? It was impossible. Not only did he know them, but he also mastered his spirit aura to a level that surpassed hers. He was cutting through her defense as if it weren't even there. Yet, she could barely even scratch his. How could his spirit energy be that much stronger than hers?

"How?" Kari muttered.

"Not only did I learn from them, but I also created new techniques. I took my spirit energy further than anyone," Jiaorong said, breaking free from the rest of the vines. "I can use those I bed as human cauldrons to cultivate my spirit energy. Think on that before I kill you. Every time I fucked you, you made me more powerful."

Kari's fists tightened, and he laughed at her expense. He knew all along. He'd been using her. All the pain she went through only served to make him stronger than her.

"There is that shocked look again," Jiaorong gloated. "I loved you, and you returned my love with betrayal. Yet, here you stand, surprised I'm not easy prey. A dragon only bares its claws when it knows the strength of its enemy."

He swung his sword in the air, and a gust of wind shot from the blade. His attack struck her right arm, cutting into her flesh and sending her sword flying through the air. Its blade struck the wall, impaling the wood.

His sword was enchanted.

"Do you like it? It's a little trophy I took from the last Shagin whore I killed." Jiaorong stared at the blade of his sword, an evil grin on his face. "I have had fun, but I think it's time for you to die."

He slashed through the air, sending a series of powerful wind currents hurtling at Kari. She dropped to the ground, allowing the blasts to pass over her and tear through the wall, letting sunlight shine through the gashes in the wood.

Kari stood in time to see Jiaorong's next attack. He swung at her with a downward strike. She blocked the attack, the sound of their blades colliding echoing in the empty room. The force of the impact dislodged Kari's sword.

Jiaorong dropped his as well, then seized Kari by the throat. He lifted her off the ground, then slammed her into the wall, which buckled and bowed from the impact. He pulled her back, then slammed her into it again. The wall gave way from the blow, and Kari was thrown from the building.

She could hear the sounds from the crowd below, where they eagerly awaited the outcome of the duel. Kari spun freely through the air as she fell from the tower. She yanked a seed from her pocket, then shot a vine up toward the pagoda. It latched onto the tower, halting her fall. She slammed into the wall as she swung on the vine.

Jiaorong unleashed a wind attack from his sword, severing the vine. Kari yelped as she continued to fall. She struck the tower on the way down, which sent her into a spin before she crashed on the roof below.

The impact sent pain shooting through her body, and she struggled to her hands and knees. She heard the whooshing of wind, quickly rolling out of the way of the incoming blast. The attack struck the roof, shattering the tiles and sending the jagged pieces shooting through the air.

Kari leaped to her feet as attack after attack was levied her way. Each attack that missed her struck the roof with such a force the shockwave threatened to knock her off her feet. She ran as fast as she could and zigzagged, avoiding Jiaorong's attacks. Reaching the edge of the roof, she leapt into the air.

The sound of another attack alerted her of the impact, but she was unable to avoid it. The blast of air struck her in the back, tearing through cloth and flesh and hurtling her to the stone ground below. She wasn't even able to soften the fall as she landed face-first.

Kari remained motionless for some time. She wasn't sure if she could even move anymore, not that she wanted to.

The sounds of murmurs filled the crowd as they speculated on whether she was dead.

Face-down, there was no way she could see another attack coming. She gathered her strength, then rolled onto her back. At the top of the center pagoda, she could see the hole from whence she was ejected, she could even make out the fuzzy image of Jiaorong standing there, looking down upon her.

Without warning, Jiaorong leapt from the tower. He landed feet-first onto the roof, and, without breaking stride, ran off the edge of the hall and landed next to Kari.

That proved it—he surpassed her in every way.

"Get up," Jiaorong ordered. "This will be a poor end to our duel otherwise."

But Kari didn't move. There was no need. He was far too strong, and she didn't have the strength left in her body to stand, much less fight. Snarling, Jiaorong seized her by the hair. He dragged her down the stairs and over to the fountain.

"Look, everyone," Jiaorong declared. "This is what happens when you challenge my might. This woman is a member of the Shagin, yet even she is no match for my strength. I am your god king. The one true ruler of this land. Heaven has declared that all shall bow before me or perish."

Jiaorong dunked Kari's head under the water, intending to drown her. Her arms instinctively shot up and pawed at his hand, trying to break his grip, but it was no use. Kari flailed and fought against his strength. Her chest burned and spasmed as her lungs demanded air. She fought against her tunneling vision. If she lost consciousness, she wouldn't be able to prevent the water from entering her lungs.

Her nails dug into the flesh of his hands as the pain in her chest became more and more unbearable. Her chest spasmed and heaved. When she gasped, water flooded her mouth. She clenched her lips tightly together, trying to prevent more water from entering, but her body wanted nothing more than to scream out for air.

Her arms went limp, crashing into the water as she blacked out.

CHAPTER TWENTY-THREE

"Where am I?" Kari asked, looking around. She was standing in a garden of blooming peach trees. A gentle breeze constantly rustled the branches.

"Right where you were before you lost consciousness. Right where you're supposed to be," a voice said from behind her.

Kari turned to see Kyoko standing there, dressed in a white-and-blue ruqun.

"You're dead," Kari said bluntly.

"Yes, I am," Kyoko said. She appeared calm and at peace.

"Am I?" Kari examined her arms.

"Not yet, but you will be soon."

"It's over then," Kari said, defeated.

"It's not over, not unless you give up hope." The daughter of Alme stepped beside Kari.

"How am I supposed to beat him? What hope do I have?" Kari asked.

"I don't know," Kyoko said. "But you are the last hope for Xiang. If you don't find a way, no one will. Alone and humiliated, the wrath of Jiaorong will be immense. Many more will suffer and die at his hands. Just like me."

"He's just too strong."

"Does that matter?" The daughter of Alme plucked a petal from a nearby tree. "Why did you choose your name?"

"Because I can create light." Kari rubbed her thumb against her fingers.

"To you this means what?" The daughter of Alme let the wind take the petal from her fingertips, and they watched as it fluttered away. "The bringer of light? You call yourself a symbol of hope and life. It's the same thing in your mind."

"It's to remind me of what I should strive to live up to."

"You're afraid of the Seed. You think it is a curse, but it is more than that. The power of the Seed holds the Three Realms apart. That same power is a part of you. It is who you are, so embrace it."

Kari gritted her teeth.

Smiling, Kyoko stroked Kari's hair. "What did you say that night?"

Kari stared at her hands. "Never again."

"It's happening again, and it will continue to happen unless you find a way."

"Never again."

* * *

Kari broke free from Jiaorong's grip, then shot out of the water.

"Never again," she said, glaring him down.

"Kari," Ina cried out as she rushed out of the hall.

"Stay back," Kari ordered. Her breathing was heavy and ragged, but air was filling her lungs, renewing her strength. "If you interfere, he wins."

"But he's killing you," Ina protested.

"No, he's making me angry," Kari said. Water poured off her head, soaking into her blouse and skirt.

"Am I supposed to be frightened by a half-dead little girl?" Jiaorong asked.

"I'm not a little girl—I'm Shagin," Kari said. "Now, get ready for round two!"

Kari shot out a vine that wrapped around Jiaorong's neck. He cut through it with his sword before unleashing a volley of three wind blasts at Kari. She dove out of the way, dodging all three attacks.

This was no good. She didn't have a weapon to fight with, not that one would do her much good. His defense was too strong. If she focused her remaining energy into a single shot, she might be able to take him down with a blast of light, but that would only give her one shot before she collapsed from exhaustion. Her light powers, while strong, required too much energy, and only a small portion of the actual blast could do any damage. The attack was too much of a waste of energy. She could rely on her plant magic, that required little energy, but the attacks were too weak to be effective.

She dove out of the way of another volley of wind blasts.

That was the key. She needed to embrace who she was. Unify the two halves of her core into one, the songstress and the Bearer of the Seed. Only then would she stand a chance.

"I thought you were angry, but all you can do is run away like a coward. This is becoming embarrassing. Let us end this."

Jiaorong raised his sword, rushing at Kari.

It was now or never. This was either going to work, or she was going to die.

She held out her hand, focusing her light energy into her palm while trying to visualize and focus on control in the same way she would if she were creating a vine.

Kari screamed as Jiaorong swung his sword. She closed her eyes, throwing her arm out in response. A flash of light turned the inside of her eyelids red as something warm struck her face. She dropped to one knee from the exertion.

Jiaorong's attack had been halted, and he was forced backward. A long, deep cut ran across his abdomen. She wiped his blood from her face with her free hand.

In her other hand, she held onto a crackly yellow whip made of pure light. She had turned her light energy into a physical construct.

Her light whip, while it took a great deal of energy to create, took almost nothing out of her to maintain. And by the looks of it, Jiaorong's defenses had just become vulnerable.

Jiaorong knew it as well. He held a hand against his abdomen as he tried to stop the bleeding.

"You'll pay for that," he growled.

"No," Kari said. "It's your turn to pay for all the crimes you have committed against your people."

Kari rose to prepare herself for the final round of the duel.

Jiaorong launched a series of air blasts at Kari, but she dove out of the way. He was trying to keep his distance. He knew he couldn't get close to her without being cut to pieces by her whip.

Jiaorong did not let up his attack. He continued to launch blast after blast toward her. While the air blasts were easier to dodge than his sword, due to the unrelenting nature of his attacks, it was all she could do to avoid being maimed. She was unable to retaliate with her own offense.

Kari dodged and ran and dove out of the way as Jiaorong unleashed a whirlwind of attacks. She couldn't keep this up forever, but he theoretically could. Enchanted weapons didn't draw on the strength of the user, and while their attacks were generally weaker than other forms of magic, unless it was a poor enchantment, the weapon would never run out of energy. Kari only had one choice. She had to confront him head-on.

Kari turned on her heel, facing the oncoming whirlwind. She swung her whip back and forth, cutting through each of his attacks. Stray winds from the broken blasts nipped at her body and cut through her skin. She winced in pain with each one, but she couldn't afford to be distracted. She had to stay focused to spot an opening.

"Die, bitch," Jiaorong screamed.

Kari leapt to the side, barely avoiding a blast of wind. She began her swing, but Jiaorong saw it coming. He quickly launched another gust at her. She tried to avoid it, but it struck her side, cutting deep into her body. Blood and flesh sprayed into the wind. She screamed, her body spinning from the force of the impact. She couldn't let this be the end.

Digging in her heel, she twisted with the momentum of the blast. She shrieked and lashed out with her whip with the last of her strength, falling to the ground. The tip of her whip struck Jiaorong's throat, slicing into his flesh. He glared, his eyes wide and his brow furrowed as blood oozed from the wound.

Her whip dissipated, and she collapsed on the ground. Her chest heaved with each frantic breath, and her vision spun and blurred. With the last of her strength gone, it was all she could do to remain conscious. She lay on the ground, clutching her side as blood poured out of her body.

"This fight isn't finished!" Jiaorong scowled at her. He marched toward her with his sword raised and one hand over his neck. His legs buckled and blood pooled between his fingers, but it did not slow his advance.

Kari screamed as she tried to push herself up. She couldn't die. She had come so far. Her arms shook, giving out from under her. She slammed into the blood-soaked marble ground.

Jiaorong readied his sword to thrust his blade into her. Goddess, this was it. Her death—she had failed. Kari reached out toward Ina.

"I... will..." Jiaorong's hand fell from his neck, blood pouring from his throat like a waterfall. He dropped his sword as his eyes rolled back into his head, and he crumbled to the ground.

A chancellor ran over and checked his pulse.

"He's dead," he declared. Kari managed a pained laugh as relief washed over her.

The crowd cheered, "Xiaoxiannu, Xiaoxiannu."

Moaning, Kari tried to force herself to sit up, but to no avail. Her vision tunneled and blackened.

"The empress needs medical attention," Ina shouted.

The chancellor turned to the crowd. "I present to you, Empress Xiaoxiannu, the sovereign ruler of Xiang!"

CHAPTER TWENTY-FOUR

IT TOOK KARI TWO weeks before she was well enough to formally address her court for the first time. She had sent word for all the nobility in the nation to gather before her. The governors and their entourages filled the throne room, along with her ministers and the various lesser lords.

The prisoners who had been captured in their coup were released immediately following Kari's victory over Jiaorong. It was a victory that came with loss. Empress Dowager Xiaoxianhua committed suicide following the death of her son. Even though Kari did not wish for her death, the woman followed through with her compulsion as Jiaorong's second. It was one last life for Kari to carry in her memories.

Cai Ren had taken to acting as her high chancellor, conducting royal affairs while she healed. He spent each evening of her recovery instructing her on the various formalities of the royal court.

"My lady, perhaps you should consider abdicating the throne," Cai Ren suggested. "This is not nearly enough time for me to provide you with proper education on political matters. With the current state of affairs, you should consider turning the throne over to someone with more experience to better handle the trials we are sure to face."

Part of her knew he was right. The empire was facing one of its greatest challenges ever. Not to mention, historically, any change in dynasties was always met with resistance and bloodshed. It was a fight she didn't want, but it was her responsibility to see it through. If she ran away now, the changes she had fought for might never come to pass. She had risen to the challenge of the Tian, and she could find the strength to lead the nation. "No, this is something I must do."

"The transition won't be easy," Cai Ren warned her. "There are already murmurs of dissension. You might have won the duel against Jiaorong, but many question how that makes you qualified to lead the nation. Just what would an attendant know of rebuilding an empire? There is only one way to quell this resistance. You need to show your strength and demand their obedience. Any who refuse should be dealt with quickly. The Kitsuno Kai are ready to act on your behalf."

"No," Kari said. She was not Jiaorong. There was no way she would use force to bend the empire to her will. "We've had enough authoritative tyranny. Now we need cooperation more than ever. I will show them the strength we can achieve as we work together."

Kari took her seat in the throne room, which was filled to capacity with the various lords. Ina took the throne next to her. It was highly irregular for anyone to sit next to the emperor during court, but Kari had no intention of following tradition. It was a decision that was bound to be met with resistance.

As a reward for her help, Kari had appointed Ina as a minister in her new court. They had watched out for each other during their time as attendants. Kari couldn't imagine not having Ina with her as she now faced the new age.

"We have a long road to recovery," Kari said, addressing the court. "The tyranny of the Tian is over. Only by working together can we achieve a nation that surpasses the old kingdom in strength and prosperity. It is now required the warehouses be open so we can feed our people instead of subjecting them to starvation while we horde food and riches for ourselves. We need to promote commerce both within our borders and throughout the world. Let us reclaim our place as the trading hub of Terra. And finally, no nation can survive while it abuses its people. A tribunal will be held to hold those who helped the Tian enslave and abuse its own people. We must be accountable for our actions."

When Kari had finished announcing her plans for the future of Xiang, she dismissed her court.

"It looks like you did it," Shenrong said after everyone had left. "It's strange. I almost didn't believe this day would ever come."

"I couldn't have done it without your help," Kari said.

"Do you think there will be trouble from the Guardian?" Shenrong asked, frowning. "After all, we do have an openly out Shagin empress."

"I don't know." It was an uncertainty that kept her up at night. By the Guardian's decree, it was a crime for her to simply be alive. He had ordered the Purge. He had declared that all Shagin must be put to death, and anyone who aides a Shagin was also worthy of death. She had overthrown and usurped one of the largest and most powerful kingdoms on Terra. The entire world knew who she was now. As far as the rest of the world was concerned, she was the last Shagin, and every nation was watching her.

The Guardian would come. It would only be a matter of time before that happened. He couldn't sit by and do nothing while she openly defied him with every breath she took.

"No matter what happens, you've earned the respect of the people. He's got to see that, see the good you've done. Any Guardian who would deny us our rightful empress, especially one like yourself, is no Guardian worthy of admiration."

"We'll just have to see what comes of it," Ronin said. He was still heavily bandaged, being pushed in a wheelchair by guardsman. "I think he has enough problems with the war with Adgul to concern himself with us. If he does, we'll be ready. Our empress didn't abandon us, and we won't abandon her."

"That's enough talk of doom and gloom," Shenrong said, bowing. "You have an empire to run. I'll let you get back to it."

"I thought you would heal faster," Kari said, looking Ronin over.

"This is fast." Ronin's face furrowed. "It's the power you bear that enhances your spirit energy, far beyond that which should be capable. I'm definitely jealous. From what I hear, you took quite the beating, yet, looking at you today, you could never tell it."

"I still feel it, though." Kari rubbed her side where Jiaorong had hit her with his wind blast. The wound was no longer there, but the area was still tender to the touch.

"I am proud of you, and I know Mother would be, too," Ronin said. "Just think, a few years ago, Shagin showed their power and nearly brought the world to its knees. Now you'll get a chance to redefine what it truly means to be Shagin. You can show the world the strength of your convictions and passion."

"I never dreamed of this," Kari said. All she wanted to do was to protect her friends. Now she had the opportunity to protect an empire. "I just wanted to make a difference."

"You have, and you will continue to change the world."

Kari spent the first few days as empress just trying to learn the names of all the members of her court. For now, she was still letting Cai Ren do the heavy lifting, but she definitely wanted a more hands-on approach to her kingdom.

"Are you zoning out, Your Highness?" Ina laughed. "I will have to get used to calling you that."

"Not on your life," Kari said, smiling. She had no intention of forcing Ina to bow before her. As far as Kari was concerned, Ina went through the same hell as Kari had and they fought together to overcome it. The victory was just as much Ina's. "How's court going so far?"

"We have our first hearing tomorrow for the tribunal," Ina said. "It's a bit odd being the one judging others for a change."

"Just remember you might not be impartial to defense. Keep in mind that not everyone who aided the brothers did so willingly. Listen to the facts, and let reason and compassion win the day."

"Understood, my lady," Ina said.

Kari finished her dinner before retiring to her house. She was having the emperors' mansion renovated, but even once it was finished, she wasn't sure if she wanted to live there. There were too many bad memories in that house. If she were going to move in, she didn't want it to remind her of all the horrible things the former occupants did to her. While the work was being done, she was staying in her old house.

So much had changed since she came to the palace. From the very beginning, all she had wanted to do was to protect Suying, but, somewhere along the way, she had lost her. They had been like sisters for years, looking out for each other, protecting one another. They had both became different people inside these walls—people who were at odds with each other. Suying just wanted to live her life without fear of death or suffering, the same death and suffering they had witnessed on a daily basis. She was fourteen when she died, just a year older than the daughter of Alme. Too young. Far too young to die.

Kari would make sure no one else would have to suffer and die due to the throne. Her people would not go hungry. She would protect them, the way she wanted to protect Suying. That would be how she would honor her friend.

Jiaorong was gone, but his memory still plagued her. He had a mastery of his spirit energy. Spirit charging was a Shagin technique. Albeit, anyone could learn how to do it, but it was still a Shagin secret. It was what made them such feared warriors. Jiaorong had claimed to have taken his energy beyond what Shagin thought possible.

Going through his personal library had revealed a number of books and tomes he had written detailing his various techniques and methods of energy manipulation. One of which was dedicated to what he called dual cultivation, and his method of using others to strengthen himself. That one made her stomach turn.

She didn't want to read his writings, but in the depths of her mind was the fear others would know similar techniques. Spirit auras and energy manipulation were thought to be Shagin secrets, something only they knew. It was what gave the Renegades an edge during the Sovereign War.

She guessed it wasn't impossible for others to stumble upon spirit energy. It was an inherit element of cantrips even though most magic users were only dimly aware of the existence of spirit energy and what fueled their own powers. She wasn't even sure where Shagin first learned the techniques. The thought still made her uneasy, though.

If Jiaorong could do it, then there were others as well, and she needed to know as much as she could to be ready for them. With her identity being made public, it would be vital for her to train and improve her abilities just in case anyone came looking for the Seed.

"Lady Hikari," Cai Ren said, catching up to her. "You really shouldn't walk around without a guard or escort. While we removed a number of detractors, there could still be other members of your court who have lost due to the change in power."

"I should be all right. After all, I can handle myself," Kari said. "Besides, the guards are best served in the city fighting the bandits and thieves that have preyed on the people for so long."

"As you wish, my lady." Cai Ren sighed. "We have a serious matter to discuss."

"Can it wait until morning? I'm feeling rather tired from the day." Her body still hadn't fully recovered from the battle with Jiaorong. Cai Ren shook his head. "Very well, what's the matter?"

"An envoy from the Guardian has arrived. He requests an audience with you, and he demands you provide aid for the war effort." Cai Ren paused. "He has also heard rumors you are Shagin, and he demands an explanation."

"What am I supposed to tell him?" It had begun. Word had reached the Guardian quicker than she'd expected. She could lie about who she was—try to pass off the stories of her being Shagin as baseless rumors meant to delegitimize her rule—but she didn't want to. She was tired of hiding. Kari was Shagin, and she would show the world her people weren't meant to be feared, that they were people just like everyone else.

One day, she would bring her Shagin sisters back to the mainland. In order to do that, she couldn't be afraid of what she was. "I'm supposed to give a justification for existing. That's absurd. You can tell him that, as of right now, we are in the process of rebuilding the empire and cannot aid in his war. As far as an explanation is concerned, I am what I am. If he so desires an audience, I will grant him one in the morning."

Kari dismissed Cai Ren before retiring to her room.

Kari removed her phoenix crown, then let her hair down. It flowed freely off her shoulders. She'd been on such a long journey to get here, and the path ahead was even longer. Her entire life had changed, and, in a way, she had changed as well. Tomorrow, she would face the start of an uncertain future as she would attempt to justify her existence to the Guardian's envoy. It was a meeting she was not looking forward to.

Ultimately, it didn't matter. Whatever challenges may come her way, she felt confident she could meet them.

Four years had passed since the moment in the cave. It seemed like a lifetime ago. Kari had run away then, but she wouldn't run anymore. She had an entire empire relying on her now. It was still strange to her that she was empress, leader of millions of people. She refused to let them down.

Kari stared at the woman in the mirror above her armoire. She was beautiful with an air of confidence about her. Her bright green eyes almost glowed with determination and purpose. Light emitted from her hand, shining throughout the room. Her name was Kari, and she would bring light to the world.

ALSO BY

Thank you for reading!

Please leave a review. Every honest review goes a long ways to help the author.

Check out these other works by the author.

Records of the Three Realms

The Songstress (Book 1)

The Bearer of the Seed (Book 2)

The Annals of Skorne (Standalone Novella)

Coming Soon

The Lady of Light (Book 3)

About the Author

Joshua Killingsworth is a fantasy lover and author who has spent his life dreaming up worlds to explore. He enjoys stories of heroes set in worlds full of imagination and intrigue. When not writing, he can be found playing video games, spending time with his two kids, or hugging any and every animal he can catch.

Acknowledgements

Special thank you to Cynthia Shepp for taking my manuscript and making it shine. You are basically magic. As always, thank you to my lovely wife Anna. I couldn't have made if this far without you.